THE SUMMER GETAWAY

THE SUMMER GETAWAY

SUSAN MALLERY

THORNDIKE PRESS
A part of Gale, a Cengage Company

Copyright © 2022 by Susan Mallery, Inc.
Thorndike Press, a part of Gale, a Cengage Company.

LIBRARY OF CONGRESS CIP DATA ON FILE.
CATALOGUING IN PUBLICATION FOR THIS BOOK
IS AVAILABLE FROM THE LIBRARY OF CONGRESS.

ISBN-13: 978-1-4328-9526-6 (hardcover alk. paper)

Published in 2022 by arrangement with Harlequin Enterprises ULC.

Printed in Mexico
Print Number: 01   Print Year: 2022

This book is dedicated to all those who serve — past or present.
With my thanks. Mason is for you.

And to Colleen, who, in the middle of COVID, took the time to speak to me about what it was like to be a drill sergeant. A thousand thanks for the blunt facts, funny stories and priceless information. I enjoyed every second of our conversation. If our paths ever cross in person, lunch is on me.

Any military mistakes made in the book are mine.
Well, all the mistakes are mine, but the military ones matter more.

ONE

"I'm going to sleep with Dimitri."

Robyn Caldwell picked up her glass of white wine and briefly thought about swallowing the entire contents in one gulp. Mindy's statement was certainly gulp-worthy. But she knew pacing herself through lunch was the responsible thing to do. A lesson her friend had yet to learn.

"You are not," Robyn murmured, because shrieking wasn't attractive. Especially at "the club," where their friends and frenemies were also enjoying Thursday's lobster salad. The dining room was filled with forty or so women, all dressed in Florida chic — diamonds sparkling, gold or platinum charm bracelets clinking, necklaces resting on tanned and toned skin.

"I might," Mindy Krause said, picking up her champagne. "He's gorgeous."

"Of course. He's a thirty-year-old tennis pro. What else would he be?"

7

Mindy, a petite brunette who was six months from turning forty, sighed. "I need a Dimitri in my life."

"You have a great husband. Payne loves you and the kids, and never has eyes for another woman. Why would you screw that up?"

"Payne would never know."

"There aren't any secrets in this town. Not in our social circle."

Something Robyn had learned the hard way herself. She'd been blissfully unaware of her ex-husband's affairs until a "friend" had oh-so-sweetly informed her.

"Maybe just some kissing," Mindy mused. "I want a little Dimitri action. The fantasies make me happy, so imagine what the real thing would do."

"The fantasies are safe. The real thing could destroy everything you have. Knowing you've cheated would devastate Payne."

Mindy's mouth formed a pout. "I never see him anymore. All he does is work."

Robyn stared at her friend-slash-boss. "You two talked about how that promotion would be more work for him but that it would be worth it. You *wanted* this for him."

"I didn't know how much he'd be gone."

The unreasonable statement grated nearly as much as Mindy's whine. "This isn't a

8

good look for you," Robyn murmured. "You're changing the rules without telling your husband. That never ends well."

Mindy dismissed the warning with a quick shake of her head. "I'm not worried. Besides, if he does find out, I can just move in with you." She laughed. "You'll soon have that big house all to yourself."

"You have four kids," Robyn pointed out. "If things go south in your marriage, I'd rather have Payne move in."

"Well, that would get people talking." Mindy held up her empty glass to the server. "More, please."

The server obliged.

Mindy took another sip. "My sister called, swears she found a Thomas Pister chest in a tiny shop in Wales. It's dirt cheap, so I'm afraid it's a fake. She's looking for someone to prove authenticity. Wouldn't that be a find?"

"It would. I'd love to see it."

Thomas Pister had built beautiful chests and cabinets in the late 1600s and early 1700s. His intricate designs with stunning inlays sold quickly and for huge amounts. Depending on the condition and the materials, a good-sized chest of drawers could go for sixty or eighty thousand dollars.

"She also found a couple of early Dutch

strongboxes," Mindy added. "Those sell for at least thirty K."

Mindy, along with her three sisters, owned an exclusive antique shop in Naples. None of the other sisters lived in Florida, so Mindy was in charge of retail. Her sisters traveled extensively, keeping the shop well-stocked with unique and expensive items.

Robyn and Mindy had met in the store. Robyn was a frequent client, although her taste was slightly less upscale than much of Mindy's inventory. They'd quickly moved to having lunch every month. When a part-time position had opened up, Robyn had applied. It was only a few hours a week, but Robyn enjoyed working with the other clients, as well as checking out whatever was new in the store. The selling wasn't her favorite, but learning about different eras and the history of each piece enthralled her.

Mindy set down her glass. "How goes the wedding?"

Robyn did her best not to grimace. "So far we're just talking generalities."

"You're still not happy they're engaged?"

Robyn again resisted the urge to chug her wine. "Kip's great. He adores Harlow, and doesn't every mother want that in a future son-in-law? I just wish . . . ."

She placed her hands flat on the table.

"She's barely twenty-two. They've known each other less than a year, and getting married is such a big step. Why can't they live together for a few years? Take off for Paris or go hiking in Chile? Why get married so quickly?"

Mindy tried to hide her amusement. "And how old were you when you married Cord?"

"Nineteen." Robyn sighed. "Which is my point. I had a two-year-old when I was Harlow's age. Sure, I had my kids early, but what if I hadn't? What if I'd gone to college or spent six months in Australia or done something other than what I did?"

"So is your concern about what Harlow might miss out on or what you gave up?"

A very valid question, Robyn thought. "How can you be insightful? That's your third glass of champagne."

"Liquor brings out my best qualities."

"I don't regret my life. I love my kids. I wouldn't wish them away."

"But?"

"I want her to have options." She picked up her fork. "Not a conversation my daughter wants to have with me." She and Harlow had managed to survive the teen years with hardly a cross word, but lately, they seemed to be fighting all the time.

"Would you have listened to *your*

11

mother?" Mindy asked.

"I'm not sure. She died when I was eleven."

Mindy's brown eyes widened. "I'm sorry. I didn't know."

"It's okay. As for talking to her when I was Harlow's age, I probably wouldn't have listened, either. I want to say I would have been mature and interested in her opinion, but it seems unlikely."

Mindy touched her hand. "It's your past, Robyn. You rewrite it however you'd like."

"Thanks. The last time Harlow mentioned the wedding, she said something about wanting to dye the pool to match the bridesmaids' dresses."

"Can you even do that?"

"No idea, and I really don't want to know." She could only hope that her daughter's wedding plans became a little more normal as time passed. Or that she decided to elope. Or hey, postpone.

"Want to play tennis next week?" Mindy asked brightly.

Robyn eyed her. "I'm not interested in meeting your fantasy guy."

"Why not? Once you see him, you'll have to admit he's totally worth the risk."

Robyn gave in to the inevitable and swallowed the rest of her wine. "Mindy, you make me crazy. You have a perfectly good penis at home. One is enough. Forget about Derrick."

"Dimitri."

"Whatever. Don't risk your marriage and your family. He's not worth it."

"But I'm not doing it for him. I'm doing it for me." She smiled dreamily. "At least let me see him naked."

"See a therapist instead."

Mindy assumed Robyn was kidding and burst out laughing. Robyn faked a smile, even as she told herself to stop trying to convince her friend of anything. Based on how her children were behaving lately, she had no skills at persuasion. Oh, for the days when she could bribe them with a Popsicle.

She excused herself to use the restroom. Halfway across the room, Madison Greene spotted her. The fiftysomething avid golfer's favorite hobby was spreading bad news. The sight of her wave and quick approach caused Robyn to nearly stumble. What now?

"Robyn, darling. You look amazing. What are you doing these days? You never join me for a foursome."

Robyn smiled as they exchanged an air-kiss, not bothering to point out that she didn't golf.

"Always a pleasure, Madison," she said,

bracing herself.

"I heard Harlow's engaged. You must be thrilled. My oldest refused to get married until she was nearly thirty. It was a nightmare. But she finally did the deed."

Madison glanced around, as if checking that they were alone, which they weren't. They were in a crowded dining room, not that Madison would care. She was here to share something awful, and the more people who heard it, the better.

"Is Cord's relationship going to be a problem for you and Harlow? Boys will be boys, but it's just so awkward."

Robyn thought briefly about a quick, "We're fine," only she had no idea what Madison was talking about. And not knowing something about her ex-husband could be risky, especially if their daughter was involved.

Madison shook her head in faux sympathy. "You have no idea what I'm talking about. Oh, no. I shouldn't have said a word."

"But you did, didn't you?"

Madison blinked at her. "Yes, well, it's just I thought you should know. Cord is dating Zafina."

Why did anyone think she was the least bit interested in who her ex-husband went out with? "I have no idea who that is."

14

Thin eyebrows rose as much as the Botox would let them. "Your ex-husband is dating your daughter's fiancé's twin sister."

Robyn stood there, trying to absorb the words. Cord was dating Harlow's fiancé's twin sister?

"I didn't know Kip *had* a twin sister," she said before she could stop herself. Crap! Double crap!

Madison offered a self-satisfied smile. "I wondered why you were so calm. I'm sorry to be the one to bring you such bad news."

"Are you?" Robyn asked before she could stop herself. "It seems to me you're delighted. It must be hard having such a small life."

With that she turned away and continued her journey to the restroom. Once she was safely in the bathroom stall, she took a moment to decide if she was going to pee, as she'd originally planned, or just plain puke.

Robyn faked her way through lunch. She preferred to mull over Madison's bombshell before talking about it. She alternated between disbelief and resignation. What had Cord been thinking? Dating his daughter's fiancé's twin sister? Really? Couldn't he settle for someone only ten years younger who wasn't related to Kip?

15

Once she was home, she quickly texted her ex, asking him to stop by that evening. Within seconds, he answered with, What did I do now?

She ignored the question.

Six works for me. See you then.

She thought about texting Harlow and asking her about her father dating Zafina, but decided that wasn't a good idea. Based on her daughter's silence on the subject, she would guess Harlow didn't know. Better to find out if it was a weekend fling that could be ignored or something that was going to blow up in their faces.

"Dammit, Cord," she muttered, wondering why, four years after their divorce, she was still dealing with his messes.

In the kitchen, she got out ingredients for a citrus marinade. Once she'd juiced the oranges and the limes, she chopped basil before turning her attention to the chicken pieces. She carefully removed the skin and any visible fat. While she'd always tried to provide healthy meals for her family, since she'd started dating Jase, she'd become even more aware of the food she prepared.

She put the chicken and marinade into a large resealable plastic bag. She'd just finished when Austin, her youngest, walked into the kitchen.

"Hey, Mom," he said, stretching before slumping onto one of the bar stools by the large island. His dark blond hair fell into his eyes. He was tall and lean, with that too-skinny look teenaged boys had. Sometime in the next couple of years he would start to fill out.

"You're home early."

"It was only a six-hour fishing charter."

"That's why you were gone before sunrise."

"I had to be on board by five thirty."

"Pesky fish and their timetables."

Austin flashed her a grin. "I blame the fishermen."

"Them, too."

Austin, barely eighteen and a recent high school graduate, eyed the plastic bag. "More chicken?"

"It's healthy."

"Did you *have* to start dating a cardiologist? All we ever have is chicken and fish."

She held in a smile. "That's not true. Last week I made vegetarian enchiladas."

"I know, but I try not to think about it. Couldn't you start seeing a guy who owns a rib place? That would be better for me."

"It's not bad for you to learn to eat

healthy. You won't be eighteen forever."

"I'm figuring I'll be eighteen for about a year."

She laughed. "I think you're right. You hungry?"

"Always."

She cleaned up, then walked to the refrigerator. "Isn't there leftover Thai?" A takeout dinner she and Austin had shared. Something they would only have when Jase wasn't coming over.

"I had it for breakfast."

"There's still some of the poached salmon. I could heat that and put together a salad."

Austin made a gagging noise in the back of his throat. "I want something *good.*"

His tone made him sound like he was eight instead of eighteen. If only that were true, she thought, remembering how easy things had been when he'd been younger. Austin was a go along to get along kid. He was even-tempered, thoughtful and affectionate. Unfortunately he was also stubborn, so when he'd said he wasn't going to college and instead would work for his dad, no amount of chiding, persuading or threatening had changed his mind.

She inspected the refrigerator contents. "Grilled cheese and coleslaw?"

"Yes, please."

"Even though dinner's in two hours?"

"Like I won't be hungry then, too."

She collected three kinds of cheese, along with butter and bread. She'd made the coleslaw that morning. Jase wouldn't approve, but she would grill vegetables along with the chicken so he could eat those and ignore the creamy goodness of her coleslaw.

She sliced the cheese, then buttered the bread before heating a pan.

"I'm moving out Saturday," Austin said as she assembled the sandwich.

"You've mentioned that."

"Into my own apartment."

She pressed her lips together to keep from saying he was too young. He would point out that he was eighteen now, an adult. Working for his father gave him a nice paycheck. He could afford an apartment and had decided he was ready to be on his own. But being the right age was not the same as being a mature adult. Not that telling him that would make a difference.

She also wasn't going to mention that she wasn't ready for him to go or that she liked having him around, although both were true. Guilting her kids had never been her thing.

She used a spatula to lower the sandwich into the pan. "What are you doing about furniture? You have your bedroom set, but what about other stuff? A sofa? A table and chairs?" She mentally ran through the contents of the house, wondering what she was willing to give up. "Are you renting a moving van or something?"

"I don't need anything, Mom. The place is furnished."

"What? Why would you rent a furnished place? It's so much more expensive."

"I didn't want to deal with moving stuff back and forth. It's only for four months."

She pressed down on the sandwich. "Four months? The move is temporary?"

"Sure. Come on, Mom. I'm barely eighteen. I'm not ready to adult full-time. I'm getting a place for the summer so I can have a good time with my friends before they go off to college. You know, like a four-month party. The rent's cheap because it's not the tourist season. I got a great deal, and it's going to be awesome."

She narrowed her gaze. "You think you can just move in and out at will? Is this a hotel?"

The charming grin returned. "Oh, Mom, don't play like you're mad. You love having me around. Plus, you think I'm too young to be on my own, so this is good news."

She flipped the sandwich. He wasn't

totally wrong, but she wasn't going to admit that.

"Why didn't you tell me this before?" she asked. "You let me think you were gone for good."

"I didn't want you to try to change my mind." His expression turned serious. "I really do have a plan, Mom."

So he'd said several times — something she would believe if he would tell her what the plan was.

"College in the fall?" she asked hopefully, sliding the sandwich onto a plate, then slicing it in half. "You could do a year of community college, then transfer to —"

"Have a little faith in me."

"I want to. I love you."

"I love you, too," he mumbled around a bite of the sandwich. When he'd chewed and swallowed, he said, "Does the chicken means Jase is coming over for dinner tonight?"

"No." She leaned against the island. "Tomorrow. Austin, do you have a problem with Jase?"

"He's fine. I just like to know when he's coming for dinner."

"Why?"

He looked at her, then away. "When he's over, I feel like I'm in the way."

"Sweetie, no." She sat down next to him. "Austin, this is your home, and you're always welcome." She smiled. "Until you move out on Saturday. Then I'm getting the locks changed." She let her smile fade. "Is it something he's said or I've done?"

"No." He finished the first half of his sandwich. "Sometimes I think Jase doesn't approve of me."

She tried to make sense of that. "He's never said that. I think he likes you a lot."

"Maybe. I don't know. Until I move out, I'll be elsewhere while your man friend is here."

"I'm not convinced this is okay."

He smiled at her. "As long as you like him and he treats you okay, then I don't have a problem."

She stood and kissed the top of his head. "You're very sweet."

He glanced at the refrigerator. "Did you use that healthy citrus marinade?"

She laughed. "It's not that bad. I'm going to grill corn, and I made blue cheese potato salad."

"You're the best, Mom."

She left him to his meal and walked through the house to the master suite. After changing into cropped yoga pants and a tank top, she grabbed her rolled mat and went out through the French doors off the sitting area.

The heat hit her the second she stepped outside. The temperature was in the high eighties, and the humidity was about the same. She unrolled her yoga mat in the shade on her patio. After drawing in several deep breaths, she began the simple routine she practiced nearly every afternoon. The slow movements relaxed her and kept her flexible. Plus the rhythm of the routine helped her clear her mind.

Austin's announcement relieved her. At least he knew he wasn't ready to "adult," as he'd called it. She would miss him while he was gone, but she appreciated knowing he would be back in the fall. Of course, that was a slight complication when it came to selling the house. In the back of her mind, she'd thought maybe, when she listed the house, Jase would invite her to move in. They hadn't talked about it, but they'd been dating a year now, and . . .

Okay, she didn't know what the "and" was, but they'd been together a while. Moving in together was the next logical step. But if Austin was still living with her, that wasn't an option. Jase's two preteen girls stayed with him every other weekend. His house didn't have a bedroom for Austin, and she wasn't going to tell her son he wasn't welcome. The obvious solution was for her to find a smaller place of her own.

She looked out at the gorgeous pool, the hot tub and the waterfall. This and the kitchen were her favorite parts of the house. The rest was too big and too perfect for her taste. She'd never felt comfortable here, and once she and Cord had divorced, she'd been eager to sell.

But Austin had only been fourteen, and she'd figured he'd been dealing with enough without adding a move to the mix. Harlow had also been a consideration, still coming home regularly from college. Now Austin was out of high school, and Harlow was engaged and living with her fiancé. Moving made sense for the kids and for her financially. She was tired of the large mortgage payment that chewed up so much of her monthly income.

She sat on the mat. She would need to get a place big enough for her and Austin — something with a pretty outdoor space and relatively close to where she lived now. If the backyard was nice enough, maybe Harlow wouldn't throw a fit about not being able to be married in this one. For reasons not clear to Robyn, Harlow had become fixated on a backyard wedding.

Robyn wanted something a lot less showy than this place. Smaller and cozier, with a few modern touches. Later she would check out local inventory online. If she saw something she liked, she would view it. As for Harlow and the wedding, it wasn't anything she had to deal with right now. One crisis at a time. And in less than two hours, the current one was going be ringing her doorbell.

TWO

Mason Bishop had the wrong address. He stared at the information on his phone, then back at the house in front of him. No, *house* was the wrong word. It was a . . . something more than just a house.

Massive, sprawling, with mismatched additions jutting out haphazardly, the three- or maybe four-story mansion looked as if it had been designed while the architect was drunk. Or by a space alien who had only *heard* about where humans lived, but had never actually seen that kind of structure for himself.

The roof was red tiles, the exterior walls white stucco. The front facade had arches and windows that were traditionally Spanish — not unfamiliar in the Southern California region, or so he'd read. The addition on the left had a Dr. Seuss-like quality to it, while the one on the right was maybe early colonial.

Surprisingly, once he got past the strangeness, he found the disparate elements oddly appealing. He wanted to explore the —

His phone rang.

"Bishop."

"Hello, Mason. It's Lillian."

Right. Lillian Holton, the widow of his third cousin, five times removed, or whatever the relationship was. Lillian, who'd been writing him for fifteen years, ever since Leo, her husband, had passed away. In every letter she'd insisted he visit the house he would, due to some legal quirk, inherit upon Lillian's death. "I'm in Santa Barbara," he told her, continuing to eye the weird-ass house. "But I'm not at the right place."

A curtain on the main floor flickered. "Are you parked outside the most unusual house you've ever seen?"

"Yes, ma'am."

She laughed. "Then you're here. The garage is a ways back behind the house. It used to be the stables. I'll meet you out there."

Mason Bishop had served twenty-five years in the army. He spent two of them as drill sergeant, turning new recruits into fighting men and women. He'd been in battle, he'd been injured, he'd seen most of the world, and he'd been married twice.

27

Very little surprised him anymore. Except for today.

"I'd been expecting a three-bedroom ranch," he admitted.

The laughter returned. "I thought you might be. I'm afraid this is the house your uncle has left you."

Had Professor Lynn been his uncle? He could have sworn they were cousins — distant cousins. Which wasn't the point. He couldn't inherit this house. It was the size of a small city. Upkeep would cost a fortune. There had to be a mistake.

"It's larger than I expected."

"No one knows how big she is. Well, someone could figure it out, but I've never cared enough to measure. I'm hanging up now, Mason."

"Yes, ma'am."

Mason did the same, then looked at the monstrosity on the hill. Holy shit. What was he supposed to do with a house like that?

He drove his SUV down the long driveway, past windows and doors and more windows and doors before following a gentle curve to a building the size of the hospital on his last base. Here the architecture was pure Spanish, with the red roof tiles and white stucco, accented by a half dozen wooden garage doors.

He parked, then got out and looked around. The sky was a deep blue, with not a single cloud. There were unfamiliar trees and bushes, probably native, with several palm trees looking as out of place as he felt. When he inhaled, he smelled the ocean. The house was only a few blocks from the Pacific, and he would guess several of the balconies he'd seen had a perfect view.

A surprisingly normal back door opened, and a tall, thin woman stepped out. She had short white hair and a cautious but steady gait.

She approached him, her face bright with anticipation, her smile friendly.

"Mason, at last. You've been very elusive."

Mason was wary around people he didn't know, and he'd been chided all his life for being slow to warm up to strangers. But Lillian Holton radiated an open welcome that promised acceptance and understanding.

He took her outstretched hand. "It's nice to meet you, Lillian."

She studied him. "I can see a little of your Uncle Leo in you."

Given how distantly connected they had been, he doubted that.

She linked arms with him. "Come inside. Salvia prepared a snack. She works here five days a week to clean and look after me, as well as oversee the maids and gardeners. She's very excited to meet you. We've talked of nothing else for days."

As they walked toward the house, he was aware of her fragility. Her bones felt as hollow as a bird's. He shouldn't be surprised. She was over ninety.

They went through a big mudroom and into a massive kitchen with white plaster walls and dark wood beams. The white cabinets had to be fifty years old, and the countertops were some fancy tile. The appliances were new — stainless steel and nicer than anything he'd ever used. Not that he cooked much.

She showed him into a large room off the kitchen. Big windows opened onto a lush walled garden. A large wooden table stood in the center, surrounded by eight chairs. A pitcher of lemonade and two glasses stood next to a plate of cookies. Two chairs were occupied by sleeping cats.

"Please," she said, motioning to a tall-backed chair with a woven seat. She sat opposite him and poured them both a drink.

"How delightful to have you here at last," she said, passing him his lemonade. "I thought you were never going to take me up on my invitation."

"You were persistent."

"I can be."

Her eyes were pale blue, but he would guess they'd been much darker when she'd been younger. Her face was lined, but in a way that made him think she'd smiled and laughed a lot in her life.

Her first letter had arrived while he'd been stationed in Iraq. He'd ignored it. The second had followed two weeks later, then a third. He'd finally answered, mostly in self-defense. Otherwise, she was going to drown him in paper.

She'd explained that they were distantly related through her late husband and that he would be inheriting their house after she died. This house.

"If I'd done drugs, I would swear I was having a flashback," he admitted, trying to take it all in.

"She does take some getting used to. But you're here, and you have all the time you need." She gave him an impish smile. "I don't plan on dying for a long time."

"I'm glad. It's going to take a long time to get used to this."

She reached over and placed her hands on his. "You're going to love it here. The weather is perfect, and you'll be able to explore at your leisure. She has many secrets, as any female of a certain age

31

should."

Okay, this was getting weirder by the minute. He glanced longingly toward the door. Maybe letting go of his rental house in Texas had been a mistake. Only Lillian had guilted him into an indefinite stay while he "got to know his inheritance" and went through her late husband's research materials.

Leo Lynn, in life a tenured professor at UC Santa Barbara, had shared Mason's interest in obscure military history. Lillian had promised complete access to the reference books, notes and source materials. He'd expected a couple of cartons in the garage. Now he suspected it was a lot more than that. He'd assumed this was as good a place as any to work on his book on Major General Henry Halleck. Now he was less sure.

"Is your head spinning?" Lillian asked conspiratorially.

"I'm taking it in."

She passed him a modern-looking key. "This is for you. It will get you in any of the doors. There's no alarm." The smile returned. "We don't have trouble with anyone breaking in." She lowered her voice. "Everyone thinks the old house is haunted."

"Is it?"

"Not that I can tell, but I have hope." She rose. "Come on. I'll show you your room."

He left his untouched lemonade on the table. They went down a hall, made a turn, and walked along another hall before reaching a wide curved staircase. The treads were at least six feet across, and the banister was hand-carved. The only modern touch was one of those stair-lift chairs.

Lillian sat on it and picked up a remote. "Shall we?"

He walked up with her, keeping pace with her slow progress. On the landing, she led the way to the left.

There were a few more twists and turns before they stopped in front of a set of double doors.

"I chose this room especially for you, Mason." Her smile returned, this time tinged with sadness. "Leo and I so wanted children, but we were never blessed. I suppose we should have adopted, but somehow we never thought about it. Anyway, this would have been our oldest son's room. I hope it suits."

She pushed open the doors and motioned him inside.

His first impression was that the bedroom — more of a suite, really — was as big as his house back in Texas. His second was that the room came with a balcony and a view of the Pacific Ocean.

"It's very nice here during sunset," Lillian told him. "And beautiful when the storms come in." She linked arms with him again. "What are you thinking, Mason?"

"That this country boy from West Virginia has come a long way."

Something brushed against his leg. He looked down and saw a cat rubbing against him. The two in the kitchen had been black and brown. This one was white.

"How many cats do you have?" he asked, as the white cat jumped gracefully onto the bed.

"About fifteen, I think. They're so restful to have around, and such excellent company."

Fifteen cats? He swore silently. He shouldn't even be surprised. Roses had thorns, and his unexpectedly fantastical inheritance came with a little old lady and a shitload of cats.

Robyn's mild sense of dread at having to deal with her ex-husband was mitigated by the fact that he wasn't her problem anymore. Because of their kids, she would be tied to him forever, especially when grandchildren started showing up, but she was no longer "Cord's wife."

She didn't have to worry about him buying something impulsively, without talking to her first. Not a car or this house or anything else. She wasn't concerned about the ups and downs of his business — although to give him his due, in the past few years, there had only been ups. Their divorce settlement had relieved her of any responsibility to the family firm. He'd released her legally and was in the process of buying her out. A significant lump sum had been deposited the day their divorce was final, and every month he wrote her a check.

Because she had a smart lawyer, she was paid before any of his other bills, and should Austin want to go to college, his four years would be covered by his dad, as Harlow's had been. The house was a bit more of a complication. She was required to pay the mortgage, insurance and taxes until Austin turned eighteen — something that had happened a few weeks ago. After that, she had six months to sell and split the proceeds with Cord, or buy him out. Something she had no intention of doing. The beautiful house on the water had skyrocketed in value. Keeping it would require getting a loan for at least two million dollars. Even more significant, she didn't actually like the house.

But her thoughts on moving were for another time, she thought, as the antique clock struck six. Right now her biggest problem was guilt at not fixing appetizers or cocktails. Telling herself Cord's visit wasn't a social call didn't make the compulsion go away. She'd been raised to be a good hostess. Old habits die hard.

At two minutes after the hour, the doorbell rang. Robyn let in her ex. Cord, about six feet of Florida tan, with a rangy build and easy, superficial charm, swept in with a grin and a quick cheek kiss.

"It's humid," he said, walking toward the kitchen. "Thunderstorms tonight."

"As long as they're done by morning," she said. "So they don't get in the way of the charters."

Boating and lightning weren't a good mix.

Cord looked around the kitchen. He wore a Hawaiian shirt over worn jeans. His sandy brown hair, a shade darker than Austin's, was a little too long, but the messy style suited him. His eyes were brown, his jaw square. He was, by all standards, a handsome man. Yet when she looked at him, she only felt relief that he wasn't her problem anymore. Not directly. Fighting with him

36

because of her kids was easy — it was fighting with him for herself that had always left her feeling emotionally broken and battered. She'd never known if he was simply better at winning arguments than her, or if he knew her better than she knew herself. Regardless, she had rarely survived any of their verbal altercations unscathed.

"No cocktails?" he asked, giving her an easy grin. "So this is going to be a serious conversation."

"It is."

"And here I thought you wanted to talk about getting back together."

She had no idea if he was kidding or not, so she ignored him. Instead of answering, she pointed to the kitchen table, thinking it was the closest seating area and the one least conducive to making them want to linger. Chitchat by the pool could go on for hours, while the uncomfortable, straight-back chairs encouraged brevity.

"What's up?" he asked, taking his former seat at the head of the table.

She went to the opposite end, so they were facing each other. With Cord, it was never good to give up ground.

"Austin told me he's only moving out for the summer, to hang out with his friends. He's moving back here in September."

Cord nodded. "Makes sense. He's not really ready to be on his own."

"I still want him to consider college."

Her ex-husband slumped back in his chair. "Let that go, Robyn. He's not the college type. He loves working for me. Sure, he doesn't have Harlow's ambition to run the place, but he'll make a good living and be plenty happy. Isn't that what matters?"

"What about his future? Shouldn't he have options?"

"To do what? Be a brain surgeon? Austin's the most easygoing kid in the world. Do you see him making it in corporate America? He lacks the killer instinct. I can give him a good life. Hey, if nothing else, he has job security."

"He's eighteen. Job security shouldn't be what he's looking for."

But Austin wasn't the reason she'd wanted to talk to Cord. There was a more pressing issue.

"I had lunch at the club today," she said. "One of the women there took great pleasure in telling me that you're dating someone new."

Cord's expression was comically confused. "What do you care who I'm dating? We're not married."

"This time I do care. Not for myself so

38

much as Harlow."

"What does Harlow have to do with anything?"

Was he playing dumb, or had he actually slipped into that state of being?

"You're dating your daughter's fiancé's twin sister, Cord. Ignoring the fact that she's what, twenty-plus years younger than you, she's Kip's sister. Come on. That's bad, even for you."

Cord chuckled. "Zafina's great. We get along. She's smart and beautiful. What's not to like?"

"I don't care about your relationship with her. Have you considered this will make Harlow uncomfortable?"

"How?"

"It's her fiancé's sister!"

"You keep saying that. Why is it a problem?"

"Oh, I don't know. The ick factor? There are plenty of single women in Naples. Date someone else."

"I like Zafina." He laughed. "Hey, if we get married, then Zafina is both her sister-in-law and stepmother. That could be fun."

"Not for Harlow."

He waved away her concern. "She'll get over it. Besides, she likes Zafina." He leaned toward her. "In a weird way, Zafina reminds me of you."

"Not something I want to talk about. So, if having Harlow find out isn't a problem, why haven't you told her?"

Cord looked away. "I don't introduce the kids to my girlfriends unless it's serious."

She rolled her eyes. "Since when? If you haven't said anything, you obviously know there's a complication."

He glared at her. "Fine. I thought she'd be upset."

"And she will be. You have to tell her, Cord. She needs to hear it from you and not someone else. Harlow doesn't like to be lied to."

Her ex-husband groaned. "Can't you tell her? She'll take it better from you."

"No, I can't. Not only won't she take it better from me, I'm not willing to be yelled at for you. This is your responsibility. Tell her."

He sighed heavily. "You used to be a lot more fun to be around. Fine. I'll talk to her. She's not going to care."

"I hope you're right." She rose. "Okay, thanks for stopping by."

"That's it?"

"Did you have something else to talk about?"

"No." He stood. "You used to offer me a

drink when we talked like this. And a cheese plate."

She ignored her guilt. "I was running late. Next time."

He studied her for a second. "Are you going to marry Jase?"

"What?" Her voice was nearly a yelp. She lowered it. "No."

They hadn't even discussed living together. Marriage? She wasn't ready to marry him or anyone. Four years after her divorce, she was finally starting to consider her options. She couldn't imagine committing to someone else in that way. Living with Jase was one thing, but marriage? Not anytime soon.

"I just wondered," he said. "You're different these days."

She doubted he meant the words as a compliment.

"Good to know. If you think of it, text me after you talk to Harlow so I can brace myself."

"Sure."

They walked to the front door. Before he stepped onto the porch, he looked at her.

"You know, most of our years together were pretty good."

The statement caught her off guard. Is that how he saw things? Her view was

41

entirely different. Not that she would say that to him — there was no reason to revisit that well-trodden road.

"They were," she lied, going for the kind response rather than the honest one.

"I think about that sometimes."

With that he turned and walked away. Robyn closed the front door behind him, then leaned against it. The list of things that had gone wrong in their marriage seemed a lot longer than the list of what had gone right. Four years after the fact, she was clear on where she'd screwed up and where Cord had, as well.

They'd married too young. They'd had kids too young. They'd put all their energy into growing the business and raising their family rather than paying attention to their relationship. And when Cord had cheated, six years in, they'd dealt with the betrayal and the pain, but never the why.

Looking back from a safe emotional distance, Robyn thought maybe that had been the first big crack. They should have gotten down to the real issues between them, but the hurt had been so big, she hadn't been able to think about anything else.

Marriage was hard, and sometimes people failed. Robyn accepted that and knew if there ever was a next time, she was going get it right.

THREE

"Having fun, Iliana?" Harlow Caldwell raised her voice over the roar of the boat's engine.

The ten-year-old nodded, her wide grin saying more than any words. Both her small hands were on the wheel, with Austin, Harlow's younger brother, standing right behind her, ready to take control.

"We're doing great, Captain," Austin said, giving Harlow a mock salute.

"I'm going to tell Thea we're heading in," Harlow said. "And get everyone ready to disembark."

The charter had been a success. Three families had gone out for a day of sun, fun and fishing. Eight hours later, everyone was happy and tired, which was how Harlow liked her charters to end.

She took the stairs down from the flying bridge to where the three guys were sipping beer on the stern deck, while two of the wives sunned on the foredeck. Only Thea sat inside, skin pale and eyes closed.

There was always one, Harlow thought, who couldn't handle the motion. She'd never been seasick herself, but had seen enough of the malady.

"Hey, Thea," she said softly.

The fortysomething's eyes opened. "Are we heading back?" she asked, her tone both hopeful and desperate.

"We are. In about two minutes, we're going to get some chop. When we're in the marina, the boat will stop rocking. Come outside and face the wind. Stare at the horizon, or close your eyes, and keep breathing. Five minutes and then we're done."

Thea struggled to her feet. "I haven't felt this horrible since I was pregnant."

"I know it's been bad." And the motion sickness medicine hadn't helped. "Just a few more minutes. Once we dock and you're on steady land, your stomach will settle quickly."

"I hope so."

Harlow guided her guest to the rear of the boat and had her sit so she was blasted by the wind. Right on time, they hit the chop, and the boat began to sway. Thea clutched the side, her face going white.

"It's okay," Harlow told her. "Austin

knows what he's doing."

"If you say so."

Harlow excused herself to tell everyone else they were nearly back at the marina. She got the lines ready, then returned to check on her queasy guest. Just then, they entered the protected waters of the marina, and the rocking stopped. Thea relaxed her death grip on the side of the boat.

"Better?" Harlow asked.

"A little." Thea offered a tight smile. "I swear, I'm never getting on a boat again in my life."

Harlow patted her arm, then went up the steep stairs to the flying bridge. Iliana was in her seat, watching Austin worshipfully as he guided the fifty-foot boat through the marina.

When he saw Harlow, he stepped back, giving her the wheel. He winked at Iliana before making his way to the main deck, where he would be responsible for securing the lines.

Harlow watched for other boats and the kayakers who ignored the signs that said they weren't allowed in this part of the marina. She went past their slip before easing the engines into reverse, then backed into the space. She cut the engines and used the thrusters to snug up against the finger pier.

Austin stepped onto the dock and tied off the aft line, then jogged to the bow and secured that line, as well.

Harlow checked the upper deck for any items belonging to their guests before going down the stairs ahead of Iliana.

"Both hands," she told the ten-year-old.

Harlow thanked everyone for the day, accepted a very generous tip and handed out business cards, along with a reminder to review them online. After giving her brother his half of the tip, she tidied up the galley and saloon. Austin, crew rather than captain, got stuck cleaning the head and restocking supplies. Forty minutes later, they were done.

"What are you doing tomorrow?" she asked Austin as they walked to the main office of Caldwell Charter Boats.

"Getting ready to move into my new place."

Harlow laughed. "You rented a furnished apartment. What do you have to get ready?"

"I want a bigger TV. I'm going to ask Mom if I can take the eighty-inch one from the media room."

"You are such a guy. Why do you need an eighty-inch television?"

Austin slung his arm around her shoulders. "*Needing* it isn't the point. Having it is."

"You're weird."

"Maybe, but also your brother so you gotta love me regardless." He dropped his arm and waved. "Enid! You're here. That must mean you've finally decided to admit you're desperately in love with me. Let's sail to Tahiti, where we'll live on the beach and I'll worship you forever."

Harlow slugged her baby brother in the arm. "Stop it. You're embarrassing her."

Austin's blue eyes were bright with laughter. "She loves the attention. I mean, come on. It's me."

Harlow hugged her friend. She and Enid had been BFFs since kindergarten. They'd both recently graduated from college, with Harlow going to work for her dad and Enid prepared to enter medical school. Austin, younger by four years, had tagged along when he could — until high school.

Enid, a pretty brunette with more brains than anyone Harlow knew, smiled at Austin. "One day I'm going to call your bluff."

He winked. "Just say the word, Enid mine."

"He's all talk," Harlow said with a laugh. "Let me go see my dad for a sec, then I'm ready to head out."

"Where are you going?" Austin asked Enid. "Want a handsome guy to escort you?"

"Do you know one?" Enid asked teasingly as Harlow went into the building. The door closed, cutting off Austin's response.

She found her dad on the phone in his office. The tone of his voice and the way he was rotating his chair back and forth told her he was on with one of his women.

Since her parents' divorce four years ago, Cord Caldwell had been enjoying the single life. He was a serial dater who always had a girlfriend. The longest she'd known him to be without someone in his life was maybe three days. Her mother, on the other hand, had waited a year to start dating. She told Harlow that she hadn't met anyone interesting enough to see more than a couple of times. That had changed about a year ago, when her mom had gotten involved with Jase, a local cardiologist. They'd become a thing, dating exclusively. Her mother rarely shared details, unlike her dad, who sometimes told her too much.

She waited a couple of minutes, but her father showed no signs of ending the call. Finally she caught his eye and tapped on her watch.

"Hey, let me call you back," he said, his

tone low and sexy. "Uh-huh. Me, too."

Harlow did her best not to gag. Yes, she and her father were both adults, but she didn't like seeing this side of him. He was her parent, not a friend. But Cord had never been big on boundaries.

"What's up?" he asked when he'd ended the call.

"We're back from the charter." She tossed him the keys. "She's clean and ready for tomorrow. Austin's off, and I'm taking out the fishermen. I'll be back at five thirty." In the morning. Not her favorite, but part of the job. "You'll look over the paperwork from the lawyer?"

Her father hesitated just long enough for her to guess the truth. "Dad, why won't you read through the offer? You have to agree to the terms before we can move forward on buying the business."

"I'll get to it."

"It's been nearly a week. Can you read it tonight?"

"Sure. Tonight."

She ignored her surge of frustration. "We talked about this all last summer. You said it was a great idea for us to expand into the easy money of kayak and paddleboard rentals. I did everything you said. I found a good business to buy, I came up with a business plan, I talked to a lawyer, and now we're ready to present an offer as soon as you say go. Have you changed your mind?"

"I've been busy, Harlow. I'll get to it."

When? But she knew there was no point in pushing. Her father moved at his own pace.

"Then I guess I'll see you tomorrow," she said before walking out of his office.

She collected her handbag, then joined Enid out front.

"What?" her friend asked. "You upset?"

"It's just my dad. He's dragging his feet on the purchase."

"Of the business you want him to buy?"

"Yeah. But I'll let it go. Come on, you. We'll have the best girls' night out ever."

Enid laughed. "That's a very high bar."

"So, yes on the eighty-inch TV?" Austin asked hopefully, as he helped clear the dinner dishes.

"No."

"But you never use it."

"Your apartment comes with a TV already."

"A tiny one. It's the size a mouse would buy. Please, Mom? I'll be careful. You know I'm a responsible kid." His eyes brightened. "I'll wash your car every week in exchange.

51

How's that?"

"I'm interested in getting my car washed, but I want a set time. No texting me and saying you'll get to it soon. Every week you have to make an appointment with me and keep it. Otherwise you bring the TV back."

He considered her offer, then held out his hand. "Deal. I'll wash your car this Saturday morning before I move in."

"And vacuum the carpets."

He made a low noise in the back of his throat, but kept his hand in place. "Sure."

She shook hands with him. "Then you have yourself an eighty-inch TV for the four months you're gone."

He whooped and jumped up to touch the light fixture on the ceiling. "You're the best, Mom."

"I've heard that before. It's starting to go to my head."

Austin was still laughing as he took the stairs, two at a time, to the second floor. Robyn had just started for the family room when her phone rang. She glanced at the screen and smiled.

"I miss you," she said by way of greeting.

Her great-aunt Lillian laughed. "Then come visit me, darling."

Robyn sank onto the oversized sofa. "How are you? Feeling all right?"

"Never better."

"Salvia is taking good care of you?"

"You know she is."

Salvia had been with Lillian a decade, but still, Robyn worried. Lillian was ninety-four and getting more frail by the year. Her mind was as sharp as ever, but there had been a fall three years ago and a bad cold she'd taken months to shake.

"So how are you?" Lillian asked. "How are Harlow and Austin?"

Robyn hesitated before saying, "They're good. Harlow seems to be enjoying working for her dad, and Austin's loving his summer after high school."

Which was all true, but somehow missed the spirit of what was happening in her life, Robyn thought, ignoring the surge of guilt.

"Have you listed the house?"

"Not yet. There are considerations. Austin for one."

"He'll be happy as long as he's with you."

Robyn smiled. "Probably. But Harlow still wants to have her wedding here."

"She's too young to get married."

"Feel free to tell her that. She won't listen to me."

Lillian laughed. "Tell her to call me and I will. Oh, I know. Sell the house, but explain to the new owners they have to let you host a wedding in their backyard."

"I wish that were a possibility." She switched the phone to her other ear. "I really do miss you."

"Then come see me. I'm old, Robyn. I could die tomorrow."

Icy hands clutched her heart. "Please don't say that."

"It's true. Fly out for a few weeks. The weather is perfect, and your room is always waiting." Lillian's voice turned teasing. "I've made a couple of changes you'll find interesting."

"What does that mean?"

"Come visit me to find out."

"Now I'm intrigued."

"Excellent. I mean it, darling. I want to see you."

"Let me work on it."

"All right. I'm off to watch the sunset. I love you."

"Love you, too."

Harlow and Enid scored a corner table on the restaurant's patio. Overhead fans stirred the humid air just enough to make sitting outside tolerable.

"Tonight's on me," Harlow said, studying the specials listed on the blackboard by the bar. "We're still celebrating you getting into medical school."

Enid shook her head. "That's old news. I leave in eight weeks."

Harlow looked at her friend. "Nervous?"

"Terrified. The first year is supposed to be so hard."

"But you're the smartest person I know. You'll be fine."

"What if I fail?"

Harlow reached across the table and grabbed her hands. "What if you get all A's?"

"Unlikely."

"There's that optimistic spirit I admire," she teased. "You were nervous about high school, and you aced that. You were freaked about college because, and I quote, 'All the smart kids will be in one place.' You graduated top of your class. Medical school is no different."

"I wish that were true."

Harlow grinned. "When have I ever been wrong?"

Enid smiled. "You do have a good track record."

Harlow waved over their server and ordered two piña colada sunrises, jalapeño poppers, chicken and mango skewers and coconut shrimp.

Enid grinned. "All my favorites."

"Of course. You got into Johns Hopkins School of Medicine. You're my hero."

"I still can't believe it." She lowered her voice. "I'm really excited."

"You should be. You'll be a terrific doctor. And for the record, you don't have to study pediatric oncology."

Enid's dark eyes widened. "But I want to."

"You're still starstruck by the doctors I had when I was little. Maybe you'd prefer to be a gynecologist. Or a neurosurgeon."

"I promise to keep an open mind, even though I'm certain about my decision."

"You can't keep an open mind and be certain. They're mutually exclusive."

"You know what I mean," Enid said with a laugh.

Harlow nodded, knowing there was no reasoning with her friend on this topic. When she'd been diagnosed with acute lymphoblastic leukemia or ALL, she'd been all of seven. She'd been too young to understand how sick she was, but everything about her treatment had scared her, especially the worry and terror in her mother's eyes. Enid had been a constant in her life. Her friend had insisted on visiting regularly, bringing dolls and books to keep Harlow company. She'd been fearless when Harlow had thrown up for weeks, lost her hair and

56

been too weak to raise her head.

While Harlow's parents had insisted all would be well, Enid had looked up ALL and reported her findings to her friend. It was only then Harlow had realized how close she was to dying. The revelation had sent her parents into a frenzy, but she'd felt better knowing the truth.

Their drinks arrived, drawing Harlow back to the present. She raised her glass. "To Enid — my amazing friend."

"I'm not amazing, but thank you."

They touched glasses then sipped.

"So," Harlow said with a laugh. "About the wedding . . ."

Enid opened the timer app on her phone. "Seventeen minutes," she said, pushing a button. "You have seventeen minutes to monopolize the conversation with wedding talk."

Harlow laughed. "I love that you're not going to let me turn into a bridezilla. So, Kip says I should plan the wedding of my dreams. I can't decide if he's being supportive or avoiding making any decisions."

"It's probably both. Guys don't fantasize about their weddings the way a lot of girls do. It doesn't mean he doesn't love you."

"I know, but I wish he wanted to be a little more involved."

"Maybe when you nail down some specifics, he'll be interested."

Harlow knew she was right. "Venue and date matter the most. I'm still thinking my mom's beautiful backyard."

Enid's expression turned doubtful. "If you're planning on next summer, it could be hot and humid, or worse, raining. Do you want to risk an outdoor wedding?"

"We could get a tent."

"So, a tent in the rain? Harlow, don't you want to get married inside?"

Harlow laughed. "No, little library mouse. I like the outdoors. I want to feel the grass in my toes."

"You're not wearing shoes?"

"Metaphorically."

"Or you could find a really nice venue with green carpeting. I'm just saying."

"When I was nine, my Uncle Leo died. I didn't know him that well, but my mom was devastated. Austin, Mom and I went to Santa Barbara and stayed with Aunt Lillian for the summer. It was magical. Her house is incredible. Huge and old, with secret passageways. Anyway, when we finally came home, my dad had bought the house my mom has now. We were all surprised. I remember running out onto the patio with Mom. She said the backyard was beautiful enough for a wedding. I told her I wanted to be married there, and she said she would make that happen."

Harlow smiled. "It's my destiny to marry Kip there."

Enid laughed. "Then I sure hope your destiny doesn't include rain."

FOUR

Robyn hurried to open her front door, then
smiled at Jase.

"You made it."

"Sorry I'm late." He walked in and gave
her a quick kiss on the cheek. "I got tied up
with a patient."

"Not a problem. Dinner can keep. Austin's out with his friends, so it's just us."

She led the way to the kitchen, where she
had ingredients for drinks on a tray. It only
took a couple of minutes to mix up the
martinis. Jase, a compact man about five-
nine with a lean build, had taken his usual
seat on the sofa. He smiled when she offered him a drink.

"Thanks," he said, his brown eyes more
tired than usual. "It's been a day."

She sat across from him, careful not to
ask for specifics. Everyone had their quirks,
and one of his was being asked about his
day. Early in their dating relationship, he'd

explained the question was a real hot button for him. It made him feel monitored and interrogated. Robyn didn't understand his reasoning, but she'd respected his request she not ever ask the question.

"What's happening with you?" he asked, his way of saying he wasn't going to explain any more than he had.

"The usual," she said with a smile. "Last night Austin negotiated to borrow the big TV." Her smile widened. "He's going to wash my car every week for the summer."

Jase's mouth turned down. "You think he'll follow through?"

"Sure. Austin keeps his word."

"I'm not saying he doesn't. It's just he's kind of checked out from life. He's coasting, with no ambition."

"He's working full-time. I'm not saying I'm happy he's chosen to get a job with his dad, but it's not like he's spending the summer hanging out with his friends and playing video games."

"He is when he's not working."

Robyn tried to temper her irritation. "If he's finished with work, why shouldn't he enjoy himself?"

"He's eighteen. He needs goals."

While she agreed, there was something about Jase's tone. A condescension that made her want to throw something at his head.

"New topic," she said. "Are the girls enjoying camp?"

Jase had twelve- and fifteen-year-old daughters who were in North Carolina at a very exclusive science and math camp.

"Settling in. Now we hear from them three times a day, not eight."

"Improvement."

He reached out, inviting her close. When she'd moved next to him, he laced his fingers with hers.

"I don't want to fight," he said. "It's just Austin has so much potential. It's hard to see it wasted."

She knew what he meant, but somehow his words made her feel defensive. Or like a bad mother.

"I'm giving it some time. I'm hoping working for his dad isn't the thrill he's expecting. Austin can get stubborn, and I don't want him making decisions because he feels trapped."

"I get that." He leaned back against the sofa. "Have you decided what to do about the house?"

"I'm still leaning toward selling. It's too big and expensive. I haven't talked to Harlow or Austin yet. I might start looking for something first. If I find a suitable replacement, then the idea of me moving will be less upsetting to them."

Jase looked at her quizzically. "They're adults with their own lives. Why do they get a say?"

"They don't get a say, exactly. But Austin will be living with me for a while longer, and —"

Jase shifted away from her. "I thought he was moving out."

"It's just for the summer."

"Since when?"

Since he'd told her yesterday, but she didn't say that. "He's not ready to be on his own permanently. He'll be back in the fall."

"You're letting him move in and out? So, when he's forty, he can move back? You're letting him run your life?"

She put down her drink and told herself to stay calm. "He's not running my life. He's my kid, and I love him. If he wants to stay for a couple more years, that's fine. He's eighteen, not forty."

"You're making a mistake, letting him think you'll always be his fallback plan."

"Why do you have so much energy on the topic? It shouldn't matter to you if Austin lives with me or not."

"What does that mean?"

The sharp question surprised her. "I have my own place. Why do you care if my kids live with me? It doesn't affect you."

"I'm not ready for us to live together."

The blunt statement caught her off guard. "We've never discussed living together. What does that have to do with anything?"

"I thought that's what you were expecting."

There was something in the way he said the words — a tone that implied a weakness on her part. Or maybe it was more about him judging.

"I wasn't," she said coolly. It had crossed her mind, but now she was firmly committed to getting her own house.

"I'm not ready for that," he told her.

"So you've said."

She told herself he wasn't deliberately trying to be hurtful, implying she wanted more from the relationship than he did. She almost believed herself.

"Your expectations —" he began.

Okay. This had gone on long enough.

She cut him off by standing. "You've been in a mood since you walked in. I have no idea what's going on with you. I'd ask, but then you'd feel interrogated. By the way, not liking when people ask about your day is dumb. Asking about someone's day shows

64

interest and affection."

He started to speak, but she held up her hand. "I'm not done."

"Perhaps *I* am." He set down his drink and rose. "I'm not the only one in a mood. We should table this discussion."

"Fine with me."

She led the way to the front door and waited until he stepped onto the porch before closing it in his face. Childish? Maybe. But very, very satisfying.

She walked into the kitchen and opened the refrigerator. She'd made a healthy salad and had fish ready to grill.

"Not eating that tonight," she murmured.

She scrolled through her phone, then pushed a button.

"Hi. I'd like to order a pizza, please. A large, all meat, extra cheese."

When the order was on its way, she sent a quick text to Austin.

Jase had to leave, so the coast is clear whenever you want to come home. There'll be leftover pizza in the refrigerator, in case you're hungry.

His reply came in seconds.

When did you order it?

Two minutes ago.

On my way home.

Robyn laughed. I'll set the table.

Harlow pushed her small grocery cart through the market. Even though it was barely four, the store was crowded with shoppers intent on finding something for dinner. Some of them moved purposefully, as if sure of their selections. Others circled aimlessly, searching for inspiration. Harlow found herself in the latter group.

She'd been excited to move in with Kip. He'd given her more than half the closet space, and his apartment had parking for her car. He listened when she'd explained that leaving wet towels on the floor made her crazy, and now even put down the toilet seat. But they were still working out the kinks of living together.

Like dinner. Sadly, Kip neither cooked nor showed any interest in cooking. He didn't even like to barbecue, which meant they went out all the time, they got takeout, or she cooked. She'd discovered that the meal prep was really the least of it. First she had to figure out what they were having. Then she had to go buy the ingredients, *then* cook it. Kip helped with cleanup, but that was less than twenty-five percent of the work.

Her mom had offered some easy suggestions for planning two or three dinners. Like a rotisserie chicken. Eat half night one with a salad and some kind of potato. Use the second half in tacos the next night, then boil the bones in chicken broth to make soup.

Harlow had become an expert at using the second half of a rotisserie chicken — she could barely look at one without gagging. She'd never gone so far as to make soup with the bones, but she'd gotten plenty creative. But five weeks into living with Kip, they'd already had five chickens. She needed another plan.

She cruised the meat aisle, but wasn't inspired. Pasta sounded too heavy, and going out to eat got expensive. She thought about asking her mom for a suggestion, but that felt too much like running home. Finally she bought shrimp, stir-fry vegetables, a Thai-inspired sauce and a bag of rice.

An hour later she'd showered and started a load of laundry. The rice was in the Instant Pot, and she'd chopped up the vegetables. As she worked, her diamond engagement ring caught the light. She paused to admire the shine.

Kip texted to say he was on his way. She poured them each a glass of pinot grigio, then took a seat on the oversized balcony.

Clouds dropped the temperature into the low eighties, but also increased the humidity. Overhead, palm trees swayed in the breeze. She stretched out in her lounge chair and closed her eyes, anticipation building in her stomach. A few minutes later, she felt a soft brush of lips on her cheek.

"You're home," she said, sliding over to make room. "I missed you."

Kip, just over six feet, with dark hair and eyes, slid in next to her and pulled her close.

"I missed you more."

He kissed her, his mouth lingering on hers. She moved her lips against his, then parted them so he could deepen the kiss before shifting so she straddled him. He was already hard.

"How was your day?" His gaze was bright with wicked intent as he cupped her breasts under her tank top.

"Good. I had two families out for a day of fun."

"Anyone throw up?"

She laughed. "Not today. Non-puke days are my favorite."

He moved his thumbs against her nipples,

making her breath catch. She tossed her tank top onto the ground. Kip glanced around, obviously thinking of their neighbors.

"Harlow!"

She stood up and walked into the living room, shedding her shorts and panties as she went.

"Yes?" she asked, glancing at him over her shoulder. "Did you want to say something?"

He stepped into the apartment and closed the sliding door before sending his own clothes flying. He grabbed her wrist and spun her back to him. Their mouths locked, their bodies collided.

They made love with an intensity that, as always, took her breath away. When their breathing returned to normal, he lightly kissed her.

"So, what's for dinner?"

She laughed. "Is that really what you want to ask me?"

He grinned. "Sure. I'm hungry. For food this time."

She laughed. While Kip changed out of his work clothes, she pulled on her shorts and tank top, then went into the kitchen and checked on the rice.

"Ten minutes," she called.

Kip came down the hall, pulling on a

T-shirt. "I'll set the table."

She liked this, she thought happily. They were a good team.

They sat across from each other at the table.

"So," she said, picking up her wine. "How was your day?"

"I sell appliances, Harlow. It's not exciting."

"But you're good at it."

He smiled. "I am, much to the annoyance of the other salespeople."

"So today you sold?"

He thought for a second. "Three washers and dryers and two microwaves. I also had clients come in who are doing a full kitchen remodel."

"Ka-ching."

"It'll be a good commission."

They talked all through dinner, then he helped her load the dishwasher. At eight, he started his biweekly online game with friends, while she loaded up her wedding planning app and tried to make a few decisions. When she got overwhelmed, she checked her email and found a newsletter from the Children's Cancer Hospital, where she'd been treated.

There were the usual notes on new treatments, updates on former patients, and donation requests.

Harlow gave a little each month. Everyone there had been so good to her. She'd been sick and scared, and they'd made her feel better.

Once she'd been deemed "cured," she'd returned for follow-ups. Monthly at first, then every six months, then yearly. She could never assume she would live her life cancer-free, but the fear was less prevalent than it had been even five years ago.

She looked at Kip, intent on his game. He understood that she lived with the shadow of the disease somewhere in a corner of her life. That having been diagnosed so young, she was more likely to be diagnosed again at some point. A truth that should have sent him running, but hadn't.

Other guys had been scared off, or treated her differently. They were too careful, too concerned, too unable to cope. Kip had listened, then pulled her close and made love to her. He never monitored her health or asked if she was too tired. He trusted her to take care of herself, and that made her love him more. With him, she could imagine forever — and there was no better feeling than that.

FIVE

I'm sorry we fought.

Robyn stared at the text, not sure what it meant. Jase saying he was sorry they fought wasn't the same as apologizing for what he said or the way he'd walked out. Just as troubling, she'd been unable to let go of her irritation. He'd been all over Austin for no reason. Early on in their relationship, they'd agreed they didn't get involved in each other's children's lives. She never offered advice about his girls, and he was supposed to stay quiet about her kids. Only he was forever making comments about their choices.

She was also concerned about Austin's statement that Jase didn't approve of him. Had Jase said something to Austin?

A question she was going to have to ask her boyfriend directly, she thought, quickly texting a noncommittal Me, too, before shoving her phone back in her purse. She got out of her car and looked around Austin's apartment complex. Seconds later, Harlow appeared, pushing a flatbed cart across the parking lot.

Robyn had offered to fill Austin's refrigerator as a housewarming gift, and Harlow had come by on her day off to help.

"How much food do you think I bought?" Robyn asked with a laugh. "Maybe we won't need that."

"I know you, Mom. You bought out the store."

"I'll admit it. I totally did."

She watched her daughter approach, enjoying her easy stride and how healthy she looked. Harlow was about her height — nearly five-eight — with long blond hair and blue eyes. They looked enough alike that no one could question their relationship.

Robyn popped open the trunk and stared at the grocery bags she'd crammed into the back of her SUV. Harlow stopped beside her.

"Jeez, Mom, they're going to have to restock every department."

"I don't want Austin going hungry."

Together they loaded the bags onto the cart, then made their way to Austin's new apartment. He'd left the key under the mat, as promised.

The apartment was big and airy, with a view of the community pool. A big black leather sofa faced the eighty-inch TV from her media room. The sad little rejected TV sat on the floor. On the coffee table were game controllers, soda cans and the remains of Mexican takeout.

"My brother is a pig," Harlow said with a laugh. "At least Kip now hangs up his towels and puts his dirty clothes into the basket."

"Austin will learn."

Robyn checked out the bedroom and bathroom before returning to the kitchen. Harlow had already started setting food on the counter.

"Is there a pantry?" Robyn asked, holding a loaf of bread and a box of cereal.

"There." Harlow pointed to a tall cabinet next to the refrigerator.

Robyn opened the doors and saw a bag of M&M's and a box of Ritz crackers on a shelf and absolutely nothing else.

"That boy," she murmured. "I taught him better than this. He's going to get scurvy."

"Can you get that in a summer?"

"I hope not."

They continued to empty grocery bags. Robyn had gone with easy-to-prepare foods like frozen pizza and bagged salad. She'd bought all his favorite fruits, thinking at least then he would be getting some vitamins. As they worked, they talked about how Harlow was doing, working for her dad, living with Kip.

Her daughter's upbeat tone made Robyn think that Cord had yet to tell her about dating Zafina. Which was just like him — always put off sharing bad news.

"The lawyer sent over the preliminary offer," Harlow said, folding an empty bag. "For the kayaking business."

A couple of years ago, Harlow had come up with the idea of Cord buying a local kayak rental company. They had a great year-round clientele. She'd created a business plan and projections, some on her own and some for class projects as she finished her business degree.

Robyn had wanted to warn Harlow that Cord was unlikely to buy the business — expansion wasn't his thing. Except when it came to women, he didn't enjoy change. But Harlow had been determined. She wanted to learn from the ground up, then eventually transition to running the family charter company. Cord had surprised Robyn by agreeing.

"How does the offer look?" Robyn asked.

"Good." Harlow made a face. "Dad is dragging his feet at reading the paperwork. I know legal documents aren't fun, but he has to review them before we can move forward."

"Good luck with that."

Harlow reached for another bag. "This is your way of telling me you won't get involved?"

"It is."

"He listens to you."

Robyn thought about how Cord had yet to say anything about Zafina. "Less than you'd think."

They put away the rest of the groceries.

"You don't mind that Austin's only renting this place for the summer?" Harlow asked.

"I think he's too young to be on his own. It'll be good practice, and then he can figure out what he wants to do with his life."

Harlow shook her head. "Mom, let it go. He's not interested in college. I know you're disappointed, but just because you regret not going doesn't mean college is right for everyone."

"I had an opportunity to go," Robyn said. "I should have taken it. Austin's going to have regrets, too."

"You don't know that. Maybe he'll have a

great life."

Working for his father? Robyn doubted that. She couldn't help feeling he had dreams that needed fulfilling.

"I just want you two happy and settled," she said.

"I will be after I marry Kip." Harlow reached for her phone. "Oh, I was on Pinterest and I saw some great decorating ideas for the backyard. You'll have to tell me what you think."

"For my backyard?"

"For the wedding, Mom. Sheesh." Harlow studied her. "What?"

Robyn did her best to keep her expression neutral. "I have no idea what you're asking."

"You made a face. Are you going to go off on your rant about how Kip and I are too young and don't know each other well enough to get married? We're engaged."

"I accept the idea of the wedding." Sort of. "It's the location I object to."

Harlow stared at her blankly. "The backyard? We've talked about this a million times."

"It's complicated."

"How?"

"Per the divorce, I got to keep the house, as long as I paid for it. The mortgage and upkeep. But only until six months after Austin turns eighteen. Then I either sell the house or buy out your father. Austin turned eighteen two months ago."

Harlow's look of concern faded. "Then buy out Dad and keep the house."

"I don't have that kind of money. I'd have to refinance, and I don't want to." Robyn didn't mention how she'd never wanted to buy it in the first place. "It would be very expensive. Pretty much everything I have would be tied up in the house. That's a scary place for me to be, financially."

"But you have to." Harlow stared at her. "Mom, I want to get married at the house. In the backyard. It's what we've talked about forever."

"When you were a little girl." A thousand lifetimes ago.

"No, now. It's what I want, and Kip's totally into it. You can't sell. Why would you even consider it?" Her gaze narrowed. "This is about moving in with Jase, isn't it?"

"This has nothing to do with him." Of that she was sure.

"Then why make such a big deal about this? Get some line of credit or something. The house is worth a lot. After the wedding, you can list it." She shoved her phone in her pocket. "I can't believe you'd sell the house without warning me or anything. That's so selfish. I'm your only daughter. This is the only wedding we're going to plan together, and you don't even want me to have it at the house."

Tears filled her eyes. "How could you?"

With that, Harlow ran out of the apartment, slamming the front door. Robyn stood in the silence, knowing the fight was far from over and dreading what would be the next of many, many rounds.

Harlow finished typing up the notes from her call with a client who wanted to charter a full-day sail. The two kids under the age of five might be a problem, she thought. Depending on whether they were prone to motion sickness. Adults generally knew if they could handle the movement, but kids could go either way.

Still, an eight-hour sail would be fun, especially if Austin wanted to crew. She glanced at the clock and knew he would be docking any time now. She would ask him when he was back. She picked up her phone. Still no text from her mother, which surprised her. Why hadn't she heard something? An apology or an offer to talk?

She shook her head. Her mom was being ridiculous. For years, she and her mom had talked about her getting married there. They'd joked about an after-the-reception pool party. They'd agreed on a valet service to handle the cars.

Harlow had always planned on getting married at the house, and now her mom wanted to sell the place out from under her?

"Don't think about that right now," she murmured. Crying at work was never a good idea. She sucked in a breath and turned her attention to her email. She'd barely opened the first one when Zafina, Kip's twin sister, walked into the office.

Like Kip, Zafina was tall, with dark hair and eyes. She was assistant manager at a local waterfront restaurant. Harlow hadn't gotten to know her as well as she would like but figured there was plenty of time.

"Hi," she said, circling the desk. "You're a surprise. Were we supposed to meet about something?"

Zafina frowned. "No. I'm here to see Cord."

Her dad? That made no sense. "Why?"

Just then her father walked out of his office. "Zafina!"

There was something in the way he said the name. Something that —

Before Harlow could figure out what was going on, Zafina stepped into her father's

80

embrace, and then they kissed. On the mouth! As if they were —

"Dad?"

Cord kept his arm around Zafina. "What?"

The obvious explanation kept forming, then slipping away, because it was impossible to consider. He couldn't. They couldn't. Only it seemed . . .

"You're dating?"

Zafina gave Cord a hurt look. "You said you'd told her."

"I said I was going to. It's no big deal." Her father grinned. "Zafina and I are a thing. Isn't it great?"

Harlow stared at them, trying to understand. Since the divorce, her father had dated a lot of younger women. Harlow figured that after nearly twenty years of marriage, he wanted to play the field. But this was different. And hard to grasp.

"You're dating my fiancé's sister and you didn't tell me?"

"Don't make it sound like that, kiddo."

"But you kept it a secret." And it was gross, but she didn't say that.

"We wanted to be sure it was the real thing."

No. No way. The real thing? What did that even mean?

Zafina stepped toward her. "I know this is

a surprise, but I like your father very much. He's a good man, and we're happy."

Like as in *like*? No. Just no. "There's a big age difference."

"Hey," Cord said with a laugh. "I'm not that old."

"It's twenty years."

"I'm fine with it," Zafina told her.

Harlow was not. "But you're Kip's sister, and Kip and I are engaged. And now you're dating my dad?"

Zafina smiled. "Isn't it great?"

Not really.

"We're grabbing drinks and an early dinner," Cord said.

For one heart-stopping second, Harlow had the horrifying thought that he was going to invite her and Kip to join them — like a double date. Fortunately, all he said was, "You'll lock up for the night?"

"I will. Not a problem." She faked a smile. "You kids have fun."

They left. Harlow stood by her desk, trying to understand what had just happened. Her father was dating her fiancé's twin sister. And it was "the real thing."

No, she thought again. This was bad, and she couldn't even mentally articulate why. Her brain simply couldn't grasp the information.

Deciding ignoring what she couldn't understand would work, at least in the short term, she started checking on the boats. She made sure the cabins were locked and the lines secured. Just as she reached the last boat, the final charter for the day made its way into the marina. Austin stood on the bow, ready to jump onto the finger pier to tie off. Harlow waved him back, then caught the line.

She worked with Austin and Buddy, the captain, to help the passengers off the boat, then helped with cleanup. Once the boat was locked up for the night, she motioned Austin into the office.

"What's up?" he asked.

"First, we have a day-long sailboat charter. Young family, two kids under five. Want to take it with me?"

Her brother grinned. "Sure."

"There could be puke."

He laughed. "Always a possibility in our line of work. Put it on my schedule."

"I will. Did you know Dad's dating Zafina?"

Her brother's expression was confused. "The sister?" He grimaced. "Seriously? Dad's dating Kip's twin sister? Gross."

"Thank you. I was thinking the same thing. She came in to pick him up, and they were all hugging and kissing. I had no idea. He kept it from me."

"He's not the only one," Austin mumbled.

"What do you mean?"

Her brother shook his head. "Nothing. Forget I said that."

"Austin? Please?"

He sighed heavily, his shoulders rounding. "Kip had to know."

"What?" she shrieked.

But even as she asked the question, she knew her brother was right. Zafina would have told Kip she was dating her twin's future father-in-law.

"Maybe I'm wrong," Austin said quickly.

While she wanted that to be true, she knew it wasn't. Of course Kip had known. The twins were tight, like her and Austin. That was one of the things she loved about Kip — how much he cared about his family.

"No, you're not wrong," she whispered. "He knows."

Kip had lied to her, or at the very least, kept the truth from her.

"I never thought he'd do that," she admitted.

Lies of omission were even worse than the real thing, because they implied that someone else had the right to decide how much

84

she had a right to know. An issue for her that went all the way back to when she'd had cancer. Her parents had told her only that she would be sick for a while. They'd kept the truth from her — that she very well might die. Something she'd never gotten over.

Austin's mouth twisted. "I'm sorry."

"Me, too." She cleared her throat. "Okay, I'm going to lock up and go home."

"You'll be all right?"

"No, but that's hardly a surprise."

On her way home, Harlow nearly called her mom a dozen times, but even as she reached for her phone, she put her hands back on the wheel. She knew her mom would totally take her side against her dad, but she was less sure about what she would say about Kip. No one expected much from Cord, but Kip was supposed to be different. He was supposed to be the guy taking care of Harlow for the rest of her life. But he'd kept an important truth from her.

Once in their apartment, Harlow pulled on a one-piece bathing suit and did a few laps in the community pool. The physical exercise helped burn off some of her energy but did nothing for her hurt and sadness.

As she showered, she tried to work up some mad, but it couldn't seem to overtake the pain she felt. Kip had betrayed her with his silence. Worse, early in their relationship, she'd explained why lies of omission were such a big deal for her, and he'd said he understood.

It was his night to work until the store closed. She tried to keep herself busy with wedding planning, but realized that between her fight with her mom and this new information about Kip, she wasn't in a wedding mood. She stared at her engagement ring and told herself they would get past this. They had to — she loved Kip.

By the time she heard his key in the lock, she'd worked herself into an emotional frenzy. He walked into the apartment and saw her curled up on the sofa. His smile faded as he got closer.

"What's wrong?"

"Why didn't you tell me my dad's dating your sister?"

Kip sank down on the sofa and swore under his breath. "He told you."

Hope that he hadn't known died. "Zafina came to see him. I would say they *showed* me more than told me." She glared at him. "You kept it from me."

"I know. I was wrong, and I'm sorry, but I didn't know what to say. When Zafina told me, I was pissed. How could she do that to us? Did it have to be your dad? We had a big fight, and I'm still mad at her." He looked at her. "Harlow, I swear I wasn't trying to hurt you or keep it from you. I just kept hoping they'd end things."

"How long have you known?"

"A month."

"What?" She sprang to her feet. "You've known a month and you never said anything? You slept with me and told me you loved me, all the while keeping this from me? What else aren't you telling me?"

He stood and faced her. "That's all. I swear. I do love you, more than I've loved anyone. I didn't know how to tell you, what to say. I didn't want to upset you."

"You *have* upset me. A lot." She fought tears. "I've told you this is my thing. Don't keep secrets. Just tell me stuff. I can handle it. You don't get to say what I can know. You don't have the right."

He nodded, looking miserable. "I'm so sorry. I felt horrible the whole time."

"Not horrible enough."

"I was wrong. Really wrong. Please believe me. Harlow, I love you."

She heard the sincerity in his words and felt his pain. He swallowed, and his eyes filled with tears.

"I love you," he whispered.

She rushed into his arms. He held her like he would never let go.

"I'm sorry," he repeated over and over.

"It's okay."

"I didn't know what to say."

She felt her own tears on her cheeks as she gave in to a strangled laugh. "It's not an easy thing to talk about. WTF? My dad is dating your sister? That's the same as you dating my mom."

He drew back. "I think your mom is great, but that is never happening."

She smiled. "I know. I'm just saying, why did he have to do that?"

"Why did Zafina? Come on. Find somebody else." His humor faded. "I really am sorry."

"I got that. I'm letting it go. You not telling me," she clarified. "I'm still freaked about my dad."

"You and me, both."

Six

Robyn held the oval platter carefully, looking for any cracks or nicks. On first glance, the piece was in excellent condition. She turned it over and saw the familiar stamp with an anchor and the words *Davenport* and *Stone China* on the back. She looked at Mindy.

"Davenport Flying Bird," she said with a smile. "1805 to 1820."

Mindy cheered. "I was hoping you'd say that. We have about two dozen pieces in the crates my sister sent. Supposedly they're all the Davenport Flying Bird pattern. It's too busy for me, but collectors are passionate about it."

Robyn studied the exotic bird, the blossoms in orange, yellow and blue. "I see the appeal. I'm not interested in collecting it, but it's a beautiful pattern. I'll go through what she sent and catalog it, then look at the wish lists to see who will want to know about what pieces."

Mindy offered clients a chance to keep a "wish list" on file, detailing items they were interested in buying, should they come up. The computerized lists allowed for easy searching when new items came in. Robyn had a feeling they would quickly sell everything that had been sent.

"I've never gotten into china," Mindy said, opening another box. "I appreciate that you know as much as you do about it."

"Compliments of my Aunt Lillian. One of the rooms in her house has hundreds of teacups and saucers from all over the world. Some of them date back centuries. We used to spend hours up there, trying to date pieces. She has a few full sets of dishes, but mostly it's the teacups."

Mindy grinned. "One of these days, I'll have to go with you when you visit her. I'm dying to see her house."

"It's pretty special." More significant than the house was Aunt Lillian herself. "I should go see her this summer. She's mentioned it a couple of times."

"How old is she?"

"Ninety-four."

Mindy grimaced. "Visit with her while you can. You'll feel awful if she passes away and you didn't make the time. This is our slow season. Take off time whenever you want."

Robyn wasn't looking for more guilt in her life, and she knew her boss was right. "I'll look at my calendar."

Mindy unwrapped a set of bowls, also in the Flying Bird pattern. She put them on a shelf, then glanced at the screen on her phone. Her mouth curved into a smile.

"Dimitri," she said.

"You're texting?"

"Some. Just little flirty stuff." Mindy sighed dreamily. "After our last lesson, we talked for nearly half an hour. The man is so good-looking. When he touches me, I go up in flames."

"He shouldn't be touching you," Robyn said flatly. "This is trouble. He's a practiced seducer, and you're getting involved in something you can't handle."

Mindy smiled. "Oh, I'll handle it just fine."

"Ugh."

Mindy laughed. "Come on. This is good for me. My life is ordinary. Why can't I have a little fun?"

"It's not the fun I object to. It's the screwing up your marriage."

Mindy waved away the concern. "Payne will never know, but obviously you have strong feelings, so we'll talk about something else. How's the wedding planning?"

Robyn unpacked a few more plates. "Not great. Harlow's mad at me."

"That's hardly new. She can be, um, difficult. Or is *demanding* a better word?"

Robyn laughed. "Either works. I mentioned selling the house, and she went off. She thinks I should take out a loan to pay off her father and keep the house until she gets married. Apparently she's set on a backyard wedding, and I'm the bitch in the way of that."

"Would you qualify for a loan on your own?" Mindy asked. "You work here, but it's only part-time."

"I don't know. I haven't talked to anyone."

Robyn had savings and monthly income from Cord buying her out of the business, but Mindy was right about her job. It was only a few hours a week and didn't pay all that much. What if she didn't qualify for a loan? While it would solve her Harlow problem, it would not be happy news. Her plan for the new house was to buy something smaller, and not on the water, so the price would be significantly less. She was hoping to just pay cash with her half of what she got from selling her current place.

"Maybe I'll talk to Payne about buying your place," Mindy said. "We've discussed getting a bigger house, and yours is beautiful. The view alone is a stunner."

"You're welcome to bring him over to walk through anytime," she said, rather than point out that buying a new house with her husband while planning to have sex with her tennis instructor seemed ill-advised.

Robyn's discussion with Mindy — the one about whether she would qualify for a loan — replayed in her mind as she drove home. The reality of it was startling.

When she and Cord had first married, they'd started the charter business together. She'd worked side by side with him, taking out one of the two boats they owned every single day. She'd continued working as a charter captain while pregnant, finishing up a fishing trip, then driving herself to the hospital to give birth to Harlow.

She'd strapped on her newborn and had gone back to work within six weeks. In the evening, she did the company's books. By the time Austin had come along, they'd had more boats and could afford help, but she'd still done the books until about six years ago.

In the divorce, Cord had bought her out of half the business — something he'd fought, but the judge had agreed that she'd worked just as hard to establish the company as he had. The supporting paperwork, including proof that she had indeed taken out a fishing charter the day she'd given birth, had helped.

Cord had pushed to pay her off over ten years instead of five. The monthly payments covered her expenses, including the mortgage, but didn't leave a lot left over. Robyn had never thought much about her income stream or the fact that in six years, she wasn't going to have that check to support her.

"Why don't I have a plan?" she muttered to herself as she drove toward her neighborhood.

Selling the house was a huge first step. Once she had her own, smaller place, she wouldn't be spending more than half of her monthly checks on the mortgage alone. She could save that money. She also needed to look at her job situation and work more hours.

She saw Austin's SUV in the driveway. She pulled inside the garage. Once in the house, she called out his name.

"In the kitchen," he yelled back.

She found him frowning at the contents of the refrigerator.

"Close the door, please," she said, setting down her handbag.

He laughed and complied, then walked

over and gave her a bear hug.

"Hi, Mom."

"Hi, yourself." She smiled up at him, because two years ago, Austin had shot past her in height. "Not that I don't love seeing you, but why are you here?"

"I'm hungry."

"I filled up your refrigerator less than a week ago."

He released her. "The guys ate everything."

She thought of all the groceries she'd bought. "I suspect not everything."

"You're right, but all the good stuff." He slid onto a stool at the island. "Besides, I miss you, so I came by."

"To stare into the refrigerator?"

"It helps me think." Austin's expression was hopeful. "Want to fix me some dinner?"

"You're taking advantage of me," she said, although without a lot of energy.

"I know, and I feel bad about it. Part of the problem is my frontal cortex isn't fully mature, so I don't measure risk the same way I will when I'm twenty-five."

"Ah, the lack of maturity defense."

"It's not a defense if it's true. Please? I was out with a charter all day, and I'm starved."

She tossed him a nectarine. "Eat this while

I make dinner. It'll be an hour."

"You're the best." He bit into the nectarine. "Mind if I watch TV?"

"Help yourself."

He walked toward the family room. She started the oven preheating, got a pot of water on the stove, then went to change out of her work clothes. Despite her teasing, she was happy to have company.

She returned to the kitchen and dropped pasta into the boiling water, then cut up raw chicken and some vegetables for a casserole. When the pasta was done, she drained it and put it in a large bowl with the chicken, veggies and Alfredo sauce cut with a little pasta water. Once the casserole was in the oven, she started on a salad and garlic bread. Austin wandered back.

"How's work?" she asked when he resumed his seat at the island. "You still like the job?"

He glanced at her. "Do you really want to know, or is this heading into the 'go to college' conversation?"

She laughed. "Can it be both?"

"I guess. Oh, Harlow's on a tear."

She continued dicing tomato without reacting. "From what?"

"Dad's dating Zafina. She's —"

So Cord had finally told his daughter. "I

know who she is. Someone at the club told me they were dating."

"It's not right. What was he thinking?"

When it came to women, Cord didn't think. He acted, consequences be damned.

"He's too old for her," he added. "I don't get it. What's his plan? To make Harlow and Kip's relationship all about him?"

"All good questions," she said lightly. "Dinner in ten minutes."

He got up and washed his hands. As he set the table in the kitchen, he said, "I'm glad you're dating appropriately, Mom. I couldn't take both of you doing weird stuff."

"As long as we do it one at a time?"

He chuckled. "That would be great."

She set the salad on the table. "Austin, we need to talk about the house."

"Okay. What?"

"I want to sell it and buy something smaller."

He looked at her expectantly. "And?"

"And that's it."

"Okay. I figured you'd be doing that. You never wanted to buy this place, and it's huge. It's gotta be expensive. I'm glad you kept it while I was in high school, but sure, now you want to sell." He swallowed. "You're still going to have room for me, right?"

"Yes. I will have room for you."

"Then you should do it."

"Harlow's not happy. She wants to get married in the backyard and says I should keep the house until her wedding."

He rolled his eyes. "Harlow needs to get over herself. She's not the one who has to pay the mortgage. She's my sister and I love her, but sometimes, she's too entitled."

Robyn pulled the casserole out of the oven. "You mean like letting your friends eat all your groceries, then expecting your mom to make dinner?"

He grinned. "Exactly like that."

"I was a jerk," Jase said when they were seated at the restaurant.

Robyn stared at him. "Interesting opening line."

He gave her a self-deprecating smile. "I thought I'd state the obvious and see how it went from there."

After his non-apology apology text, she hadn't heard from Jase for a few days. Then this morning he'd texted her and asked her to meet him for dinner at a local seafood place.

She'd taken her time agreeing, not sure if there was a point to them continuing to see each other. No doubt the smart decision was to rethink their relationship — the only problem being she'd missed him enough to make her realize she wanted it to work out between them.

"Last time," he continued. "When I was at your place. I know I was difficult."

"Moody," she offered helpfully. "And a little judgy."

He looked at her without smiling. "Yes to both. It's been a hell of a couple of weeks."

He took one of her hands in his. "I lost a patient. She's been in and out of the hospital. She's had a couple of heart attacks." He drew in a breath. "I can't get into the details."

"Of course not."

"She died the day I came over. It hit me hard. I knew it could happen, but when it did, I wasn't ready. Her family was devastated. She had eight grandkids."

Regret filled her. "I wish you'd told me. I don't need specifics, Jase, but some small amount of information would be very helpful."

"I know. If it was just that, I would have been okay. But there's more."

Their server appeared to tell them about the specials and get their drink orders. When he left, Jase's gaze met hers.

"It's Galen."

His oldest daughter? "Is she all right?"

He dropped his head for a second. "She's anorexic."

"What?" Galen had always been thin, but anorexic? "When did you find out?"

"We got a call from the camp. She hadn't been eating. I knew she was skinny, but she wore baggy clothes and we thought she was fine." Tears filled his dark eyes. "We got her into a special program in Miami. I've been getting her settled these past few days. Plus we had to deal with Grayce. We talked about bringing her home, but in the end, let her stay in camp. She has friends there, and the counselors are watching out for her."

Now she reached for his other hand. "Jase, I'm sorry. This is such a nightmare."

"What if she's not okay?" he asked, his voice trembling. "What if this is my fault? I work a lot, her mother works a lot. We've had trouble keeping a nanny. Maybe there wasn't enough consistency."

Robyn doubted consistency was the problem, but didn't say that. From what she could tell, both girls were scheduled every moment. There was no time to just be, to think, to imagine, to get bored. She would also guess they needed their parents around a little more.

"You know the situation now," she said

instead. "That will help. It's going to be a process." Not exactly helpful, but she didn't know what else to offer. She'd never had to deal with the disorder.

Jase released her hands and cleared his throat. "The whole time I was gone, I kept thinking about your kids being so normal. Okay, Austin didn't go to college, but he's a solid kid. He fucking eats."

Jase held up a hand. "I apologize for swearing."

"It's okay."

He shook his head. "It's not. I lie awake at night and think of all the things I used to worry about happening when Galen went to high school. I figured drugs, or some guy knocking her up. I never thought she'd stop eating. I never thought she might die."

Robyn had no idea what to say to him. "I'm sorry," she murmured.

"Me, too." He looked at her. "I've been thinking about you so much. Through all I'm dealing with, I wonder how you'd handle it. You're not like us — you didn't push your kids to achieve. You're relaxed. Austin's refusal to go to college would devastate me, but you went with the flow."

Their server appeared with their drinks, then left. Jase wrapped his hand around his scotch.

"Look at Harlow," he added. "She's working for her dad. Not exactly at a 'change the world' profession, but she's happy. Engaged. Normal. I envy that."

Robyn was trying to stick to the positives, but it felt like there were little digs buried in his compliments.

"Maybe it's because you weren't pushed yourself as a kid," he continued. "You married young and got pregnant right away. You didn't go to college." He smiled ruefully. "I used to think that was a problem. I worried we wouldn't have anything in common because you weren't educated, but I was wrong. I might have gone to medical school, but you're the one who knows how to raise happy, healthy kids."

"Like an idiot savant?" she asked dryly, telling herself not to take what he was saying personally. He was in a bad place and not thinking about his words.

"What? No. Of course not. More like an earth mother. Like how mother bears know how to look after their young. It wasn't bred out of you."

"Or erased by too much learning."

He set down his drink. "You're angry. What did I say?"

She held up a hand. "Let it go, and I'll try to do the same." She didn't want to fight with him. Not tonight. He had too much going on. Later she would slap him upside the head, but right now, she was going to play nice.

He looked confused. "But I was complimenting you. I think you're a great mother."

"Because I'm hearty, uneducated peasant stock?" she asked before she could stop herself. He was really starting to annoy her.

"Robyn, no."

She told herself to change the subject, then blurted, "What did you mean when you said you worried we wouldn't have anything in common?"

He leaned back, obviously uncomfortable. "That we, ah, come from different worlds. I'm a doctor surrounded by professionals. My ex-wife is a principal. Just job stuff."

"Not *just* job stuff. You're way too uncomfortable for that."

"You have to admit our circumstances are different. I'm a doctor."

"Yes, you've mentioned that once or twice."

"You work in retail. Part-time. You don't have any ambition. At first I thought you were dating me because you wanted to marry a successful doctor. To give you security."

Her mind went in fourteen different directions, leaving her unable to articulate a single one. His stark assessment of her life was the most painful, but his assumption that she was looking to marry a rich doctor was the most annoying, so she went with that one.

"You thought I was trying to trap you?" she asked, careful to keep her voice low. "I wasn't."

"I know that now."

Did he? "Why go out with me if you thought that?"

He stared at her blankly. "You're beautiful. I knew the sex would be great. Finding out we had something to talk about was unexpected but very welcome."

Anger blossomed. She thought of all the times he'd gone to work events without her, saying she would find the evening boring. Had he been ashamed to be seen with her? What about dinners at his club — one that was far more exclusive than hers? The rare occasions they went, everyone watched them. She'd barely met his friends and had never been introduced to his extended family.

How, after a year together, had she only figured out just now that her boyfriend was ashamed of her?

"Let me recap," she said softly. "You assumed I only wanted to date you to hang out with a —" she used air quotes "— rich doctor with the ultimate goal of trapping you into marriage. You felt I was beneath you, what with me being an uneducated and possibly unintelligent stay-at-home mother with no hope except to find a rich man to support me. You think I'm attractive and you're interested in sex with me, so you figured it was a good trade-off as long as you were clear we weren't going to end up together permanently. I mean, what would your friends at the club say? Right?"

He blanched. "Robyn, you're taking this all wrong. Or maybe it's me. I don't know what I'm saying. I'm sorry. I've hurt your feelings. Please, can we start over?"

She picked up her bag. "We can, Jase. We can go back to the moment when we met. It was at Mindy's store. Do you remember? Let's go back to when you asked me to lunch. This time, I'm going to say no and then pretend we never met."

She rose and walked out, more grateful than she could say that she'd driven herself. She handed her ticket to the valet, asked him to hurry, then waited for her car. Jase didn't walk outside. A good thing, considering that by the time she got into her car, she was already crying.

SEVEN

Harlow hosed down the sailboat, washing the salt water from the deck. The familiar chore allowed her to get lost in her thoughts, which was usually okay, just not today.

She missed her mom. She'd stopped by the house a couple of times, but her mother hadn't been home. Texting was the obvious solution, but somehow that felt like surrendering. She knew Kip would tell her that communicating with her own parent shouldn't be measured as a win or a loss. While in theory, she agreed with him, the need to stand strong, to be the one in the right, was impossible to ignore. Which left her feeling sad and lonely.

She and Enid had planned to hang out the previous evening, but her friend had picked up another shift at the restaurant, leaving Harlow with no one to help her through the multiple crises in her life. In her head, she knew her BFF had to save money for medical school, but her heart felt unloved.

Harlow turned off the water and coiled the hose. She checked that the sailboat was ready for the next charter and the door to the cabin was locked before heading back to the office, where she would face yet another email from the lawyer helping her with the kayak company purchase. At some point she was going to have to pin down her father so they could move forward. But he was being elusive, and she wasn't up to fighting. Not today.

She scanned her emails, added a couple more charters to her calendar, then wandered into her father's office. He was typing, but looked up and smiled when he saw her.

"How'd it go today?" he asked.

"Good. They enjoyed themselves and want to book an overnight for next week."

"I like that."

She slid into the chair on the visitor side of his desk and tried to see her father as a stranger would. Cord was forty-six, but he looked younger. He was fit, tanned, with an easy smile. She guessed he was good-looking. The dad-factor made it hard to judge. He always had a girlfriend, most of them a lot younger, which hadn't bothered her until he'd started dating Kip's twin.

"How's it going with Zafina?" she asked.

He frowned. "Why would you ask?"

"I don't know. I just wondered. You two met when? At my graduation party?"

"No. We met when I had dinner with Kip's parents back in March. She was there."

Harlow grinned. "That must have been awkward, Leah and Zafina at the same dinner. They don't seem as if they'd like each other."

"I didn't take Leah. It was just the four of us. Zafina and I hit it off. After Kip's parents left the restaurant, we went to the bar and made a night of it." He smiled. "And that was all she wrote."

"Wait, what? You started dating Zafina in March?"

He nodded, leaning back in his chair and putting his feet on his desk. "That's nearly four months with her. I hadn't realized." He grinned. "That might be a personal best."

"But you didn't break up with Leah until the end of April. I remember because she called me crying about it. She wanted me to change your mind. As if." She stared at him. "Wait. You were cheating on Leah with Zafina?"

Her father's expression turned smug. "I like to keep my options open."

"Dad, that's awful."

How could he? Good men didn't cheat. Only losers did. Her dad was a decent guy — she'd always believed that. He was her father.

"Hey." His feet slammed to the floor. "Don't look at me like you're disappointed."

"I *am* disappointed. I may not like all your girlfriends, but you should at least treat them like human beings. It's bad enough that you're dating my fiancé's sister, but now this? I don't understand. Is this who you really are?"

She had more she wanted to say, but before she could get her mad on, Austin stuck his head in the office.

"Dad, we have an appointment."

Cord looked at him. "What are you talking about?"

"I've asked for some time to talk to you. You're always busy, so you said to make an appointment. I did. For now." He pointed to the computer. "It's on your calendar."

Cord brushed him off with a wave of his hand. "This isn't a good time."

Harlow stood. "I'm out of here. You two go ahead."

Austin stepped into the room, but Cord shook his head. "No. I'm not doing this now. I have to go."

To cheat on Zafina, too? But Harlow only thought the question.

Her father tucked his cell phone into his shirt pocket and grabbed his sunglasses. "Harlow, lock up before you go. Austin, we'll talk another time."

With that he headed out of the building. Harlow watched him go, feeling awful about what she'd just learned.

"He's being especially jerky today," she said.

"I got that. What were you talking about?"

"He admitted he cheated on Leah with Zafina. For like two months. I can't accept that. Our dad's not supposed to be like that."

Her brother shrugged. "Yet he is."

"Why are you so calm? This is disgusting and upsetting and a lot of other words I can't remember right now. My stomach hurts, and I want to hit him. Where's your emotion in this?"

"You're surprised by him."

There was something in the way Austin spoke — as if he were the older sibling, waiting for her to catch up.

"So you knew?"

"Not the specifics, but Dad's not the faithful type."

"Since when?"

Austin turned away. "Since he got his freedom." He walked out of the room. "See you tomorrow."

"Austin, wait. What do you know that I don't?"

His only answer was laughter. Then she heard the front door close, and she was left alone with too many questions and not enough answers.

Mason turned at the marina and began his slow run back to Shoreline Park. He'd found several options for his morning run, but so far, this was his favorite.

He'd never spent much time on the West Coast and hadn't known what to expect. The topography was beautiful, with the mountains to the east and the ocean to the west. Most mornings were cool — in the fifties — with some days never warming up as the marine layer settled in for a good long stay. But on other days, it was sunny by nine. He was beginning to think there was nothing more beautiful than the Pacific Ocean on a perfect, sunny day.

He was still having trouble wrapping his head around the changes in his life. He was living in the most unusual house he'd ever seen, getting to know an old woman, while battling fifteen cats who draped themselves on his bed, or rubbed against his leg, meowing, shedding on everything he owned. The cats came and went, despite his closed bedroom door, which meant there were secret passages in the house.

He hadn't explored much, wasn't sure he should. Yes, technically he would inherit the house when Lillian passed away, but knowing that and believing it were two very different concepts.

He ran at a steady pace. He wasn't the fastest runner around, but he could go far longer than the six miles he clocked most days. Ten years ago, he could have gone faster, but he was older now, and time was a mean old bitch.

A half mile from the car, he slowed to a walk, giving his body time to cool down. He glanced to his left, still surprised there was actual ocean there. The street-level view was different from the one from his bedroom, but still impressive. Sometimes he had trouble believing any of this was real.

Two days ago he'd met with Gregory, Lillian's lawyer, at her suggestion. Mason had found out that yes, he really was going to inherit the house, along with his uncle's papers and personal effects. The contents of the house, along with the cats, would go to Lillian's great niece.

The lawyer had explained that all the expenses — taxes and utilities — would be covered by the estate for a year. There was also a stipend to cover emergency repairs. That gave Mason time to figure out what to do with the house. Keeping it wasn't an option. Yes, he was a published author, but his books weren't exactly bestsellers, so his main source of income was his military pension.

He had no idea what the market was for a house like that, nor was he going to ask Lillian. That seemed tacky at best and money-grubbing at worst. She seemed healthy enough, so he would continue to wish her a long life. Once she passed, he would deal with selling the house.

He reached his car and pulled out the bottle of water he'd brought with him. After gulping it down, he drove back to the house, his stomach growling in anticipation of breakfast.

Salvia cooked breakfast and lunch every day. The morning meals were delicious and hearty affairs, with omelets, pancakes, fruit and homemade bread. After twenty-five years of army food, Mason was ready to build a shrine in Salvia's honor.

Inside he was immediately assaulted by the smell of coffee and cinnamon. Salvia, a small, dark-haired woman in her forties, smiled at him.

"Good morning, Mr. Mason. How was your run?"

"Morning. It was excellent." He inhaled. "What's cooking?"

She smiled at him. "Cinnamon rolls. I'm also going to make you an egg and sausage scramble. Miss Lillian said to meet her in the breakfast room after your shower."

Interesting. While he and Lillian had talked a few times since his arrival, they'd yet to share a meal.

"Twenty minutes," he told her.

Eighteen minutes later, he returned to the main floor.

Lillian sat at one end of the wooden table, a calico cat on her lap. Several others roamed the room. He ignored them as he walked to the other place setting near her.

"Good morning," he said, pulling out a chair.

"Mason! It's good to see you." Lillian set the cat in the chair next to her and smiled at him. "Thank you for joining me."

"Of course. I appreciate the invitation."

Lillian laughed. "I wanted to give you time to settle in before suggesting we dine together. I assumed the situation would be a little overwhelming."

114

"It is."

The table was set with ornate flatware, cloth napkins and blue-and-white dishes. He reached for a fancy coffee server. "May I?"

"Please."

He poured them each a cup of coffee. Lillian added cream. One of the cats started to walk across the table, but she shooed it away.

"Not when we're eating," she said firmly, shaking her finger at the cat. "Remember, we're civilized."

"But the rest of the time they're allowed up here?" he asked with a grin.

"Of course. This is their home, too."

Each cat wore a collar with a small tag with a phone number and its name. After a couple of days, he'd realized the cats were all named for English kings and queens. So far he'd met Elizabeth, Mary, Charles I and Charles II, Victoria, Edward and Henry.

"Who takes care of the cats?" he asked.

"Salvia feeds them. My vet sends a technician every four weeks to make sure they're all well." Her smile faded. "With so many, it's easy to miss when someone's not feeling right. She also takes care of vaccinations and routine exams. If there's a problem

115

between visits, Salvia takes whoever to the vet."

"You have a system."

"I do." Her smile returned. "You should respect that."

"Absolutely." He looked at a black-and-white cat by the door. "I've never had a pet."

"How is that possible?"

"I was in the army and I moved around a lot. Plus I was gone all day. It never seemed feasible."

She laughed. "You're getting a trial by fire now, Mason."

"I am." He wasn't sure how he felt about that, but so far the cats weren't awful.

Salvia walked into the breakfast room and set down a plate of sliced, fresh fruit and a basket of hot, gooey cinnamon rolls.

"I'm going to start on the scramble," she said before returning to the kitchen.

"You must try one," Lillian said, motioning to the cinnamon rolls. "Hers are extraordinary."

He bit into one. The roll was hot, the frosting thick and not too sweet. The combination of flavors, the way the dough nearly melted on his tongue, was perfection. Mason had never been all that interested in food, except as fuel, but lately that was changing.

"Delicious," he said when he'd swallowed. "If I eat as many as I want, I'm going to have to up my run for the next few days."

"Every fine chef wants her food to be enjoyed. I'm afraid I'm not very fun for Salvia. I don't have much of an appetite anymore." She sliced off a tiny piece of cinnamon roll before popping it in her mouth. "As wonderful as I remember. So, Mason, how are you settling into the house?"

"Still finding my way around," he admitted.

"You should explore. There are many surprises."

"I have a door in my room that opens onto a wall."

She laughed. "There are several of those, along with staircases that go nowhere and a few secret rooms." She picked up her coffee. "You spoke with Gregory."

"As you suggested."

"Yes. It went well?"

He wasn't sure how to answer. "There was a lot of information."

She looked at him. "Selling makes the most sense. The upkeep on a house like this is very expensive, and what use would you have for it?" She looked around. "Robyn and I have talked about what it would take to convert it to a hotel, but I'm not sure that's even feasible."

"Robyn?"

"My great-niece."

The woman getting the contents and the cats. He hoped Robyn had a big enough place to hold all the furniture, knickknacks and critters.

"Will you sell?" she asked.

He wasn't comfortable with the line of questioning. "Maybe we should talk about something else."

"Because you selling the house means I'm dead?" The smile returned. "Mason, I'm ninety-four. I've long made peace with my passing. You should, as well. As to the house, the local historical society is very interested in buying. They're already raising money. You'd get more from some developer, but I hope you'll consider the historical people. They have big plans for the building."

He had no idea what to say. "Thank you for the information."

"You're welcome. Gregory has all the details, and with a little luck, none of this will be an issue for years to come."

"That's my hope as well."

"You're very kind." Her gaze turned speculative. "Did you leave anyone special back in Texas?"

"I don't have any family."

"I was thinking more of a significant other."

"No."

"Then I must try harder to get Robyn to visit. She's divorced with two wonderful children. Harlow is twenty-two, and Austin is eighteen."

He reached for another cinnamon roll. "Don't go there, Lillian. I'm a bad bet when it comes to women."

"How interesting. Why is that?"

"I've been divorced twice. I'm good at a lot of things, but relationships aren't one of them."

"What did you do wrong?"

"More things than we have time to talk about."

She laughed. "A very polite way to tell me to mind my own business. All right. I'll stop questioning you, but I'll continue to wonder."

"Works for me."

Salvia returned with a serving bowl in the same pattern as the dishes. She set the scramble between them and handed the serving spoon to Mason. He offered it to Lillian, but she shook her head.

"Help yourself. I'm not going to have eggs this morning."

Mason eyed the combination of egg,

sausage, cheese, onions and green peppers. How could she pass this up?

He put a large serving onto his plate.

"Twenty-five acres of land come with the house," Lillian said as he ate. "When I'm gone, you should have a survey done and hold back a few acres for yourself. Something with a nice view of the ocean. You'll have plenty of money to build a house. Unless you plan to move back to Texas."

He hadn't known there was land. No way he could afford a house on the ocean, but if he got the land for free and some money from the sale of the house, maybe he could swing it.

"I would probably stay here," he said. "There's nothing for me back in Texas."

"Santa Barbara is a beautiful little town. You must go see the mission and do some wine tasting. There's also great shopping, but I suspect that's not your thing."

He chuckled. "I'm not a shopper."

They talked through breakfast. When they were finished, Lillian insisted he take a couple of cinnamon rolls up to his room. He ate one as his laptop booted. He glanced at his screen, but had no interest in his book. Instead he stared out at the view of the Pacific.

The water was a deep blue today, with a

few whitecaps from the breeze. As he watched, a seagull landed on his balcony's railing. Out of nowhere, a white cat raced to the closed French door and stared out, making a cacking sound in the back of his throat.

"You think you could catch that?" Mason asked the cat. "Or is this just wishful thinking?"

The cat ignored the question. When the seagull flew away, the cat jumped onto the desk and gave Mason a headbutt. Mason turned over its tag.

"Hello, Charles II," he said, rubbing under the cat's chin. "Are you a mighty hunter?"

Charles II began to purr.

"I think you're happy being taken care of. It's a whole lot better than fighting for every meal."

Mason knew that from personal experience. While he'd never had to hunt for his food, he'd been on a couple of tours that had been intense. Facing death on a daily basis had a way of changing a man, and not always for the better.

Like Charles, he was living a different kind of life — lately a very surreal one, in a house on a hill.

"With a strange old lady and too many

damned cats."

Charles II leaned against him and continued to purr.

EIGHT

Robyn stood in the far bay of her four-car garage. Three dressers and a dining room table filled the space. Estate sale finds she'd bought over the last couple of years with the idea she would refinish and sell them. She'd made a nice profit that way a few times. She'd played with the idea of starting a business, only somehow she'd never gotten past the buying a few pieces stage.

She'd always regretted that she hadn't gone to college. She'd browsed the catalog online, but hadn't ever registered, let alone taken a class.

She had a job with Mindy — a silly part-time job that was maybe sixteen hours a week. It was fun and she enjoyed it, but she wasn't working to pay the bills or further herself or anything remotely serious. She was a complete and total failure at her life. Worse — she had no plan, and when the money Cord was paying her ran out, she had no income.

What was wrong with her? How had this happened? How had she become so directionless and pathetic?

Thirty-six hours after her enlightening, albeit painful, conversation with Jase, she was still reeling from seeing herself from his perspective. While it was easy to make him the bad guy — a title he totally deserved — she couldn't help thinking that he wasn't wrong. She had few salable skills and no serious job, let alone a career. She was drifting, and in six years, she was going to get an ugly financial wake-up call.

She ran her hand along the top of one of the dressers. She'd been divorced four years. *Four!* Why hadn't she planned for her future? Sure, she'd needed to keep the house while Austin finished high school, but what about everything else? She could have earned her degree by now, if she'd been serious about it. She could have learned a trade. Or gotten a real job.

But she hadn't. She'd maintained her lifestyle, lunched with her friends, baked for Austin and mourned her marriage. She'd kept her country club membership up to date, had replaced a three-year-old car because hey, that was what they always did. She'd ignored the ticking clock that was her

124

payments from Cord, and she'd wasted four years of income.

The truth was humiliating and humbling, not to mention a little scary. What was she supposed to do now? Her skills — beyond Jase's assessment of her parenting style — included managing the company's books, although she'd stopped doing that six years ago, and captaining a boat. Also something she'd stopped doing six years ago.

Her stomach flipped over a couple of times. She was scared, she was angry (mostly at herself), and she was determined to get her act together. Step one of any plan was to not make a rash, impulsive decision. She knew better than to react out of fear. She had limited resources and didn't want to waste any of them. She had to know what she was doing.

She went into her small home office. At her desk, she consciously slowed her breathing before looking at the lists she'd made. She'd brainstormed options, written down the pros and cons of each.

Selling the house was her number one priority. She knew a couple of agents through her friends at the club and had already set up an appointment with the one she liked best. Their preliminary phone call had confirmed that her best chance at getting top dollar was selling in the fall, when the snowbirds returned to Naples.

Although she would love to dump the house this second, she had to make a financially smart decision. Better to wait and end up with more money.

As for her monthly expenses, she'd already canceled her membership at the club. It was a ridiculous amount to spend, just to go to lunch with her friends. Austin didn't use the facilities, and Harlow used her dad's membership.

She was reviewing a few other places where she could cut her spending. As for her future — she was giving herself until the house went on the market to figure out what she was going to do with the rest of her life. She would be thoughtful and practical and smart. Seeing the truth about herself hadn't been pleasant, but she was grateful to finally have clarity.

Her phone buzzed. She glanced at it and saw yet another text from Jase.

I'm sorry. I messed up and I hurt you. Please talk to me and let me explain. I don't want to lose you.

Talk to him? No, she couldn't do that. She was too embarrassed and upset. What he'd said to her had been shocking. The things he thought about her had been awful. She would never marry a man for money, and he should know that.

She picked up her phone, then put it down as she reminded herself she wasn't going to do anything impulsive. She needed to think her answer through and —

"Screw that," she muttered and began to type.

We're done, Jase. I can't be with someone who's ashamed of me.

She paused, flushing at the words. How could he think so little of her? She knew how to dress, she was comfortable in any social situation. She was well-read, well-traveled, she could talk about wine.

Tears burned, but she blinked them away before adding, I also can't be with someone who thinks so little of me. You won't hear from me again, and I would prefer not to hear from you.

She drew in another calming breath, ignored her racing heart and pushed Send.

"Mom?"

Robyn usually enjoyed her daughter dropping by, but right now she wasn't up to the drama. Not that she could share her feelings — they would send Harlow into full frenzy mode.

She faked a smile and walked out of her office to find Harlow in the living room.

"Mom!"

Her daughter dropped her bag on the coffee table and ran to her.

"It's so awful," Harlow said, flinging herself at her. "Everything is a mess, and I don't know what to do."

Robyn hugged her, wondering if her daughter's crisis was real or imagined. With Harlow, it was hard to know.

"We'll figure it out," she said with a confidence she didn't feel. She stepped back. "Start at the beginning."

Harlow sank onto one of the sofas. "Dad's dating Kip's twin sister, Zafina. She showed up at the office, and they were obviously together. It was gross. She's too young for him, and hello? My fiancé's twin sister? Why would he do that to me? Plus Kip's known all this time, and he didn't say anything. I was so mad at him, but he said he just didn't know how to tell me, which I guess makes sense." Her lower lip began to tremble. "I don't know what to do."

Robyn sat on the opposite sofa. "That's a lot."

"It is. It's too much. Why is she interested

in him? He's a dad with adult children. Plus, he cheated on Leah to go out with her." Harlow grimaced. "My father cheated on his girlfriend. I don't want to know that about him. It's awful, and I don't know what to think. Why would he tell me that? Why would he *do* that in the first place?"

All excellent questions, Robyn thought, horrified that Cord would be so cavalier with his own daughter. Telling her about Zafina was one thing, but admitting he'd cheated was selfish and unnecessary. There were things that no child should have to deal with, regardless of their age. His flaws were his problem, not Harlow's.

Harlow looked at her. "Did you ever cheat on Dad?"

"Of course not."

"See? That's my point. You'd never do that. People shouldn't cheat. Why not just break up with Leah?"

Robyn tensed as she waited for the next obvious question. *Did Dad ever cheat on you?*

How was she supposed to answer that? She wasn't going to lie to protect Cord, but she wasn't interested in telling Harlow the truth.

Fortunately Harlow was too caught up in her own feelings to think of asking that.

129

Instead she said, "I didn't want to know about him and Zafina."

"I know. It's hard to deal with."

"What if they're still together at the wedding? No one will care about me and Kip — they'll all be talking about my dad's date. It's supposed to be our day, but he'll make it about him." She shuddered. "I know I already said this, but it is really gross."

"It is, and I'm sorry."

"Me, too." Harlow looked at her suspiciously. "You're not surprised about Zafina."

And here it comes, she thought glumly. "Someone at the club told me last week. I spoke to your father and told him he had to come clean. That you were going to find out, and it was better to hear it from him."

"You knew!" Harlow sprang to her feet, glaring. "How could you not warn me? You're my *mother*!"

Her daughter was about an inch taller than her, with the same long blond hair and athletic build. When Harlow had been younger, people had commented on how much they looked alike. Cord had joked that her genes alone had created their oldest — with no help from his.

Harlow's hurt and anger were a tangible presence, a manifestation of her strength.

Robyn focused on how good it was to see her daughter so strong and healthy. Years ago, while Harlow had been fighting leukemia, Robyn would have given anything to know her child would survive to adulthood.

Harlow took two steps away, then swung back. "Everyone knew but me?"

"I told you what happened," Robyn said calmly. "I spoke with your father. He agreed to tell you himself. As he's the one who created the problem, he should be the one to fix it. I didn't want to get in the middle."

"That's not fair."

Robyn really wasn't in the mood for this. "I find it interesting that you complain I don't treat you like the adult you claim to be, yet whenever something doesn't go your way, you get in a snit. So, which is it? Do you want to be treated like an adult or like a child? It's hard to tell from your actions."

Harlow glared at her. "I can't believe you said that."

"I can't believe how you're yelling at me for something that isn't my fault."

They stared at each other. Harlow blinked first and resumed her seat on the sofa.

"You're being difficult," Harlow muttered.

"So are you." Robyn told herself to be the bigger person. "I know this is hard for you. Your father's relationships don't last long.

I'm sure they'll have ended things by the wedding."

"The wedding you don't want me to have."

Robyn felt her self-control beginning to fray. "Could we please have a pleasant conversation without you sniping at me?"

Her daughter flushed slightly. "You *don't* want me to marry Kip. Why is that sniping?"

"You know why. Harlow, I've had a few very bad days. I can't deal with much more. Can we table this until later?"

"Of course," her daughter said stiffly. "I'm sorry I bothered you with something so insignificant. It's only my life."

"It's my life, too," Robyn snapped. "Not everything is about you. For once could you please give me a break? Just this one time. It's been twenty-two years of making everything about yourself, so maybe I'm due for a small amount of consideration."

Harlow's eyes widened. "You're saying I'm selfish?"

"You tend to see things from your point of view and no other."

"That's not true. I don't do that. Give me one example."

"Seriously? Sure. Me keeping the house for the wedding."

"But we talked about it. You promised I could be married here."

"I never promised you anything like that," Robyn told her. "Yes, we talked about it, and I'm sorry you have your heart set on it, but there is no way I can keep this house."

Tears filled her daughter's eyes. "Why are you saying that? It's not true."

Robyn didn't want to get into a discussion of her bad decision-making over the past four years, but there was no way to avoid a few ugly facts.

"I'd have to buy out your father to keep the house. That means getting a new mortgage."

"So?"

"I won't qualify for one. I don't have enough income or assets."

Harlow brushed the tears from her cheeks. "Then why didn't you plan better?" She stood and grabbed her purse. "You could keep it if you really wanted. You're not even trying. You've never wanted me to marry Kip, and now you're doing your best to ruin my wedding."

Robyn rose, knowing it was better to be standing as she faced the attack. "Amazingly enough, this isn't about you. I can't keep the house because I can't afford it. No bank will give me a loan, so unless you have two million dollars lying around, the house has to be sold. I don't have a choice. Do those words mean anything to you? Do you understand what I'm saying? Or can't you think of anyone but yourself?"

"This isn't fair, and you're being awful on purpose." More tears spilled down her cheeks. "Fine. Forget it. We'll get married at the club. Sell the house. Move away. I don't care what you do. Don't even bother coming to my wedding."

With that she ran out of the house, slamming the front door.

Robyn stood alone in the living room, absorbing the sharp pain of her heart cracking in two. She and Harlow had fought before, but her daughter had never been so uncaring and mean. She knew the words were spoken in anger, but for once, she wasn't going to make excuses. Harlow was selfish and entitled. She had been for a while now.

"I'm the mother, so it's probably my fault," Robyn muttered, walking into the kitchen. She wasn't hungry, but wine sounded like a good idea.

She'd just pulled the cork out of a nice merlot when her phone buzzed with a text message. She glanced at the screen and saw a picture of a perfect California day. The sky was blue, as was the ocean that seemed to stretch out forever. There were palm trees and bougainvillea and flowers trailing along the balcony off Lillian's bedroom.

Three dots appeared, followed by another text.

Wish you were here. And yes, I am trying to tempt you.

Robyn stared at the familiar scene. She'd sat there with her great-aunt countless times. There would be a light breeze, zero humidity and absolutely no pressure for her to do anything.

A thought formed. She pushed it away, but it returned, a little more insistent.

She could go to California for a few weeks. Hang out with Lillian, plan her future, escape from everything here. It was the slow season, so Mindy wouldn't care. Robyn didn't need to get the house ready to sell for at least two months. Austin was in his own apartment, so he would be fine. Honestly, what was keeping her in Florida?

I'll admit to being more than a little tempted.

Excellent. Book a flight and let me know

when you'll be here.

Could she do it? Should she?

Robyn thought about everything that had happened in the past few days. She was stressed, scared and sad. Heading to California was a lot like running away — even if it was just for a few weeks. But maybe that wasn't such a bad thing. Lillian had always been there for her. Time to think would be good — she could figure out what she was supposed to do with her life. She had frequent flyer miles to pay for the flight.

Give me a couple of hours and I'll let you know.

Lillian's reply was instant.

I can't wait to see you.

Me, too.

Harlow stumbled into her apartment, half-blinded by her tears. She'd cried the entire way home, not sure what had upset her more — that she wasn't getting married in her mom's backyard or the actual fight. Her mother had been so awful. Selfish and mean. How could she act like that? This was her only daughter's wedding. That should be more important than anything.

For years she'd pictured herself getting married on the huge patio by the pool. She'd imagined the twinkle lights, the way the chairs would be set up. In her mind, the weather would be perfect, the guests beautifully dressed. Until the last year, the groom had been a vague stand-in, but now it was Kip. This was supposed to be her moment, and her mother was ruining it.

She threw herself on the sofa, where she cried until there weren't any tears. Even though she had to pee, she didn't get up. Why bother? Nothing would ever be good again.

"I hate her," she said aloud.

That decided, she walked to the bathroom and took care of business, then washed her face before curling up on the bed. She was still there, feeling sorry for herself, when Kip walked in two hours later.

"Harlow?"

"In here."

She clicked on the nightstand light and sat up. The second she saw him, the tears returned.

"What happened?" He rushed to the bed and sat next to her. "Are you hurt?"

She buried her head in his shoulder. "I had a fight with my mom. She's a terrible person, and I hate her."

He held her close, his body warm and protective. "You don't hate her."

"I do. I mean it this time. I'm never going to forgive her." She sniffed and looked at him. "She says we can't get married in the backyard, and it's all I've ever wanted."

More tears fell, and her throat got tight.

"Since I was a little girl. But she doesn't care about that. She's ruining the wedding."

Kip brushed away her tears. "You know I love you, and I'll do anything to support you, but I don't believe your mom told you we can't get married in her backyard."

"She did. She's selling the house. She won't even try to keep it."

Kip's concern faded. "It's a lot of house, Harlow. It has to be expensive to maintain, plus the mortgage."

She slid away from him. "You're taking her side?"

"I'm pointing out that her wanting to sell isn't unreasonable."

She glared at him. "We're talking about our wedding."

"Yes, and your mom, who loves you and has always taken care of you."

"Not this time."

"What did she say specifically? Did she give a reason for selling now?"

Harlow thought about their fight. "She said she'd have to refinance — because of the divorce. She can live in it until six months after Austin's eighteenth birthday, and then she either has to sell it or buy out Dad. I told her to do that. What's the big deal?"

"What did she say?"

Harlow looked away, the first flicker of guilt igniting in her chest. "That she couldn't afford it. That the bank wouldn't give her a loan."

Kip looked at her without speaking, as if waiting for the words to sink in.

"She's lying," Harlow said, scrambling to her feet. "She has plenty of money from my dad. He's buying her out of the business. She gets a check every month."

"Which probably covers the mortgage and a few expenses. The house has a water view, Harlow. It's worth what? Two million? Four? Where is she supposed to come up with that kind of money? She doesn't have a good-paying job. There was only a small lump sum at the divorce. Do you really believe she's lying about her financial situation?"

His tone was so reasonable. Harlow didn't like it.

"Why do you keep taking her side?"

"Because I don't think you're really that

mad at your mom. I think you're furious with your dad for going out with my sister and cheating and not being your hero. But for some reason you can't fight with him, so you fight with your mom instead." He faced her across the bed. "This is hard to say, but I know you value the truth, so here goes. Sometimes you act like you're fifteen. It's not your best quality."

Fury and embarrassment flooded her. He was wrong about all of it. She wasn't fighting with her mom because of her father. That was ridiculous. But also not the worst thing he'd said.

"You're telling me I'm immature?"

His gaze was steady. "Sometimes. Mostly about your mom. Why are you making such a big deal about her selling the house? What you're asking is unreasonable."

"It's not!" she shrieked. "I've been planning this since —"

"You were a little girl," he said, interrupting her. "Yes, I know. We all know. Your mom can't afford the house. There's no other conversation to be had. Talking about this endlessly, having to admit she couldn't qualify for a loan, must embarrass and upset her."

She was about to smack him with one of the throw pillows on the bed when his

140

words sank in. She suddenly saw herself as he must see her. Whiny, juvenile and unreasonable. Not exactly the characteristics any guy wanted in a bride-to-be.

She felt trapped by her own words and behavior. There was no way out of the situation without admitting she was wrong, and she didn't want to do that. The only escape was to escalate the fight and make him the bad guy. A stretch, but she could do it. She could —

"Don't," Kip said softly. "Please don't."

She stared at him. "What?"

"Whatever you were going to do. Let's just talk about what's really wrong."

Shame washed through her. She looked away. "Nothing's wrong."

"We both know that's not true. Let's talk about your dad."

Tears returned. She folded her arms across her chest and hunched her shoulders. "He was so casual about the cheating. He said he liked to keep his options open. As if that's something to be proud of — like he's some kind of player. I didn't know he was like that." She looked at him. "He's my dad. He's supposed to be better than that."

"I'm sorry he told you he cheated."

She shook her head. "You're not sorry he did it?"

"Yes, but I'm more concerned about you. Now you know something you can't ever unknow. It changes how you look at him. You're hurt and you feel let down, plus you have anger you don't know where to put."

She dropped her arms to her sides and rushed around the bed. Kip drew her close.

"I'm sorry," she whispered, her cheek pressed against his shoulder. "I'm sorry I'm such a bitch. You're right. I feel awful and confused. I'm so mad at my dad."

"And you're taking it out on your mom."

She groaned. "I am. I don't know why I do that."

"Because she's safe. She's always going to love you."

Was it as simple as that? Did she believe her mother would be there for her, no matter what?

"This sucks," she said with a sigh, then stepped back. "Do you cheat?"

Kip's gaze locked with hers. "No. I never have, with anyone. I don't do that."

She thought about pushing back but believed him. "I don't either. I don't get it. Just break up. Why be such a dick?" She wiped her face. "I'm a wreck."

"Are you hungry?"

"I am now."

"Then let's get something to eat." He

smiled. "We can talk about wedding venues. Don't we have an appointment at the club next week?"

She nodded. "I guess it's more than a backup plan now."

A thought that made her sad, but Kip's points had been valid. If her mom couldn't afford the house, there was nothing to be done.

"I wish it was different," she said as they walked out of the bedroom. "I really did want to get married in her backyard."

"I know you did, but the wedding is just one day. Our marriage is forever."

"I know."

"I was talking to *my* mom a couple of days ago and mentioned the appointment at the club."

Harlow glanced at him. "What did she say?"

"She's excited and wondered if she could come along to our first appointment." He grimaced. "I know it's not ideal, but she wants to be a part of things."

His mother wanted to join them? But it was their wedding, not hers. It wasn't like she was paying for it.

But Harlow knew her behavior that night had been pretty bad, so she forced herself to smile and say, "Sure. She can come along. I'll ask my mom to join us, too. They can get to know each other better, and maybe they'll have some great suggestions."

He paused by the front door and smiled at her. "I know you don't believe that, but thank you for saying it."

She grinned. "And agreeing to let you bring your mom."

"That too."

Robyn switched from the 405 freeway to the 101. Normally she would have flown to LAX and then taken a commuter plane directly to Santa Barbara. But she'd booked her flight at the last minute with miles, which had limited her options. Rather than pay for flying the last leg, she'd opted to drive. Yes, it would take longer, but she was fine with that. She would be through the San Fernando Valley well before late afternoon traffic.

She'd needed less than a day to get ready to leave. After clearing her trip with Mindy and arranging for her house-sitting service to collect the mail and check on things, she'd let Austin know she would be out of town, reserved her flight and packed. She'd thought about telling Harlow, but had decided against it. If, or when, her daughter got in touch with her, she would let her know. Until then, she was going to enjoy a few drama-free days.

She glanced at the temperature gauge and saw it was a balmy seventy-eight degrees. After rolling down the windows, she breathed in the humidity-free air and laughed. Southern California might have some issues, but humidity wasn't one of them. Even better, the bugs were small and reasonable — unlike Florida, where they were practically big enough to drive and join a gang.

With each mile, she felt herself relaxing. She loved spending time with Lillian. They would hang out and talk. She could explore the house — always a favorite pastime. When her head cleared, she could think about her future.

She passed through Carpentaria, then Summerland, before entering the outskirts of Santa Barbara. As she got closer to her exit, she felt almost giddy with anticipation. Everything about being here was right.

Ten minutes later, she pulled into the familiar driveway and drove back to the garage. After climbing out of her car, she took a moment to stand there, breathing in the hint of salt in the air.

The back door opened, and Salvia hurried toward her, arms outstretched.

"Miss Robyn, you're here! I'm so glad to see you. When Miss Lillian told me you were coming, I was happy, happy."

Robyn hugged the other woman. "Me, too," she said with a laugh. "How are you?"

"Always good. Miss Lillian is well." Her smile widened. "Never cranky, that one, always a kind word."

Robyn left her bags and walked inside with Salvia. The kitchen was exactly as she remembered, updated, but still appropriate for the house, and filled with cats.

"How many are there now?" she asked, pointing to a light gray cat sunning on a wide windowsill.

Salvia sighed. "Fifteen. They've all been fixed, so we shouldn't have more, but they just appear. I think they tell each other about the crazy house on the hill."

"If I was a cat, I'd want to live here," Robyn said with a grin and hugged Salvia again. "I'm so glad to be here."

"She's excited to see you. Go on up. I'll bring drinks and appetizers." Salvia's mouth twisted. "Try to get her to eat. She's reached the age where she has no appetite, so she's thinner, but still healthy."

Robyn wanted to ask more but told herself she should get the answers from Lillian. She thanked Salvia and made her way through the house.

She took the hallway leading out of the kitchen, passing a dining room and a sitting room. The ceilings were high — nearly twelve feet, and each room was massive. She ignored a small staircase, knowing it ended on a landing that was walled in on three sides, and all the closed doors. Some were closets, some opened onto blank walls.

The house — inspired by the Winchester House in San Jose — was a marvel of architecture and whimsy. There were secret passages, beautiful views and rooms filled with priceless furniture and artwork. On her last visit, Robyn had discovered a painting she'd been sure was a Renoir. Lillian had promised to get in an expert.

She walked into the five-hundred-square-foot foyer and started up the curving, grand staircase. At the top she saw the chair that Lillian now used to gracefully ride up and down the stairs. Getting her great-aunt to admit she needed the chair lift had been a year-long undertaking, but certainly worth the fight. Robyn slept easier knowing Lillian wasn't risking a fall.

She ran the last few feet to Lillian's room, knocked once on the partially open door, then let herself in.

"I'm here," she called, walking out onto

the huge balcony with the perfect view of the ocean.

She ignored the expanse of water and the two cats grooming themselves in the sun, and went toward the chaise in the center. Her aunt stood and smiled.

"You made it. Come hug me so I know you're really here."

Robyn rushed forward and embraced her, noting how she seemed more fragile than she had before — not entirely unexpected, given her advancing years, but still troubling.

"I've missed you," Robyn whispered fiercely. "So much."

"As I've missed you, darling. Come, sit. Let me look at you." Lillian stepped back. "Ah, to be young and beautiful again."

"You'll always be beautiful."

"You're sweet to lie."

Robyn pulled a second chaise close and made sure her aunt was comfortable before taking a seat. Lillian squeezed her hand.

"Tell me you're staying forever."

Robyn laughed. "Almost a month."

"Excellent. I look forward to every second." Her gaze sharpened. "What convinced you to come see me?"

"Once again, I'm running away to you." Robyn did her best to keep her tone light.

Lillian's gaze sharpened. "That's why I'm here. Now tell me what happened."

Salvia appeared just then, carrying a tray. Robyn pulled a table between their chairs, then grinned when she saw the classic mai tais, each with a pineapple and cherry garnish. There was also a fruit and cheese plate.

"I'm going to make some coconut shrimp," Salvia told Robyn.

"Sounds delicious. Thank you."

Robyn handed her aunt a drink, then pushed the cheese plate close to her. She picked up the second glass and grinned. "Now I know I'm home."

"I should drink something more sophisticated, but I can't help it. I love these, and Salvia's are the best. All right, you have your drink and snack. Tell me what's going on."

Robyn took a sip, mostly to buy time. She wasn't sure how much to share about the disaster that was her life.

"Things are good," she hedged.

Lillian sat up and faced her. "Robyn, I've known you all your life — from the time you were a little baby. I loved you then, and I love you still. You're my favorite person in the world, and there's nothing you can say to change that. So what exactly are you running from?"

149

The words made her feel warm and accepted, and a little foolish. Robyn opened her mouth, closed it, then blurted, "My life is a mess. I've been an idiot. No — I've been irresponsible and ridiculous, and I'm so ashamed."

She explained about the house and how she didn't have a job that paid anything and how she'd wasted four years. That she'd been living off of Cord's payments with no plan for her future and that she should have gone to college when she was eighteen or even after the divorce, but she hadn't. She talked about Austin's summer move-out, the fight with Harlow, and how she would be listing her big house in early September. By the time she wound down, they'd finished their drinks, and much of the cheese plate was gone.

Salvia showed up with a second round and coconut shrimp. When she'd left, Lillian smiled.

"That's a lot."

"I know. I'm trying not to feel overwhelmed."

"There's no need, if we take things one at a time. So, college."

"I should have gone after high school."

Lillian dismissed that with a wave of her hand. "What's that saying? Don't 'should' all over yourself. I don't think either of us would wish away your beautiful babies. Start from where you are now. Do you want to go to college?"

"Yes."

"What would you study?"

"I should —" Robyn stopped when Lillian rolled her eyes. "I know what you're going to say, but I have to be practical. I'm forty-two."

"Pretend you're not going to be practical. What would you study?"

"Art history."

Lillian sipped her mai tai and smiled. "An excellent choice for you. Tell me about your job with Mindy. It's going well?"

"Mostly. I mean, I love the work, but sometimes Mindy is difficult. She's my boss and we're friends, which is awkward. Sometimes I'm not sure how much I like her. She's making terrible decisions in her personal life."

Mindy was yet another place in her life where she'd taken the easy way out. She hung out with her because of the job, she had the job because she hadn't bothered to figure out her future, she had no future because . . .

"You're shoulding again," Lillian said gently.

"I am. Sorry. I'll try to stop. It's just, I feel I'm being forced to confront my every mistake. It's a big list."

"Then we'll start small. Your job."

"I'm not working enough hours. Managing the inventory doesn't pay much. In sales, I'd at least get a commission."

"You could open your own store."

Robyn glared at her great-aunt. "We've talked about this, and you've promised never to die, so no."

"Darling, I won't live forever."

"Yes, you will. I insist."

Lillian chuckled. "I'm sorry, but you don't have that kind of power. Besides, I've lived a good life. I'm ready when the time comes. You know you're inheriting the contents of the house, so start thinking about what to do with everything."

"I don't want to," Robyn said automatically, even as she thought about what a daunting job sorting through the rooms would be. There were museum-grade pieces and artwork, and some things that were total crap.

"It would take a while," Lillian said mildly.

"At least a year."

"That year is in the will. I'm hoping the house gets sold to the local historical society."

Robyn nodded. Lillian had mentioned that before.

"Some things should stay with the house," Robyn said, picking up a piece of shrimp. "Some belong in a museum. Did you get someone in for the Renoir?"

"Hmm, I don't think so. You could take care of that for me while you're here. And maybe start categorizing things. Even being generous in what stays and what goes to museums, you'd still have enough for ten antique stores."

She was right, Robyn thought. Something she'd never considered. "I'll refresh my memory on what's here. Work will help me clear my mind and figure out my future."

"Excellent. Will Harlow visit while you're here?"

Not a happy change in topic.

"No. She's working, and we're currently not speaking."

"That will change," Lillian told her. "She loves you."

"And I love her, but lately all we do is fight." Robyn shifted on her seat. "It's my fault. I told her she was too young to get married, and that didn't go over well. I probably said it wrong. And I spoiled her when she was little."

"She was sick and nearly died. You're allowed to be indulgent."

"For a while. I let it go on too long. I was thinking about this on the plane. Once she was better, I was so happy that I never required anything from her. I just wanted her to be a normal kid, having fun. I didn't put limits on her the way I should have, and now she's entitled and selfish."

She remembered the ugly words she and Harlow had exchanged about the need to sell the house.

"I wish we didn't always fight," she admitted. "When I was her age, I was working with Cord, taking out charters seven days a week with a baby strapped to my chest."

Lillian smiled. "A wonderful visual, so thank you for that. You have to remember Harlow's matured at a different rate from other girls her age. She lost two years of her life to cancer — that would have arrested her emotional growth. She'll catch up."

Robyn grabbed Lillian's hand. "I love you so much. You were raised in such a different time with a worldview I can't imagine, yet you are providing insight about my children."

"I do my best."

Robyn released her and picked up her drink. This was exactly why she'd come here. To hang out with one of her favorite people and know she was loved and cared for. Lillian had always provided wise counsel and a place to recover, whether when Robyn had been eleven and had just lost her mother, or carting her five- and one-year-olds after she'd learned that Cord had cheated on her.

Robyn heard footsteps and expected to see Salvia with another appetizer. Instead a man, about six feet with short, dark hair, walked onto the patio. She'd never seen him before, yet he moved with an ease that said he was comfortable in his surroundings, only stopping when he saw Robyn.

"I didn't know you had company," he said, his voice low with a hint of command.

Lillian waved him forward, holding out her hand as he approached. "Mason, I was hoping you'd stop by." She smiled up at him.

Robyn did her best to keep her mouth from dropping open. Lillian obviously liked the man. Yes, he was good-looking, and people shouldn't be alone if they didn't want to be, but he had to be at least fifty years younger, and was she being judgmental to think some version of ew?

Lillian turned to Robyn. "You two finally get to meet. This is Mason Bishop."

"Is it?"

Lillian laughed. "I can tell you have no idea who I'm talking about. Darling, this is the man who's going to inherit the house."

NINE

"Are you sure?" Robyn asked before she could stop herself. Unexpected resentment mingled with fear and jealousy. "Have you confirmed his identity or spoken with your lawyer?" She turned to Mason. "Any proof that you're related to Leo?"

Lillian's eyebrows rose, but she didn't speak. Mason's calm expression never changed.

"Nice to meet you, Robyn," he said with absolutely no edge to his voice. "I saw Lillian's lawyer a couple of days ago. As for confirming my identity, Lillian reached out to me. Not the other way around."

"He's right, I did," her great aunt assured her. "Years ago. We've been corresponding, me more than him, but you know how men are." Lillian leaned toward her. "Please don't be angry. I should have said something. I just thought your meeting would be a lovely surprise."

Robyn tried to understand. She'd always known the house was going to a relative of Leo's, but the specifics had been vague at best. Lillian had implied she didn't know anything, either.

Apparently that wasn't true. Apparently they'd become good friends, and now he was here.

"You've been in touch with him for years, and you never said anything?"

"Oh, dear." Lillian's mouth turned down. "I've hurt you."

"I'm not hurt." Not exactly. The situation was just confusing and not at all what she'd expected, and she didn't like any part of it. She looked at Mason. "How long have you been living here?"

"Nearly two weeks."

"What?" Robyn scrambled to her feet and faced her aunt. "You've had someone living here for two weeks and didn't think to tell me?"

Suddenly Harlow's fury over lies of omission made a lot more sense.

"What else is happening that I don't know about?" She glared at Mason. "Are you taking advantage of her? Have you stolen money from her?"

"Robyn!" Lillian's voice was sharp. "You're being ridiculous. Mason is family, just like you. I invited him. The terms of the will are clear."

"I don't care about the house. I care about you."

Mason stiffened. "I'm not taking advantage of your aunt."

Robyn wanted to ask how she could possibly believe him — she didn't know him. She looked at Lillian. "I'm calling the lawyer."

"Excellent idea." Lillian rose. "Let me get you his number. The sooner we clear this up, the better."

Mason stood in his bedroom, telling himself he didn't care what Robyn Caldwell thought of him. He was here legitimately, and if she had a bee up her ass about that, she'd have to get over it.

Which sounded great but was total bullshit.

Lillian had mentioned her niece several times, had even hinted they were both single, a fact Mason had ignored. He knew his flaws, and he just wasn't very good at relationships. When Lillian had told him Robyn was coming for a visit, he'd barely paused to nod. What did he care? No, having her here wasn't the problem. The problem was that she obviously hated him.

He'd seen it in the way she'd looked at him — as if he were slime on her shoe. She'd wanted him to not exist, or disappear, which would have been no big deal if she hadn't been so . . . So . . .

Incredible.

He swore under his breath, telling himself to get his shit together. Yes, Robyn was stunning. Athletic, with long blond hair and eyes as blue as . . . Hell, he didn't know. The sky maybe?

She looked like a woman who wouldn't take crap from a man. She looked like the kind of woman you gladly sold your soul for, even if you knew it was going to end badly. Which proved his theory that life was a woman with a mean sense of humor.

He had no idea what had just happened. He generally enjoyed women. Some were more desirable than others, but he'd never once in his life felt a kick in his gut just from looking at one.

Charles II appeared from under the bed and jumped up to Mason's desk, his expression imperious. When Mason didn't pet him, Charles meowed loudly.

"Do you always get what you want?" Mason asked, stroking the cat. Charles butted his head against his hand. "Yeah,

yeah, I know. Behind your ears. I remember."

The cat was a distraction but not enough of one. Mason was aware that Robyn was somewhere in the house. Probably talking to the lawyer or calling the cops. He could deal with either. For a brief second, he imagined she was changing her clothes the way some women did every fifteen minutes. What if she was naked? Even if she wasn't, she would be at some point. Like in the shower.

That fantasy went right to his groin, giving him a painful boner faster than he could say the word.

He pulled open the balcony doors. Unfortunately the outside temperature wasn't cool enough to do anything about his erection. He forced himself to think about his book and the research he still had to do. When that didn't work, he recalled the disdain in Robyn's eyes, and that seemed to do the trick.

He returned to his desk, moved Charles to his bed, then opened his laptop. Work was always a place to escape, he reminded himself. He could get lost in the —

He heard a knock.

Mason stared at the door for several seconds before crossing to open it. He'd been expecting Salvia or even Lillian, but instead Robyn stood in the hallway.

Up close, her eyes were even bluer than he remembered. She was about five-seven, and that hair. Gold-blond and falling straight down to the middle of her back. He would have given his left nut to touch it.

"Mason," she said, then paused.

The sound of his name on her lips about brought him to his knees. "Ma'am."

Her eyebrows rose. "Excuse me? Ma'am? Is that what you called me?"

"It seemed appropriate." Actually it had been a defensive move, but he wasn't going to admit that.

"Wow. Okay, then. Should I call you Mr. Bishop?"

"If you're up to it, we can progress to first names."

"Seeing as your third or fourth cousin — Lillian wasn't clear — was married to my great-aunt, and we're going to be living in the same house for a while, I'm in favor of first names."

He nodded because standing this close to her, hearing her speak for so long, had turned his brain to mush. He stepped back, indicating she was welcome to enter, only realizing after the fact he'd invited her into his bedroom. Not the wisest move considering his current lack of dick-control.

She walked in, then held out a bottle of wine. "A peace offering."

One corner of her mouth turned up in a self-deprecating smile. "I'll admit I took it from the wine cellar, so while it's a peace offering in spirit, I actually boosted it from my great-aunt."

"I'm sure Lillian won't mind."

The smile widened. "She would, in fact, approve. Lillian believes most problems in life can be mitigated with a cocktail or a glass of wine."

He took the bottle, set it on his desk and turned back to her. She'd moved to the bed and was petting Charles II. She glanced at him over her shoulder.

"Are you a cat person?"

"No. I've never had a pet. They seem all right, even if there are a lot of them."

"The cat population varies."

"Lillian says right now it's fifteen."

Robyn sighed. "Last time I was here, it was about eight. She better keep her promise and live forever."

"Because of the cats?"

"You inherit the house. I get the contents and the cats."

"That's a lot to take on."

"It is." She faced him. "I want to apologize

163

for my behavior. I have a lot of excuses, but honestly none of them matter. I'm genuinely shocked at how I acted. That's not me, except I did it, so I guess it is." She shook her head. "There have been too many unpleasant revelations about my character lately. What's up with that?"

He loved her voice. If it was a blanket, he would wrap himself in it and carry it with him wherever he went. As she talked, she moved her hands and tossed her head, causing her long hair to sway in a way designed to seduce the hardest of hearts.

She wore jeans tight enough to be interesting and one of those silky button-up shirts elegant women always seemed to have in their wardrobes. The dark purple color suited her, but then, Robyn was the kind of woman who would look good in tent flap.

She was still talking, and he forced himself to listen to the words rather than just admire the view.

"My point is," she continued, "I was rude and unfriendly, and I accused you of taking advantage of my aunt, without a single shred of evidence you'd ever considered that. I'm ashamed, and I'm sorry."

"No problem."

She looked at him. "You're not mad?"

"No."

"But I said terrible things."

"Which you regret. I understand. You didn't know about me, and having me show up was a shock."

"You're very understanding."

"I'm not here to hurt your aunt," he told her.

"So I gathered. How long have you two been corresponding?"

"About fifteen years."

Perfectly arched eyebrows rose. "She never said a word."

"But you knew I existed."

"I've always known the house would be passed on." The sexy smile returned. "There was speculation about you." The smile faded. "I was such a bitch."

"You weren't."

"Mason, I was awful. It's been a very odd couple of weeks." She raised a hand. "I'm not using that as an excuse. I'm just saying. So much has happened that has turned my world upside down."

Her phone chirped. Robyn pulled the phone from her back pocket and read a text. Her happy, intimate smile had him wanting to put his fist into the face of whoever had caused that particular smile.

"My son," she said. "He wants to know if I got here okay."

The instant jealously faded as quickly as it had exploded. A kid he could handle.

She tucked the phone in her back pocket. "I said I was fine and that we'd talk later. I can't wait to tell him about you. He's going to be so excited."

"How old is he?"

"Eighteen. I also have a twenty-two-year-old daughter."

He did the math. "You had your kids young."

"I was twenty when Harlow was born."

"You don't look forty-two."

She laughed. "Thank you. Some days I feel older than Lillian, but that's emotionally rather than physically. Ironically, my kids are nearly as much trouble now that they're grown as they were when they were little. It's just a different kind of trouble. Do you have children?"

"No."

"A wife?"

"I'm divorced." Twice, but why go into that?

"Me, too. A divorced woman with two grown kids." She looked at him. "I ran away."

"From?"

"My life. It's temporary, but it's what I did. I couldn't deal with everything. Doesn't

166

that make me sound useless?"

"You came here to figure it out."

"You can't know that."

"Isn't it true?"

The smile reappeared. He felt the gut punch down to his groin.

"It is. I have no idea why I'm telling you this, but I'm going to anyway. My ex-husband is dating my daughter's fiancé's twin sister." She laughed. "I'll pause and let that sink in."

Mason replayed her words, trying to get the information straight. "How old is her fiancé?"

"Twenty-six."

"And the ex?"

"Forty-six."

"She's twenty years younger."

"There is that."

Mason didn't get why guys did that. Sure, the sex, and then what? He'd always enjoyed a woman he could talk to — one who challenged him.

"And the twin sister? Your daughter can't be happy."

Robyn nodded. "She's not. She's really close to her dad, but he kept this from her. Plus Cord is the kind of guy who thinks it's funny to talk about how if they get married, Zafina will be both stepmother and sister-in-law to Harlow."

"Worse. He'd be his own daughter's father and her brother-in-law."

Robyn's amazing blue eyes widened and her mouth dropped open. "Oh, no," she breathed. "I never thought of that. You're right. That's so much worse. Her father is her brother-in-law? Shouldn't that be illegal?"

"Absolutely."

She still looked shell-shocked. "The only good thing is that Cord doesn't tend to stay in relationships long."

"I can see how finding out about that would make for a bad week for you."

"It did. My boyfriend also told me I wasn't good enough for him." She paused. "Ex-boyfriend."

"Not good enough for him? That's not possible. Who does he think he is?" Mason forced himself to stop talking. There was a little too much energy in his voice.

What an asswipe. Any man who was lucky enough to be dating Robyn should get on his knees every damned day and thank God.

"He's a cardiologist."

"I don't care if he runs the EU. He's a moron."

She smiled at him. "You're defending me, and you don't even know me. I could be an awful person."

"No one who's an awful person is willing to consider the possibility that she's awful. Self-awareness requires intelligence, and your apology was sincere. Besides, you're willing to be responsible for fifteen cats."

"That's quite the assessment."

"I'm good at figuring out people."

"Apparently." She pointed to the bottle of wine. "Technically that's a gift, but I'd be happy to split it with you at dinner."

"I'd like that."

"Me, too." She started toward the door, then turned back to face him. "It was nice to meet you, Mason. I'll try to talk less next time."

"I like the talking."

"Most men don't."

"I'm not most men."

She nodded and left. When he was alone — except for Charles — he sank into his desk chair and waited for the room to stop spinning. If Robyn Caldwell was half as interesting as he thought, he was in trouble. The kind of trouble that ripped a man's heart from his chest and threw it on the side of the road. And because he was the biggest fool on the planet, he couldn't wait.

TEN

Robyn unpacked, then took a quick shower. Her conscience clear, she was able to enjoy her surroundings and appreciate that she had such a beautiful place she could escape to. Once dressed, she opened the French doors to her balcony. The familiar view of palm trees, rooftops and the ocean beyond made her smile. Later, there would be a spectacular sunset.

Two gray cats strolled in. She petted both of them and checked their name tags. "Victoria and Mary," she said with a laugh. "Nice to meet you. Charles II is hanging out next door."

Neither cat seemed especially interested in the information. They walked out on the balcony and settled down in the sun. Robyn watched them, careful to keep her gaze straight ahead. No peeking toward Mason's room next door, which shared the balcony with hers. She wondered if he knew they were neighbors.

He was an interesting man, she thought, stepping into flat sandals. Attractive and a thoughtful listener. He'd been gracious about her apology, which she appreciated. He had a nice face — strong and masculine. Good-looking enough to be appealing, but not so pretty that he would want more mirror time than her. Not that she was looking for anything. No way. She was barely out of her relationship with Jase. Even more compelling, until she figured out her mess of a life, she was staying away from men. The last time she'd gotten serious about someone, she'd given up college and her dreams. Yes, she'd been eighteen, but still. She'd thrown away so much to be with Cord, and while she didn't regret her children, she couldn't help wondering how things would have been different if she'd thought about what she wanted as much as she'd thought about what he expected.

"You can't change history," she murmured aloud, putting on a pair of diamond studs.

Her phone buzzed. She glanced at the screen and saw a text from Mindy.

Can you talk? Say yes! You have to say yes!

Robyn laughed as she quickly called her friend.

"What's going on?" she asked by way of greeting.

"Dimitri and I kissed!" Mindy squealed. "I can't believe it. It was amazing. I'm still shaking. He kisses like a god. I melted and nearly begged him to take me."

Robyn sank into a chair. "You didn't. Mindy, this is bad."

"Don't say that. I'm so happy, I'm floating."

Robyn knew her friend wouldn't listen, but she had to try to get through to her. "You're risking your marriage for a few kisses? Come on, I don't care how great he is, he's not worth it. You could lose everything."

"I won't. Payne will never find out. You're spoiling my news."

"I'm not happy about your news."

"You're supposed to be on my side."

"I am. This is me trying to save you."

"I don't want to be saved. I want to throw myself in Dimitri's arms and enjoy every second. Can't you be happy for me?"

Robyn didn't know how to answer the question. "I think you're making a huge mistake, but I'll always be here if you need me."

"Thank you. How's life in Santa Barbara?"

"It's sunny and seventy-five with about forty percent humidity."

"Ugh. It's about ninety-eight here, and the humidity matches." Mindy laughed. "But I have Dimitri, and that's all that matters. Gotta run. Talk to you later."

She hung up before Robyn could warn her to be careful. Not that she would listen — Mindy was on a course, and Robyn had a bad feeling nothing was going to come between her and her illicit affair.

There would be consequences, Robyn thought, remembering how she'd felt the first time she'd found out Cord had cheated on her.

He'd gone to a trade show for the weekend, and she'd decided to surprise him in his hotel. Which she had, but there'd also been a woman with him in his bed. What Robyn remembered the most was how stupid she'd felt for traveling all the way to Orlando to do something nice and instead had learned her husband was a lying bastard who couldn't keep his dick in his pants.

She hadn't said anything. Instead she'd run back to her car and had driven home, then packed up the kids and gotten on a plane to Santa Barbara. Travel with a five-

and a one-year-old hadn't been easy, but Leo and Lillian had welcomed her. They'd enjoyed the kids, giving her time to figure out what to do about her marriage. They'd offered her a home for as long as she wanted, and had told her the money for college was still available, if she was interested. She could stay with them and go to UC Santa Barbara. Something she'd seriously considered.

Cord had kept calling her, but she'd refused to speak to him. A week after she arrived, he'd shown up, full of remorse, begging her to forgive him. He'd vowed that it was a onetime thing and it would never happen again. He told her he was devastated, not only for what he'd done, but for how he'd hurt her. He'd reminded her how much they loved each other and talked about their life together. He'd said exactly what she'd wanted him to say. In the end, she'd gone back to Florida with him. As far as she knew, he'd continued to be faithful for another few years. At least, that was her best guess.

She shoved her phone into her sundress pocket, only to have it buzz a second time. She grinned when she saw Austin had texted her again.

Back on land. So about this Mason guy. Is he an ornithologist?

When the kids were little, Robyn had explained that someone else would be inheriting the house. They'd speculated about who he was and what he was doing at that moment. Austin, learning about different professions in school, had latched on to the idea of the mystery inheritor being an ornithologist.

He doesn't strike me as a bird watcher, but I'll ask at dinner. You doing okay?

I miss you. Don't tell the guys I said that, btw. It's not manly.

Robyn smiled. Your secret is safe with me. I miss you, too, kid. She returned her phone to her pocket and left her room to go downstairs.

She found Lillian and Mason in the large, open living room, heads bent together as they talked. They turned at the sound of her footsteps. Mason stood while Lillian smiled.

"Unpacked and settled?" she asked. "Do you need anything?"

Robyn kissed her cheek, then took a seat

across from Mason. "Just your love and your company."

"You have both."

"Good." Robyn smiled at her. "I've apologized to Mason for my behavior, and now I apologize to you. I was rude and difficult."

Lillian waved a hand. "All forgiven and forgotten." She picked up her glass. "Mason made me a cocktail."

"Would you like one?" Mason asked.

"I'll wait for dinner and that bottle of wine we're splitting."

Mason nodded and settled back in his seat.

"Did you talk to the children?" Lillian asked Robyn.

"I texted with Austin. He's doing well. Harlow and I still aren't speaking right now."

"That girl," Lillian murmured. "She's being difficult."

"She would say it's my fault for not supporting her wedding."

"She's too young to be getting married. In my day, it's what a woman did, but now there are so many options."

"I agree," Robyn said lightly, knowing she'd ignored her options and only had herself to blame for the outcome.

The large French doors were open, allowing the ocean breeze to flutter through the room. Sunset was an hour away, but the sky had already taken on a deeper shade of blue.

"It's going to be a pretty one tonight," she said.

"Yes, it is." Lillian smiled. "My favorite time of day, even if I do miss Leo." She turned to Mason. "We were always together for the sunset. It was, as you young people like to say, our thing."

"It's good to have a thing," he said.

Robyn glanced at him. "Are you here for vacation or something longer?" She did her best to keep her tone friendly so no one would think she was having another meltdown.

"Mason's here for the duration," Lillian told her. "He's a writer."

"Oh. What do you write?"

Mason looked more uncomfortable than pleased with the change in topic. "I'm not a writer. Not the way you're thinking."

"He's published books," Lillian said proudly.

Mason shrugged. "I've written a couple of nonfiction books on obscure historical battles. It's a hobby of mine. Until two years ago, I was in the army for twenty-five years."

"A military man," Robyn said, surprised by the information. "So you could straighten out my kids in eighteen seconds."

"I doubt there's anything wrong with them."

She grinned. "Then you would be mistaken."

Their eyes met. His were dark — mostly unreadable but with a hint of humor. His career explained his air of confidence. He looked like he could handle any situation, and that was probably true.

"I've been trying to convince him to go through Leo's papers," Lillian said. "Robyn, my dear, tell him he must."

"You must. Especially if you enjoy history. You know Uncle Leo was a professor at UC Santa Barbara."

"Lillian mentioned it."

"He loved his work and research. There are boxes and boxes of I have no idea what. I know there's source material." She smiled. "You might find something that inspires you."

For a moment nearly too brief to measure, his gaze sharpened, before returning to normal.

"I wouldn't want to intrude," he said.

Lillian looked at Robyn, who turned to him. "Please, intrude. I'm happy to deal with everything in the house, except for Leo's papers. They're not my thing. Maybe they're yours."

He nodded. "You knew him?"

"Yes." Robyn reached for Lillian's hand. "I was born in the area and lived around here until I was fourteen. My mother passed away when I was eleven. My father was devastated and unable to cope, so he dropped me off with Lillian and Leo. It was supposed to be for a few weeks, but I ended up staying four years."

"Those were the best years," Lillian told her.

"I agree." Robyn turned back to Mason. "My father was a charter boat captain. He eventually settled in Naples, Florida, and sent for me."

Mason glanced around the room. "It's a beautiful place to grow up."

"It is. The house was never boring."

They chatted for a few more minutes. Then Salvia called them into dinner. Mason helped Lillian to her feet, and offered his arm. Robyn followed them to the massive dining room with the table that, when extended, could seat twenty-four.

Tonight it was just the three of them, clustered at one end. Salvia had already opened the bottle of wine Robyn had brought Mason.

Once Lillian was seated, Mason moved to

Robyn's chair and held it out. Before she sat down, she leaned toward him.

"I really am sorry about before. You've now seen me at my worst. It only gets better from here."

His dark gaze locked with hers. "If that was you at your worst, then we have nothing to worry about."

She took her seat. When he settled across from her, they looked at each other and smiled. It was the kind of smile that spoke of shared secrets and an intimacy that comes from familiarity and trust.

How odd, she thought. She barely knew the man. She shouldn't feel connected to him. Or attracted.

Jet lag, she told herself firmly. She'd been up since predawn to catch her flight to LAX, and then she'd had the drive. There was nothing between her and Mason — she was just a little tired.

Harlow left for work early so she could swing by her mom's house. They hadn't spoken in nearly a week — probably the longest they'd ever gone without some kind of contact. At first she'd expected her mom to get in touch with her, but she'd been silent. As time had passed, Harlow had started to think more and more about the

180

conversation. Unfortunately, the more she replayed what she'd said, the more uncomfortable she became.

As she drove the familiar route, she thought maybe she'd been wrong to insist her mother keep the house. She supposed there was a possibility that it was kind of expensive — a point Kip had made. Waterfront in Naples didn't come cheap. Given that her mom didn't really work and the buyout from her dad came in monthly payments, Harlow supposed it was possible that her mother qualifying for a home loan on her own was unlikely.

Which meant Harlow had been a bitch for no good reason — a concept she didn't want to think about but couldn't seem to ignore.

She pulled into the driveway and walked to the front door. It was a little after seven, but her mom was always up early. Harlow used the keypad on the front door to let herself in. Just in case she was wrong, and her mom was still asleep, she walked quietly into the kitchen to see if there was coffee brewing.

But the large, open kitchen was empty. Harlow looked around, surprised at the lack of coffee, the empty fruit bowl, the —

She spotted a couple of forms on the

counter, along with a pile of mail, and walked over. A quick scan told her they were from a house-sitting service, giving a report on the house.

Doors and windows all secure. All bathrooms and the kitchen checked for leaks. The outdoor sprinklers are working. There was a date and a time, along with a name. The box for "confirming email sent" had been checked.

Harlow ran through the house to the master. Her mother's bedroom was empty, and there were clothes missing in her closet.

"She can't be gone," Harlow said aloud. Only she was. She'd left without saying anything to anyone.

"I don't understand," she said into the silence.

She walked outside, careful to lock the front door. In the car, she stared at the house she still thought of as home. How could her mother have gone away without telling her?

Harlow blinked away the familiar burn of tears. How ridiculous. She was twenty-two years old. She didn't need her mother!

But what had been rage a week ago had morphed into shame and longing. Now she battled a touch of worry. Her mom could be anywhere — what if something happened to her? How would anyone know?

Harlow told herself to take a breath. She would talk to Austin when she got to work. If he didn't know, then she would call Jase. She didn't have much contact with her mother's boyfriend, but he should know where she was. And if they were off together, his office would have information.

That decided, she backed out of the driveway and headed for the marina. It was already hot and humid, despite the early hour. As she drove, she thought about the empty house and how one day it would belong to someone else. Back when her parents had told her about the divorce, her mom keeping the house had offered consistency. She'd been comfortable knowing her home, her room, her life weren't going to change too much. She'd been going off to college, but she liked knowing the house was still there for her to come home to — at least while Austin was in high school.

But it had to have been different for her mom. She might have kept the house, but she'd lost her marriage. Harlow knew her mom had been sad but determined. At no point had Harlow thought they might get back together.

Harlow arrived at work and went in search of her brother. He was crewing for one of the other captains, and she found him inspecting the child-sized life jackets.

"Hey," he said when he saw her.

"Mom's not at the house." She heard the panic in her voice. "Do you know where she is?"

"Yeah. She's in Santa Barbara visiting Lillian. Didn't she tell you?"

"No. We're not speaking. I can't believe she would leave without saying anything."

Austin's mouth thinned. "Jeez, Harlow, what did you do this time?"

"What does that even mean?"

"You're . . ." He paused. "You're difficult lately. More so than usual. It's like you're always mad."

"I have no idea what you're talking about."

He shrugged. "Whatever. Mom's in California. Now you know."

"You're pissed at me. Why?"

"Because you're mean to Mom. A lot. What is she doing that's so bad?"

"I'm not mean. She only thinks of herself. Selling the house when she knows I —"

Austin shook his head. "Seriously? Tell you what — you pay for it just one month and then we'll talk."

"You know it's expensive?" She wouldn't have thought him that aware.

"Sure. We've talked about her selling it

184

and moving someplace cheaper. I'm fine with that. Dad's money is going to end someday. You're already gone, I'll be gone, and then what? Who's looking out for her?"

Harlow wanted to say that he was just being a suck-up, only Austin had always been the steady one who could see both sides of a situation. A sometimes annoying but mostly satisfying characteristic.

"I just didn't think she'd take off without talking to me," she grumbled.

"Then text her." He frowned. "Not right now. It's four-thirty in the morning there."

"I'll think about it."

His mouth twisted. "Why do you always have to take the hard road?"

"I can't help it. That's kind of my thing."

"Dumbass thing, if you ask me." But he was smiling as he spoke.

Harlow lunged for him. He caught her easily, twisting her until she was bent nearly in half, then tickled her. She squealed and wriggled away.

"Don't do that!" she said, but she was laughing as she spoke.

"Can't help it. Tickling you is kind of my thing."

She leaned against him. "Don't tell, but I miss her."

"Me, too. Having my own apartment isn't

the party I thought it would be."

"I'll text her."

Austin shook his head. "You're too stubborn. One day you have to suck it up and admit you don't know everything."

"One day," she agreed with a grin. "But not today."

She stored her bag in her locker, then got to work, checking out her boat before her charter. When that was done, she went into the office to complete the paperwork. Her dad was at his desk.

"How's it going, kid?" he said when he saw her.

"Good. I have a charter in a bit."

"We're busy. That's good."

She thought about asking about the business plan. He'd promised to review it, but hadn't said anything yet. But instead of mentioning that, she found herself saying, "Dad, was your divorce mutual?"

He looked at her, his expression quizzical. "What brought this on?"

"I don't know. I was thinking about it. When you told me and Austin, you two didn't get into details. Everything was already worked out."

They'd obviously been planning it for a while. Harlow remembered how angry she'd been when she'd figured out that her parents had been waiting for her to graduate from high school before making the announcement. She'd felt so betrayed, with the lie of omission burning deep. Now, looking back, she saw it as an act of kindness. Her parents hadn't wanted their decision to disrupt her senior year.

She looked at her father. No, not her parents. Her mother. She'd been the one to make that call.

"Dad, did you cheat on Mom?"

Her father's brows rose. "Why would you ask that?"

His falsely hearty tone was answer enough. She felt her shoulders slump as questions assaulted her. Who? When? How many times? The weight of it all nearly pushed her to the ground.

"Did she know? Is that why you got a divorce?"

He looked away. "There were problems, Harlow. Marriage is complicated."

She straightened, then repeated. "Dad, did you cheat on Mom, and is that why you got a divorce?"

He looked at her. "Yes."

Her stomach lurched. "Okay," she whispered.

"There were other factors. Your mother —"

She held up a hand. "I've got a charter, Dad. I have to go."

She walked out of the office. On her boat, she drew in a couple of breaths, trying to make sense of what she'd learned, only to realize that wasn't possible. With a few simple words, her worldview had shifted. For reasons unclear, she'd always assumed her mom had been more at fault for the divorce than her dad. Maybe because, as Kip had pointed out, it was easier for her to be mad at her mom.

But she'd been wrong. And if she'd been wrong about that, then what else was she assuming that wasn't true? And what other unpleasant surprises were lurking, waiting to pounce?

ELEVEN

Robyn walked through the back gardens at Lillian's house. The landscape — more native plants with a couple of formal English-style gardens — couldn't be more different than her yard in Florida, but the setting was still incredibly beautiful. She loved the scent of the salt air, the balmy seventy-degree temperature, the promise of a beautiful sunset.

Three days in, she'd adjusted to the time difference and was enjoying her escape from her real life, with only the occasional qualm about what she'd left behind. Although she was texting regularly with Austin, she hadn't heard from Harlow. She often picked up her phone to text her daughter, only to put it back down. She wasn't angry or even hurt, but she still felt . . . unsettled. She'd assumed that when her kids were adults, she would know how to parent them, but no such luck. She was still awash in indecision.

Logically if she missed her daughter, she should text her. But Robyn didn't want to reinforce Harlow's selfishness. So she put it off again.

She paused by several roses. The flowers — pink and red and yellow — were completely out of place, yet so pretty. A team of gardeners worked the property year-round. Although Lillian had tried to entice her into learning about the various plants, Robyn hadn't been interested.

She brushed her hand across a cluster of hummingbird sage, then continued along the path. By the garage was a large deck with coast live oaks around it. There was an old barbecue, a table, chairs, and several chaises. When she was younger, that deck had been a favorite reading spot. She could get lost in a book without interruption.

She turned in that direction, thinking it would be a good place for her to plan what to do with the rest of her life. Lillian had done a good job of planting the antique store seed — no pun intended. There was enough furniture to fill twenty stores. Preparing an inventory was daunting, but she knew there were hundreds of treasures in the house.

A number of them belonged in museums, and she would want a few for herself and the kids, but the rest could be sold. It was an incredible gift — much like the offer to pay for her college. The difference was, this time she wasn't going to dismiss it.

With luck, Lillian would live another decade, which meant Robyn had time to come up with a plan. She could either get more hours from Mindy or find a full-time job. She could also start on a business degree with a minor in art history. That was the longer, more complicated path. There were several online courses that helped people start a small business. She could complete those and then only study art history. Or she could complete those and get her experience through work.

She was fine not having more specifics right now because she liked her options. They were sensible and had tangible goals. She would —

She heard an odd clink of metal against metal. The gardeners weren't here, so it was something else, and it was coming from the back deck.

She rounded a cluster of ornamental grasses and saw Mason tightening screws on the old barbecue.

"Hello," she said, stopping on the edge of the pavers. "I didn't mean to interrupt. I heard a strange noise and came to investigate."

He straightened and looked at her, his expression curiously guilty. "You probably wonder what I'm doing."

"Working on the barbecue?"

He cleared his throat. "Yes, that. Obviously." He brushed his hands against his jeans. "I thought I could get it working."

Okay, sure. That much was clear, so why was he acting strangely? She was about to ask when he blurted, "I can't take it anymore. Last night we had salad for dinner. The night before we had soup." He sounded desperate and unhappy. "Soup isn't dinner. Except for breakfast, half the meals are vegetarian, and the portions are tiny. I'm hungry all the time. I need meat."

Robyn tried not to laugh. "You sound like my son."

"He's a smart kid."

She gave in to her amusement. "Poor Mason. Trapped with women who don't obsess about meat."

"I don't either. Unless I don't have it. Then it's on my mind."

She thought about the meals Salvia served. The portions were small, and there really hadn't been much protein.

"We had coconut shrimp the day I arrived," she teased.

"Yeah, it was great. And since then lettuce every day. And kale." He shuddered.

She grinned. "Fine. We'll get you some meat. I can talk to Salvia."

"I don't want to make trouble. I was just going to cook my own."

"You can cook?"

"I can barbecue." He smiled. "Fire good."

Unexpected and powerful awareness rushed through her, making her a little dizzy. That smile. Confident, easy, sexy. This was the real Mason Bishop, she thought, trying to catch her breath. The man underneath the polite and slightly distant facade.

"Aside from tossing meat onto a grill, what culinary skills do you have?" she asked, mostly because conversation might distract her from her sudden attraction.

"I can do almost anything with eggs. Spaghetti."

"Do you make your own sauce?"

"Seriously? No, I buy the sauce."

"Homemade is better."

"So is sex with someone other than myself, but life isn't always that —"

He dropped the wrench and stared at her, his expression horrified. Color bled from his face, then returned, darkening his cheeks.

"I apologize, ma'am," he said stiffly. "That was unacceptable and uncalled for. I forgot myself. It won't happen again."

Gone was the friendly, sexy smile, gone was the teasing. His body was stiff, his shoulders squared, his gaze direct. He'd retreated to military bearing.

She had no idea what to say to make him feel better. More significant to her, she wanted to see the sexy smile again.

She walked toward him, consciously keeping her body language relaxed.

"I've had children, Mason. So the sex thing isn't all that foreign to me. And yes, I agree, it's better with someone else, although I have to admit Jase, the cardiologist, was incredibly uninspired. You'd think that a man who spent all those years studying human anatomy would have a clearer understanding of where the clitoris is, but he always seemed lost and then confused when he found it. So sometimes, alone is better. But that may just be a girl thing."

He swallowed. "I wouldn't know about that, ma'am."

"I'm assuming you mean you wouldn't know about the experience from the female point of view. I'm hoping you don't mean you're confused by what a clit is for and how to find it."

His gaze shot to hers. "I know what it is and what to do with it."

"Just checking. So we can be done with this now. We've both said too much, which evens the playing field. You're going to stop calling me ma'am or I'll put ants in your bed. When I get back to the house, I'll put together a grocery list. Do you shop, Mason?"

"At the grocery store? I do, ah, Robyn."

"Good. You buy today and I'll buy next time. How does that sound? We'll start with steaks, and later in the week I'll marinate some chicken and pork chops."

He relaxed a little. "I am sorry for what I said."

"Don't be. I'm not that delicate."

"I don't want to offend you."

She smiled. "Do you like pineapple?"

"Yes."

"Good. I have a recipe for a pineapple-based marinade that's pretty delicious. It's Austin's favorite." She glanced at Mason. "He's my youngest."

"I remember."

"He's moved out, but just for the summer. He'll be moving back in September. Sort of an adulting trial run. I miss him."

"I'm sure he misses you, too."

She motioned for him to continue with

the barbecue and sat in one of the chairs. "He's drifting, and it's all my fault."

Mason listened to Robyn nearly as much as he watched her. Not only because he enjoyed the sound of her voice but to make sure he hadn't totally screwed up what had been a great moment.

Why had he talked about masturbating? In front of her, of all people. He swore silently. It was a boneheaded move. A rookie mistake. Robyn was classy — upscale and beautiful and refined. He should be able to handle that — he'd always been able to assess his surroundings and fit in. Even when he wasn't comfortable, no one knew. But thirty seconds alone with her and he'd been talking about his dick. Dammit.

"Austin doesn't have any direction," she said, her voice low. "I blame myself for that, too."

"He's eighteen — that's on him."

"No, he's legally an adult, but no eighteen-year-old is truly mature." She paused. "Cord and I divorced four years ago. We waited to tell the kids until Harlow had graduated from high school. Part of the settlement was that I kept the house so Austin would have continuity. Same neighborhood, same friends. Plus, it gave Harlow a place to return to on breaks."

"Sounds like a plan."

"Four years ago. Four."

She seemed a little obsessed with the time thing. He took a seat in one of the wrought iron chairs.

"Harlow went to college. Austin finished high school." She looked at him, her mouth twisting. "You know what I did in that time? Nothing. Zip. I have a piddly-ass part-time job that doesn't pay anything. I got a new car because mine was three years old. I kept my membership at the country club."

Her voice rose a little with each sentence until it approached a pitch only dogs could hear.

"I lived on the payments from my ex-husband. We started the business together, so he's buying me out. I have no plan, no safety net, no skills, and in six years the money runs out. I wasted four years, so I'm worried Austin learned the wrong lesson from me. I could have gone to college after high school. Lillian and Leo offered to pay for it, but I married Cord instead. So many bad decisions."

She sighed. "I've been thinking about my daughter a lot. She had cancer when she was little. She's fine now, but for a couple of years, we thought every day we could lose her. After she was better, I didn't push her hard enough. I indulged and spoiled her because she was alive and happy."

"That's not an unexpected response to having a sick kid."

"I know, but what if I let myself off the hook, too, because of what we'd been through? Did I give myself too much of a break, thinking I endured the worst thing ever? And if so, how do I get myself on track?"

Tears filled her beautiful blue eyes. Tears that made him want to slay whatever dragon might be bothering her. Or at the very least, wash her car. Something tangible that would make her feel better.

That was the guy side of him. The soldier he'd grown to be understood that pity was another way to get lost. Self-pity was a waste of time and effort. Pity made a person feel weak, a slick road to acting weak.

"What are you going to do about it?" he asked a little more loudly than he'd planned.

She jumped slightly. "Excuse me?"

"You have six years to get your life in order. That's more notice than most folks get. You have money, you have resources, you have time. Come up with a battle plan. Execute. Accomplish. Make things happen."

One corner of her full mouth twitched.

"So no hug?"

Her words were so unexpected, he couldn't process them. When he did, he started laughing. She joined in, the sound bright and clear. God, she was incredible. Later, when he was alone, he would think about the fact that she'd said "clit" in front of him. He would do a lot more than think about it, but that was for another time.

"Not a lot of hugging in the army," he told her.

"Probably for the best. There could be some misunderstandings." She stretched out her long legs. "You're not wrong. I do have six years to figure it out. I just wish I'd figured out the problem four years ago."

"You can only go forward. What's your goal? And none of that 'I want to be happy and save baby seals' crap. Realistically, where do you see yourself?"

Her eyes widened. "I really was going to join Greenpeace."

He grinned at her. "Sure you were."

"Okay, not that, although I support their cause." The smile faded. "At some point, I hope not for years, Lillian will leave us, and then I have the contents of the house to deal with."

"And the cats. We need to all be clear on that. Cats equal you."

She laughed again. "Oh, Mason, I'd thought Charles II was winning you over."

"Him, I like. It's the other fourteen I'm less sure about."

"Fine. I get the contents and the cats. At that point, I have more than enough inventory to open an antique store."

"Back in Florida?"

"I don't know. It's where I live."

He wanted to point out she could live here, but didn't know how that would sound to her. Besides, it wasn't as if anything was going to happen between them, so why did he care where she lived?

"In the meantime, because I want Lillian to live forever, I'm coming up with my plan. Right now it involves getting some business experience and working more hours. While I'm here, I'm going to do a preliminary inventory of the house. Just broad strokes. A real inventory would take a year. Is that good enough for you, Soldier?"

"It's a start."

"A start is more than I had yesterday."

Harlow told herself not to read too much into Kip's decision to pick up his mom and bring her to the club, leaving Harlow to arrive on her own. She told herself the move made sense — Judy had never been to the club and was uncomfortable about finding her way. It was the kind thing to do and spoke well of Kip as a person. Harlow had read somewhere that a woman should pay attention to how a guy treated his mother because it was an indication of how he would treat his wife later in life.

Which sounded great, but left Harlow arriving alone. She was still dealing with the knowledge that her father had cheated on her mother, the fight with her mom, and now having her future mother-in-law inflict her opinion on a possible wedding venue. She'd felt unable to say Judy couldn't tag along, but suddenly wished her own mom was there, as well.

Harlow opened the large door and walked into the air-conditioned comfort. In deference to their appointment, she'd put on a light blue summer dress and high-heeled sandals. She'd spent the morning of her day off running errands and doing laundry. After she was done here, she was hoping to talk Enid into hanging out for bit — assuming she could catch her friend between her two jobs.

Harlow sat on a bench by the entrance and texted Kip that she was here. The reply came immediately.

It's Judy. We're nearly there. The golf course is so beautiful.

Harlow knew that Kip couldn't text and drive, but giving his phone to his mother? It was one thing to hand it to Harlow, but his mom?

She held in a shudder, then slipped her phone back in her bag. Five minutes later, Kip and his mom walked in and walked toward her.

"Rusti's meeting us at two," Harlow said. She turned to her future mother-in-law. "Hi, Judy. Thanks for joining us."

She did her best to keep her tone friendly. She'd agreed Judy could come, so she couldn't be upset that the other woman was here. As for her mother not being with them, well, apparently she was still in California, not bothering to communicate with her only daughter.

Judy, about five-three and overweight, looked around. "This place is really nice, Harlow. It's a private club?"

"Uh-huh."

"You pay a membership fee?"

"Yes. Monthly, and there's probably an initiation fee. I'm not sure. I'm on my dad's membership."

Judy's lips pressed together. "But you still

have to pay for everything you do, like tennis or golf or eating here."

Kip smiled at his mom. "It's a country club, Mom. That's how it happens."

"But why do you pay a membership fee and then pay for everything else? What's the point of that? Why not golf on a public course and eat in a restaurant? It would cost less."

"It's exclusive," Harlow said with a smile. "Here you can make reservations for tee times and spa treatments."

"But you're still paying double."

"Mom!" Kip looked at her. "Maybe less questions?"

"All right. I just don't understand the whole point of clubs like this."

Kip shot Harlow a frustrated look. She smiled back when what she was thinking was, *You wanted to bring her.* Once again she thought that her mom would have smoothed things over with Judy or distracted her.

Rusti appeared right on time. She was a petite redhead with the personality of a born people pleaser.

"I'm so excited you're considering having your wedding here," she said in her Southern drawl. She shook hands with Kip and Judy. "I've known Harlow forever. We played tennis together when we were little. My parents are members, and my grandparents." Rusti laughed. "It's a family thing."

She smiled at Harlow. "Come on, Miss Bride. Let's go look at the facilities. On the way you can tell me how far along you are in your planning."

"I'm just starting."

Rusti gave her a knowing look. "Oh, no. Overwhelmed by options?"

"A little."

"Once you make a few choices, everything gets more manageable. The venue informs the date and the number of guests. The wedding dress is a big one. The rest is easy. If you have your wedding here, you can choose as much help as you want. I've had brides I see once six months out and then not again until the day before the ceremony. Other brides like to pitch a little tent in my office and live there." Rusti laughed. "What makes you happy makes me happy."

Harlow felt herself relaxing. "Thanks. I'm not sure what kind of bride I'm going to be."

"The best kind," Kip told her.

"You're sweet," Rusti said. "And such a cute couple. All right. This is our main ballroom." She pulled open double doors

and led them into a giant ballroom overlooking the water.

"Depending on weather, the glass doors
can be open or closed. Open means more
space and mingling. Dance floor on the east
side." She pointed. "Buffet is available, but
a plated dinner really makes the evening.
The ceremony would be next door, overlooking the gardens."

She grinned at Harlow. "We don't want a
view that outshines the bride. A fifty-
thousand-dollar deposit holds the space
and, of course, applies to the cost of the
wedding."

Judy blanched. "Did you say fifty thousand
dollars?"

"Mom." Kip looked at her. "It's okay."

"It's not okay. It's fifty thousand dollars.
That's a down-payment on a house."

Rusti smiled at Harlow. "Are you comfortable with this?"

Harlow ignored the flush of embarrassment heating her face. "It's fine, Rusti. My
dad wants me to have the wedding of my
dreams. Let's keep going."

Rusti took them into the garden. The heat
and humidity slapped them, making Harlow want to duck back indoors. But she
nodded and listened as Rusti explained the
options. Once they returned to the ball-

room, Rusti mentioned looking at menus, just to give them some ideas.

"The fifty thousand doesn't include a meal?" Judy asked in disbelief.

Kip shot Harlow a look of apology. "We're going to go," he said. "I'll check in with you later."

Harlow nodded, once again wishing her mom was here. She would know what to say and how to defuse the situation.

She looked at Rusti. "Sorry about that. Kip and his family aren't country club people, so it's hard for her to understand."

"Of course. Don't worry about it. So, what do you think?"

"I don't know," Harlow admitted. "It's beautiful, and we could invite everyone we want. I do like the idea of being able to hand off a lot of the work."

"That's why I'm here."

"I need to think on this. It's a big decision, and I want to make sure it's the right one."

Rusti's smile never faltered. "Let me get you a list of the dates that are currently open. We book up fast, so there aren't many. You might want to put down the deposit while you're considering other options. It's fully refundable up to six months before the wedding."

"Great idea," Harlow murmured, thinking she didn't have fifty thousand dollars. She would have to talk to her dad. Sure, he'd said he would pay for her wedding at the club, but did he have a clue as to the cost?

"I'll be in touch," Harlow told her. "Thanks so much for your help."

She made sure Rusti had her email address to send the dates, then made her escape. In her car, she looked back at the club. Yes, Judy wasn't used to country club prices, but Harlow had to admit that even to her, fifty thousand seemed steep for a deposit. It wasn't as if she and Kip could contribute, and her mom wasn't in much better shape. There would be cash when the house sold, but maybe her mom should keep the money for her future.

As she drove away, she thought about the business she and her dad were supposed to be buying, if only he would read the offer the lawyer had sent over. That was two hundred and fifty thousand dollars.

How much money did her dad actually have to spend on things like buying a business and her wedding? They'd talked about both, but with Cord, she was never sure he was listening. Maybe it was time to have a serious conversation with him about many things, including the fact that he'd cheated on her mother.

"Probably best to start with the money stuff," she murmured aloud. "That will be a whole lot more pleasant than talking about Dad being a hound dog."

Twelve

In the end, Harlow went for easy rather than expedient. She drove into town and parked near the upscale shopping area. From there it was a quick walk to the boutique where Enid worked most afternoons before starting her shift at a local bar.

Enid, manning a professional steamer, smiled at her.

"Hi. How did it go? Are you getting married at the club?"

"I don't know." Harlow hugged her, then glanced at the still wrinkled black cocktail dress. "Pretty."

"Linen." Enid lowered her voice. "I can't keep the wrinkles out. Don't buy this one."

"Thanks for the tip. Anyway, it went all right. Kip's mom freaked at the deposit. We didn't get much past that."

Enid returned her attention to the dress and began steaming. "Most people freak at those kind of prices."

"Then Kip should have warned her. It was really uncomfortable. I wish my mom had been there."

"She's still in California?"

"I guess."

Enid looked at her. "You haven't talked?"

"No. She just went away without a word. For all I know, she's never coming home."

Enid's mouth twitched. "Ah, there she is. My little ray of sunshine."

Despite how her afternoon had gone, Harlow smiled. "Okay, I'm not always the most positive person on the planet, but this was bad. Judy was uncomfortable the whole time."

"A lot of people don't have country club lifestyles. Kip doesn't come from money like you."

"I don't come from money. We're not rich."

"Richer than most. Haven't you and Kip talked about what it was like when he was growing up?"

"What do you mean?"

"His dad works in a machine shop. His mom's a checker at the grocery store. He sells appliances. I'm not saying it's bad — but it's not the way you grew up."

Harlow stared at her friend. "How can you know all that about him?"

"We talk sometimes when the three of us go out with friends." Enid shrugged. "Kip and I have a lot in common. You're the richest person we know."

"But I'm not. I don't have money."

"You have access." Enid moved the cocktail dress to a rack, then began steaming a silk blouse. "If you need something, you ask your dad." Her expression darkened. "I'm working two jobs to save for medical school. If I'm lucky, I'll graduate only a hundred thousand in debt."

"But you had scholarships."

"I did, and a few grants, but it's not enough. I'm not complaining. I'm just pointing out that you and Kip come from different financial worlds."

Harlow tried to take it all in. She knew Enid was right, but the way she'd said it . . . as if Harlow had had it easy.

Okay, maybe she'd been spoiled as a kid, and she'd never had to worry about getting a job after college or paying for anything.

"Hey, don't be mad," Enid said quietly. "I didn't mean to upset you."

"I don't think about money."

Enid's smile was sad. "You don't have to." She motioned to the blouse. "Would you think twice about buying that if you liked it?"

"No."

"It costs what I'll take home this week. Kip works on commission. He doesn't show up for the job, he doesn't make anything. You should absolutely have the wedding of your dreams, but don't be surprised when Kip's family has trouble keeping up."

Harlow wrestled with emotions she couldn't define.

"Am I selfish?"

Enid put down the steamer and hugged her. "No. That's not what I'm saying. I'm just pointing out that we're not all as lucky as you."

Harlow looked from the blouse to her best friend. "Do I make you feel bad?"

"Never. I love you. Always." Enid hugged her again. "I'm saying it all wrong."

"I don't think so." Harlow mulled over what her friend had told her. "Kip and I have never talked about money. It's never been an issue, but now I'm wondering how much I don't know about his financial situation. He always pays for stuff like it's no big deal."

"He's a really good salesperson. He's usually number one at his store."

Harlow nodded slowly. "I know, but if we're getting married, shouldn't we plan for our financial future? Like the wedding. Having it at the club is going to be really expensive. Maybe the money would be better spent on something else."

Enid sighed. "I've destroyed your wedding."

"No, you've said some things I need to hear. I need to think about them."

Kip's mom being unable to handle the country club wedding was one thing, but Enid talking about money was another. Enid had been her friend forever — she'd been there when Harlow had been a little girl with cancer, even though Enid had been exactly the same age. They'd weathered high school and boys and going to different colleges. Theirs was a bond that could never be broken, so if Enid had something to say, Harlow was going to listen.

Harlow shifted her bag to her other shoulder. "Are you working at the bar tonight?"

"Until midnight."

"Okay, then I guess I'll see you later in the week."

"Absolutely."

They hugged one last time, then Harlow left. As she got in her car, she glanced back at the boutique. Enid needed a hundred thousand dollars for medical school. Based on the deposit and what she could guess the reception would cost, Harlow would say her wedding would cost about that. A hundred thousand dollars for a single day as opposed to four years of medical school. How could they be the same amount?

If she had that money, she would give it to her friend, she thought. But it wasn't hers, it was her dad's, and he wasn't paying for Enid's tuition. But if Enid were his daughter, he would gladly cover the cost of Johns Hopkins.

Life was complicated, Harlow thought as she drove toward the apartment she shared with Kip. The one where he paid for most of the rent and all the utilities and all the dinners out. Harlow kept the place stocked with groceries and paid a nominal amount each month toward everything else.

Hardly fair, she thought, not sure how the arrangement had come to be. After all, she and Kip made about the same amount. He even had a car payment, while her car had been a gift from her parents.

They should talk about money, she told herself. And maybe set a few financial goals. She should also speak to her dad about the company he was going to buy, along with a budget for the wedding. Conversations she wasn't sure how to start.

As she stopped at a light, she instinctively reached for her phone so she could text her mom. But then she put it down. She had no idea if her mom was mad at her, or just waiting her out, and because of that, she didn't know what to say. Did her mom think she was selfish about money and maybe everything else?

There was only one way to find out, Harlow thought, accelerating when the light turned green. But she wasn't willing to take the chance — not just yet.

Robyn sat on her deck, reading an article explaining the terms in a basic retail space lease. From what she could understand, triple net meant she would be responsible for the lease payment, insurance, maintenance and repairs.

"Maybe instead of opening an antique store, I should save enough to buy a building and lease it out," she murmured to herself. It seemed like a quicker way to make money.

Her phone buzzed. She glanced down at the screen, hoping the text was from Harlow, but instead, Mindy had sent a quick update on her relationship with Dimitri.

The latest make out session lasted nearly an hour. I'm boneless and we haven't even done anything. This is the most fun I've had in years.

"Moron," Robyn said aloud.

"That seems harsh."

She saw Mason stepping out onto their shared balcony. She had to admit, seeing Mason made her feel a little fluttery in her tummy.

"Not you," she said, waving her phone. "My friend Mindy."

"A likely story."

She laughed. "It's true. Mindy's being incredibly stupid. She's starting an affair with her tennis instructor, and it's not going to end well. Eventually Mindy's husband will find out. She has three great kids, a beautiful house, and a husband who adores her. She could lose everything. So she's the moron."

"It doesn't sound smart."

"It's not. Plus, the tennis pro is a total player. Seducing his students is a hobby for him." She motioned to the empty seat next to her. "You're welcome to join me, although I'm not sure I'm done ranting about Mindy, so consider yourself warned."

"I'm prepared to be ranted to." He smiled. "If not about."

Mason sat to her right. He looked good,

she thought, studying his short hair and relaxed posture. He was easy to be around, and despite the strangeness of their surroundings, he fit in.

He had unexpected skills. Once he'd gotten the barbecue running, he'd fixed a faucet in one of the bathrooms and a window that had refused to close. When he wasn't jogging or puttering, he was working on his book, or joining them for meals. He was well-traveled, funny and willing to share the spotlight. Unusual in a man, in her limited experience.

"You don't approve of cheating," he said.

"Never." She closed her laptop. "I'll ask the obvious. Did you ever cheat on your wife?"

"Not either of them. Or any woman." He looked at her. "Why not just leave?"

"I know, right? That's what I think. Cord cheated. The first time I found out, the kids were little. Harlow was five and Austin was one. I ran here. Leo and Lillian took me in and offered me a home, if I wanted to stay."

"You didn't."

"No. Cord begged me to come back, and eventually I agreed." She looked at him. "Judging?"

"Not at all. I have no idea of your circumstances or what you needed or wanted. I'm sure you made the best decision you could."

Which was the kindest spin possible. "I still loved him, and I wanted to stay. Our marriage had been good until he messed up. I suppose a part of me wondered if he meant it when he said it had been a onetime thing, born of opportunity."

"It wasn't?"

"I have no idea. I think he was faithful for a while, but then he wasn't." She gave him a wry smile. "I got suspicious, so I searched his office. He'd rented an apartment, which certainly speaks to motive."

"I'm sorry."

"Me, too. The thing that really gets to me is I'd been talking about going to college. The kids were older, and I had the time."

Mason shook his head. "He told you it was too expensive."

"How did you know?"

"Lucky guess."

Because he understood people, she thought. "You're right. He said it was an unnecessary expense. I didn't need a degree. The money could be better spent elsewhere. I was such a fool." She glanced at him. "And to answer the question you're too polite to ask, I took him back, because Harlow had just gone through two years of treatment for cancer, and we were finally going to be a normal family again."

He nodded slowly. "You didn't want to give the kids one more trauma."

"That was a lot of it. I also knew that while Harlow was sick, neither of us had paid attention to our marriage. He begged for yet another chance, and I gave it to him. I told myself we'd do better."

"You loved him and trusted him. He's the fool."

"That's very sweet. Thank you."

"It's true. Some men can't see what they already have. They're in it for the chase — the rush to acquire. They can't be content. He did what he did because of himself, not because of you."

"Thanks, but I could have been a terrible wife."

"Not possible."

"You can't know that."

His gaze locked with hers. "I'll ignore the fact that you're beautiful, smart and funny. You've been here a week. In that time you've checked out each cat's health, you've talked to Lillian's doctors and gone over her diet with Salvia. And that's only the stuff I know about. You care, Robyn. I'm not saying you're perfect, but there's no way you're a bad wife."

His words stunned her. His obvious admiration should be unsettling but wasn't. She admired Mason, and knowing he liked her made her feel good. Special.

"Thank you," she said quietly. "You're seeing the best version of me."

"According to you, I've also seen you at your worst."

She laughed. "Ah, yes, the night of my being bitchy. Not my proudest moment."

"It wasn't that scary."

"So speaks the soldier."

His life had been so different from hers, she thought. He was confident, comfortable with who he was.

"I gave up so much of myself to be married to Cord." She held up a hand. "That's on me, not him. I was young and in love and wanted to be with him. I was eighteen. We married in less than a year and started the business together. We had Harlow right away."

She sighed. "She wasn't planned. Austin came along four years later. I was a wife, mother and business partner. I'm not sure there was time for anything else, and after a while, I forgot to find out."

"What about now?"

"I want to start thinking about what I want. Actually it's not just a want. It's a need." She had to be responsible for herself and her future. Going along to get along was just plain dumb. "Harlow's already on her own. Soon Austin will be ready to leave. I need to figure out my next act — a cliché but not a bad one."

"Change is hard."

"I know. And scary. Plus I worry about making a mistake. It's so much easier to see what other people are doing wrong."

"Like your friend Mindy?"

"Absolutely."

"Some people can only learn by making the mistake and living with the consequences. Some people can't be told."

He was right about that. She'd never articulated the thought so clearly, but she knew it to be true. "Harlow can be told, but Austin has to do it himself," she said. "Funny how they're so different. Harlow is all drama, and Austin is the calm one, so I would think it would be the reverse."

She looked at Mason. "Once again I've dominated the conversation."

"You haven't. I enjoy listening to you talk. You're always interesting."

She laughed. "I wish that were true. Tell me about yourself. Did you join the army right out of high school?"

He nodded.

"Okay, why?" She smiled. "Family tradition? You knew you'd look good in the uniform?"

That earned her a chuckle. "I grew up in West Virginia. There was the coal mine, the general store and not much else. The army offered opportunity."

"You served twenty-five years?"

He nodded.

She thought about everything the country had been through in that time. He'd seen a lot.

"Did you regret leaving your hometown?" she asked.

"Naw. My dad told me to get out while I could. He died twenty years ago — old before his time with lung disease. I haven't been back."

Her gaze locked with his. "I'm sorry."

"He wanted me to have more than he did. I know he was proud of me."

"That's a good feeling." She'd always known, whatever mistakes she made, Lillian was proud of her. "Any kids?"

He shook his head. "No."

She waited, sensing there was more. Mason glanced over her shoulder.

"My first wife and I wanted kids. She got pregnant easy, but couldn't stay pregnant. After losing four babies, she got quiet and sad, then one day she left."

Robyn instinctively reached out her hand to his arm. "I'm sorry. That had to be awful."

"Yeah, it sucked. I didn't expect her to take off the way she did. I thought we'd talk to more doctors." His smile was self-deprecating. "I was still naive."

"Some women do want to stay and figure it out."

"I've heard that."

She realized she was still touching him and drew back her hand.

"My second wife had three kids. I was excited about being a stepfather. Their dad had run out, so they were just as eager to have me around."

"That sounds nice."

"It was, until I figured out she was only interested in having someone to help with the work and pay the bills." He glanced at her. "Any man would have done."

She winced. "So not you specifically?"

He nodded. "It was a blow to find that out. I hated leaving the kids, but I wasn't willing to be a meal ticket. So that ended. I figured after two failures, I should probably not get involved anymore. I'm a bad bet."

"I think that's harsh."

He flashed her a smile. "You don't know me well enough to voice an opinion." His tone was gentle as he spoke.

"I know you some. I know you're very tolerant of cats, even if you're not sure you like them. Although you do seem to be falling for that white cat."

"Charles II. He likes when you use his full name."

She laughed. "See? You're proving my point. You're a good guy."

"I'm not saying I'm a bad one — I'm just pointing out I seem to be lacking whatever skills it takes to make a romantic relationship work."

"And possibly learning the wrong lesson. Maybe your lack of skill is in who you pick."

He grinned. "Very likely."

She appreciated learning about him. Not just the information but how he explained his past. She couldn't remember Cord ever telling a story where he wasn't the hero.

"What about you? Want to share a few facts about yourself?"

She raised her eyebrows. "You don't think telling you my ex-boyfriend not knowing his way around my girl parts was enough of a share?"

His mouth twitched. "That was interesting, I'll admit. And an example of you being kind. You offered a distraction."

"A really good one," she teased.

"It was excellent. Any other men between your ex and the hapless doctor?"

"Just a few dates. It's tough with kids, plus for a while everyone I met knew Cord, and that wasn't comfortable. Like you, I think I'll stay single."

"I doubt that will last for long."

She appreciated his faith in her but wasn't sure it was warranted. "Any more house exploring?"

"I've looked around a little. I keep finding doors that lead nowhere. I did find a staircase in the back of what I thought was a closet, but it didn't go anywhere, either. You're the expert. Want to take me on a tour?"

"I'd like that a lot. Bring Charles II. I hear he knows all the best places to hang out."

THIRTEEN

Harlow checked the spreadsheets a third time. Buying the paddleboat and kayaking company made sense financially. They had a solid customer base and room for growth. The concession stand was something new, but she would figure it out. Eventually she was hoping to offer prepacked lunches for their boat charter customers. Maybe even sell a few branded items like baseball caps and towels. There was money to be made, if only she could get her dad to talk to her about buying the business.

The price was what they'd talked about, and the preliminary agreement was back from the lawyer, only she couldn't pin down her father.

"The man frustrates me," she murmured, saving the spreadsheet. He also disappointed her emotionally. First dating Zafina and then cheating on her mom. She sighed. Okay, those had occurred in the opposite order in real time, but from her emotional perspective, the cheating was the most recent thing.

"Fathers," she grumbled.

She finished her paperwork for her charter, then reviewed her schedule for the week. In the back of her mind was a vague sense of unease. There wasn't any one specific item bothering her — it was more low-grade worry on an assortment of topics.

The visit to the club had pointed out how very little she knew about Kip's life before her. They just didn't talk about their past very much. At some point, they needed to share a little more. First up — financial goals. She'd assumed they were going to save for a house, but they'd never discussed it. What if Kip didn't see himself as a homeowner? She couldn't imagine that, but some people preferred to rent.

What about their attitudes toward spending and saving? If they made about the same, shouldn't they split expenses evenly? And what about getting her on the lease? Or leasing a place together?

She also had to talk to her dad about the wedding. She had no idea what he expected to spend and if he would ask her mom to pitch in. A few weeks ago, she would have assumed they could each pay the same amount, but now she wasn't sure how much money her mom had. Thinking about that made her mind circle back to how much it would cost to get married at the club. Did she really want to spend that much? Did Kip? What were his expectations for their wedding? He'd never said. Was it because he was a typical guy who only wanted to be told when to show up, or was there something else going on?

Her phone buzzed. She glanced at the screen and saw a you have a sec text from Kip.

She smiled as she called him.

"I was just thinking about you," she said when he picked up.

"That's good." He chuckled. "I wasn't sure if you were back from your charter."

"About a half hour ago. I'm locking up tonight, so I'm waiting for the rest of the boats to come in. I should be done in about an hour."

"Good. Can't wait to see you." He paused. "My mom called."

Harlow ignored a sinking sensation. "Okay."

"She's upset about how things went at the club. She wants to have you over for dinner. Not to talk about it," he added hastily. "Just to have a nice evening together."

Harlow liked Kip's parents well enough, she supposed. They never spent much time over there. While she mostly wanted to refuse, she not only knew that wasn't an option, she thought maybe this would be a good time to learn more about Kip's childhood.

"We can do that," she told him. "Ask her what I can bring. She shouldn't have to cook dinner on her own."

"Really?" He sounded surprised. "You don't mind?"

"Of course not," she lied. "Please let her know I'm not the least bit upset about her reaction to the club. In fact, I appreciate it. Getting married there would be a lot of money. Maybe we should look at other venues."

"I'll let her know. Thanks, Harlow. You're being great."

"Because I love you," she said, her voice teasing. "See you in a bit."

She hung up just as Austin walked into her office, looking more than a little grumpy.

"We're back," he told her. "I'm going to clean up the boat, then I'll clock out."

"Bad trip?"

"No. It was fine. Just a bunch of men fishing. They want to drink beers, lie about how successful they are, and catch fish. Easy duty." He glanced down the hall. "Dad and I were supposed to talk tonight when I got back."

"He took off about a half hour ago. I'm locking up." She walked over to Austin. "I'm sorry. I didn't know you had an appointment."

"He keeps blowing me off. I have stuff I want to talk to him about."

Austin was uncharacteristically intense as he spoke.

"Can I help?"

"No. Thanks for the offer, but this is between me and Dad." His mouth twisted. "This is the third time he's either not shown up or told me he was too busy. I miss Mom. She listens."

Harlow nodded. "She does, and I miss her, too."

"Then text her."

"I should. I will."

"Liar."

"It's hard to give in when we had a fight."

"You mean it's hard to admit you were wrong." His mouth curved up. "You were the wrongest."

"I'm not going there."

He laughed. "Harlow the Harpy."

"Don't call me that."

"Harp, harp, harpy."

She pointed to the front door. "Go clean up your boat. I'll inspect it in twenty minutes."

He grabbed her in a neck lock, kissed the top of her head, then released her. She watched him go, grateful that at least one relationship in her life was uncomplicated. Now if only she could find a second one that was equally easy, she would consider herself very, very lucky.

Mason told himself that anticipation was good. It made life interesting and gave people things to look forward to. Expectations were different — especially unrealistic ones, which his would be, if he was dumb enough to have any. The chance to explore the house with Robyn was plenty. Spending time with her was going to be fun. Whatever he felt when she was close was his business and his problem. But damn, there was something about her.

He stood by the rear staircase, where she'd told him to meet her. He was three minutes early because being on time was the same as being late in his mind — a characteristic neither of his wives had appreciated. He was prepared to wait all day. But about thirty seconds before the hour, Robyn appeared on the landing.

She smiled when she saw him — an easy, welcoming smile. Friendly. He smiled back, taking in the long blond hair, the big blue eyes and the way just looking at her was a kick to the gut . . . and the groin.

"Hi," she said as she approached. "Are you excited about our house tour?"

"I couldn't sleep last night."

She laughed, a sweet, happy sound he couldn't get enough of. "Somehow I doubt that."

"You're right. I'm a good sleeper. Years of training. Get it while you can."

"It's an admirable superpower," she teased. "Come on. Let's head upstairs. I thought we'd start on the fourth floor. This is the only staircase to that part of the house. It's smaller than the other levels because it only covers the northeast section. Interestingly, you can't get to the roof from it. You have to use one of the other staircases and go up through the third floor."

"Nothing about this house surprises me."

She laughed. "I'm happy to tell you that you are in for many surprises today."

They went up to the fourth floor. Each staircase narrowed progressively, with the final one barely three feet wide.

"You wouldn't want to bring a king-sized

bed up here," he said when they reached a small landing with a hallway heading off in each direction.

"I agree, and yet there are some very large pieces of furniture on this floor." She started toward the left. "I think they used ropes to pull it up from outside. Although the windows aren't that big, either."

The narrow hallway lacked the high ceilings of the other floors. There were closed doors and empty built-in shelves. If the house was haunted, it all happened up here, he thought.

The hardwood floors looked like they hadn't been walked on very much. She led the way to the end of the hallway and opened an unassuming-looking door.

"Prepare to be amazed."

He stepped into a huge room with soaring ceilings and tall windows on two sides. The walls were painted with old-fashioned tableaus of exotic locations. Display cases held dozens and dozens of globes. Small, large, plain, enameled, bejeweled. Large tables were covered with piles of maps. Bins held rolled maps. There had to be hundreds, maybe thousands of maps. Many looked old and hand drawn while a few were more contemporary.

He turned in a slow circle, trying to take

233

it all in. When he glanced up, he saw constellations painted on the ceiling, along with the points of a compass. He looked at Robyn.

"I don't know what to say."

She smiled. "Told you. We refer to this as the map room, but it really needs a better name." She motioned to a bookshelf in the corner. It was crammed with books of different sizes. No, he thought, walking closer. Not books.

"Journals?" he asked.

"Yes. Handwritten travel journals. It's all very random. Some are detailed. Some barely say anything. A few have wonderful drawings. It's as if someone went around the world and bought up old travel journals, then brought them all here."

She crossed to the table and pointed to the map on top. "It's the United States, just before the Louisiana Purchase. See the detail and how the western part of the country is barely drawn in?"

He stared at the delicate sheet. "You can't just leave this here. It needs to be preserved. Shouldn't it go to a museum or something?"

"Possibly, but Mason, this is just one map. There are hundreds even older and more important. And this is just one room. The house is filled with treasures like this."

He looked around. "That's a huge responsibility. I'm glad I only have to deal with the house."

"I figure it will take that year you have until you sell the house. But I'm not worried. Lillian has promised to never die."

"Let's hope she keeps the promise." He'd grown to like Lillian and spending time with her.

"Come on," Robyn said, starting for the door.

"Wait. I'm not ready to leave. I want to look around."

Her expression turned indulgent. "We have to keep moving. I want to give you a taste of the house. Now that you know this is here, you can come back later and explore."

He nodded, then followed her out of the map room. On the way back to the staircase, she showed him a few other rooms. Most were empty, with a few still furnished as bedrooms.

There was an old-fashioned bathroom complete with a pull-chain toilet and a claw-foot tub.

"I think the water's turned off on this floor," Robyn said as she started down the stairs. "To cut down on leaks."

They had to go to the second floor to find

another staircase to take them to the third. Here the hallways were wider and taller, the doors more ornate. He'd walked around on this floor a little. There were bedrooms and a big room with a billiard table.

Robyn showed him the dumbwaiter that worked on a manual pulley system. The opening was big enough for a decent sized cart. From there, she led him into a room lined with shelves, all filled with dishes. No, he corrected himself. Teacups and saucers. Thousands of them. Some small, others oversized. Every shape, every color. Some looked too delicate to touch.

"What if there's an earthquake?" he blurted.

Robyn winced. "Don't even think that. A lot would be lost, and I would cry."

"Then I take back the question."

"When we get downstairs, you need to go outside, turn around three times and spit."

"To appease the earthquake gods?"

"Yes."

He chuckled. "Sure. I'll take care of it."

She picked up a teacup done in blue and white. The pattern was a little fussy for him, but then he'd never been much of a teacup kind of guy. Give him a sturdy mug and he was happy.

"I recognize about half the patterns,"

Robyn said, putting the cup back on its saucer. "Lillian knows a few more, but some are a mystery. The older ones are probably hand-painted by obscure artists, or maybe just ordinary people being creative." She pointed to the cabinets under the shelves.

"More teacups?" he asked.

"In some of them. Others have complete sets of dishes. A few are rare and would go for a lot of money."

"Lillian doesn't seem to be lacking in resources."

"She's not. There was family money on both sides, although I would guess keeping up this house is expensive."

She reached for a rose-covered teacup. "This was one of Harlow's favorites," she murmured. "When she was little, she would beg me to let her hold it." Her smile turned wistful. "She was always very careful."

"You miss her."

She put down the teacup and looked at him. "I do. I was so hurt and angry when I got here, and now I can barely remember our fight. She was always my best girl. I told you she had cancer when she was little."

"You did."

"It was awful. She was seven when she was diagnosed. Acute lymphoblastic leukemia or ALL. Cord and I were terrified we

237

were going to lose her. Lillian flew out and took care of Austin the first few weeks. He was so young. We tried to keep his life as normal as possible, but there was no protecting Harlow."

Her blue eyes darkened with emotion. "Obviously she recovered, and she's been cancer-free ever since. There's no reason to think she won't live a normal, healthy life. But sometimes, she's difficult. Lillian's theory is that Harlow's emotional development was arrested while she was dealing with the cancer, so even though she's twenty-two, it's more like she's still a teenager."

This conversation was well above his pay grade. "What do you think?"

"That we indulged her, and that's hard to reverse. She can be a bit entitled."

"That's not unique to her."

"She's engaged."

He tried to judge her feelings on the subject from her tone, but couldn't. "Congratulations."

"She seems young."

"You married young."

"Yes, I did, and I want to say that was a different time. Harlow has so many opportunities." Her smile turned wry. "I did, as well, and I ignored them because I was in love. I just wish . . ." She drew in a breath. "I'm not sure how well she even knows Kip. It feels like things have happened so fast between them."

She picked up another teacup. "When she was twelve or thirteen, we talked about her getting married in the backyard. The house Cord and I had together is large with a beautiful view of the water."

"The house you're going to sell?"

"That's the one."

She would make money from that, he thought, surprisingly disappointed by the thought. What did her having money matter? She was already out of his league. He was just a middle-aged man on a military pension.

"That's what we fought about," Robyn admitted. "She was so angry I wasn't keeping the house. She wouldn't believe that I can't get a loan. She said some things that —Well, we haven't spoken since."

"I'm sorry."

She shook her head. "Why am I telling you this? Please don't apologize. I'm the one who's emotionally dumping on you." Her smile strengthened. "You're a good listener."

He'd prefer to be her fuck buddy, but he would take what he could get.

She led the way out of the room. "I should have made something of myself. Look at you, Mason. You started with nothing and finished your military career shaping future soldiers. That's something to be proud of."

"You talk like you have no value."

"I don't bring much to the table."

"That's not true. You're intelligent, articulate, funny." He stopped before he said something stupid like "sexy."

She paused and faced him. Tears filled her eyes. "Thank you. That's very nice of you to say and embarrassingly nice to hear. I haven't been getting a lot of positive feedback lately, especially from myself." She cleared her throat. "I'm not being dramatic, just honest. And now I'm being overly emotional. You must think I'm a total mess."

Impulsively, he reached for her. She shocked the hell out of him by stepping into his embrace. He pulled her close and hugged her, wrapping his arms around her. She held on, resting her head on his shoulder for a second, before they both stepped back.

"Thank you," she said, brushing her cheeks. "You give good hugs."

"That's the goal."

They walked down the hallway together, passing a couple of cats as they went.

"Freaking about inheriting?" she asked.

"I try not to think about it. When Lillian first started writing me about the inheritance, I thought it was a three-bedroom ranch. I couldn't figure out what she was so excited about."

"And when you saw the house for the first time?"

"I knew I had the wrong address."

She laughed. "I wish I'd been here to see the look on your face."

She opened another door, and they stepped into a room with a grand piano, a harp, a stage, seating areas, dozens of musical instruments in their cases and piles of sheet music.

"Do you play?" she asked.

"Never learned."

"Me, either. When I was maybe ten or twelve, Lillian and Leo had the local high school orchestra come in and play. The acoustics are amazing in this room."

He looked at the gilded ceiling, the painted cherubs on the walls. "You were right. I was surprised when I saw the house."

"Ha! I knew it."

She pressed a panel on the wall behind the piano. A section popped open, exposing a narrow staircase.

He moved close. "Where does this go?"

241

"Down to the basement." She reached inside and turned on a light. "It's a little winding, so watch your step. We'll come out by the wine cellar."

She entered the secret passage, then held out her hand to him. "Come on, Mason. It'll be fun."

He laced his fingers with hers, enjoying the feel of her palm against his. The house wasn't the only surprise, he thought, following her down. The more he got to know Robyn, the more he liked her. A situation that wouldn't end well for him.

FOURTEEN

"You ready?" Kip asked.

Harlow looked up from her phone. She and Kip were having dinner with his parents that night — not anything she was looking forward to.

"One second. I heard from my mom." Just a quick Hi, how's it going? but at least they were talking again.

Harlow knew she had to apologize but thought that might be better done in person. So she shot off a fast, I'm good. When are you coming home? then grabbed her bag and left with Kip.

"Feel better?" he asked, backing out of his parking space.

She nodded. "I'm sorry my mom and I fought." And that it had been mostly her fault. Funny how time had given her a little perspective. She wanted to talk to her mom about the wedding and tell her that her dad was still dating Zafina and maybe figure out a way to ask about the cheating.

"Being a grown-up is complicated." She leaned back in her seat. "There's a lot of responsibility."

"There is."

She looked at Kip. "We should talk about money."

He glanced at her, obviously confused. "Why?"

"We never bothered coming up with a plan. You asked me to move in and I did, but we need to figure out where we are. I'm not on the lease, and I barely pay anything. I don't even know how long you're going to be in the apartment. Where do you see us in a year? Five years? What are our financial goals?"

He slowed for a traffic light. "You're right. We should talk about it. Just not on the way to my folks', okay?"

She laughed. "I wasn't suggesting we get into it now. But I do want to talk about money on our next day off. We're both debt-free, so we should —"

Beside her, Kip tensed.

She looked at him. "What's wrong?"

He glanced at her, then back at the road. "I'm not debt-free."

"What do you mean?" He hadn't been to college, so there weren't any student loans.

"You mean the car? That's no big deal."

Most people had a car payment. Not everyone had a new car handed to them when they graduated, the way she had. Or a job in the family business.

"Not just the car." There was an edge to his voice, and his hands tightened on the steering wheel. "I'm getting it under control. The credit card stuff. It's taking me a bit, but I'm working it."

A knot formed in her stomach. "How much are we talking about?"

"A few thousand."

She waited.

"Twenty."

"What?" Her voice was a yelp. "You owe twenty thousand dollars in credit card debt? How did that happen?"

"Oh, I don't know. Maybe first-class tickets to Cancun and a five-star hotel for a week."

She told herself to take a breath and think before she spoke. Attacking Kip wouldn't make him want to tell her the truth.

"I'm sorry," she said quickly. "I was surprised, not accusing."

"I'm not a bad guy."

"I know. Is it really all from the trip? Did we spend that much?"

"The trip was about ten grand."

She flinched. "Kip, why didn't you say something? That's a ridiculous amount to spend on a week's vacation."

"I wanted you to have a good time."

"We could have spent less. At the very least, I could have paid for part of it. You shouldn't be paying for everything. We're engaged. We need to be a team." She hesitated. "Twenty thousand plus the car?"

He slumped in his seat. "Maybe a little more. We're nearly at my folks' house. Could we talk about this later?"

No! She wanted to demand the truth, but knew that wasn't a good idea. "Sure. Let's talk preliminaries when we get home and then go over the details by the end of the week."

He didn't look enthused at the prospect, but nodded.

They arrived at his parents' house. For the first time, Harlow really looked at the neighborhood. The homes were relatively small and close together. No water views — not even a canal. Most were well-maintained, with bikes and skateboards tucked up on the porches.

She thought about the house where she'd grown up with the oversized rooms and ocean view. After the divorce, her dad had bought a luxury condo. Obviously the family business was successful, which was a good thing, but Harlow found herself unexpectedly aware of the financial differences between herself and Kip. She'd always thought he hadn't been interested in going to college, but now she wondered if there were other reasons he'd skipped furthering his education.

She doubted his parents could have paid for it. Maybe they'd expected him to move out when he turned eighteen. Maybe no one in his family had ever gone to college. As Kip parked, she thought about all she didn't know about her fiancé and vowed to start asking more questions.

They went inside and greeted his parents. Harlow was relieved not to see Zafina or her dad. While Kip watched sports with his father, Harlow went into the kitchen with Judy.

"How can I help?" Harlow washed her hands at the sink.

"Maybe finish up on the salad," Kip's mother said.

Harlow began slicing tomatoes. "Thanks for inviting us over for dinner," she said with a smile. "You're such a great cook."

"Just easy things." Judy glanced at her. "Not like when we had dinner with your mother. That was a fancy meal."

Harlow tried to remember the menu. There had been cheese, crackers and nuts to start, a simple, cold cucumber soup, followed by grilled fish and salad. She and her mom had worked on the menu together to find the right mix for the first meeting with the in-laws-to-be.

"I guess it's going to take time for us to find our way with each other," Judy said with a smile. "Blending our traditions. How we celebrate birthdays, opening presents on Christmas Eve, that sort of thing."

Harlow set down the knife. "You open presents on Christmas Eve?" she asked, hearing the outrage in her voice. She cleared her throat. "I mean, is that really what you do?"

"Of course. After our ham dinner."

"You eat ham on Christmas Eve?" She shook her head. "Never mind. It sounds nice, but why presents on Christmas Eve? Santa hasn't been there."

"We've never really been into the whole Santa thing. It's a bit ridiculous, don't you think?"

Harlow thought of the beautiful stockings Lillian had needle-pointed for everyone and how even now, her mom filled them with silly things like pens and candy and socks.

"No stockings?" she asked, trying not to

let her disappointment show.

"Your family celebrated Santa?"

"We went to midnight services, then home to bed. In the morning, we opened presents from our family and had stockings from Santa." *I love Santa.* But she didn't say that because she knew it would sound ridiculous.

Harlow continued slicing the tomatoes, doing her best to sound cheerful instead of horrified. "Different traditions are interesting. In some ways, your Christmas Eve tradition will solve the problem of what part of the holiday we spend where."

"Oh, after you're married to Kip, we'll spend the entire holiday together," Judy said firmly.

Harlow swallowed hard and made a mental note to add the holidays to her list of things to discuss with Kip.

When dinner was ready, the men turned off the game and joined them at the table. Harlow thought about how Kip always helped her with dinner when it was just the two of them, but here only the women cooked. She now added *sharing chores* to the list she and Kip needed to work through, then took some salad and passed the bowl to Judy.

"This is nice," her future mother-in-law said. "Having you here. I want you to be comfortable in our home, Harlow, running in and out whenever you want." She served herself some of the chicken casserole. "I've been getting lots of calls from your cousins, Kip. Everyone is excited about the wedding."

He looked at his mom. "They can't all come. There's too many."

"We'll have to see, won't we? How can you invite only part of the family?" Judy turned to Harlow. "I have three sisters, and Hank's from a big family, too. We're the only ones in Florida, but between the Iowa branch and the Texas folks, Kip has about twenty cousins."

Harlow stared at Kip. "Twenty? You never, ah, mentioned that."

"I know it's a lot. Most of them are older than me, so they're married, with kids."

Harlow didn't want to think about that. "We haven't firmed up the guest list," she murmured, "but we were trying to keep it under two hundred."

"Now that you're not having your wedding at that ridiculous country club, you can have it in a park," Judy said cheerfully. "Your mom and I could cook a simple menu, so it wouldn't cost much. That way, you can invite everyone."

Harlow did her best to keep from shrieking. "I'm not sure."

"The park makes sense," Hank told her. "Why wouldn't you want to do that? Isn't it fancy enough?"

Judy turned on her husband. "Hank, don't."

"You told me about that country club. Fifty thousand for a deposit? Come on, that's highway robbery." Hank picked up his beer. "I say have it at the park and be done with it. We're talking about one day. What does it really matter where you get married?"

Harlow tried to keep breathing. "It matters to me."

Kip put his hand on hers and squeezed her fingers. "You two need to back off. Harlow and I will make the decisions about the wedding. We'll let you know when we've picked a location and what the guest list is."

"The less you pay for the where, the more you have for the who," his father grumbled.

Judy shot him a warning look.

"I'm shutting up," he told her. "It's her parents' money. If they want to waste it, that's their decision. I know, I know. You've told me enough times."

OMG! Kip's parents talked about how *her* parents spent their money? Harlow stared at her food, not sure what to say.

Judy freshened everyone's iced tea. "Let's talk about something else. Kip, you'll never guess who called the other day. Tracey, and she wanted your number. I didn't give it to her."

Kip's face drained of color.

"Who's Tracey?" Harlow asked.

Hank frowned. "Kip's ex-wife. Who else would she be?"

"I know nothing about grandfather clocks," Robyn admitted with a laugh as she removed the clean towel from the top of the bowl and checked the dough.

Sure enough, it had risen. She scooped it onto the floured countertop and used a sharp knife to divide it into twenty-four pieces.

"The one on the second floor might be from the early 1800s. I think it's an English marquetry longcase." She glanced at her aunt. "It belongs in a museum, Lillian."

Her aunt smiled from her comfortable chair as she patted the tuxedo cat dozing on her lap.

"Then you should get on that, my dear."

"Call up a museum and offer it to them?"

"I'm sure there's a procedure," Lillian teased. "Leaving it on the doorstep like an abandoned puppy won't do."

"Plus it's really big."

Robyn stretched the first piece of dough into a square, folded the corners under and shaped it into a ball.

"It's good to see you back in the kitchen," Lillian said. "Making bread."

"You're the one who taught me how. Every time I work with dough, I think of you."

She remembered being in this kitchen back when she'd been so small, she'd had to stand on a chair to see what her aunt was doing. Lillian had taught her how to make cookies and brownies, crunchy French loaves and delicious cakes. She'd passed on that knowledge to both her kids, although Austin had been a lot less interested than Harlow.

Thinking of her daughter made her grateful she'd reached out. They'd only exchanged brief "hi, how are you" type comments, but it was a start. Fighting less with her daughter was on Robyn's to-do list. She just had to figure out how to make that happen.

"I remember the first time you brought Cord here," Lillian mused. "He was determined to help you in the kitchen."

Robyn chuckled. "He kneaded with great enthusiasm."

253

"He wanted to please you. That boy was crazy about you."

"We were young and in love," Robyn said lightly, knowing that hadn't been enough to sustain them.

"You have regrets," Lillian said kindly.

"Sure. About a lot of things. Sometimes I wonder if I'm more to blame than him. Not for the cheating — that's on him, but for giving in rather than standing up to him."

"You didn't want to rip apart your family. You thought, after surviving cancer, Harlow needed both her parents. Austin, too."

"You make me sound reasonable."

"You were."

"You're right that I forgave him because of Harlow and Austin. I felt like they'd already been through so much. I didn't think they'd survive a divorce. But what if that's not true? What if I was really protecting myself?"

"Is that bad?" Lillian asked.

"Yes. It means I'm weak."

"It means you're human."

Robyn finished with the rolls. She draped plastic wrap over them and washed her hands.

"You always see the best in me."

Lillian laughed. "Of course, my dear. I love you. What else would I do?"

Robyn's phone rang. She glanced at the screen, then grinned as she answered and put the call on speakerphone.

"Austin, you're calling instead of texting. Has there been a shift in the earth's rotation? Are the stars not aligning? I'm here with Lillian, by the way, so say hello."

Her youngest chuckled. "Hey, Lillian."

"Hello, dear boy. I miss you. Come see me."

"I'd love to," Austin admitted. "I miss you both."

Robyn heard something in her son's tone, but didn't want to probe in front of her aunt.

"We miss you, too," she said. "How are things?"

"Okay. Work. Hanging out with my friends."

Lillian shifted the cat off her lap and rose. "I'll leave you two to talk," she said. "I'm going upstairs to take a little nap."

Robyn kissed her cheek. "I'll check on you later."

Lillian walked out of the kitchen. Robyn turned her attention back to the call, taking him off speaker and putting the phone to her ear.

"Austin, are you okay?"

He sighed. "Dad's sticking me with all the

shit jobs, like he's trying to prove something and I don't know what. Plus, I've been trying to talk to him for a month, and he keeps blowing me off."

"What do you want to talk to him about?"

"Stuff. My future."

Which told her nothing. "I'm right here. I can listen."

"Thanks, Mom, but this is stuff I need Dad for. Besides, some of it is me finding out if he'll ever listen to me. I know you'll always take the time."

"Austin, your dad loves you."

"That doesn't mean he has time for me."

She ran through a list of potential "dad only" problems. "Is someone pregnant?"

The line went silent. Robyn held her breath, too terrified to even pray.

"Mom, jeez. I don't have a girlfriend right now."

"That doesn't mean you aren't having sex. You know to wear a condom every single time, right? Every time. You whip it out, you put on party clothes."

She practically heard him clench his teeth. "We aren't talking about this."

"Your penis? Is this where I remind you I saw it before you did?"

"Mom!" He exhaled. "No one's pregnant."

"Okay. Just checking. I love you, Austin. I'm always here if you need me. Do you want me to come home?"

"No. I'm okay. I just need to think some things through. I love you, too. And Mom? Don't tell Dad to talk to me. I want him to make time on his own. If he won't, then that's a message, too."

"Every fiber of my being screams at me to get involved, but I'll respect your wishes. Why don't you call me before you go to sleep and I'll read you a bedtime story?"

"I'm eighteen, not five."

She laughed. "Just checking. Because I would if you wanted me to."

He chuckled. "That's both really sweet and totally terrifying."

He ended the call.

Robyn stood in the kitchen, wondering if her youngest needed her to come home. And while she fretted, she thought about how she and Harlow were now exchanging brief texts, but weren't yet speaking. Despite how Harlow made her crazy, she missed her oldest. Why couldn't they be friends the way they used to be?

"Didn't someone tell me it got easier as they got older?" she murmured, thinking she really had to remember who had said that so she could call them a liar. Things were different, but in no way were they easier. Not in the least.

FIFTEEN

Harlow had no idea how she got through dinner. She must have faked her way well enough because no one stared or asked if she was okay. She thought maybe she'd eaten something, although she couldn't be sure, what with her stomach flipping and spinning as she tried to make sense of what she'd learned.

Kip had an ex-wife. Kip had been married before. He'd proposed, had a ceremony, gotten a divorce, and he'd never said a word to her.

She sat next to him, in his car, as they drove back to their apartment, not sure what to do or say or think or feel.

"You're mad," he said into the silence. "You have every right to be. I'm sorry. I should have said something."

Something? He should have said *something.* "I think a more specific, 'I've been married' would be more appropriate," she said quietly, knowing if she gave in to the hurt and fear growing inside of her, she might be overwhelmed by emotions she couldn't begin to handle.

"Harlow," he began, then sighed. "Yes, I was married before."

The blunt words hit her right in the heart. Tears filled her eyes as pain ripped through her.

"You never said," she whispered. "You never told me."

"I didn't know how. I was ashamed. I thought you'd think less of me. After a while, I didn't know what to say. It didn't mean anything."

"You were married. That means something." She closed her eyes. "You've done all these things with someone else. An engagement, a wedding." The tears ran faster. "None of this is special to you."

"No! Harlow, don't. It wasn't like that. We were both nineteen. We eloped. There was no engagement, no wedding. We got married, and six weeks later, we realized it was a mistake, so we got a divorce. End of story."

But it wasn't the end of the story, she thought as he pulled into his parking space. It was just the beginning of a nightmare. Kip had been married before. She was having trouble wrapping her mind around that truth.

"You should have told me."

"Yes, I should have. I was wrong. I'm more sorry than you can know."

She thought about how the evening had started, with him admitting to thousands of dollars of debt, and now this. She felt cold and sick and lost. She needed her mom, only her mom was a continent away, in Santa Barbara.

Still crying, she got out of the car and started for their apartment. Kip put his hand on the small of her back. She quickly stepped to the side, away from him.

"Don't," she said, her voice thick with pain. "Don't touch me."

"I know you're upset," he began.

She wiped her face and glared at him. "Upset? I'm not upset. Upset doesn't begin to describe how I feel. You lied to me. You lied!"

"I didn't."

She hurried toward their apartment and fumbled with the key. After letting herself inside, she ran to the bathroom and locked the door. Once she was alone, she pulled out her phone.

She needed to get away from Kip. She needed to figure out what was going on.

With her mom gone, the house was empty — appealing under other circumstances, but not these. She didn't want to be by herself. Enid was living at home for the summer to save money, so that wasn't an option.

Harlow quickly texted her brother.

Can I sleep on your sofa for a couple of nights?

Three dots appeared right away. Sure. I'll even loan you a pillow.

Despite her pain, she smiled as she answered. Thanks. See you in a few.

She walked out of the bathroom and found Kip waiting for her in the hall.

"I didn't lie," he repeated.

She moved past him. "Don't go there. You lied by omission."

That was what got her. He knew how she felt, but he'd done it anyway.

Once in the bedroom, she pulled an overnight bag out from under the bed and opened it.

Kip swore. "You're leaving?"

"I can't think around you."

"We have to talk."

She looked at him, grateful for the bit of mad welling up inside of her. Anger was strength. Anger was safe. At least if she was pissed, she wouldn't feel stupid and small and broken.

"You're right, we do need to talk, but not tonight." She wiped away her tears and glared at him. "You've had nearly a year to talk, Kip. You've had months and months to tell me about being married before and your credit card debt and who knows what else. So you know what? I get a break here. I get a little time to find my way through all this crap, and you just have to deal with that."

Frustration twisted his expression. "You can't run off at the first sign of trouble."

"A year," she repeated. "You said nothing. Don't tell me what I can and can't do. When it's been a year for me, then you can judge."

"Harlow, please."

She returned to the bathroom and collected her cosmetics. After tossing them in the suitcase, she grabbed a stack of T-shirts from the dresser, then heard the front door open and close.

She dropped the T-shirts and ran into the living room. Kip was gone. He'd left. He'd done this to her, to them, and he'd walked out first. Like he wasn't wrong.

The shock of his leaving knocked the air from her lungs. She sank down on the floor and gave in to sobs that shook her body. She cried as if her heart was broken —

probably because it was. She was still crying when she heard the front door open, footsteps, then strong arms pulled her into a warm hug.

Only it wasn't Kip. Instead her brother held her tight.

She clung to him, the only solid point in a rapidly spinning world.

"He left," she managed, her voice shaking. "We had a fight and he walked out."

"I got worried when you didn't show up, so I came to check on you. I'm glad I did. What do you want to do?"

She looked at her brother. "I want to come stay with you."

"Let's go."

"Hello?"

"Robyn. Glad I caught you."

It took her brain a second to process the familiar voice. Recognition was followed by a sense of dread.

"Jase?" She swore silently, reminding herself to check who was calling before answering.

"I wasn't sure you'd pick up."

She wouldn't have if she'd known it was him. "Why wouldn't I?" she asked, telling herself it was a question and therefore not a lie.

"I know you're upset with me, and with good reason, but I wanted you to know I miss you."

Information she didn't need or want. "Okay."

"Losing you has shown me how important you are to me. I made a terrible mistake, and I'm sorry."

She wasn't sure what to do with that information. "You've already apologized. It's fine."

"It's not." His voice dropped. "If it was fine, you'd still be here in Florida, instead of wherever you are."

"How did you know I was gone?"

"I ran into your house-sitter."

"Oh." Sucky timing, she thought. What were the odds? "I'm in California, visiting my Aunt Lillian."

He sighed. "I was hoping you were closer so I could convince you to give me a second chance."

"Jase, we're done. I don't mean that harshly, but it was never going to work between us. You saw me as someone who was after your money. There's no way to get over that."

"How many times do I have to tell you I was wrong? You're not that person. I get it now."

"Even without that, we wouldn't have made it long-term."

Yes, he'd hurt her feelings, but the truth was that since landing in California, she hadn't thought of him at all. As for missing him — not even for a second. Whatever she'd thought she had with him either hadn't existed or had faded way faster than it should have.

"I wish you the best," she said quietly. "And I hope Galen is doing better."

"She is. We're hopeful. Robyn, can't I convince you to give me another shot?"

"No. I'm sorry."

"Me, too."

He hung up.

She tossed her phone on the bed, then flopped down on her back. Why was it the second she didn't want the man, he was all over her? Jase's pursuit was so perverse as to be almost comical.

"Men," she muttered, then stood and shook her phone. "Not taking your call again."

With her notebook, she went to her aunt's room, knocking on the half-open door before entering.

"It's me."

"Out here, darling."

Robyn walked through the large sitting

266

room and bedroom to the patio. It was overcast and chilly, but still beautiful. Today the ocean was gray rather than blue, and the seagulls seemed especially loud. The only spots of color were the flowers in pots.

She checked that Lillian was well-protected by warm blankets, then sat next to her.

"I think that painting in the laundry room is a Picasso." She showed Lillian the picture she'd taken. "I'm not sure which surprises me more — that you have a Picasso or that it's in the laundry room."

Her great-aunt laughed. "The location does seem unusual. I'm sure it got there by accident."

"It wandered in one night when no one was looking?"

"Perhaps not that, but no one would put a Picasso in the laundry room on purpose."

Lillian reached out. Robyn took her hand, trying not to wince at her aunt's tiny bones and tissue-thin skin.

"You're making progress on the inventory," Lillian said. "First the clocks, now the Picasso."

"I'm getting an overview. You have more treasures than I realized. As I said yesterday, you should start donating to a few museums now so you can enjoy their fawning."

"I do love a good fawning," Lillian admitted. "As to what should be donated, I leave that to you. When you get a couple of hours, we should take a look at my jewelry."

Robyn squeezed her fingers before releasing them. "I'm not going through anything personal," she said firmly. "You promised me at least another twenty years."

"Darling, as much as I love you, I'm not going to make it until I'm a hundred and fourteen. Nor would I want to. But the jewelry can wait." Lillian pressed her lips together. "Forgive me, but I can't help asking. Would you consider staying here permanently?"

Robyn stared at her. "You want me to move here?"

"I do. I know it's selfish, but I love having you around."

She didn't know what to say. Live here permanently? That was certainly an interesting offer.

She enjoyed being close to her aunt. She also enjoyed having time to think about her future. She still battled shame and embarrassment over her irresponsible behavior, but lately she was spending more time being practical and working on a plan for her future. She wanted to eventually open an antique store. Hopefully Lillian would live many, many more years, but between then and now, Robyn planned to move forward with her education and her retail experience, while keeping herself on the financial straight and narrow.

"I've never thought about making this my home," she admitted. "I have Harlow and Austin to consider. Harlow's on her own, but Austin's planning on moving back home in the fall. He works for his father, so I couldn't ask him to move here with me."

"He could get a job here. I'm not sure about Harlow." Lillian sighed. "I'm asking too much."

"You're not. It's just a lot to think about." Move permanently to Santa Barbara? She was tempted. "What about Mason? Wouldn't that be awkward?"

"The house is big enough for twenty of us. Besides, I thought you liked Mason."

Robyn thought about how capable he always seemed. He was strong without being dominating. She liked that he could simply be in a space without having to talk all the time. Plus the man was sexy. Not that she was going to admit that to her ninety-four-year-old aunt.

"I do like him, but visiting is one thing. Living here is another."

"It's still my house," Lillian pointed out.

"I get to say who lives here."

Robyn smiled at her. "Yes, you do."

"You could go to UC Santa Barbara."

The college she'd almost gone to when she'd been just out of high school. "Now you're really tempting me."

"I'm trying."

She thought about living in this beautiful house and taking classes at UCSB. "I'm still coming up with a plan," she said.

"Just offering options. I think Mason should be one of them."

"I wonder how he would feel about you planning his life."

"Just the sex part."

Robyn laughed. "That's kind of a big step. I'm sure he'd want a say."

"I think he'd be pleased. He watches you sometimes. There's a sexy, brooding aspect that is very fun for me, as the observer."

Robyn stared at her aunt. "What do you mean?"

Lillian's smile turned sly. "He's attracted to you. Haven't you noticed? I'm guessing you're also attracted to him."

She was, but they weren't going to talk about that. "You're meddling."

"Yes, I am. So . . . any interest?"

"Lillian! We're not having this discussion."

"Why not? Talking about it is all I have

270

left. Are you afraid if you get involved, you'll surrender yourself? You're not twenty, Robyn. Mason isn't Cord. You don't have to give up yourself to be with a man."

Robyn shook her head. "You're far too insightful. Why can't you talk about the past, like most old ladies?"

"You know I'm right."

"You are. I gave up too much when I married Cord. Not because he asked, but because I thought being in love meant doing what he wanted. I was too young." Her mistakes were the reason she worried about Harlow — something her daughter didn't understand.

"Isn't it smarter to be strong enough to be your own person rather than avoiding love completely because you're afraid of what you have to give up?"

More insight and it wasn't even lunchtime. "I thought we were talking sex," she said, her voice teasing. "Now you want me to fall in love?"

"I want you to be happy, my dear. I want you to have the life you deserve, with a wonderful man who loves you, a career you enjoy, and dozens of grandchildren."

"I want that, too, and I'm doing my best to figure out how to make it happen."

■ ■ ■ ■

Harlow finished work, then swung by the grocery store for the ingredients for spaghetti. Her mother would be disappointed to know her only daughter was going to settle for jarred sauce, but there wasn't time to make anything from scratch.

In Austin's apartment, she boiled water for pasta, then cooked the sausage she would add to the sauce. She'd just finished making the salad when Austin walked in.

"Hey," he said with a smile as he crossed to the kitchen. "You weren't kidding earlier when you said you'd fix dinner."

"I owe you for letting me stay here."

"It's been two nights, Harlow, and you're sleeping on the sofa. It's no big deal."

"It is to me."

More than a place to sleep, she thought. Austin hadn't asked any questions. Not here and not at work. He also hadn't said a word when she'd ignored Kip's texts and phone calls.

"Besides," she said, faking a smile. "Tonight's my last night. I'm heading home tomorrow."

"You sure you want to do that?"

"No, but I can't avoid him forever."

"You're not leaving him?"

She flinched at the words. Leave Kip? "I love him."

"Just checking." He leaned against the counter. "I'm quitting my job."

"What? Austin, seriously? Why? What will you do?" Panic seized her. What if he left her and moved away?

"Because Dad won't listen. I've made a bunch of appointments, and he won't sit down with me."

"What do you want to talk about?"

"My future. I'm not like you. I don't want to take over the family business. I don't have a fancy degree and a business plan. I just need time to figure a few things out, and I wanted to talk to him, only he won't listen."

"I'll listen. Austin, don't quit."

"I've made up my mind."

Which was Austin's way, she thought. He took his time making a decision, whether it was about what color shirt to buy or what to do about college. Once he made his decision, he couldn't be swayed.

"What are you going to do?" she asked.

"I'm going to drive across country to see Mom for a couple of weeks while I figure out my next step."

Harlow felt a stab of envy. "I wish I could come with you."

"You can. Road trip. It'll be fun."

She smiled. "I have a job with responsibilities."

"Adulting sucks."

"Sometimes, yes. And speaking of that." She pointed to the table. "That needs to be set, and you have to start the barbecue so we can cook the garlic bread."

"I'm on it."

He washed his hands, then went out to the grill on the balcony. Twenty minutes later, they sat across from each other at the small table off the kitchen.

"You're serious about going to Santa Barbara?" she asked.

"I am. I'm going to try one more time with Dad. If he talks to me, then I'll give notice. If not, I'm quitting right there."

"I get your point. I just wish you didn't have to go. I'll miss you."

"The road trip offer stands."

"Thanks, but my life is here. I talked to Kip today. We agreed that I'll come back, but we're not going to discuss what happened for a few days."

She'd explained she needed more time and space, and he'd promised to give her both. He'd also apologized for walking out. She'd wanted to push back on that, but she'd been packing a bag, so she was just as at fault.

For the twentieth time, she thought maybe her mother was right. Maybe they were too young to get married.

Her brother looked at her. "What *did* happen between you two?"

She'd been avoiding saying the words out loud — as if speaking them made them real. But she knew she would have to deal with it eventually. Might as well start now — in a safe place.

"A couple of nights ago, I found out Kip was married before."

"What?" Austin started to stand, then sank back on the chair, his eyes dark with anger. "Are you shitting me? He was married and you didn't know?"

"I had no idea. He never said anything." She explained about dinner with Judy and Hank and how Judy mentioned that Tracey had called.

"I felt so stupid," Harlow admitted. "I asked who she was. I was humiliated, and then I was hurt, and then I went numb. I don't know how I got through the dinner. I don't remember any of it. On the drive home, Kip kept saying he was sorry and that he hadn't lied."

"Bullshit. He has to know how you feel

about lies of omission." His hands curled into fists. "I'm going to beat him up, starting with his face."

Harlow leaned toward him. "Thank you and no, you won't."

"Why not?"

"Because it doesn't help me."

His shoulders slumped. "I want to do something."

"I know. I wish you could fix it, but only I can do that."

"What are you going to do?"

"I have no idea."

"You don't have to go back to him, Harlow. You can stay here or move into Mom's house. She would let you."

"She would." Even if they were barely speaking beyond a few texts. "I miss her."

"Me, too." Austin looked at her. "I'm sorry. I thought Kip was a good guy."

"Yeah. Now I worry about what else he's not telling me. He also told me he has some credit card debt." A lot of debt.

"Not everyone has folks who pay for stuff."

Harlow thought about Enid and medical school. "I'm starting to get that." She poked at her salad. "I know this sounds stupid, but Kip's mom told me they open presents on Christmas Eve."

Austin stared at her. "What about Santa?"

She smiled. "That's what I said, and she pointed out that he's not real."

"It's not about him being real, it's about the stockings. You're not giving up your stocking."

"It's strange, right? Christmas Eve is when we go to church."

"I guess falling in love means making compromises."

He was right, but Harlow wondered at what point compromising became giving in and losing things that were important to her. How was she supposed to know when withholding information was just Kip not knowing how to handle a situation rather than being deceptive?

"I don't know what to do," she admitted. "All I know is I need to go back to see how I feel when I see Kip." Maybe that would answer her questions.

"Do you want him to make it right?"

She considered the question. "I do."

"Do you think he can?"

"I'm not sure."

And that, she thought sadly, was potentially a bigger problem.

SIXTEEN

Mason knew how to work through gunfire, a couple going at it in the other room, cold, heat, rain and hunger. He'd once spent three days trekking supplies to a remote hospital, physically pulling an oxcart four miles over a ridge, when his truck had broken an axle and waiting for the repairs would take too long. He knew how to get the job done in nearly every condition. He was sharp, he was focused, he could power through with the best of them. What he didn't know how to do was not think about Robyn.

She was everywhere, even when she wasn't. A statement that, he admitted, made no sense, but was true. The cut flowers left in fancy vases around the house reminded him of her. As did the paintings he'd started noticing. Just yesterday, going through Leo's desk, he'd found a dozen pictures of Robyn, from toddler right up to maybe fifteen years ago, when she'd been photographed with a couple of good-looking kids he would guess were Harlow and Austin.

He saw her first thing in the morning when she walked barefoot — regardless of the weather — onto the balcony they shared. He sat across from her at dinner, and inevitably caught sight of her exploring the old house during the day.

He could live with the low-grade desire that never left, the eagerness with which he hung on her every word. He'd let go of male pride about eleven seconds after meeting her. No, the real problem was, with her in the house, he couldn't write.

Oh, he could type long, convoluted sentences about battle conditions and how many horses were killed, but he was going through the motions. He liked reliving history, smelling the gunpowder, hearing the screams.

These days that wasn't happening. He was obsessed with a woman and could only wait for the fever to pass.

He'd never felt like this before. He'd wanted women, of course. He'd wanted and not had. Regardless, he'd managed to get through his damned day without acting like an idiot. He tried telling himself that if he could get her into his bed, he'd be fine.

Only he knew that wasn't true. Worse than wanting her was knowing that if someone offered him the chance to fuck her one glorious time or spend the rest of his life hanging out with her, seeing her smile, but only as a friend, that was the one he'd pick.

He stared at the pathetic three sentences he'd written in the past two hours, then slammed his laptop shut. He'd already gone for one run that morning, but maybe a second would clear his head. He had to figure this out. He wasn't obsessive over anything, so why now? And why her?

He heard a light knock on his half-closed door. Instantly his heartbeat tripled in time.

"Yes?"

Robyn pushed open the door and smiled at him. "The wind's come up from the right direction, finally. I've chartered a small sailboat. She's thirty-two feet, so it's going to be lively out there. I wondered if you wanted to join me."

She had on slim-fitting jeans, deck shoes and a long-sleeved T-shirt. Her long blond hair was in a ponytail. She looked sexy and wholesome, and need poured through him until he couldn't breathe.

"Sailing?"

She smiled. "That is generally what I do

on a sailboat. You might have other experiences."

"You're mocking me."

"I'm teasing. I'm a good captain. It'll be fun. Say yes."

"Yes."

She laughed. "Just like that?"

With her, he would agree to anything.

She looked him over. "You'll need to put on tennis shoes. Long sleeves to protect from sunburn. Sunscreen everywhere and a hat. Meet me by the car in fifteen minutes?"

"I'll be there."

She turned to leave, then faced him again. Her expression shifted to concern. "Do you get motion sickness?"

"Not as a rule."

"On boats?"

"I don't boat much. I'm an army guy. We travel by land."

She eyed him. "I'm not addressing the military thing. As for you throwing up, I guess we'll risk it. Motion sickness medicine can make you drowsy."

"I won't throw up."

The smile returned. "If only wishing made it so."

Sixteen minutes later, they were heading down the hill, Mason in the passenger seat.

"Have you ever been on a sailboat?" she asked.

"No. A couple ski boats. Fishing. This is the first time I've lived by water."

"Then you're in for a treat. Powerboats are great. They go fast, they have more room inside, the ride can be smoother, and you have a lot more control. But sailing is magical. It's how the Vikings explored and conquered Europe. It's how Drake became the first Englishman to sail the Straits of Magellan. I grew up sailing." She flashed him a grin. "As opposed to boating."

"I get the difference. You're saying a sailboat is romantic."

"I am. Thanks for getting that. Some people don't."

He wondered if her ex-husband was one of them. Or the cardiologist who hadn't known what to do with her clit.

Don't think about that, he told himself. Because he'd come up with about two dozen things to do down there, should he ever have the opportunity.

She circled the marina until she found a parking space. "I still have my six-pack license," she said. "Just so you know."

"You're licensed to drink beer?"

She laughed. "No. A six-pack license says how many people I can have out on the boat. I haven't kept up my other licenses. Harlow has more. Austin seems happier crewing."

"I miss my kids." She shook her head. "Not the subject for today. Come on, Mason. Let's pretend we're Viking warriors."

"I should have brought a gun."

She laughed. "No shooting. I take it back. We'll relax and let the wind take us where she will."

"As long as we're back by dark."

Her gaze locked with his. "You have my word."

They went into the rental office. Robyn filled out the paperwork and chatted with the kid behind the desk. They flung around terms he didn't understand, but he could tell Robyn was impressive. When she pulled out a credit card, he got there first with his.

"I insist," he told her. "You're doing all the work."

"That's very nice, Mason. Thank you. I'll repay you by making dinner. Just tell me what you like."

Her, champagne and the sound of the ocean were all he needed. In fact, he could skip the champagne and the ocean.

They went outside, toward a row of slips where sailboats bobbed in the water. He immediately had second thoughts.

Robyn glanced at the paperwork the guy had given her, then punched a code into a security pad. The gate unlocked, and they went through it.

Everything was fine until they stepped off the sloping gangway. The entire dock shifted and swayed.

"Is this thing floating?"

She looked at him. "Of course. It's a dock. What would it be anchored to?"

Land? Pylons? Elon Musk had a rocket that could deliver shit to the space station. Couldn't someone invent a dock that didn't move?

Robyn pointed to an impossibly small sailboat. "That's our girl."

He stood on the dock while Robyn stepped onboard. She made the transition look easy. She stored the paperwork in the tiny cabin below — just the thought of which made him sweat. Then she checked the lines and the gas level in the small outboard. Finally she faced him.

"You up to this?"

Up was not a choice of words he would use, but he didn't correct her.

"Sure," he said with more confidence than he felt. He started toward the boat.

"Grab here." She stepped close, pointing

to a metal handle. "Swing your leg over. Be prepared for the movement."

Shouldn't the boat and the ocean move at the same rate, in the same direction? But they did not. His weight immediately set the boat to bobbing back and forth. Robyn shifted to the other side, amusement bright in her beautiful blue eyes.

She pointed to a bench in the middle of the boat. "Sit here while I run through a few things."

He managed to cross the small open area, avoiding hitting his head. Once he was seated, she sat across from him.

"Still want to go sailing?"

"Yes."

She watched him as she spoke. "Would you be more comfortable wearing a life jacket?"

Absolutely, he thought. "Do you?"

"Only if I think I'm going to end up in the ocean."

"So, no."

She smiled and stood, showing him how the bench seat concealed storage. "They're in here." She pointed to the rear of the boat. "That's the stern. We use that long stick, the tiller, to steer."

"I thought the wind pushed us."

"It does, but we can influence our direction." She slapped the large metal pole sticking out of the middle of the boat. "This is the mast. The mainsail goes toward the back. Depending on your tolerance, we might use a jib as well. That will go toward the front. Now let's talk about the boom."

She loosened a line and showed him how the boom swung back and forth. "I'll shout out a warning when you need to duck. The standard phrase is 'coming about.' For you I'll probably just yell 'duck.' "

"I'm good at following orders."

"An excellent and rare quality in a man. In this case, you need to listen. If the boom hits you, it's gonna hurt. Even more to the point, it could push you into the water, and then you'll be sorry you're not wearing a life jacket." She smiled. "I will say I've never lost anyone overboard, so you'll be fine. Ready?"

No. Every instinct screamed at him to get back on land where he belonged. But the thought of spending a couple of hours alone with Robyn on this tiny piece of fiberglass was more compelling. He liked the idea of her being in her element. He wanted to see her with the wind in her hair, sailing, laughing. He wanted the experience — apparently more than he wanted to live.

"Ready."

She directed him to loosen the aft line but hold it in place so the boat didn't drift. They used the small motor to back out of the slip. Once free of the marina, she raised the mainsail, shut off the engine and headed out into the ocean.

For the first twenty minutes, Mason tried to absorb the experience. Sailing was quieter than he'd expected, and he quickly adjusted to the movement. Once his stomach settled down, he was able to enjoy it. Every now and then a wave struck their bow, and he could taste the salt water on his tongue.

Seagulls swooped down and called out greetings. The small boat skimmed across the water, faster than he would have thought possible.

"This is great," he said.

She gave him a blinding smile that kicked him in the head and the dick. "Feeling brave enough for me to put up the jib?"

"Sure." Not that he had any idea what would happen.

She motioned for him to slide back toward the tiller, then put his hand on the stick. "Keep us pointed in this direction. I'll get the sail ready."

She pulled a huge bag out from the tiny cabin, then hooked the sail to the mast, pulled it up and tied it off. The boat jumped forward and started to lean. Wind caught the sail, billowing it out.

"Watch your head," she said, raising her voice to be heard. "We're going to come about. I'll give you two seconds warning, then duck and shift to the other side."

"You mean move seats?"

"Uh-huh."

"Why?"

"Now. Duck and move."

He dropped to his knees so the boom swung over his head. He scrambled to the other side. Robyn joined him, hanging on to the tiller and the line controlling the jib. She let it out a little more, and the boat leaned into the wind, the far side dipping perilously close to the water.

He wanted to ask what happened if they went in, but decided he didn't want to know. Instead he watched Robyn, obviously in control and enjoying herself. If she wasn't worried, he wasn't.

She scooted closer, then handed him the line. "Hold on tight. I want you to see what happens when you draw in the line versus letting it go. You can feel the difference in how the boat moves."

He did as she suggested, feeling the response in the sail and the movement of the boat. A waved doused them with cold water. The rope slipped, but he didn't let go.

They sat like that for a long time. He could see other boats in the distance and to the east, the shoreline. Once he thought he spotted Lillian's house, but that could have been a trick of the light. After a while, Robyn had them shift to the other side as they circled through the ocean. The sun moved across the sky, marking time, but he could have stayed out here forever.

Eventually she took down the jib and stuffed it into the cabin. The boat immediately slowed and righted itself. Robyn handed him a bottle of water.

"Hungry?"

"I'll wait."

She sat across from him, one hand on the tiller. "How's your stomach?"

"Pretty good, but I don't want to test it."

"Smart. I have very thick pork chops marinating back home. I was thinking baked potatoes and fresh tomatoes from the garden."

His mouth watered. "I could eat that."

"Good. Being on the water always makes me hungry. I like to think I burn enough calories that I can afford the big dinner."

"You worry about your weight?"

"Worry is strong. I think about it."

"Then you have no idea how good you look."

The words fell out before he could stop them. Her gaze met his.

"I could say the same about you."

Holy shit! Had she really said that? Had she meant it? She thought he was . . . what? Interesting? Sexy? Or simply not hideous?

She looked past him to the horizon. "I love it out here. When my kids were young, we'd go sailing. Just the three of us." Her mouth turned down. "My ex isn't into sailing as a sport. Oh, he charters them and has crew for the bigger sailboats, but it's not his thing. He's into getting there fast."

"Physically and metaphorically?"

She laughed. "Exactly." The humor faded. "Austin's having a sucky summer with his dad. I'm not sure what he expected from the job, but he's definitely not happy. He's not saying much, but I can tell."

"And Harlow? Are you two speaking yet?"

"We've exchanged a few greetings. She says everything is fine, but I worry."

"You're a good mom."

"I hope so. I've made mistakes. When Harlow had leukemia, it was a terrifying time. She knew she was sick, but we didn't tell her that it was really serious."

"As in she could die?"

Robyn nodded. "We wanted to protect her and thought telling her the truth would scare her."

"Makes sense."

"Maybe, but it was a flawed plan. What we didn't know was that her best friend was a smart little girl who knew how to look up information. When Enid came to visit Harlow, she knew the risks. Somehow they got talking about it, and Harlow discovered the truth."

He winced. "That couldn't have gone well."

"It didn't. We felt awful, Enid was devastated, and I'd never seen Harlow that mad. She felt we'd betrayed her. It took her a long time to get over that, and she still has a thing about lies of omission."

"Understandable. How much do you beat yourself up over that?"

"I've let it go."

He looked at her. "It's just me and the seagulls. You can tell us the truth."

He thought she might resent the implication that she was lying, but instead she sighed. "You're right. I blame myself, and I wonder about the emotional scars left behind. The cancer was tough enough. What if we made it worse?"

"You did what you thought was right. You

had the best of intentions."

"The road to hell and all that?"

He shrugged. "When you knew better, you did better."

"You're quoting Maya Angelou to me?"

"I'm a man of many depths."

She laughed. "You are and I like that."

Seventeen

Harlow stared at her phone, fighting a sinking feeling. Austin had texted with the news she'd been dreading.

> Dad just blew me off again. I'm done. I quit. I'm going to go see Mom.

> I'm sorry he's being a jerk. Can I help?

> I'm fine. Just pissed. BTW, so is he, so watch your back. Love you.

> Love you, too. Drive safe and let me know you get there okay.

> Now you sound like Mom.

She smiled. There are worse things.

She got out of her car and walked to the apartment she shared with Kip. When she'd left her dad, he'd been in a decent mood.

She would guess now all that had changed. While she understood her brother's frustration, she was sorry to see him go. They would be shorthanded for the rest of the summer, and that was going to be a problem for everyone.

Finding good employees was always a challenge. Working on a charter boat meant a lot of grunt work. The pay was good, and you got to spend your day on the water, but there were also things like customers getting drunk or seasick. Weather could be an issue, and all employees needed a working knowledge of boating. Plus having to pass a drug test.

A month into the summer, nearly everyone who wanted a job had a job. Finding a replacement for Austin would take some effort.

She unlocked the front door and stepped inside. The faint scent of roses lingered in the air-conditioned air. The big bouquet — waiting for her when she'd come back two nights ago — sat on the dining room table. Harlow fingered the soft petals.

Kip was trying. After he'd apologized (again) for not telling her about Tracey and for walking out after that dinner with his parents, they'd agreed to give each other time to process, then have a big meeting next week, when they both had the day off.

She wasn't looking forward to that, but knew it was important. She and Kip had to be honest with each other. No more secrets. She could deal with the truth, but first she had to know what it was.

Her phone buzzed. She glanced down.

Your brother quit. Just up and quit. I need to redo the schedule. Can you get back here?

She only hesitated a second before texting back, On my way.

She spent the drive trying to solve the problem. Only as she pulled into the marina did an unexpected solution occur to her.

She reached for her phone.

Can you call me right this second? It's not an emergency but it's important.

Seconds later her phone rang.

"What's up?" Enid asked.

"Did I interrupt you at work?"

"Nope. I'm just leaving the boutique, and I'm on my way home. For once I'm off tonight. I'm going to throw myself on the sofa and not move until morning. So, what's

295

important but not an emergency?"

"You like boats."

"You mean in general? Sure. I always have fun when we go out."

"You've helped with the big charters before. You don't get seasick."

"No. Plus I look adorable in crop pants and a striped T-shirt. What does that have to do with anything?"

Harlow explained that Austin had quit and they were short-handed at work. "I haven't talked to my dad, but I know he'll be interested in hiring you. I'm pretty sure it pays more than the boutique, plus there are usually tips we all split, and you'd be done in time for your night job. Want me to mention you?"

"I'd love that. I can crew. More money would be fantastic. I'll clean up the puke. I don't care."

Her enthusiasm made Harlow wish for the money to pay for her friend's medical school. "I'll talk to him right now. I'll call you when we're done. Give me half an hour."

Harlow hurried inside. The second she walked into the main office, she could hear her dad.

"Dammit all to hell. How could he do this?"

Something hit the wall. Harlow heard the thunk but not the sound of something breaking, which was good. At least he hadn't tossed a lamp or a glass.

She braced herself for her father's mood and walked into his office. He spun to face her.

"What is he thinking? You have to talk some sense into him. I can't believe he did this to me. Just up and left with no warning. He knows better. If he thinks he's going to come back and work here sometime in the future, he can forget it. He's irresponsible and still a kid. Going to visit his mommy? What is he? Five?"

Harlow waited out the rant, knowing her father wouldn't listen until he wound down a little. As Cord continued to pace and rage, his face red, his body language tense, she remembered her parents fighting when she'd been a kid.

Her mother had always kept her voice low, but her dad's voice would steadily rise until he was yelling loud enough to shake walls. Sometimes he'd throw things, scaring Harlow and Austin. They would huddle together in her room. If it got really bad, they hid in her closet.

When the house got quiet, their mom would pull them close and tell them everything was fine.

"I know it's tough when your dad gets mad," she would say. "But it's only noise, and noise can't hurt you."

Harlow had tried to believe her, but she hadn't been convinced. Over time she'd learned that her father didn't do well if he didn't get his way, and it was smarter to let him tire himself out. Once he calmed down, he could be reasoned with, but until then, he was like a kid having a tantrum.

"He's eighteen," her father fumed. "I gave him a good job. I paid him more than I should, and this is how he thanks me? He's always been a mama's boy. I don't know why I bother."

Harlow didn't point out that Austin had been crewing since he was fifteen. The only reason he didn't have a captain's license, beyond a six-pack, was that he'd never bothered to take the tests. He wanted to work here in the summer, but as he'd said, running the company had never been his thing.

About twenty minutes later, Cord ran out of steam. He sank into his chair and stared at her.

"We're screwed."

She took the visitor's seat and shook her head. "You're being way too dramatic, Dad.

We'll figure it out, just like we always do. Yes, we're short-handed, but that's not why you're mad. You're mad because he left."

Her father stared at her. "I guess. I don't know why he did it. He stood right there, looked me in the eye and quit."

"He's been trying to talk to you for weeks, and you wouldn't listen. He made appointments with you, and you wouldn't take the time. This is on you."

He scowled. "Anything else you want to criticize?"

"I'm not being critical. I'm pointing out what happened. And while we both know we'll be okay staff-wise, you've taught me it's always smarter to be prepared. I know who we could hire to replace Austin."

Her father immediately perked up. "Who?"

"Enid."

She was ready to explain why that was a good idea, but before she could start in on her list, her father relaxed, leaned back in his chair and grinned.

"Well, look at you. That's a great idea. Enid. I should have thought of her myself. She knows the boats, she's good with people, and she'd look hot in the uniform." His gaze swung back to her. "Does she want the job?"

"Yes. It pays more than the one she has now. She's saving for medical school, Dad, so the money's important to her. She also needs to be done by four so she can get to her night job. You'll need to keep that in mind when you schedule her. No sunset charters except on the days she's not working at the restaurant."

He nodded as he turned to his computer and started typing. "Easy enough. Get her in here first thing to fill out the paperwork. I've got a half-day charter from ten to three tomorrow. I'll put her on that. While she's in the office, she can give me her schedule."

Harlow kept her expression neutral. "I'll take care of it. Anything else?"

Her father waved toward the door. "Nope. See you tomorrow."

She knew there was no point in waiting for a thank-you. Her father didn't believe in them. Once she was in the hallway, she did a little dance. Even a half-day charter would pay more than the boutique. Enid was going to be relieved.

Once she was in her car, she called her friend.

"Be in the office about eight tomorrow to fill out the paperwork. And bring your restaurant schedule. I'll refresh you on everything, and you'll be on by ten." Harlow paused. "Oh, wait. That means you're not giving the boutique any notice. Is that a problem?"

Enid laughed. "No. Business is slow, my manager said. Someone needs to quit or people will be laid off. No one quit yet. I'll let her know the happy news."

Her friend's voice dropped. "Thanks, Harlow. This is fantastic. More money and more fun than steaming clothes."

"Happy to help. Let's go get Mexican to celebrate. My treat."

"I owe you. I should buy."

"No way. I want to celebrate my friend, so it's on me. I'll pick you up."

Enid laughed. "I'll be here. Can't wait."

Robyn stepped out of the shower and reached for a towel. She was tired and hungry — hours on the ocean plus skipping lunch — but also happy. She'd enjoyed herself. Mason had been an excellent sailing companion. On the way back, she'd shown him how to tack into the wind, and he'd picked up the basics quickly.

Despite his lack of experience, he'd been fine. No seasickness. Nor had he been anxious out on the open ocean. Unlike Florida's West Coast, where the water was warm, shallow and frequently calm, between

California and Asia stood nothing but some atolls and thousands of miles of water. A few hundred yards off the shore, the ocean floor dropped about ten thousand feet. There was always current and wind. Even an experienced sailor could be intimidated in a small boat.

But Mason had been fine. He'd trusted her, done what he was told and been an excellent conversationalist.

She remembered what Lillian had said about Mason watching her. As she started to dress, a little shiver rippled through her. Anticipation, she thought happily. Possibilities. They were both adults. Both single. Both aware of each other. It was nice.

She blew out her hair, then walked barefoot back into her bedroom.

Her phone rang. The screen showed Mindy's name. Instantly her stomach sank as she wondered what kind of trouble her friend was in now.

"Hey," she said, answering the call.

"We did it. We slept together."

Robyn dropped into a chair. "No. Why?"

"You're supposed to be supportive and ask how it was."

Robyn leaned back, closing her eyes. She wanted to say Mindy would regret the act forever, but there was no point in repeating herself.

"How was it?"

Mindy sighed. "Less wonderful than I'd hoped. I mean, his body is incredible, and it was very exciting being with someone other than Payne, but no fireworks. I couldn't relax. We went to his place, which is very nice. He did all the right things, but I don't know. It felt weird."

Robyn opened her eyes. "Are you okay?"

"I feel guilty. That should make you happy."

"This isn't about me being happy. I never wanted you to feel bad. I wanted you not to do it in the first place." She pressed her lips together to avoid saying something she would regret. "I'm sorry it wasn't wonderful."

"You don't mean that. You're sorry I did it."

"I am. Mindy, you have to stop before something bad happens."

"I want to see him again. Why did I even call? You won't listen."

"I am listening. I just want you to be safe."

"Dimitri won't hurt me."

"What he does or doesn't do isn't the point. I'm worried about you and your marriage. Please remember how much you love Payne."

"I know what he means to me. I need this. I wish you could understand that." Mindy sighed. "I have to go. I'll talk to you later."

The call ended. Robyn tossed the phone onto her bed, then crossed to the French doors and stepped onto the balcony.

The temperature had warmed considerably, and this late in the afternoon, it was nearly eighty. She stood in the sun, breathing in the salt air, telling herself that if she couldn't convince her friend to listen to her, then she could at least be available when it all hit the fan. And it would.

After a few seconds, she glanced toward Mason's room and saw him sitting on the balcony, reading. Or at least holding a book. When she spotted him, she saw he was watching her, his expression unreadable.

Their eyes locked, and in that moment, all thoughts of Mindy vanished as unexpected need filled her.

Surprised by her reaction, she was torn between moving toward him and retreating to her room. Mason solved the problem by smiling at her. A friendly, easy smile that made her lips curve up in return.

"I can't stop thinking about the pork chops you promised me," he said. "Between skipping lunch and being out on the water for a few hours, I'm starving."

"Me, too," she said, thinking she was hungry for more than food, but hey, better to keep the conversation on an even keel (no pun intended).

"You okay? You seem concerned about something."

"My friend who's being an idiot."

"Mindy?"

"That's the one."

He motioned to the chair next to his. "Want to talk about it? I can't promise to offer advice, but I'm a good listener, and the view can't be beat."

She sat next to him, then put her bare feet on the ottoman. "Mindy slept with her tennis instructor. I knew she wanted to, but I didn't think she actually would. It's so dumb, and when her husband finds out, her life will be ruined. I've told her and told her, but she won't listen."

"Some people secretly want to screw up."

"You're right, they do. More deep thoughts."

He laughed. "Just an observation."

"A good one. I just wish . . ." She shook her head. "No, you're right. I can't fix this. She has to figure it out for herself."

"You're a good friend."

"I try. I don't always succeed."

"You're being too hard on yourself."

"You can't know that."

"You put in the effort when it comes to relationships." One corner of his mouth turned up. "Let's just say I've had a lot of experience figuring out people quickly, and I'm good at it."

She supposed it was a skill he would have developed, given his former career. "Then I'll accept the compliment. Thank you."

"You're welcome. I had a good time today."

"Me, too. You did great, by the way. I think you have some sailor in you."

"Yeah, let's not put it that way."

She grinned. "I thought all the branches supported each other."

"We do, but I'm not a sailor."

"So we need a more civilian word? Sail person?" She tilted her head. "That sounds weird and gender-related. I have nothing. We'll have to brainstorm."

"All I'm getting is boat guy and water curious."

"You don't take yourself too seriously, do you?" she asked.

"I try not to."

"But you had a serious job."

"One is what I did, the other is who I am.

They're not the same."

"You didn't define yourself by your work?"

His expression turned thoughtful. "I did, but I can separate the two."

"You're an interesting man, Mason Bishop."

"You're an interesting woman."

They stared at each other. Robyn was pretty sure she read interest in his eyes. She hoped so, because she was definitely leaning in that direction. She dropped her gaze to his hands and wondered how they would feel on her body. Anticipation made her want to squirm.

"Okay," she said, coming to her feet. "I need to check on the pork chops."

He rose, as well. Their chairs were pulled relatively close together, so standing, she and Mason were practically touching. Stepping to the side made the most sense, and was even the polite thing to do, but she couldn't seem to move. Not when looking into his dark eyes felt really good.

He was taller than her, and broader. Fit, with plenty of muscle and that capable air she liked so much. He was always controlled, which made her wonder what he was like when he was out of control.

Hunger burned and not for pork chops. She wanted him to kiss her, but wasn't sure how to get the message across. After a second of frustration, she realized *she* could kiss *him.* Why did the man have to initiate things? She knew he thought she was attractive, so it wasn't as if he was going to run screaming —

"You're killing me," Mason said, his voice a low growl, right before he put his hands on her upper arms, leaned down and pressed his mouth to hers.

Surprise morphed into pleasure as his lips lingered against hers. There was plenty of warmth and the right amount of pressure. He didn't demand or take things too far or grind into her. Even more exciting was the heat that quickly built up inside of her.

She got lost in his kiss, in the feel of his hands settling on her hips, the warmth of his body and how much she wanted to rub against him like one of the cats. The image of that was just disconcerting enough to allow her to pull back and breathe in a little sanity.

They stood less than a foot apart, looking at each other. She wondered if she looked as stunned as he did.

"That was nice," she murmured.

One eyebrow rose. "Not the way I would describe it."

His voice was low and gravelly, with more

than a hint of passion.

"What's a better word?" she asked, trying not to smile.

"Seismic. Epic. Life-altering."

"Those work, too."

He drew in a breath. "They're different than *nice.*"

She stepped toward him and lightly brushed her mouth against his. "I'll go with *epic.* It was very epic. And now I have to go see about some pork chops."

She walked back into her room, then slipped on sandals. As she made her way downstairs, she realized she was smiling and humming and generally acting like a very happy woman. Which, it seemed, she was.

Unexpected, but very, very epic.

EIGHTEEN

Harlow was hot and tired. Her charter had run over by two hours — not all that unusual, but she hadn't slept well the night before, so the longer day had bothered her more than usual. Plus, the heat and humidity were getting to her. She grabbed a bottle of water from the refrigerator in the break room, then made her way to her office, where she booted her computer.

Maybe she was dehydrated, she thought, typing in her password. Or exhausted. She'd spent the past couple of days working on long charters with Enid, making sure her friend knew everything she needed to for her job.

Fortunately her BFF was a natural sailor. As Harlow had suspected, Enid was great with the clients, and the various captains liked her, so it had been an easy transition. Her dad had calmed down about Austin leaving and was now wondering aloud why he hadn't hired Enid years ago.

Harlow watched her email load. She was off for two days, something she was usually grateful for, just not this time. Oh, she wanted to not be working, but now she and Kip were going to have their sit-down, and she wasn't in the mood for that at all.

She knew getting to the heart of what was going on was important, but she didn't think she could survive the "discussion" that would go with it. What if they had bigger problems to deal with? Although she couldn't imagine something worse than him having been married before. That little shocker was part of what kept her awake.

What was she supposed to do with that information? How was she supposed to feel? Yes, Kip and Tracey had eloped, so he hadn't had a big wedding, but still. She wasn't going to be his first wife. For the rest of their lives together, she was his second wife. Nothing was going to be new for them.

Worse, he hadn't told her. She'd reached the point where she understood the omission was a bigger deal than the marriage itself. Which explained her wanting to avoid the serious conversation she knew they had to have.

She worried about what else was he hiding. What if whatever it was turned out to be so bad, she had to end things? She didn't think she could handle that. Not with both her mom and Austin gone. She would be totally on her own, with all the crap going on.

She should have gone with Austin, she thought, opening an email about a charter request. Not that her dad would have given her the time off. So that was a nonstarter. Still, it would have been nice to see Aunt Lillian and spend a few days at the house. She could have cleared her mind and hung out with her mom and talked to her about Kip and what was happening.

She saw an email from the attorney handling the purchase of the kayak business and felt a jolt of guilt. She hadn't even thought about the kayak business in days. No wonder he was writing her — she'd practically dropped off the face of the earth.

But when she opened the email, she discovered he wasn't chiding her. Instead he'd sent paperwork officially rescinding any interest in purchasing the company.

"What?"

Harlow stared at the email, then printed the attachment and scanned it.

"I don't get it," she said aloud. She walked into her father's office.

Cord was just hanging up the phone.

She waved the paper in her hand. "We're no longer interested in buying the company?" She couldn't believe it. "What happened? You never said anything."

Her father's expression turned peevish. "Dammit, Harlow, what did you expect? That I would buy it?"

"Why are you mad? I'm asking a legitimate question. I sat in this office with you, and we talked about this for hours. I spent my senior year coming up with a business plan, forecasts and even an evaluation. I ran everything by you. You said it was a great idea."

He sighed heavily. "Look, it *is* a great idea. For a college project."

"But you're not buying the business?" She genuinely didn't understand.

He swore. "That business costs two hundred thousand dollars. You think I have that kind of money just sitting around here? Where? In a drawer?"

His derisive tone made her feel she'd done something wrong. "You said you wanted to do it. We had a plan. You said you were fine with it."

"I said what you wanted to hear. Listen to yourself, Harlow. You think I'm going to spend that kind of money for some crap rental place just so you can learn to run it?

You want to take over this company someday, learn it from the ground up. I'm not buying you a business to practice on. Jesus, kid, get real. I'm willing to give you a fancy title and overpay you because you're my daughter. That's how it works in a family business. But there are limits."

She flushed at his assessment. The attack seemed to come from nowhere, and she couldn't think of a defense.

"Why didn't you say any of this before?" She tried to keep her voice steady. "Why did you make me think you were really interested?"

"I don't know. I didn't want to disappoint you. I didn't think you'd move forward so fast. I thought you'd lose interest. You didn't, so I shut it down."

"You lied to me."

He glared at her. "Don't start. I didn't lie. I let you believe it was going to happen because I didn't want to disappoint you. I'm not the bad guy. You're the one with unrealistic expectations."

But he *had* lied. He'd let her think he supported what she was doing. He'd let her think it was real when the entire time he hadn't been interested in buying the business at all. He'd seen her as foolish and entitled. A spoiled brat who expected her daddy to buy her a business.

Humiliation and shame rushed through her as she realized that description wasn't far from the truth. She *had* expected that, just like she'd expected her mother to keep a house she couldn't afford so Harlow could have her dream wedding.

"I wish you'd told me sooner," she said.

"I'm telling you now. It's done."

"I see that."

She returned to her office. Once she sat, she became aware of the tremors radiating out from her core. She ignored her shaking hands and scanned her email, making sure she'd handled all the charter requests. Then she logged out and shut the computer down.

She got her bag from the locker room, then went to her car. Once she was home, she could deal with everything that had just happened.

She made it about a mile before she started crying. She had to pull into a drugstore parking lot to wait out the tears. If they would ever stop. She covered her face with her hands and sobbed.

She'd been so sure, she thought, struggling for breath. She'd thought she was doing something meaningful. She'd been proud of the hard work she'd put into her business plans. The cash flow had been great. She'd figured it would take two years to recoup the cost of buying the business, with a growing profit every year after that.

Only her father had never been interested in her plans. Worse, he saw her as some entitled kid who expected things handed to her. No, that wasn't the worst part. The worst part was that she *had* been that person, and apparently she still was.

She found a couple of napkins in the console. She wiped her face, blew her nose, then leaned back.

Nothing made sense. She and her father had always talked about her coming to work for him. She'd take over while he sailed off to the Bahamas. They'd had a plan — they were going to be a team.

She'd started working at the company when she was fourteen. She'd gone out on charters, had learned everything about managing the business that he would teach her. She'd shown up early and stayed late. She'd majored in business because it had made the most sense. She'd been so sure this was what she had wanted that she'd never bothered to interview anywhere else. She loved the company. She thought she belonged there. Now she wasn't sure of anything.

Did her father even want her working with

him? She flinched as she remembered him saying she was overpaid with a fancy title. He was the one who handled payroll, so she didn't know. Was she getting more than the other captains?

Too many questions and no answers. Harlow looked out of her car, not sure where to go now. She didn't want to go home — Kip would already be there. Yes, he should be the person she should want to run to, but things were weird between them right now. Enid was working, and her mom and Austin were gone. She was all alone.

Sitting in her car wasn't really an option, so she wiped her face again, then drove toward the apartment. She told herself she would be fine. She would get through the evening, then spend tomorrow figuring out why everything was falling apart in her life. While she wanted to blame everyone else, she had a bad feeling she was at least partially responsible.

She paused before opening the apartment door. Game face, she told herself, then put her key in the lock.

"Hi," she called, faking cheerfulness.

"Hey, beautiful." Kip stepped out of the kitchen and moved toward her. "How are you?" He paused and frowned. "You've been crying."

She mentally searched for a decent lie, then nearly groaned when one occurred to her. "I heard that a cancer patient I knew years ago died. We didn't stay in touch, but it still got to me."

She was so going to hell for that one, she thought grimly. And she deserved it, but she didn't retract the words.

Kip held her tight. "I'm sorry, babe. That has to be so rough. How can I help?"

"I'll be okay. Let's not talk about it."

"Sure." He kissed her, then released her. "I made that grilled shrimp salad you like. Whenever you want to eat, I'm ready."

"Thanks. Let me go shower off the salt water, and then we can have dinner."

He smiled. "Want some help?"

She took a step back. "I'm okay."

The smile faded. "You sure you're just sad about your friend? Nothing else?"

"I'm tired, but I'll be fine. See you in a few."

She lingered as long as she could in the bathroom, but finally forced herself out. In the living room, Kip had her favorite chardonnay waiting. They sat on the sofa, talking about their respective days. Harlow spoke about her charter, careful not to mention her conversation with her father. She knew she would have to tell Kip at some point, just not tonight. It was all too humiliating.

They moved to the table. Kip tossed the salad and set it, along with a French baguette, on the table. Harlow served them each some salad and started to take a slice of bread, only to stop and stare at her plate.

"There are beets in the salad," she said.

"You like beets."

"You hate them." She looked at him. "Like six weeks ago, you threw a fit in that restaurant because they put beets in your salad. You practically had our server in tears."

He chuckled as he took his seat across from hers. "It wasn't that bad."

"It was. You yelled. You said you hated beets, that you'd told her you hated beets and there they were, in your salad."

He speared one of the beets and put it in his mouth. "I don't like red beets. These are golden. They're good."

"They're the same!"

The statement came out with a little more shriek than she'd planned, but honestly, now he liked beets?

"They're not," he said, studying her quizzically. "Golden beets are sweeter."

"But you were horrible. You were mean to our server. We talked about it. And now you're just eating beets?"

319

"Harlow, you're not making sense."

She told herself they shouldn't be fighting about a stupid vegetable, but she knew it wasn't the beets. It was everything else. It was the credit card debt and Christmas Eve and the fact that he'd been married to another woman and never told her!

"I can't do this," she whispered, pushing back from the table.

She ran to the bathroom and locked the door. Kip followed instantly, rattling the knob.

"Harlow, what's wrong? Let me in. Please, honey."

She sank onto the floor, her back against the tub. Tears spilled down her cheeks, but she ignored them as she pulled her phone out of her pocket. She blinked until she could see, then quickly texted her brother.

Where are you?

The answer came seconds later.

Just checked into a motel in the Panhandle. I moved out of the apartment before I left, so I got a late start. What's up?

I want to come with you.

She thought about the closest airport to

his route. Can you pick me up in New Orleans tomorrow?

Sure. Do you know your flight info?

Not yet.

Seconds later her phone rang. She answered it instantly.

"I haven't booked my flight. I'll do it right now and let you know."

Austin sighed. "What's going on?"

"A lot of stuff I can't talk about yet."

"Harlow?" Kip pounded on the door.

"Just a second," she called, then turned her attention back to the call. "I'll tell you when I see you. It's just one crappy thing after the other."

"Are you okay?"

"Never better," she lied. "I'll see you in New Orleans."

"Okay. If you need me to come back, I will."

Some of her pain eased. "I know. Thanks, but not necessary. See you tomorrow."

They hung up. She scrambled to her feet and opened the bathroom door. Kip stood right outside, looking both worried and pissed.

"What's going on?" he asked. "Why did

you freak out about the beets?"

She stared at the man she loved and wanted to marry and wondered how it had all gone to shit so fast.

"It wasn't the beets," she told him. "It was everything else. There's too much, Kip. You and Tracey are a big part of that. I need to figure out what it all means."

He grabbed her free hand. "It doesn't mean anything. I love you."

"I love you, too, but something's wrong, and I don't know what it is, let alone how to fix it."

He dropped her hand. "Are you breaking up with me?"

"No. I'm going to go see my mom for a few days." Longer than that, but she didn't want him to worry more than necessary.

"You're running away?"

Exhaustion swamped her, leaving her unable to fight. "If that's how you want to see it. From my perspective, I'm visiting my mom and giving myself time to think. Austin left this morning. He's going to pick me up in New Orleans."

Kip stepped back. "Just like that? You're going to walk away from me? From us? Are we still engaged?"

She could feel his pain and knew this was killing him. "I want to be," she said, her voice steady. "I love you, and I want to spend the rest of my life with you."

At least she was pretty sure she did. There was still the debt to be discussed. And Tracey. And at some point, she had to tell him what happened with her dad. Speaking of which, she had to let her father know she would be gone. He probably wouldn't take that well.

"Let me go see my mom," she said. "Let me think about everything. I'll come back. I promise." She pressed a hand to his chest. "Look at me, Kip. I mean it. I promise I'll come back to you."

His shoulders slumped. "I don't have a choice, do I?"

He didn't, but she wasn't going to say that. She kissed him. "Thank you. Let me book my flight. Then we can finish dinner."

She wasn't hungry, but it was the only peace offering she had.

Mason knew he was an idiot, but he was okay with it. Less than twenty-four hours had passed since he'd kissed Robyn, and honest to God, it was all he could think about. He'd thought about it all through dinner, occasionally sharing a look with Robyn before they both smiled and looked away. He'd dreamed about it, and it had been his first thought this morning.

Kissing her had been better than he'd imagined, and he'd imagined plenty. She was beautiful, sexy, responsive and fun. He liked how she was kind and smart. His only question was why her ex had let her go. Okay, that and why the boyfriend hadn't married her. Robyn was the kind of woman that came around once, if a man was very lucky. Walking away wasn't an option.

Not that he would have a choice. Ignoring his shitty track record with women, Robyn was so far out of his league as to make his interest in her laughable. He was very clear on what he brought to the table. He was a good guy who gave a hundred percent. He was loyal, honest and hardworking, but he wasn't special. Robyn deserved special.

At eleven he stopped pretending to work and made his way to Lillian's sitting room. She'd asked him to meet her there. Given the cats, the house and Lillian's interest in countless subjects, the meeting could be about anything. He was smiling at the thought of a rousing discussion on desalinization to solve the world's water problems when he saw Robyn sitting across from Lillian.

As their eyes locked, he felt a surge of heat that could be embarrassing for him and upsetting for a woman in her nineties. He immediately thought of the last time the Taliban had nearly blown his ass to hell and back, which quickly took care of any arousal.

"Right on time." Lillian motioned to a chair close to Robyn's but not so close that he wouldn't be able to think. "Thank you both for coming."

Robyn's expression turned quizzical. "So, this is an official meeting?"

Lillian smiled at them both. "I suppose it is. Doesn't that sound exciting? I want to talk about what happens when I die."

Robyn immediately paled, while Mason's gut clenched.

"No," he said firmly, surprising himself and possibly them.

Lillian raised her eyebrows. "Are you saying don't talk about that subject, or forbidding me to die?"

"Can I forbid you to die? Because if I have that power, I'm going to use it."

Lillian's expression softened. "You're a very sweet man. I knew I would like you. We're all going to die, Mason. I've just had the luxury of time to plan."

"I don't want to talk about this," Robyn murmured.

"And yet, here we are." Lillian smiled at them both. "Now, we all understand how

Leo's will works. Mason gets the house, and I'm leaving Robyn the contents." She looked at her niece. "I've been thinking about that, dear, and I was wondering if you'd let Mason have a few books. The works on military history. That sort of thing."

"I don't need them," he said quickly.

Robyn looked at him, her gaze filled with sadness. "Don't say that. Some of the first editions are hard to find. You'd enjoy them. I'd rather they went to you than to a book-store where they might sit, unappreciated."

"But talking about this upsets you."

One corner of her mouth turned up. "The thought of Lillian dying upsets me. I think you taking the military books is a good idea."

"Excellent." Lillian nodded. "So that's resolved. Robyn, you're moving forward with the idea of opening an antique store." Lillian turned to Mason. "I'm trying to convince her to move in with us and open a store here in Santa Barbara. What do you think of that?"

All Robyn, all the time? "I'm in."

"Let's see if we can convince her with our individual powers of persuasion." Her smile turned conspiratorial. "About the house. I'll set up a meeting with the historical society so you'll be comfortable with them."

"I appreciate that," he told her.

Robyn opened her mouth to speak, then closed it and turned away. "I can't do this."

"Robyn, love, what's wrong?" Lillian sounded concerned.

"I love this house so much. I grew up here, and it's always been in the family. In a single day, I'm going to lose you and it?" She gave a strangled laugh. "I'm being unreasonable. I'm sorry. I know you can't keep the house. It's just I never pictured it belonging to anyone else."

She blinked several times. "I sound like Harlow, wanting me to keep my house for her wedding. It's silly. I'll get over it."

"Robyn," Mason began, only to stop when she turned to face him, tears filling her eyes. The sight of her pain made him want to protect her. Only there was nothing any of them could do about Lillian dying.

"I can't talk about this anymore," she whispered. With that, she ran from the room.

Mason rose, then hesitated, not sure what to do.

Lillian picked up her cup of tea. "If I were you, I would strongly consider going after her."

"Good idea."

NINETEEN

Robyn ran to her bedroom balcony and clutched the railing, as if holding on as hard as she could would somehow give her strength.

Tears dripped down her cheeks. Which was totally ridiculous. She'd always known the house was going to a relative of Leo's and would have to be sold. No normal person could afford it. So why was she feeling such intense loss — as if something precious had been torn from her?

She heard footsteps and tried to control her tears.

"I'm sorry," she said, not wanting to face Mason. "I have no idea where all this came from. One second I was fine, and the next . . . I don't know. Everything just hit me." She wiped her face, then sucked in a breath. "If I wasn't so close to the emotional edge, I would try to make a PMS joke, not that I'm feeling especially hormonal. Totally dumb, because I always hated it when Cord accused me of reacting to something simply because I had my period."

She winced as she realized this was perhaps not the most appropriate conversation. Before she could figure out what to say or how to explain indefinable feelings, he pulled her into his arms.

"This sucks," he said bluntly. "Lillian being ninety-four, Leo having to leave the house to me, you having to deal with all of it. You're reacting because this is life-changing. It has nothing to do with PMS. It just totally blows."

His expression was two parts concern, one part regret.

"Don't be sorry that you'll inherit the house," she told him. "It's good. Except for Lillian dying."

"And the fact that you're stuck with the cats."

She laughed. "There is that."

He brushed moisture from her cheeks. "She's a great lady, and I don't want her to die for at least twenty years."

"She's already told me she won't make it to one hundred and fourteen."

"I'll take a hundred and twelve."

She sighed. "I know you can't keep the house. The historical society will take good care of it."

He watched her carefully.

"I mean it," she told him.

"Lillian told me to keep some of the land for myself and build a house on it."

"That's a great idea." She thought of all the acres around the house. "You could get a perfect plot with an ocean view. I'm envious."

He chuckled. "I'll let you have the one next to mine for cheap."

"I may hold you to that."

Before she could say anything else, her phone buzzed.

"That might be one of the kids," Mason said, stepping back. "You should check."

"I'm not sure if you're being considerate or if you're happy to have me distracted from your generous offer."

Amusement danced in his eyes. "Can it be both?"

She smiled and looked at her screen. The text was from Cord.

The kids are missing.

Her stomach dropped, and she nearly went to her knees. She dialed his number.

"What happened?" she demanded.

"Hey, hi. I didn't think you'd call."

His calm voice was at odds with the message. "You said our children are missing. What does that mean?"

"Austin quit. Just up and quit, which pissed me off, then Harlow decided to take a few days. It's the middle of summer. Who does that? It's your fault. You spoiled them."

The relief was nearly as intense as the fear and was quickly followed by anger.

"Dammit, Cord. Don't tell me my kids are missing when you know they're not. You fighting with them isn't my problem."

"They're both gone, and I don't know where."

"Have you tried texting them?"

"No. I'm pissed. Why would I text them?"

She thought briefly of throwing her phone off the balcony, but stopped herself. The gesture would only be satisfying in the moment.

"You're a lunatic and not in a charming way," she said, her heart rate finally returning to normal.

"You're going to text them, so tell them they're both in trouble with me."

"Tell them yourself. Goodbye, Cord."

She hung up and quickly texted Austin. He answered her in seconds.

Waiting in the cell lot at the New Orleans

airport. I was driving out to hang with you and Lillian for a bit. Harlow decided to join me. I'm picking her up. We should be there in maybe three days.

There was a lot of information in those few sentences, she thought. And while she had a thousand questions, this wasn't the time.

Drive safe. We can't wait to see you both. Love you.

Love you, too.

She tucked her phone back into her pocket, only to see that Mason had left to give her privacy. Which was very polite and just like him.

She knocked on the half-open French door to his bedroom.

"Everything all right?" He stepped outside, his expression concerned.

"Cord, my ex, was being a jerk. He does that sometimes. Austin and Harlow are driving here. Guess you're going to meet my kids. It's all good." She hoped. She had no idea why Austin had quit, and it wasn't like Harlow to simply take off.

Something big must have happened. Only

she and Harlow hadn't progressed beyond "hey, how are you" in their texting.

"The cats will be much easier than kids," she said.

He smiled. "One or two maybe. Fifteen will be a problem. Plus however many more she accumulates."

"You're right." She drew in a breath. "Okay, I'm feeling marginally better. I'm going to apologize to Lillian."

"After that, can I buy you a drink?"

She met his dark gaze. "Is that a literal, we leave the house, you buy me a drink, or a euphemism for having a cocktail with Lillian?"

"Your choice."

"Let's have drinks with her. I'm still feeling fragile, and I'd like to spend as much time with her as I can. Plus I want to let her know the kids are coming. She'll love to hear that."

"Done."

She put her hand flat on his chest. "You're a very good man, Mason Bishop. I'm glad you're here."

"Me, too."

Harlow rested her bare feet on the dash of her brother's 4×4 Toyota pickup. It was the vehicle he'd wanted when he graduated from high school, big enough for friends, surfboards, camping or scuba gear. She wasn't sure how a big pickup would fit in in California, but Austin always made it work.

She glanced at him. She'd driven that morning, and he'd taken over the afternoon shift. Getting from one coast to the other was surprisingly easy. He'd gone north to Interstate 10, then west. Except for the brief detour to the New Orleans airport, they would literally stay on this road until they reached Santa Monica.

"Ready to talk?" Austin asked, never taking his gaze from the road.

She leaned back against the headrest. "There's not much to say."

"You walked out on the job you've been working for since you were a kid, you didn't bring your fiancé, and from what I can tell, you're still not talking to Mom. It sure seems like something happened."

When he put it like that, she thought, looking out the side window. "I thought I had everything figured out," she admitted. "I was wrong."

"That's pretty much the case for everyone. Not just you."

She managed a faint smile. "You saying I'm not special?"

"You're special to me. Is this still about

Kip being married before?"

"Some. There's other stuff." She thought about the incident with the beets, but didn't know how to explain that without sounding like a crazy person. "Mom kept telling me I didn't know him that well. What if she wasn't wrong? Everything happened pretty fast, and I was at college last year, so maybe we didn't have enough time to get to know each other. Tracey's huge, and the credit card debt."

She held up her hand. "Not that he has it, but that he didn't tell me. I know it's hard to talk about, but he should have been honest with me before he proposed."

"Would it have changed your mind about marrying him?"

"No." At least she didn't think it would have. "I might not have talked about a wedding at the club." She looked at her brother. "Am I entitled?"

"No more so than most. Harlow, you're a product of how you were raised. We never wanted for anything, so are we entitled? Probably. You're not a bad person."

"Just selfish?" she asked, her tone bitter. "Look at Enid. She's going to medical school. Because I was sick when I was a kid, she wants to be a pediatric oncologist."

"Isn't that a good thing?"

"Yes. She'll be amazing, but she can't afford medical school without huge loans. Is that fair? Why do I get a new car after college when Enid gets stuck with over a hundred thousand dollars' worth of debt?"

"It's *not* fair. She has a different family, and they don't have a lot of money. It's just life."

"I don't like it."

He smiled.

She glared at him. "You think I'm naive."

"A little, but it makes you likeable. Kip can't have been happy you left."

"He wasn't. He thinks I'm leaving him."

"Are you?"

"No. I love him. I need to think, and not just about him." She glanced at her brother, then back out the side window. "Dad never intended to buy the kayak business. He told me he wasn't going to spend that kind of money so I could learn on the job."

Austin glanced at her. "But he helped you come up with a plan."

"I guess he wanted me to feel good about my senior project. I'm not sure he was thinking." She still couldn't reconcile all the time and energy he'd put into their discussions only to tell her it was all a lie.

"He said I was spoiled, and while he was happy to overpay me and give me a title I didn't deserve, the rest of it wasn't happening."

Austin reached across the console and squeezed her hand. "I'm sorry. Dad can be an asshole. Look at his cheating."

"And sleeping with my fiancé's sister." She blinked away tears. "I don't know what's real anymore. I believed him. I trusted him. I thought we were a team, but we weren't. Imagine what he was saying to Zafina about it all."

She sat upright and swung to face her brother. "What if Zafina told Kip? Did he know Dad was just stringing me along?"

"Kip wouldn't do that."

"Are you sure? He was married before and didn't tell me. Compared to that, this is nothing. He could know."

"Don't go looking for trouble."

"I don't have to. It's right there in front of me." She covered her face. "He's probably talked to his parents about it. They're all thinking I'm some little princess who expects to get married at a country club where the deposit for the ballroom is fifty thousand dollars."

Embarrassment and humiliation made her squirm. "Why did I trust him?"

"Dad or Kip?"

An excellent question, she thought glumly.

Right now she couldn't trust either of them.

"I'm going to ignore all my problems until we get to California," she said.

"Uh-huh."

She shoved his arm. "I mean it. Now tell me why you wanted to talk to Dad."

"No way. You'll freak."

"I don't freak."

"You freak all the time. You're incapable of emotional maturity."

"You can't talk to me like that. I nearly died from cancer."

"More than a decade ago. That's the best you have?"

She grinned. "I use what works. How about this? I'll keep my freak-storm inside."

Austin looked at her, then returned his attention to the road. "I want to go to college."

"That's hardly freak-worthy. It's also something you should have thought of six months ago."

"I wasn't ready. I'm still not. I need the year. But I'm going to apply."

She sensed there was more to his announcement.

"I want to join the navy. Through ROTC."

"What?" Her voice was louder than she'd expected. She cleared her throat. "What?"

"Freak much?"

"That was volume, not freak. We're not a military family."

"I know, but that could change. I've been thinking about UC San Diego. If I can get in, I'll join ROTC."

Her brother in the navy? "You want to fly jets? Like that old movie?"

"I want to captain a destroyer."

She stared at him. "Are you serious?"

"Yup. Mom doesn't know."

"Oh, I'll let you tell her. That will be a freak-storm for the ages."

"She'll be fine with it."

Harlow laughed. "Uh-huh. Have you met our mother? You joining the navy? She's going to lock you in a closet and never let you out."

"You're wrong. She'll be okay with it. Dad wouldn't listen."

Suddenly Austin's quitting made sense. "That's what you wanted to talk about," she said.

"He's good at ignoring us."

"He is. So what's the plan?"

"I'm going to hang with Mom and Lillian for a while, then head down to San Diego and talk to a few people. If everything works out, then I'll ask Lillian if I can move in, get a job and establish residency." He glanced at her. "That way college is a lot cheaper."

He sounded confident, she thought. "You've been thinking about this."

"I came up with the idea senior year, but I knew I wasn't ready, so I waited. By next September, I'll be anxious to go. In the meantime, I should be able to get a job with a charter company." He grinned. "And work on my surfing."

"I'm impressed," she admitted. "You're going to do this."

"I think so."

She meant what she said — she *was* impressed. And a little envious. A month ago she'd been as confident about her future, but now she was less sure about everything. She'd completely misread her father's interest in buying the business. She was confused about Kip, worried how she would fit in with his family and starting to think she might be a whole lot more of a spoiled brat than she'd ever considered. It was kind of a lot. And unlike her brother, she wasn't sure she was up to the challenge.

Living all over the world had not prepared Mason for life in Santa Barbara. Every morning he gazed at his incredible ocean view, wondering how a poor kid from West Virginia ended up here. He'd thought adjusting to civilian life after more than twenty years in the army might be tough, but it had been nothing when compared with learning his way around Lillian's house, where cats were always willing to trip him. More often than not, he had a sense of having slipped into an alternate universe — where a beautiful neighbor spilled her secrets and occasionally kissed him. He had no idea how he'd gotten so lucky, but he'd be grateful every day for the rest of his life.

Between the weather, the views, Lillian and Robyn, the sprawling garden and the fact that Charles II seemed to have adopted him, he was out of his depth and loving every second of it. But there was at least one constant he could count on — Costco.

He liked bulk buying. A man never knew when he might need twenty-five D-cell batteries. He enjoyed the bakery, where the pies were big enough to feed a squad. He always fantasized about one of his books showing up on the big tables. Unlikely, but fun to think about.

Today he headed directly for the meat. Robyn's kids were coming, and she'd wanted steaks. When he'd offered to do the shopping, she'd given him a list. They were about to jump from three people living in the house to five, and she'd warned him Austin and Harlow both liked to eat.

Thirty minutes later, he'd filled his cart. He'd bought fruit, salad, four whole chickens, steaks, two pies, a cake and the giant cookie assortment. On the way out, he grabbed three bouquets.

He loaded everything in his car and started back toward Lillian's house. A Toyota 4×4 followed him up the long driveway.

He pulled in front of the garage and got out. The truck pulled in next to him, and two kids got out.

He recognized them immediately. Austin looked less like his mom, but there was still enough there for Mason to like him. Harlow looked enough like her mother to make him wonder if there had been a father at all. He saw how Robyn would have looked twenty years ago and decided he liked the more mature version better.

"Hello," he said, crossing to Austin and holding out his hand. "I'm Mason."

"Oh, right." Austin grinned. "Harlow, this is the guy who's going to inherit the house."

Harlow eyed him from a safe distance. "Nice to meet you."

Mason walked to his trunk. "Let me get these groceries inside, then I can help you with your luggage."

"There are only a couple of bags," Austin

342

said easily. He glanced in Mason's trunk. "Costco, huh? Did Mom send you with a list?"

"She did, but I also bought cookies."

"Good man."

Instead of taking care of his own suitcases, Austin grabbed one of the boxes and started for the house. Harlow hesitated before taking another and following her brother. Mason was a couple of steps from the back door when he heard a happy shriek from inside the kitchen.

"You're here!"

Mason walked into the house in time to see Salvia hugging both of Robyn's kids, squeezing them tight and speaking rapidly in Spanish.

"We're happy to see you, too." Austin swung Salvia around before setting her down. "You look good."

"I feel good." Salvia patted his cheek, then turned to Harlow. "You're so beautiful. Your mama said you were engaged."

Harlow held out her left hand. Salvia cooed over the ring.

"Impressive, and the style suits you." She embraced Harlow. "My babies are back."

Austin glanced at Mason. "She gets enthused."

"I see that."

Salvia released Harlow and raised her hands. "Mr. Mason, you bought so much food."

"Yes, more mouths to feed."

Salvia sighed happily. "All right, go, go. I'll put this away. You two find your mother. She's in the music room. Then go see Miss Lillian. I'll make a snack. I'm sure you're hungry."

"Still bossy?" Austin asked, kissing her cheek. "I like it." He started for the back door. "Harlow, come get your bag."

"I'll bring it in," Mason said easily. "If you want to go find your mom."

Harlow studied him for a second, then nodded and walked further into the house. Mason went outside with Austin.

"How was the drive?" he asked.

"Good. It's long but easy enough." Austin pulled a couple of duffels and a suitcase from the pickup. "So, you're the mysterious heir."

Austin's words were friendly enough, but Mason had the sudden thought that as far as the kids were concerned, he could be taking something from them. Something that had been a part of their lives for as long as they could remember.

"I'm Leo's distant relative. At least that's what Lillian and her lawyer tell me."

344

"We always knew you existed. I'm disappointed you're not an ornithologist."

"That's what your mother said. What is it with you and birds?"

Austin grinned. "Birds are cool, man. But an army guy is okay, too. So you don't have to worry."

"I wondered how I was ever going to sleep again."

Austin laughed. "Now you know."

TWENTY

Harlow wound through the old house toward the music room. Even after two years' absence, the route was familiar. Lillian's house had been a part of her life for as long as she could remember. Everything welcomed her — the ancient Persian carpets on the floor, the intricate carvings around every door and window, the Tiffany lamps, the antique sideboards, the paintings and the cats she passed along the way.

Just being here made her feel better — as if all her worries and problems were a little more solvable. Maybe it was the energy of the house, or maybe it was being a couple thousand miles from Florida. Either way, she felt lighter and more capable.

The door to the music room stood open. The huge space — with what she'd been told were perfect acoustics — was filled with music stands and chairs, a grand piano, a harp and shelves filled with all kinds of musical instruments. In the far corner were two complete drum sets. Off to the side was a small recording booth. As kids, she and Austin had written and performed a radio show that they'd burned onto a CD for their parents.

That memory made her smile, as did the sight of her mom flipping through sheet music.

Harlow couldn't speak. An unexpected flood of emotions froze her in place. Longing and love filled her, along with shame and confusion as she thought about the last thing she'd said to her mother. She'd been so selfish — telling her she didn't care if her mother couldn't afford to keep the house and basically disinviting her from her wedding.

She must have made a noise, because her mom turned. Robyn's eyes widened as she smiled with obvious love and delight.

"You're here!" She hurried toward Harlow, arms open wide.

Harlow flung herself at her mom, needing to feel the familiar, comforting embrace. They hung on to each other longer than usual. Harlow let herself breathe in the feeling of being loved and cared for.

"How was the drive? Did you take turns?" Her mom drew back and looked at her, eyes wide with concern. "Sweetie, are you all right?"

"Better now," she managed.

"You've lost a little weight. Are you eating enough?"

"I haven't been very hungry."

Her mother placed a hand against her forehead — an instinctive, maternal gesture that made Harlow laugh.

"I'm not sick, Mom. Just dealing with a bunch of crap."

"Want to talk about it?"

"Yeah, but let's go see Lillian first. I'm feeling better now that I'm here."

"The house has that effect on people." Her mother hugged her again. "Your great-great-aunt should be dozing on her balcony about now. However beautiful you remember the view being, it's even better in person."

They linked arms and walked toward the stairs.

"I've been doing a little inventory," her mother said. "There are more treasures than I realized. I found a Picasso in the laundry room."

"Oh, no. Not that weird half face painting. I just thought it was quirky. It's a Picasso?"

"I'm pretty sure. I'm getting together a

list of the more important paintings. At least the ones I can identify. Lillian and I have been talking about donating them to different museums."

They went downstairs. Harlow paused when she saw the chair lift.

"She's using this?"

"Yes, and it's a relief. She's not getting younger. I like knowing she's not trying to climb the stairs every day."

Changes, Harlow thought, knowing they were inevitable but often unwelcome.

"But she's feeling all right?"

Her mother smiled reassuringly. "As spry and sharp as ever."

"Good." Harlow thought about the other big change in the house. "How long has Mason been here?"

"At least a month. He moved in before I got here."

"He just moved in? He's mooching off Aunt Lillian?"

Robyn looked at her. "Lillian invited him. He's part of Leo's family, and this is going to be his house. She's been after him for years to come live here. He finally said yes."

Which sounded reasonable, but Harlow didn't like it. Still, she'd learned something about jumping to conclusions over the past couple of weeks.

They walked into Lillian's sitting room, then out onto the balcony. She turned from the view of the ocean to Lillian.

Her great-great-aunt sat on a chaise, a blanket pulled up to her waist. She seemed smaller than the last time Harlow had seen her. Her white hair was more wispy. But her blue eyes were just as focused, and she beamed with delight when she saw Harlow.

"You made it! My darling Harlow. You're more beautiful than the last time I saw you."

Harlow sank down next to the chaise, where she carefully wrapped her arms around Lillian.

"I've missed you," Harlow whispered. "Thank you for always being here to welcome me."

"Of course, my love. Where else would I go?"

Holding her, Harlow became aware of Lillian's fragility. Her bones felt delicate, and the older woman had obviously lost weight. She shot her mom a frantic look, but Robyn didn't seem worried.

Before Harlow could figure out how to ask if Lillian was all right, Austin and Mason walked out onto the balcony. Her brother jogged to Lillian's other side and pulled her into a gentle bear hug.

"Finally, we're together again. I've missed you."

Lillian laughed and patted his cheek. "Look at you, Austin. More handsome by the day."

"It's a curse," he said solemnly. "But my heart will always belong to you."

Harlow sat close and reached for her aunt's hand. "We're happy to be here. And to see you."

"I won't ask how long you're staying," Lillian told her with a smile. "Whatever you tell me won't be enough." She lowered her voice. "I'll warn you. I'm trying to convince your mom to move in with me."

Harlow and Austin exchanged a look. She knew he'd be fine with the idea. He was hoping to establish California residency. But Harlow didn't like thinking of both her mother and her brother being so far away. She would be all alone in Florida.

But instead of blurting out something she would regret, she patted Lillian's hand and said, "You can be persuasive. I doubt she'll be able to resist you."

Lillian's gaze sharpened. "Are you all right, dear?"

"I'm great."

Harlow looked toward her mother, then nearly fell off her chair when she saw Mason lightly brush her mom's arm in a gesture that was both caring and slightly possessive. Instead of swatting him away, her mother smiled up at him affectionately.

WTF?

Anger and disappointment boiled up inside of her. Not her *mother,* too. Couldn't anyone be a decent person for five minutes?

She sprang to her feet and walked toward the door. "I'm going to get my suitcase."

"It's in your room," Austin told her. "You okay?"

"Fine." Harlow knew her voice had an edge, but she was about out of control. "Mom, could you help me?"

"Sure. Lillian, I'll leave you in these gentlemen's capable hands."

"A wonderful idea. Mason, it's after two. Let's have cocktails."

Robyn joined Harlow in the hall. "I think your aunt is having a few too many cocktails these days, but the woman is ninety-four. I probably shouldn't say anything."

Harlow waited until they'd stepped into the room she always used here. For once she ignored the big bed, the French doors that opened onto a small balcony and the overstuffed chair where she'd spent hours reading. Instead she spun toward her mother.

352

"How could you?" she asked, letting out her anger. "My God, it's disgusting. I don't get it. Am I the only person on the planet who hasn't cheated? Is it because of Dad? Is that it? I know that he wasn't faithful in your marriage. That was awful, but now you're acting the same? Why? He did it, so you want to try it? Or have you been doing this all along?" She paused, then shook her head. "Never mind. Don't answer that. I don't want to know."

Her mother stared at her. "What are you talking about? Harlow, are you sure you feel all right? You're acting very strange."

"Strange? How about disappointed, because that covers it." Her eyes burned. "Mom, I never thought you'd cheat on Jase. You and Mason were all over each other. You've been here two weeks and you're sleeping with him? It's gross and wrong."

Her mother's expression tightened. "Ask a few questions before jumping to conclusions. Not that it's your business, but Jase and I broke up before I left Florida, and I'm not sleeping with Mason."

Harlow's anger deflated, and embarrassment took its place. "You broke up with Jase? Why didn't you tell me?"

"When was I supposed to do that? After you told me not to come to your wedding?

After you stopped talking to me or texting me? You seem to enjoy assuming the worst about me, Harlow, and I have no idea why. Maybe instead of getting mad because you think I'm cheating on my boyfriend, you should consider that not everything is about you."

Harlow saw movement out of the corner of her eye. Austin had stepped into the bedroom. His was next to hers, and they shared a Jack and Jill bathroom. He was watching them both, but didn't speak.

"I don't know what to say," Harlow admitted.

"An apology might be a good start, but I know better than to expect that."

Her mother walked out. Austin waited until she was gone to look at Harlow.

"We haven't even been here an hour. Why are you always all over her? She didn't do anything wrong. This one's on you."

With that, he left as well, closing the bathroom door behind him, leaving her alone and feeling very, very small.

Robyn decided to work on her hurt and frustration with a little physical labor. A couple of rooms on every floor were, for lack of better description, filled with junk. Broken chairs, boxes of old paperwork, abandoned craft projects, cracked bowls and stained carpets. Two days ago she'd ordered a big bin from the trash company. It was due to be delivered by the end of the week. Until then, she could spend some time sorting the junk into *save* and *toss* piles.

She walked from Harlow's room to the junk room on the main floor, hoping the movement would make her feel better. But she arrived just as upset as she had been.

Why did it have to be like this between her and her daughter? Why did Harlow assume the worst? She would never cheat on Jase, and Harlow had to know that.

Only Harlow knew about Cord and his cheating, so that had to be upsetting. And, as her daughter had said, gross. No kid, no matter how old, wanted to know about a parent cheating. Worse, Cord was dating Kip's sister. Yet another point of concern on the queasy scale. Harlow had a lot to deal with, and she hadn't had much time to process it.

"Maybe I should give her a break," Robyn murmured.

"I'm not sure she deserves one."

Robyn spun and saw Austin walking into the room. She pressed a hand to her chest.

"You scared me."

"Huh. Usually you're happy to see me."

She laughed. "And I am today, as well. I can't believe you drove cross-country by yourself."

"Harlow was with me."

"For part of it. You're only eighteen. I worry."

"As we've discussed, my judgment center isn't fully developed, Mom. You need to accept I'm going to make bad choices."

She hugged him. "I do accept it, but I don't like it. I've missed you."

"I've missed you more."

She stared into his blue eyes. "Want to talk about why you're here?"

"Can I have a little more time to process?"

"You can. Are you willing to tell me why you quit your job with your dad?"

Her son's mouth tightened. "He wouldn't listen. I tried to talk to him, but he wasn't interested."

Her heart squeezed tight as she felt his pain. "I'm sorry. Despite his actions, he loves you very much."

His posture relaxed. "You always support him, even though he would never act the same way about you."

"I find pleasure in being the bigger person. No matter what happened between me and Cord, he's still your father, and I respect the connection."

"If not the man?"

"I didn't say that."

"You didn't have to. He can be a jerk." He shoved his hands into his shorts front pockets. "When he wasn't interested in what I had to say, I quit. I closed the apartment and turned in my keys, then packed up to drive here. Oh, I checked on the house. All good."

She didn't bother pointing out she'd hired a house-sitting service. Austin was the kind of man who would always check on the house, even when not asked.

"I'm glad you're here. What's your next step?"

He laughed. "I don't get twenty-four hours to settle in?"

"It's a mom thing. How about if you reassure me you have a plan? Then I can relax."

"I have a plan."

"Okay, then. I'll be around whenever you're ready to talk."

He kissed her cheek. "Thanks, Mom. I love you."

"I love you, too. Now go unpack, then hang out with Lillian."

"What are you going to do?"

"I was going to clean out this junk room to help me deal with Harlow-generated emotions, but I'm feeling better."

"Because of me. I'm like a unicorn. Basically I'm a magical creature."

She laughed and pushed him out of the room. "You're a weird kid, and I'm not sure what I was thinking, bringing you home in the first place."

They went upstairs together. Austin went toward Lillian's suite while Robyn retreated to her own room. She was pleased to see Mason reading on their shared balcony. She pulled a chair close to his.

He closed his book. "Kids all settled?"

"They will be."

"Did they tell you what's going on?"

She frowned. "What do you mean?"

"They both just followed you across the country. There has to be something driving that."

"We haven't talked yet."

Which sounded better than the fact that she and her daughter were already fighting and Austin needed more time before he was ready to share what was on his mind.

She sighed. "I think I might have screwed up as a parent."

"No way." Mason shook his head. "I've seen a lot of kids their age, and you did just fine. I say that as a professional."

She laughed. "Thank you. Somehow that

makes me feel better. Still, they are going to change the energy in the room."

"Is that good or bad?"

She leaned back in her chair. "Mostly good." She looked toward the horizon. "It's a beautiful day. Were you serious about selling me some land?"

He seemed surprised by the question. "Sure. If you want it. Would you move here?"

"I don't know. Maybe. My children don't need me as much, and aside from them, there's nothing keeping me in Florida." When Lillian was gone, she would be busy going through the house. That would take a while. It made more sense to open a store near her inventory.

"I like the idea of a little house overlooking the ocean," she said, smiling at him. "I promise to be a good neighbor."

"I'm not worried about that. I just hope I can afford to build a house for myself. Everything is more expensive out here."

She tilted her head. "Why wouldn't you have enough money? You're selling this place to the historical society."

"I know, but they're a charity group. How much can they pay?"

He didn't know. She hadn't realized that until this second. "Mason, it's a forty-thousand-square-foot house on twenty-five ocean-view acres. Even if you hold back five or six acres for yourself, you'll get at least ten million from the historical society. You'd get more from a developer, but he would just tear the place down and put up luxury condos, so we don't want that."

Mason stared at her, unblinking. His eyes were wide, his mouth slightly open.

"What did you say?"

"Ten million dollars. That's a guess, by the way. They could be offering you more, but you could probably speak to Lillian's lawyer and find out. I'm sure they've talked numbers. Gregory will know better than me."

She smiled at him. "Are you in shock?"

"Yes."

"Do you need a minute?"

"More like a week, but yes."

She rose. "I'll leave you to consider your newfound fortune. But think about what I asked before. I really would like to discuss me buying a half acre or so."

She couldn't afford it right now, but after she inherited, she could sell a few of the more expensive pieces and pay cash. Even if she stayed in Florida, she liked the idea of having a little something of her own out here, on the coast.

"Ah, sure. It's yours." He stood and looked at her, then at the house. "I have to go."

He walked into his room and closed the French doors behind him. Robyn smiled. Poor guy. Yes, it was only good news, but if he hadn't been expecting to be rich, then he'd need a minute to adjust.

A big inheritance could change a person. Some people went crazy and ran through their money in months, then ended up with nothing to show for it but a fancy watch and a racehorse. Mason wouldn't be like that. He would make smart choices. Yet another reason she enjoyed his company. He wasn't a man who would disappoint a woman. Something, she'd recently discovered, that was getting harder to find.

TWENTY-ONE

Not sure how to apologize for being bitchy (again) and not wanting to face everyone, Harlow had begged off dinner, pleading exhaustion. She'd retreated to her room, had fallen asleep by seven and hadn't stirred until nearly six the next morning. She woke up feeling better about herself and the world.

She moved two cats that were on her bed, then walked to the bathroom to brush her teeth. After pulling on shorts and a T-shirt, she went downstairs and started coffee. She poured a little cream and coffee into two mugs, then quietly slipped into her mom's room.

The bed was empty, but the light was on in the bathroom. Harlow put a mug on Robyn's nightstand, then slid into bed. Leaning against the headboard, she reached for her coffee when her mom appeared.

"Morning," Harlow said, pointing to the

mug. "I brought you coffee."

"Which is why you're my favorite daughter."

Her mom, still dressed in a loose nightgown, got back in bed and stuffed pillows behind her back. When she was settled, she grabbed Harlow's free hand and squeezed, then smiled at her.

"I love you, baby girl."

Harlow's eyes filled with tears. "I was horrible yesterday. You should hate me."

"You'll have to live with my love."

"I don't deserve it."

"The love comes for free, no matter what you do. I may not always approve, but I'll always love you." She released her hand and picked up her coffee. "All right. Enough with the mushy stuff. Why are you here? And by here, I mean California, not my bed."

The change in tone made Harlow smile. "You're telling me to get to the point?"

"You came a long way for some reason. I'm curious."

Harlow had been thinking about that herself on the drive out. The list was long, and it all needed to be said, but first she had to apologize.

"I was a bitch about the house," she began. "I'm sorry. I shouldn't have expected you to keep it just for my wedding. Especially when money's an issue. I'm sorry about what I said before." She glanced at her mom, tears once again blurring her vision. "I need you at my wedding."

Robyn smiled. "I'll be there, even if I have to hide in the bushes."

"Why am I such a brat?"

"I don't know. Maybe I spoiled you too much when you were sick."

She noticed her mom didn't say she *wasn't* a brat. Harsh, but true. "So I get to blame you for being emotionally stunted?"

"You're not stunted. We all forget to look past ourselves sometimes."

Harlow had the feeling she did that more than most. "Kip and I checked out the wedding facilities at the club. With his mom."

"How was that?"

"Weird. She nearly lost it at the cost. The deposit on the ballroom is fifty thousand."

Her mom flinched. "Okay, or a car."

"I never talked to Dad, so I have no idea what the budget is going to be."

"That's a good place to start. I'll kick in some, as well, but first find out what he's willing to spend."

Harlow tucked her leg under her, angling toward her mom. "You don't have to pay for my wedding."

"I'm going to help, sweetie. I want to. Right now I'm figuring out my financial future and coming up with a plan. Selling the house will help."

Harlow nodded rather than get into it with her mom. The money from the house was going to be a big part of her mom's income. No way she wanted to take any of it for her wedding.

"What else?"

Harlow told her about what had happened with her dad and the kayak business.

"I thought he meant it," she admitted. "I feel so stupid. Like a kid playing dress-up. It's just we talked about it like he really wanted to buy the business. But he made it clear he didn't. This whole time, he was lying to me."

Her mother put down her coffee and hugged Harlow. "Okay, that's awful. I don't get it. Why not tell you from the start that he wasn't going to buy the company? Why string you along? It wasn't as if you were thinking about going to work somewhere else. He didn't need to bribe you into coming into the company. You two always talked about running it together. I'm sorry. I don't know what he was thinking."

The words and the hug made her feel better. "I put so much effort into something that was never going to happen. Plus he talked about overpaying me because I'm his daughter. I don't know, Mom. Maybe I don't belong there."

Robyn's gaze was steady. "Don't make any sudden decisions. You've wanted to work with your dad since you were a little girl. Why should that change? You see how he expects things to be. Now think about what *you* want. I'm not sure you'd be happy working somewhere else."

"I've never even tried." She sighed and put down her coffee. "There's more. Dad and Zafina."

Her mother's expression tightened. "I don't know what to say about that."

"Because there aren't any words. If they get married, she could be my stepmother and sister-in-law. He could be my dad and my brother-in-law, which is even more disgusting."

"I'll admit that one stopped me, as well. I wish there was a way to break them up."

Harlow laughed. "Me, too." Her humor faded. "There's also stuff with Kip."

She sucked in a breath as she gathered the courage to admit what she'd found out. "It's a lot. His family celebrates on Christmas Eve. They open presents and don't go to church. Judy didn't let the kids believe in

Santa, so no stockings."

Her mother looked at her. "Sad, but work-able. What do you really want to tell me?"

Harlow wasn't surprised her mother guessed there was more. "Kip has credit card debt. Over twenty thousand. We were supposed to talk about it, but we never did. Other stuff happened."

"The debt is big news, and it's unfortu-nate, but not the end of the world. You need to understand his history and decide if he's learned his lesson and won't do it again or if this is a pattern."

Harlow nodded. "You're right. We have to talk about it." She plucked at the hem of her T-shirt. "Kip was married before." She raised her gaze to her mother's face. "He eloped when he was nineteen. The marriage didn't last long. I found out when I had din-ner with his parents. I didn't know, and his mother said something about Tracey call-ing." The tears returned. "He was married and he never told me."

Her mother pulled her close and held her.

"You said I didn't know him very well. What if you're right? I love him, Mom, but what if I can't trust him?"

Harlow sniffed and drew back, wiping her face. "What if there are other secrets? Worse ones? What if everything's a lie?"

"Everything isn't a lie."

"But some things are."

"Yes."

"How do I figure this out?"

Her mom looked at her. "I don't have an answer right this second."

"But you always know."

"This is bigger than regular stuff, sweetie. Kip's a good guy, and I believe he loves you, but I don't know what to say about him having been married before. It's not that he was married, it's that —"

"He didn't tell me," Harlow finished. "Those stupid lies of omission."

"You're not wrong to be upset. This is really significant. Have you talked to him?"

"Not much. Between that and Dad and a stupid fight about beets, I ran."

Robyn laughed. "I ran, too, so I'm not going to judge. Sometimes the immature response is the right one." She hugged her again. "I'm really glad you're here. Let's hang out as much as we can. I've missed you."

"I've missed you, too. I love you, Mom. You're my rock."

"And you're my little pebble."

Mason sat at his desk until nine in the morning, then called Lillian's lawyer. After about thirty seconds on hold, he was put through and was able to ask the list of questions he'd come up with last night, while he wasn't sleeping. Thirty minutes later, he hung up and carefully put his cell phone down in front of him.

He'd been shot at more than once in his life. He'd parachuted out of a flying plane twice, had been in a Humvee that had overturned. He'd been married and divorced twice. He'd scared the shit out of kids to turn them into soldiers, and he'd told sobbing recruits it was time to go home.

But he'd never faced anything remotely like what Robyn had so blithely mentioned yesterday and that Gregory had just confirmed. He, Mason Alexander Bishop, born in a house that barely had running water, whose family had spent a couple of generations in the coal mines, was going to inherit a house that would be sold to the historical society for twelve-point-seven million dollars.

The lawyer had made it clear Mason could get triple that amount from a developer. Maybe more. But Lillian was hoping he would agree to the deal with the historical society so the house could be saved.

There had also been a discussion of tax implications, which would reduce the amount Mason would eventually put in his bank account, but he was okay with that. Ending up with eight million was still something he couldn't wrap his mind around.

Him. Eight million in cash money. How was that possible?

He went in search of the one person he could talk to. He found Robyn in the pantry, studying the shelves. She looked up at him.

"I'm planning menus. I figure Salvia has enough to do with the sudden influx of guests. You're right about Lillian's love of salads and soups for meals. Between you and kids, we're going to need more substantial food." She stopped talking. "Are you all right?"

"No. I spoke to Gregory."

She nodded and led the way through the kitchen and out to the far back little patio area where he stored the barbecue. They settled on chairs opposite each other. Mason leaned forward, his arms resting on his thighs.

"I never thought it was real," he admitted. "Any of this. When Lillian first started writing me, I thought she was a loon."

"Who owned a three-bedroom rambler," she teased.

He glanced at her and smiled. "Yeah, that. When I first got here, I couldn't take it in. Not really. As for inheriting, that was a concept. Nothing real. Then Lillian mentioned me keeping some land for myself, and I liked that idea."

He'd come to love the area and could see himself settling here. He didn't need much — a small house with a view of the ocean would be more than he'd ever expected.

"Gregory said Lillian and the historical society have agreed on twelve-point-seven. After taxes, I'd end up with about eight million." He looked at her. "Dollars." He ran a hand over his hair. "That's not me. That's not my life."

"It doesn't have to change much, Mason. You'll build a house and write your books and maybe get a car you've always dreamed about." Her tone was gentle. "It's a lot to take in. Give yourself a little time."

"I want her to live forever. I like her. I'd rather have her than the money."

Her expression softened. "Now you're just trying to make me throw myself at you, and it's working."

"She's the only family I have." He thought about all the time he'd wasted. "Why didn't I answer her right away? I could have gotten to know her years ago."

"You know her now."

Feelings churned inside of him. "I don't know how to deal with this."

"Just let the information sit. Nothing's going to happen for a while."

She stood and held out her hand. When he took it, she pulled him to his feet, then stepped into his embrace.

Holding her felt good, he thought, breathing in the scent of her hair. She'd used shampoo scented like coconut and vanilla. Her curves pressed into his body, distracting him from his swirling mind.

Giving in to the impulse, he tangled one of his hands in her long, blond hair and pulled her head back just enough for him to kiss her.

She wrapped her arms around his neck and sank into him. Her lips parted, then her tongue welcomed his with a sensual dance that had him hard and hungry in seconds.

He released her hair and dropped his hands to her rear. Her breath caught, and she rubbed against him, groaning slightly as she moved. Unable to help himself, he moved from her mouth to her jaw, then nibbled his way down her neck.

The sound of her faint moans nearly made him come in his pants. She shocked the shit out of him by pulling his hands around to her breasts. They kissed and he explored her curves until they were both breathing hard.

"Touch me."

The whispered command had him fumbling with her jeans. Need made him clumsy, but he managed to get the zipper down. She parted her legs even as he slipped his hand against the warm skin of her belly before sliding it into her slick, swollen heat.

She stared at him, her need raw and exposed, her mouth parted. The image of her so aroused, because of him, burned in his brain. He would die remembering this moment, and everyone in the room would wonder why he was smiling.

He moved steadily, watching her, waiting. Seconds later, her orgasm ripped through her. She came, whispering his name, clinging to him, begging him not to stop. She rode his hand and fingers through to the end, then stood there, gasping for breath.

She stared at him with a combination of satisfaction and concern. As if she wasn't sure what had just happened. No — that wasn't right. As if *worried* about what had just happened. Of what he must think of her.

"I've never . . ." She pressed her lips

together. Color stained her cheeks. "I can't believe I asked you to . . ." She cleared her throat. "I'm usually more contained and . . ."

He put her hand on his hard dick. "I want you," he said, staring into her eyes. "I want you, and I can't believe you let me do that to you. It was incredible. You're incredible. Honest to God, I'd give my left nut to have a condom on me right now."

"Do you have one back in your room?"

Her question nearly killed him with desire. "No."

"You might want to fix that sometime in the next few days."

Before he could take in that happy bit of news, the world went totally berserk as Robyn undid his belt, opened his jeans, then dropped to her knees and took his dick into her mouth.

Just. Like. That.

"You can't," he began, but she'd gone to work on him, so there was no way he could keep speaking.

The warm heat of her mouth, the steady movement of her hand, conspired to send him toward the edge. It had been so damn long since he'd had company for this, plus it was Robyn. Faster than he would have liked, he lost it, shuddering into his release, giving her all he had.

She kept her mouth on him, moving gently, licking him, teasing until he started laughing.

"I'm done. I'm done."

She drew back, and he helped her to her feet. They stared at each other, both smiling.

"That was unexpected," he admitted.

"Yeah, it was."

There were probably things he was supposed to say, he thought, aware that she was fully dressed, but he was standing there with his shrinking dick hanging out.

Somewhere in the distance, the back door slammed.

"Mom? You out here?"

Harlow's voice carried to them.

"Timing," Robyn whispered, as she fastened her jeans. "I should probably handle this while you get dressed."

As he pulled his jeans into place, he watched her walk away. Her conversation with her daughter carried to him.

"I figured I could go to the grocery store," Harlow was saying. "We'll need a bunch of stuff."

"I was thinking the same thing, but I thought maybe I'd send Mason in to do the shopping."

375

That made him grin.

"No, I'll go," Harlow said. "I never trust guys to buy food."

"All right. Let's make a list, and you and Austin can go."

Their voices faded as they walked into the house. Mason gave himself a few minutes before he followed. Later, he would swing by the drugstore. As long as Robyn was in his life, he was never going to be unprepared again.

TWENTY-TWO

Robyn spent the rest of the day alternating between satisfaction and shock. Her Mason-generated orgasm had been pretty spectacular, but she still couldn't believe they'd done that right there on the patio. Or that she'd asked him to touch her.

She busied herself with planning a few meals and coming up with a shopping list, then hung out with Lillian for a couple of hours. But sometime in the late afternoon, she knew she was going to have to face Mason and talk about what they'd done. Better when it was just the two of them than, say, over dinner with her aunt and kids.

To that end, she made her way to his office, knocking once on the half-open door. When he called, "Come in," she entered, then carefully shut the door behind her to ensure privacy.

Only once that was done, she was alone in

a room with a man who could reduce her to quivering with a few kisses. Memories of how he'd touched her, how he'd made her feel, made it impossible to think.

Her gaze locked with his. He looked as shell-shocked as she felt. He circled his desk, cupped her face and lightly kissed her.

"I've been thinking of you all day," he murmured.

"Me, too."

"It's made it difficult to work."

"The battle will still be there tomorrow."

He smiled and stepped back. "You're here because we need to talk."

"Yes."

"I agree." He pointed to an aging tapestry-covered sofa pushed against the far wall. "I'm not sure what Leo was thinking when he chose that for his office, but it seems to get the job done."

They sat down, angled toward each other. She took in the strong lines of his face and the slight smile that tugged at his lips. His eyes were bright with interest and affection.

"You okay?" Mason asked. "Any regrets?"

"I'm doing well, and no regrets. A bit shocked by my behavior, but that's on me, not you."

"What did you do that was out of character?"

"Sex on the patio, for starters."

He smiled. "That was unexpected and very nice."

"It was. But . . ." She paused, thinking she should have planned this conversation better. "Mason, there's something about you. I'll admit that. You're very appealing, and being around you makes me feel really good." She sucked in a breath. "But maybe we should slow things down a little."

His gaze never wavered. "We should. Your kids just showed up, and there's a lot happening. We have time. I'm not going anywhere."

"You're not mad?"

"No." He lightly touched her arm. "And while I won't talk about how wet and swollen you were, I'll be thinking about it." He leaned toward her and lowered his voice. "A lot."

She shivered, liking the need that built up inside of her. "That surprises me," she admitted, trying not to smile. "I would have thought you'd be remembering how it felt when I sucked your dick."

The surprise and appreciation in his expression were a nice reward for speaking her mind.

"Damn," he murmured. "You just keep getting better and better. For what it's worth, I'll be thinking about you sucking on my dick more than I should."

"Good."

It occurred to her that it would be really easy to slide onto his lap and feel how aroused he was. From there it was a quick journey to getting naked. She wanted to explore all of him and have him do the same with her. She wanted —

"What you're thinking is killing me."

She blinked, drawn back to the present. "How did you know?"

He sagged back against the sofa and closed his eyes. "Lover, it is all over your face."

Lover. The single word caught her by surprise. There was need in his voice, but also affection. Lover. She'd never thought of herself that way. As someone's lover. A wife, a girlfriend, a companion, but not a lover.

"Thank you, Mason," she whispered, then kissed him. She briefly rested her hand on his thick erection before hurrying out of the room. Safely in the hallway, she paused to smile.

She was going to be his lover, and it would be glorious.

Mason gave up on sleep a little after midnight. He couldn't stop thinking about Robyn, which meant he was constantly hard, and that didn't help the situation at all. Plus the whole eight million dollars thing had his mind racing. He pulled on sweats and a T-shirt and made his way to his office. While he doubted he could work, maybe reading research material would put him to sleep on the ugly sofa.

He'd barely opened the box of notes when Austin walked into his office.

"I saw the light," the kid said. "You're up late."

"So are you."

"I'm on a mission. Want to join me?"

"Sure."

They went up one of the back staircases, climbing two floors before heading down a hallway. Austin led the way to yet another staircase, one Mason didn't think he'd used before. The passage narrowed until it ended at a big metal door. Austin lifted the bar securing it, then pushed out onto a section of roof.

The night was cool and clear. This part of the roof was flat, about thirty by thirty, with wrought iron fencing to keep them safe. But what really caught his attention was an odd little building right in the center.

Mason followed Austin inside and saw a

large telescope pointing at the sky.

"Your own observatory," Mason said.

Austin nodded as he began opening panels to allow them to see the stars. "Harlow and I found it when we were kids. Lillian had forgotten it was here. She got some guy out to make sure it was working, then had a professional from UC Santa Barbara teach me how to use it. Since that summer, I've studied up on astronomy a little. I've also gotten decent at celestial navigation." He grinned. "Not that I'd want to cross the ocean using it."

"Sailors used to."

"Brave men."

Once the panels were open, Austin approached the telescope. "In a couple of weeks, we'll start to see the Perseids meteor shower. It's a good show. And if you want to get up early, we can see Venus and Mars just before dawn." He made a few adjustments. "But tonight, we're going to look at Antares. That's in Scorpio."

He looked through the telescope and made another adjustment. "The midnight culmination of Antares is around June first. That's when it's highest in the sky at midnight." Austin flashed him a grin. "I respect when the name of something tells you what it is."

"That would help."

"The further south you are, the easier it is to see Antares. In the Southern Hemisphere, it's visible all year long. For us, it's just a summer fling."

He stepped back so Mason could look through the telescope. He saw a bright, reddish star.

"It looks like Mars," he said.

Austin nodded. "It does."

Mason looked in the telescope again. "You come up here a lot?"

"When I'm here, a few times a week. The sky is always changing. We get lots of clouds, but when it's clear, it's beautiful."

"How about Florida?"

"I don't have a telescope there. How'd you end up in the army?"

"In my hometown, it was the military or the coal mine."

"I don't think I could work underground."

"Me, either. Like you said before, it takes a brave individual."

"So you chose the army."

Mason nodded, wondering if this was why Austin had sought him out. "I wanted to be part of something, see the world."

"Did you?"

"Much of it."

Austin looked at him. "Still, not much of

a choice."

"I could have gone to work at the local gas station. Getting out of town was better."

"I get that. I have too many opportunities. My mom's always telling me I can do anything."

"So you went to work for your dad?"

"Not anymore. I quit."

"What's your next move?"

"I've got a few ideas." He looked through the telescope again. "What's going on with you and my mom?"

Mason kept his body language casual even as he scrambled to figure out how to answer the question. Maybe he'd been wrong about why Austin had invited him up here.

"I like and respect her."

"She's a good mom. She really cares, and she listens. My dad doesn't." He straightened. "He cheated. It went on a long time. I found out when I was eight."

Mason did his best not to react. "How?"

"I saw him with another woman at a restaurant. I'd gone with a friend to a birthday party across town, and there was my dad. I started to walk over to their table. Then he kissed her, and I knew."

"Did he see you?"

Austin shook his head and looked away. "Nah. He was too busy sticking his tongue in her mouth. I went to the party and didn't tell anyone. A few months later, I told my dad what I'd seen. He said I was too young to understand, but if I said anything to my mom, I'd make her cry."

Mason's gut hurt for the young man standing in front of him. "That's a lot to take on when you're eight."

"Yeah. He's a jerk. She was faithful to him all those years. She took care of him, worked in the business. I swear, she willed Harlow not to die of cancer. Mom's a force. She deserves better."

He turned back to the telescope. "Don't cheat on her."

"I won't. I've never cheated on anyone. It's not who I am."

Austin looked at him again. "It'll take me a while to figure out if I believe you."

"That's fair."

"Wear a condom. No bullshit about how it's not as good. Treat her right."

"You're a hell of kid," Mason said. "I respect what you're saying, and I agree. I won't hurt her."

"Don't say that. You have no idea what you're going to do to her. Shit happens." He stepped back from the telescope. "Okay, so this is called the Summer Triangle. It's made up of Altair, Deneb and Vega and used to be called the Navigator's Triangle before GPS."

Harlow curled up on her bed, her earbuds in place, her phone in her hand as she Face-Timed with Kip.

"I miss you," he said, looking and sounding miserable. "When are you coming home?"

"I don't know. I just got here. I need some time to think."

"You're scaring me, Harlow. I don't want to lose you."

"That's not what this is about." At least she didn't think so. At this point, she wasn't sure of anything. "Trust me." *And stop pressuring me,* only she didn't say that.

"Harlow." His voice cracked. "It's like you're never coming back."

"I am. Now tell me what's going on with you. How's work?"

"Good. Busy. I've beat my sales target for the reporting period."

"Congrats. That's amazing. Not a surprise, though. You do really well there."

"Are you trying to make me feel better, or do you really believe that?"

"I believe it. You're my guy."

He sighed. "Sure. Okay, so what's new with you?"

"I haven't been here very long, so not much. Lillian looks frail. That scares me. She's like ninety-four. I didn't know real people lived that long." What else? "I took a career assessment this morning. It said I should consider teaching, management and something with marine biology."

He managed a chuckle, and his gaze locked with hers. "You must have said you liked boating."

"I did. At least the management part is interesting."

"Why did you take the assessment?"

"Just to see what it would say. I never considered working anywhere except with my dad. What if that doesn't work out?"

"I know you're mad at him right now, and with good reason, but running your dad's company has always been your dream."

She stretched out her legs. "I think maybe that's the problem. It's my dad's company. I didn't earn my way in, and he's not treating me like I'm a serious employee. I'm his kid, and that's how we've both been acting."

She paused for a second. "Kip, did you know he wasn't going to buy the kayak company?"

He frowned. "No. How would I know that?"

"I thought maybe he told Zafina and she told you."

"What?" he yelped. "I wouldn't not tell you that."

"I wasn't sure."

He swore. "You don't trust me at all, do you? You really think I'd keep that from you? I'm not that guy."

Her chest tightened. "I know. I'm sorry. It's just with everything you didn't tell me about other stuff, I wasn't sure."

He was quiet for a long time. "You're never going to let the Tracey thing go, are you? It's going to hang over my head for-ever."

"It's not just that you were married to Tracey," she admitted. "It's the debt and that you knew about my dad and Zafina and didn't tell me."

Because he didn't want to show himself in a bad light, she thought. He wanted to be the hero. She sat up suddenly as she realized another uncomfortable truth. Kip was act-ing just like her dad.

"Harlow, please don't make me sound so shitty," he said sadly. "I love you, and I take good care of you. I'd never try to hurt you."

"No, but you *are* willing to make deci-sions for me. You're deciding what I can handle and what I can't. Marriage isn't supposed to be like that. We're supposed to be a team, but you're treating me like a child."

"I'm not. I'm taking care of you."

Wasn't that the same thing?

His mouth twisted in frustration. "I can't talk about this now. I have to go to work."

"Kip," she began, then sighed. "Okay. Have a good day."

"You, too."

He hung up. She removed her earbuds and stared out the French doors. She was more sad than angry. Kip didn't want to face their problems, but until they were willing to deal with the truth, they couldn't move forward with their future. Assuming they still had one.

Robyn stepped into her daughter's room.

"Your brother says you're moping," she said cheerfully. "I'm not sure if that's true, but either way, I thought you could help me go through the teacup room."

She half expected her daughter to protest, but Harlow surprised her by scrambling to her feet and saying, "That sounds like fun." She tucked her earbuds into the nightstand drawer, then shoved her phone into her shorts pocket.

"What are you looking for?" Harlow asked as they headed for the stairs.

"I want to go through the sets of dishes. There might be one or two I want to keep for myself. The rest will eventually be sold, unless you're interested in one."

"Really?" Harlow ran up the stairs. "I'd love a set. There are a couple I really like. And if I could have the Spode pattern 312 teacups and saucers, I would love that."

Spode pattern 312 was beautiful, with gilding, pink roses and blue-and-yellow forget-me-nots. The design dated back to the very early 1800s.

"I think I saw a creamer in the same pattern," Robyn told her. "I wonder if there's a sugar bowl somewhere."

"We'll look."

They went into the teacup room. As always, the sight of the beautiful cups and saucers made her happy. Delicate and elegant, they had once graced tables in regular houses with real people. They had been part of celebrations and sad days, held, filled, washed and dried. Somehow they had survived for years. Some for more than two centuries.

Harlow picked up a cup with the Spode pattern 312. "I feel like I'm holding a newborn chick." She wrinkled her nose. "I guess hatched is a better word rather than born."

"I'm more confused about when you would have held a chick at all."

Harlow laughed. "I must have somewhere. Maybe summer camp."

"I don't remember seeing baby chicks on the streets of Naples."

They grinned at each other, then settled on the floor in front of an oversized buffet. Several dish sets were stored in the long, low cabinets.

Robyn pulled open the left door, while Harlow drew back the right. The sturdy shelves overflowed with dishes.

"A lot to look at." Harlow reached for a bowl.

"In every room. Doing inventory is a daunting task." Robyn held out a pretty white-and-yellow plate. "I've been telling Lillian she can't ever die because I love her, but also because I'll be overwhelmed by going through the house."

Harlow looked at her. "What will you do with it all?"

"Some will go to museums, some will stay with the house. The rest I'll sell."

"You're going to start your own antique store?"

Robyn thought about how she'd been looking for a future, when it had been waiting for her right here. "Uh-huh. I'm starting online small business classes. When I head back to Naples, I'll find a job with more hours and get to know all aspects of an antique store."

She would watch her money and move to a smaller house, but she thought it was manageable. At least it was a plan, which was more than she'd had when she'd left Florida.

"That's a lot."

"It is, but it feels right." She set the plate on the floor and pulled out a mismatched bowl. "How are you doing?"

"I don't know. Kip and I are fighting."

"About him being married before?"

"Among other things. He's mad because I said I need time, but not telling me about Tracey is huge." Harlow hesitated as if there were more.

"I get that," Robyn told her, wondering how to encourage her daughter to share her thoughts. "It's an odd piece of information to withhold. You were going to find out eventually."

"I know, right? Plus to hear it from his parents. It was a nightmare. I had to sit through dinner, pretending everything was fine."

Robyn ached for her and wished there was a way to take on some of her daughter's pain. But Harlow was an adult and had to manage her own life.

"I'm glad you're thinking things through," she said. "It's so easy to get caught up in emotion and make a decision you later regret."

Harlow nodded. "I just wish there wasn't so much right now, you know? Dad didn't tell me the truth, either."

Robyn knew she had to be careful with her words. "Sometimes your father doesn't like to give bad news. But however it happened, you know he loves you."

"I've started wondering if he and Kip are more alike than I realized. Kip knows about me being sick as a kid, and he's been fine with it. He always treated me like I was capable. But he didn't tell me about being married, or Dad dating Zafina. Maybe he's protecting me more than I thought. I know Dad's treating me like a child. Is Kip doing the same?"

"It could be Kip is, as you said, protecting you." Robyn sucked in a breath and took a big ol' risk. "It could also be your behavior."

"Mom!"

"You can be emotional and difficult."

Harlow stiffened. Robyn braced herself for a tantrum. Then her daughter surprised her by relaxing.

"You're right. I do lead with my feelings. Like with you selling the house."

"That was a big deal for you."

Harlow looked at her. "Mom, you can't tell me I'm immature and then defend my position."

"I know, but it's hard not to get between you and the bad stuff. A remnant from when you were sick. I try to take the hits for you. Some of this is on me."

"You're blaming yourself for my entitlement issues? No. Only one of us is responsible for that." Harlow pressed her lips together. "Sometimes I'm ashamed. I can be such a bitch."

"Well . . ." Robyn began, her voice teasing.

Harlow sighed. "You know I'm right. Except I feel like Dad tricked me on buying the business. I did everything I was supposed to do. He was totally on board the whole time, then poof. Everything changed. He's so frustrating."

Harlow looked at her. "How did you stay married to him for so long?"

"Being his wife isn't the same as being his daughter." Robyn touched her cheek. "And that is all I'm willing to say on that topic."

Harlow's gaze turned knowing. "You're protecting him. Not because you're still in

love with him, but because he's my father."
She smiled. "You're a good mom. I hope
when I have kids I'm just like you."

The unexpected compliment had Robyn
blinking back tears. "Thank you. That's very
sweet."

"Not that I'm having kids for a while. Like
ten years. I'm not ready. I can barely handle
my life, let alone someone else's. Do you
think —"

Robyn's phone rang. She pulled it out of
her pocket and glanced at her screen.

"It's Mindy, calling instead of texting."
She answered the call. "Hello?"

"It's me. So, the house in Santa Barbara.
Is it some crazy oversized thing that takes
up a couple of city blocks?"

"That's the one. Why?"

"I'm here." Mindy's voice cracked.
"Robyn, I'm in so much trouble. Payne
found out about Dimitri. The look on his
face about killed me. He got so quiet and
was so hurt. It was like he ripped out my
heart. We fought, then he wouldn't talk to
me anymore. I didn't know what to do, so I
left the kids with my mom and flew out
here, to be with you. I hope that's okay."

Robyn opened her mouth, then closed it.
She had no idea what to say. "Um, sure.
Are you in front?"

"I'm in the Uber. I didn't want to let him go until I was sure this was the house."

"It is," Robyn said with a brightness she didn't feel. "Drive around back. Keep going until you see a bunch of cars in front of the garage. I'll meet you downstairs."

She hung up and scrambled to her feet. "Mindy's here."

"Your boss Mindy?"

"That's the one." Robyn hesitated. Harlow was going to learn the truth soon enough. "She had an affair, and her husband just found out. I tried to warn her, but she wouldn't listen. It's a disaster. And now she's here."

Harlow took a couple of steps back. "Wow, that's a lot. Okay, well, good luck dealing with your friend."

"Escaping while you can?"

Harlow grinned. "It seems the sensible thing to do. I'll spend some time with Lillian."

Leaving Robyn to deal with the mess Mindy had made of her life. How fair was that?

Twenty-Three

Harlow found her aunt in her sitting room, photo albums strewn around her. With a smile, Lillian patted the space next to her. "Come sit with me, and we'll go through memories together."

"I'd like that." Harlow settled close and hugged her aunt. "Mom's boss, Mindy, just showed up. I think there's going to be some drama later on."

"Other people's drama is the best kind." Lillian reached for an old, battered photo album. "Let's look at this one. Your uncle is very dashing."

They flipped through pages of pictures. Scribbled notes on the side dated them back to the 1960s.

"You got some good height on your hair," Harlow said, smiling at a picture of her aunt with bangs, a headband and shoulder-length hair that flipped up at the ends. "Your skirt is a little short."

"I was daring, and miniskirts were all the rage." She patted Harlow's arm. "Look at your uncle."

"So handsome. You're a cute couple."

"We were very much in love, right until he died." Lillian sighed. "I won't tell you we never fought, because we did, but we learned from our mistakes and did better."

She turned the page. Harlow stared at the pictures of large crowds with signs about the right to vote.

"What are these?"

Lillian peered at the photographs. "Your uncle and I spent two summers down South, helping register Black folks to vote. It got a little dicey every now and then, but it seemed like the right thing to do."

"You were part of the civil rights movement?"

"They didn't really call it that back then, but I suppose we were."

Harlow studied the pictures more closely. Her aunt and uncle had risked their lives in a social movement that changed the country, and she was whining because her father hadn't been honest about buying her a business?

"I need to work on my priorities," she murmured.

"Why?" her aunt asked.

"I was just thinking how upset I am about my dad, but these pictures put everything in perspective."

She explained about the kayaking business and how she'd thought her father wanted to buy it.

Lillian listened attentively. When Harlow finished, her aunt said, "It seems to me you acted in good faith. He's the one who changed the rules."

"I was entitled. I should have thought it through."

"But you did. You researched the company and understood the numbers. You didn't do anything wrong, Harlow."

"Then why do I feel stupid and young?"

"Because you were betrayed by someone you trust. That always hurts. You've always been tenderhearted."

"You're being too nice, Lillian. I don't feel tenderhearted. I think I can be difficult."

Lillian brushed aside that comment. "I remember when you were a little girl. Maybe ten or eleven. You'd beaten the cancer, but you were still recovering from the treatments. You and Austin and your mom came here for the summer. Leo and I loved having you."

Harlow remembered that time, as well. She'd grown stronger out here, running around with her brother, sailing with her mom. She couldn't recall specifics, but in the back of her mind, there was a sense of sadness about the trip. Something had happened — she just wasn't sure what.

"We were here a long time," Harlow said. "Did I go visit the local elementary school? I sort of remember that."

"You might have looked it over." Lillian carefully avoided her gaze.

"Why would I have done that?"

"You were interested."

She'd been ten. No kid was that interested in another school — especially in summer. She also recalled her mother crying. Robyn had tried to conceal it, but Harlow had found her in tears more than once. There had also been quiet conversations behind closed doors.

"Dad never visited us," she said slowly. "Not until the end when he showed up to tell us he'd bought us a new house with a swimming pool and a view of the water."

The house her mother lived in now. The one she had to sell. A house she'd never really liked.

"Dad bought that house while we were gone. The first time we saw it was when we came home. All our stuff was moved in. But Mom never left here that whole summer."

Harlow stared at her aunt. "Did my dad buy a house and move us into it without my mom ever seeing it?"

Lillian closed the album. "Well, this is awkward. I'm not sure what Robyn would want me to do. I suppose the truth doesn't matter now, so I'll tell you. That's exactly what he did. Your parents were having a difficult time, and he wanted her to be happy."

A month ago, Harlow would have accepted that statement and moved on. But now she knew more. She knew that her father was a chronic cheater who didn't respect the women he was with. Now she knew her father had cheated on her mother, and that was the main reason their marriage had ended.

She thought about the long months of her cancer treatment and how her mother had been there for every second of it. She thought about how her mom had brought her and Austin away for the summer. She remembered visiting the school and her mother crying and hearing, "You'll always be welcome here," from her aunt and uncle.

Twelve years ago, while she'd been dealing with cancer treatments and her mother had been by her side, her father had cheated, and her mom had found out. Things had gotten so bad that her mother had taken her and Austin across the country while she figured out what to do next.

Somehow their dad had convinced her to give him another chance. Harlow wasn't sure if the house was a bribe or what, but somehow it played into all this.

"I didn't know," Harlow whispered. "About any of it."

"You were a child, darling. You weren't supposed to know."

Her mother had protected her and her brother. She'd never let on there were problems or what Cord had done. She'd made the summer happy and wonderful, allowing Harlow to heal. And in the end, she'd taken her children home because that was where they would be happiest.

"I don't know if I could do that," Harlow admitted. "Sacrifice myself for my kids."

"You would. It's biological. When you have children, everything changes."

She thought that might be true. Everything had changed for Robyn. Even if Cord had sworn he would never cheat again, she'd suffered through the pain of it. She'd been betrayed by the one person who had vowed to love and protect her forever. Once shattered, how could that trust be rebuilt? How could she have gone on for so long?

Harlow had known in her head that marriage was hard and love required a lot, but until this exact second, she hadn't understood what that really meant. The bigness of loving someone else. The responsibility of having children. Thinking about that now put her own problems in perspective.

"I have a really great life," she said aloud.

Lillian smiled. "That makes me happy, sweet girl. It's all I've ever wanted for you and your brother. To have a really great life."

After three hours of listening to Mindy sob, cry, and swear she couldn't understand what had gone wrong, Robyn escaped. Her claim of needing to get dinner started was actually the truth, which helped her say the words sympathetically, as if she really didn't want to leave her friend.

Not that she didn't care about Mindy and how she'd screwed up. She did. Mostly. It just wasn't a surprise. Of course Payne was going to find out — Mindy wasn't an experienced cheater and liar. She was a bored novice who had done something incredibly dumb, and now she was paying the price for it. As was Payne.

In the kitchen, Robyn went through the contents of the refrigerator and pantry, then thought about how many people they now had to feed. Assuming Mindy stayed for a few days, which seemed likely, there were six adults, including an eighteen-year-old male who ate enough for three regular people.

They'd already gone through all the chicken Mason had bought at Costco, not to mention the cookies and the pies. There were three steaks in the freezer, but that wasn't nearly enough.

She made a menu and grocery list for the next couple of days, including breakfasts and lunches. She was just finishing it when Harlow walked into the kitchen.

"How's Mindy?" her daughter asked, looking concerned. "I could hear her crying from the hallway."

"It hit the fan, and she's sorry about that, but I'm less sure she regrets actually sleeping with Dimitri." Robyn held up her hand. "That came out more harshly than I intended. Ignore my mood."

Harlow surprised her by hugging her. "Mom, this *is* a lot. You came out here to think about your own life, when suddenly you're dealing with me and Austin and now Mindy."

"Thanks for understanding. I'll be fine. I've already talked to Salvia and told her the invasion is my responsibility, not hers. She's here for Lillian. She's going to get someone in to help with the extra cleaning, starting tomorrow. We'll handle our own cooking, shopping and kitchen duties. I'm going to need you and Austin to help with that."

"Sure. Let's start now. What do you need?"

The cheerful attitude was a bit unexpected, but Robyn wasn't going to question it. "If you could do grocery shopping, that would be a big help. I'll reimburse you for the food."

Harlow scanned the list. "This is very doable. I'll get Austin to come with me."

"Thank you." Robyn looked at her. "I'm sorry our time together got cut short."

"Me, too, but we'll be able to talk when this settles down. Do you think Mindy will be getting a divorce?"

"I have no idea. She's suddenly realized how important her marriage is to her, but it might be too late. I'm not sure Payne will forgive and forget."

"I wouldn't," Harlow said flatly. "Kip's used up all his extra credit with me already. If I found out he'd cheated, I would break up with him and then back his car off a pier."

Robyn held in a smile. "You might want

to stick with ending things and avoid the felony."

"Fine. I'll break up with him and *think* about backing his car off a pier." Harlow waved the list. "I'm heading out now. Austin's in his room, right?"

"Last I heard."

Her daughter left. Robyn returned her attention to what she had on hand for dinner. There were four nice-looking avocados for guacamole and several freshly picked tomatoes for salsa. She had tortilla chips in the pantry, along with spaghetti, beans and plenty of spices for her to make her own taco seasoning. Harlow and Austin would bring back lettuce for salad. As she didn't think Lillian was up for taco spaghetti for dinner, Robyn would make fresh gazpacho to go with her salad and maybe a small cheese plate.

She went to work, prepping the salsa and leaving it out for the flavors to meld. She would make the guacamole last. She combined chili, garlic and onion powder along with oregano, paprika and cumin to make taco seasoning and put it in a jar. She'd just started dicing onions when Mason walked into the kitchen.

The second she saw him, she dropped her knife onto the counter and walked into his outstretched arms. He hugged her tight, holding her as if he would never let go, which was exactly what she needed. She clung to him, pressing her face into his shoulder.

He felt good — strong and steady. She ignored the tingles and jolts that came from being this close to him. Right now comfort was more important than sex.

"Did we get a ghost?" he asked, speaking into her ear. "I can hear a woman crying somewhere in the house."

She laughed, thought for a second she might start crying, although she had no idea why, then laughed again.

"Mindy showed up."

"Ah, the stupid friend."

"Payne, her husband, found out. He's devastated. They had a big fight. He's crushed, Mindy feels guilty and didn't know what to do next, so she left her kids with her parents and flew out here."

"You okay with that?"

"I'm not sure I have a choice. Lillian's very understanding. She pointed out the house was plenty big, and as long as the emotional drama isn't coming from one of us, she's happy to be a spectator." Robyn leaned against him again. "I put her on the third floor."

"You want her comfortable but not *too* comfortable."

"Uh-huh." She drew back again. "Am I crazy, or is her trip here really impulsive?"

His dark gaze was steady. "She's dealing with a potentially life-altering reality, and it's her own fault. Under those circumstances, running makes sense."

"I get that, but why here? She has sisters. Plus, she knew I didn't approve of the affair. It's not like I'm going to tell her what she wants to hear."

"Maybe she wants the hard truth," he told her. "Maybe she thinks it's time she faced the consequences of her actions."

"You're so rational."

"Years of training. Know what to do and do it right. It's not very interesting or fun, but it gets the job done."

"I think it's very interesting and appealing."

One corner of his mouth turned up. "But not fun."

She smiled. "You're fun in other ways."

"So are you." He looked around the kitchen. "Where are the kids?"

"Grocery shopping. More people means more planning."

"It does. I'll wash my hands. Then you can put me to work."

Because he would step in to help where he was needed, she thought, grateful for him in more ways than he could know. He wouldn't complain or protest the job was beneath him. He wouldn't tell her there was a game on or that she took things too seriously. He would simply do the job.

Not a characteristic every woman would appreciate, but as far as she was concerned, it was sexy as hell.

Mason set the table, then found the large serving bowls Robyn needed. When the kids got back, he helped put away the groceries.

"Dinner's in about forty-five minutes," Robyn said. "Mason, would you make Lillian's cocktail? I don't want her feeling left out in the sudden frenzy."

"I always enjoy spending time with her. What about you? Can I bring you a cocktail?"

She smiled at him. A warm, happy smile that always kicked him in the gut.

"I think I should stay sober for a while longer," she said with a laugh. "But I'll be having wine with dinner."

"Then I'll go hang out with Lillian."

"I'll join you," Harlow said, falling into step with him. "Give me a second to go wash up. You'll be on her balcony?"

"Yes."

"I'll do the grunt work for Mom," Austin said.

Mason raised his eyebrows. "Grunt work?"

The teen grinned. "No offense."

"None taken."

Mason walked to the stairs with Harlow. He wasn't sure why Robyn's daughter wanted to join him and Lillian. Maybe she was just being friendly, or perhaps she wanted to get to know him better in an effort to protect her mother. Either was fine.

He thought about what Austin had told him — about knowing that his father had cheated on his mother from the time Austin had been a kid. That had been a tough burden to carry. At least Harlow hadn't learned about her father's shitty behavior until recently, according to Robyn.

"I'm making a salty dog for Lillian," he said. "Want to try one?"

"I would. Thanks."

He found Lillian in her usual place on the balcony — on her chaise, blanket on her legs, eyes closed. He paused, not wanting to wake her up. Then she opened her eyes and reached for his hand.

"Mason! I was hoping you'd come see me."

He bent down and kissed her cheek. "I'm

410

going to make you a twist on a salty dog. Using tequila and lemonade."

"Lovely. You'll join me?"

"Of course."

Salvia had left fresh lemonade in the small refrigerator in the sitting room. He salted the rims of three glasses, then mixed two drinks and carried them over to Lillian. She took hers and smiled at him.

"This is a treat. I don't usually get you all to myself."

"You're very flattering. Harlow's going to join us in a bit."

"That will be nice, too."

He took a seat. She sipped her drink, then sighed. "Very nice. Unexpected. I love the salt." Her smile turned sly. "I like that you don't assume I'm supposed to be watching my salt intake."

"You don't seem to have many dietary restrictions."

"I've been blessed with good health."

He told her about Robyn's plans for her dinner.

"I love a gazpacho," Lillian told him. "That's perfect. I'm not sure what taco spaghetti is, and to be honest, it sounds dreadful."

He laughed. "I'm looking forward to it."

"I used to eat foods like that. No interest

anymore. But I'm glad everyone else will be happy." She lowered her voice. "Have you met Robyn's friend?"

"No, but I've heard her crying."

"The tears seem a little late, if you ask me." Lillian took another sip. "But I'll be polite at dinner. Are you all right with the added company?"

He wasn't sure what she was asking. "Shouldn't I be?"

"This isn't what you thought you were getting into. First Robyn, then Harlow and Austin. Now her friend Mindy. It's a houseful."

"This house can handle it."

"That's true. But you've lived alone for a long time. Is it too much?"

"I like having people around."

"Good."

Harlow walked in. She'd changed out of her shorts and T-shirt into a summer dress. Mason fixed her drink, then handed it to her. She thanked him and flopped down into a chair.

"You can hear her crying up and down the hall," she said. "I feel bad for Mom having to deal with her."

Robyn did seem to be the person everyone ran to, he thought.

Harlow sipped her drink, then looked at

him. "Austin tells me you go jogging every morning. Mind if I join you?"

The request surprised him. "I'm out of here by six."

"I can do that." Harlow smiled. "So, tomorrow morning by the garage at six?"

"I'll be there."

"Me, too."

"I Since he is you ber...
him. "Austin told me you go jogging every
morning, Mind if I run you"
The researcher spread him: "I want to
bare break.
I' glad on that B. Elslow said, 3, '50
morrow I gonna to the gone at
I do th
Ms. Do

TWENTY-FOUR

"Isn't it like five-thirty in the morning?" Enid asked with a laugh. "Why are you up?"

"I'm jogging with Mason and Austin at six. I thought I'd call you first and see what's going on."

"Everything is great. I'm working more hours, and your dad gave me a raise."

Harlow exhaled slowly, grateful her father hadn't taken out his temper on her friend. "Just checking. It's easy to leave stuff out in a text."

"Hey, I wouldn't do that." Enid lowered her voice. "He misses you, by the way. Keeps asking if I've heard from you."

Harlow knew they were still talking about her dad. "Funny, because he never texts me himself."

"You don't text him, either."

"Taking his side?"

"Nope, just pointing out the obvious. I'm good at that."

Harlow grinned as she walked back and forth in her room, warming up her muscles. "I'll send him a quick hi. How's that?"

"Very mature of you. And speaking of missing, how are things with Kip?"

"About the same. He wants me to come home, and I need more time."

"But you're still together."

"Of course. I love him."

"Just checking. I know he's pulled some stuff, but he does love you." Enid paused. "I gotta get ready for my charter. You should go back to bed."

"I'm going running. As a future doctor, you should be excited about my commitment to exercise."

"You're already pretty active. I don't worry about you that way. Talk soon."

"Absolutely."

Harlow hung up and tossed her phone on the bed. For a second she thought about putting in a quick call to Kip, but she decided against it. She was still processing their last conversation. Texting was safer.

She put on shorts, a tank top, and running shoes. She went into the bathroom, where she pulled her hair into a ponytail and slathered on sunscreen. When that was done, she collected her phone and a hat, then knocked on her brother's door.

"You ready?"

He opened it, already dressed. "Just waiting on you, sis."

They went downstairs together and found Mason waiting by the cars.

"We can take mine," he said, opening the driver's door.

Harlow pushed Austin toward the front passenger seat, then got in back. "Where are we going?"

"There's a path that goes by the marina. I like to run there. You up for five miles?"

"Sure," she said, hoping she was. Her runs at home were closer to three or four miles, but she figured she could push herself. "What about you, Austin? Want us to leave you behind?"

"Very funny. I can keep up."

They were quiet as they drove down the hill, then out to the water. Mason parked in a public lot, and they got out.

"We'll go slow to warm up," Mason told him. "Stretch at the end. I'll keep a steady pace. Shout out if it's too much for you. No point in getting hurt just to try to look good."

"You're taking charge?" Harlow asked.

Mason looked at her, amusement darkening his eyes. "Yeah, I'm taking charge."

She grinned. "Just asking."

"Good. Let's go."

He started for the path. Once there, he broke into a slow jog. After a couple of minutes, Harlow glanced at her brother.

"You hear from Dad?"

"No. You?"

"No. I talked to Enid this morning, and she pointed out I could get in touch with him. I'm not sure I'm ready to be that mature." She didn't mention Enid saying he claimed to miss her, knowing that might hurt Austin's feelings.

"You should make up with him," her brother said. "You're going back to work with him. It's what you've always wanted."

"I did. Now I'm less sure." She looked at Mason. "Did you hear what happened with my dad?"

"Some."

She filled him in on the low points of finding out he hadn't ever planned to buy the business.

"I'm not sure what to do with all that," she admitted. "I feel played, which is yucky, but it's more than that. I was so entitled. It's not a comfortable feeling."

"You didn't like being entitled?" he asked as he increased his pace.

"Everyone likes being entitled," Austin said. "Knowing the world will do your bidding is great. It's finding out that you're selfish and thoughtless that sucks."

Harlow winced. "Is that how you see me?"

"No. That's how you see yourself."

She groaned. "It's early. Don't be insightful. I just wish I knew what to do with my life."

"You'd never want a job with another company," her brother told her. "You love the business."

She did, but did that make it the right place for her? "I've never worked anywhere else. I wouldn't know what that was like."

"Maybe that's the problem," Mason said. "You lack perspective. And maybe a little courage. New things can be threatening. What do you want?"

"To not be stupid." She glanced out at the water. The sun had barely cleared the mountains and was starting to shimmer on the water. "To be proud of what I do in a day. To offer something of value."

"Those are all on you. Where you work doesn't matter. If you want to be proud of yourself, then take pride in your job and how you do it. If you don't want to be stupid, stop making boneheaded decisions."

"You make it sound easy."

He looked at her. "It is. Do the right thing or don't. Live with the consequences."

"You ever screw up?"

He surprised her by smiling. "All the damn time."

"I'm going to San Diego," Austin said. "To check out the university and poke around a little. I'll let Mom know, then head out. Want to come?"

Harlow shook her head. "There's a lot going on here, and Mom shouldn't have to handle it all herself."

Mason's expression turned approving. "See, there you go, making the right decision."

She smiled. "Why do I feel what you're really thinking is something along the lines of what people said to their dogs? 'Good girl, Harlow. Good sit.' "

Mason chuckled. He glanced at Austin. "Going to check out the ROTC office?"

"It's on the list."

"You're really considering joining the navy?" Harlow asked. "For real?"

"Yeah. I think I'll do well there. I can handle the discipline, and I've always enjoyed being on the water. I want to serve. It feels right."

"It's a way of life," Mason told him. "And a lot more than a job."

"That's what I want."

"When you talk to your mother, make

sure she knows where you're going and why," Mason said firmly. "Clear?"

Austin looked at Harlow. "Do you believe this guy?"

"He's not wrong. Tell Mom. She can handle it."

She liked that Mason was looking out for her mom, and that he was honest. Right now telling the truth seemed to be in short supply.

"I'll tell her I'm looking at UC San Diego," Austin said. "But I'm not telling her about ROTC until I know that's what I want. She's got enough going on without me stressing her. If I do it, there will be time for her to deal."

Harlow grinned at him. "Okay, little brother. You'll have twenty-four hours after your return to cough it up. Otherwise, I'm going to let Mason rip you a new one."

Austin glanced in his direction. "Fair enough. I'm pretty sure he could take me."

Mason chuckled. "Damned straight I could."

They finished their run and took a few minutes to stretch before getting in the car. Back at the house, Harlow went to her mother's room. She knocked once and waited for the cautious, "Come in," before entering.

Her mother stepped out of the bathroom and immediately relaxed when she saw Harlow.

"I thought you were Mindy," she admitted in a low voice. "I was up with her until after midnight."

"I'm sorry. Not fun."

"No, but she obviously needs to talk." Her mom smiled at her. "How was your run?"

"Good. Mason kept us in line."

Her mom grinned. "How did you react to that?"

"Surprisingly well." She laughed. "I know this sounds strange, but I really like him." Her smile faded. "I'm sorry I assumed the worst."

Her mother hugged her. "Forgotten and behind us. Want to help me with breakfast?"

"Absolutely. But before we go down, I want to say something."

Her mother waited.

Harlow drew in a breath. "I hope you're going to sell the house. It's too big and too expensive, and you've never liked it. Keeping it would be ridiculous. You hung on to it so Austin wouldn't have to move while finishing high school, but there's no point in hanging on to it now. I'm sorry I pressured you about it. I won't do that again."

Her mom smiled. "That's very sweet. I

appreciate your support and that you can see my side of things."

Harlow hung her head. "You don't have to be nice to me. I was so awful. My God, selfish much?"

"Let it go, sweetie. I have." Her mom stepped back. "Where will you hold the wedding?"

Harlow winced. "Yeah, I'm not thinking about the wedding right now. Kip and I have a lot of things to work out before we start planning the ceremony."

Her mother studied her. "Are you two going to be all right?"

Harlow wanted to confess that she wasn't sure, that she was scared, mad and confused when it came to Kip. Only everyone else was dumping on her mom right now.

"We'll be fine," Harlow said easily. "Let's go make breakfast for the herd."

Her mother looked at her. "You sure you're okay?"

"I'm getting through it," she said honestly, walking to the door. "And I'll be stronger for the struggle."

Robyn would have thought that eventually Mindy would run out of fluids. Who knew a person could cry that much for that long? But after three days of rehashing the same material over and over again, Robyn was losing her patience.

"He was so angry and hurt," Mindy said, sobbing into a tissue. "The look on his face."

Robyn patted her friend's knee, then stood. "Okay, don't take this wrong, but I need a break. Why don't you shower and meet me downstairs? We'll go for a walk or something, to clear our heads."

Mindy blinked at her, obviously not sure if she should be offended or obedient. Fortunately, instead of shrieking or throwing something, she nodded slowly.

"I would like to take a shower."

Robyn fled the bedroom before Mindy could change her mind. She raced to the main floor and ducked into the kitchen for more coffee and possibly an escape route.

Harlow was at the big kitchen table, working on her laptop. She looked up as her mom entered.

"What's wrong? You look . . . I don't know. Upset maybe?"

"More afraid," Robyn admitted, pouring coffee into a mug. "I'm not sure how much longer I can listen to Mindy have the same stupid conversation." Robyn crossed to the table and took a seat. "What are you working on?"

"Trying to figure out what to do with my life."

Robyn laughed as she settled across from her daughter. "Gee, I've been doing the same thing. Want to compare notes?"

Harlow nodded. "Absolutely. You're going to open an antique store, right?"

"That's the long-term plan. Hopefully very long-term."

"Are you going to move back to Naples?"

The question surprised Robyn. "Why would you ask that?"

Harlow closed her laptop. "I don't know. You like it here. Austin's down in San Diego, looking at going to college there. I'm an adult. I wasn't sure you wanted to go back to your old life. I mean, Mason's here."

"I'm not moving anywhere because of a man," Robyn said firmly. "I did too much I didn't want to do when I was married."

She paused, wishing she'd phrased that statement a little differently. "What I mean is —"

Harlow touched the back of her hand. "I know what you mean, Mom. It's everything from not going to college to agreeing to live in the house Dad bought." She hesitated. "You gave him more chances than he deserved, and in the end he cheated again."

Their eyes met. "I wish we weren't having

424

this conversation," Robyn admitted. "Mostly because I wish you didn't know what happened." She was pretty sure her daughter only had broad strokes, but they were enough. "What happened between your father and me is our rock to carry. Not yours. I don't want this to be an added stress."

"It's not that, exactly. More eye-opening. I get what you mean about defining yourself through Dad. Mason wouldn't be like that."

"I know. I'm just cautious."

"But you like him?"

Robyn smiled. "I do. Very much."

"Me, too. Don't take this wrong, but Jase wasn't exactly warm. Mason likes people. He doesn't take a lot of crap from anyone. I respect that." She smiled. "And back to my original point, which was a really good one, you don't have to come back to Florida. Things are different now."

Robyn leaned toward her. "Lillian's asked me to move in with her. I think she would like the company."

"Are you considering it?"

"I hadn't been. I'd assumed I was needed at home. But you're right about Austin. If he's getting ready to go to college, then I can relax about him. Which leaves only you." Robyn studied her daughter. "I'm not sure I'm comfortable with you on the other side of the country."

"I don't like it, either, but you can't live your life based on me."

"Okay," Robyn said slowly. "What does that mean?"

"I'm trying to grow up," Harlow said lightly. "Be less selfish. You're still young, Mom. You have to think about what you want."

"And when you have my first grandchild? Don't you think I want to be there?"

Harlow's eyes widened. "That is not happening for years. Like years and years. That's a far, far out in the future thing."

Robyn hid a smile. "Okay, no pressure."

"Jeez. Kids! Way to spoil the mood."

"So if you're not looking to get pregnant, what are you going to do?"

Harlow surprised her by sighing. "I don't know. I'm still working through what happened with Dad."

"Your dad has flaws, but so does everyone. Harlow, I know what he did was wrong and you're the one suffering, but I would hate to see you throw away the dream you've carried for so long because of that. Your dad won't want to work into his eighties. In a few years, he'll be ready to cut back, and you'll want to be there to take his place."

Harlow rested her chin on her hand. "Maybe. I don't know. I've never worked anywhere else, Mom. I haven't even ever filled out a job application. Maybe I should get some experience with another company before going back to work for Dad."

Robyn did her best not to let her shock show. She'd never heard her daughter talk like this. "Where would you go?"

Harlow raised the top of her laptop and turned it so Robyn could see the screen. "There's a charter company in the Keys that's about the same size as Dad's. I know the owner's son. We were at college together." She smiled wistfully. "I met his dad a couple of times, and he joked about hiring me away. I don't know if he was just being nice, but maybe I should talk to him."

Robyn glanced at the website and back at her daughter. "I don't know what to say."

"Me, either. I'm just thinking about stuff. Maybe if I got experience somewhere else, Dad would take me more seriously. Maybe it would be good for me to not be the boss's kid and have to make it by myself."

"You've worked hard. You did great at college."

Harlow didn't look convinced. "That's

school, not real life. I want to earn my place. I don't want it handed to me."

"You're a really good charter captain."

Harlow relaxed. "I am. I do good work. So it might be time to prove that to the world." Her mouth curved up. "Plus, if you're right about Dad wanting to step down in a few years, then he'll be anxious to get me back." She closed her laptop again. "I'm not making any decisions right this second, but I'm considering options. You should be proud."

"I always am." Her little girl was growing up. Robyn knew it was inevitable, but to see it happen in front of her was unexpected.

"So about today," Harlow said. "I was thinking wine tasting."

"What do you mean?"

"You, me, Mindy and Mason go wine tasting. I talked to Lillian earlier, and she would rather stay here. So we'll drive in, taste a little wine, give you a break from Mindy and get buzzed."

Robyn glanced over her shoulder, then lowered her voice. "I'm in. Anything to keep me from having the same conversation with Mindy."

TWENTY-FIVE

Mason parked just off State Street. He'd never been a wine tasting kind of guy, but it appeared he was unable to refuse Robyn anything. She hadn't even been trying all that hard. She'd simply walked into his office, smiled and asked if he wanted to go with her, Harlow and Mindy. Mindy, who did nothing but cry all day long. Even at dinner, she frequently dissolved into tears before excusing herself and racing out of the room, the sounds of her sobs getting fainter and fainter until she locked herself in her third-floor room.

He wasn't big on female tears. Break an arm, sure. Lose someone you loved, yup. Go for it. But crying as the result of stupidity — he had no patience for it.

But here he was, getting out of his car, ready to taste a bunch of pansy-assed wines with a woman who probably cried more when she was drunk. He needed to get his head on straight. That or take Robyn to bed, make love with her for real and then not give a shit about the rest of the world.

Cheered by that image, he managed a smile when Harlow asked him if he was excited about their outing.

"Can't wait," he told her.

She grinned. "I wouldn't have taken you for the wine tasting type."

"I always enjoy learning new things."

She eyed him. "Can you be rattled, even a little?"

Involuntarily, he glanced at her mother and saw Robyn's little smirk.

"Every now and then," he admitted, returning his attention to Harlow. "But not that often."

They crossed the street and entered a wine tasting room. Mason glanced around, assuming the beamed ceiling and oddly paned windows were meant to replicate a wine cellar. Fake ivy was artfully draped along the walls, and a couple of murals looped around arched doorways.

"How quaint," Mindy murmured, looking around.

A woman in her late twenties smiled and approached them. "Welcome," she said. "You're just in time for our afternoon tasting." She motioned to a menu on a chalkboard. "You simply have to decide on how many wines you'd like to taste and if you'd prefer whites, reds or a mix." She smiled. "Then I can get you a table for four."

They were shown to a table on the shaded patio and handed tasting menus. The three women discussed what they would order. Mason pushed the menu to the side.

"I'll have a soda."

Robyn frowned. "Why? You like wine."

"I'm driving."

"I want to push back on that," she admitted. "It doesn't seem fair that you should be the designated driver."

His dark gaze locked with hers. "You can push all you want."

"You can't be moved?"

"Oh, I can be moved, but I won't be drinking."

Her eyes dilated slightly, and she swayed toward him. He had a feeling she'd forgotten they weren't alone. He forced himself to look away and asked, "What looks good, Mindy?"

"I don't know," her weepy friend said. "I wonder if I could get a few doubles."

Two hours later, Mason escorted the ladies back to his car. Robyn and Harlow were slightly buzzed, in a charming, relaxed way. Mindy had teared up twice at the table, making him look longingly for the exits.

They managed to get her into the car without her bursting into tears, and he drove directly back to the house. The sooner he was away from her, the better.

He pulled into the driveway only to see an unfamiliar rental car by the garage.

"We have company," he said, looking around to see who had rented the Toyota. Just then a guy with glasses and thinning hair stepped out of the house. Beside him, Robyn stiffened.

"Payne?" Mindy said from the backseat. "Is that Payne?"

"The husband," Robyn whispered.

"Good thing it's a big house," Mason murmured.

He put the car in Park, and they all got out. Mindy walked toward her husband, her steps hesitant.

"What are you doing here?"

He stared at her, obviously miserable. "You're my wife. Where else would I be?"

"You told me you'd never forgive me."

"I don't know if I can, but don't you think we should talk about it?"

Mindy burst into tears. Mason grabbed Robyn and Harlow by the upper arms and hustled them both inside.

"Run," he said quietly when they were in

the kitchen. "Run and hide."

Harlow grinned at him. "I thought you were some tough soldier. You're supposed to stand and fight."

"Every day, no problem. But not with the weeper around. God knows what Payne's going to start yelling." He grimaced. "What if they both start crying?"

"A nightmare," Harlow said solemnly.

"Damned straight."

She waved at them. "I'm going to check on Lillian. Then I have a FaceTime call with Kip. I'll take the secret staircases and avoid the main hallways. I suggest you two do the same."

Mason looked at Robyn. "Was I too harsh about your friend?"

Her blue eyes were bright with laughter. "No, and I admire your ability to say exactly what I'm thinking, only in a more direct way."

She put her hands on his chest and smiled at him. "Do you know what I'm thinking now?"

Heat poured into him, making him hard and hungry in less than a heartbeat.

"I believe I do."

"Did you get to the store?"

"I have a box of condoms sitting in my nightstand."

433

"Oh, goodie." She raised herself on tiptoes and lightly kissed him. "Want to go make sure they fit?"

"I thought you'd never ask."

"It's been quiet for a while now," Robyn said, sitting across from Lillian in the breakfast room. It was nearly ten in the morning, and they were having tea and scones. A very civilized way to enjoy life, she thought.

Of course these days she was pretty much happy all the time — the result of dozens of Mason-induced orgasms.

They had been lovers — real lovers — for nearly thirty-six hours. They'd spent the past two nights together, touching, exploring, learning and pleasing each other. There hadn't been enough sleep, but that was for later. Right now she was enjoying the feeling of general well-being and smug satisfaction.

"They could be sleeping," Lillian said, putting jam on her scone. "Or maybe they're having sex."

Payne and Mindy had been holed up in her room for much of the past day and a half. They'd appeared briefly for dinner, Mindy looking red-eyed and defeated, Payne seeming more confused than angry.

But since then, no one had seen them. There had been plenty of shouting and crying, but little else.

"I hope it's sex," Lillian added with a smile. "That's so much more interesting than fighting."

Before Robyn could figure out what to say to that, Austin walked in, looking tall and tanned and happy. She rushed to him.

"You're back! How was the trip? Did you like UC San Diego? Is it a contender?"

She told herself to stop talking so much. Austin being interested in going to college was its own reward. Pushing wouldn't help. Her youngest made up his own mind, in his own time.

"Mom!" He pulled her tightly against him, then swung her around. "I missed you."

She laughed. "And you missed all the drama with Mindy. Payne showed up two days ago, and no one knows what's happening. Are you hungry? Want some tea?"

He glanced at the table. "Any coffee?"

"There should be some."

She got Austin coffee, along with a couple of bananas. When she returned to the breakfast room, he was seated next to Lillian and eating a scone.

"Did you drive back this morning?" she asked.

"I couldn't sleep, so I checked out of the motel a little before six. Because it's Saturday, traffic was light, and I made good time."

He reached for a banana. "I toured the campus. I liked it a lot. I want to apply there, Mom."

Robyn told herself to act calm. Shrieking would only make him question his decision. But on the inside, she was jumping and dancing. College! At last. Austin could take time and figure out what he wanted to do with his life. He would meet new people, see there was a world beyond working for his Dad.

But instead of saying all that, she nodded and murmured, "It's a great school. Plus, San Diego is a fantastic city. Do you know what you want to study?"

He finished his banana, then wiped his hands on a napkin. His gaze met hers.

"I want to apply to the navy ROTC."

He kept talking, but she didn't hear anything else. There was a roaring sound, and she thought maybe her heart had stopped beating. Except she was still sitting upright, and if her heart had stopped, wouldn't she collapse?

Fury, fear and a sense of betrayal battled for dominance. How could he? She'd trusted him. She'd *slept* with him! And all the time he'd been going behind her back to convince her son to —

"Mom!" Austin said sharply. "You're not listening."

She ignored the pounding in her ears and the sense that she couldn't catch her breath so she could focus on her son. "I'm here."

Austin's mouth twisted. "I know what you're thinking. Mason has nothing to do with this. This isn't a new idea. I talked to the ROTC people last year. One of the times I went to visit Harlow, I went by the office and got information. It's been on my mind for a while. I just wasn't ready, you know. After high school? It seemed too soon. I wanted to be sure. It's a big commitment."

He looked at her. She could see the man he would become and the little boy he had been. Images flashed in her mind. Of him learning to ride a bike. Of him surfing when there was a riptide and how she'd struggled to drag him on shore. Of them laughing together, and the Saturday afternoon his first girlfriend had dumped him and broken his heart.

"Don't cry," he whispered.

"I'm not," she said, even as she wiped her face and found tears.

Lillian squeezed his hand. "I'm so proud

of you, Austin. You're going to be a wonderful naval officer."

He kissed her cheek, then got out of his chair and came around to Robyn's. He crouched next to her and hugged her tight. "Mom, you gotta let me go. It's time, and this is what I want to do."

What if you get killed? Only she didn't ask that because they both knew it was a possibility. On any given day, something awful could happen.

She forced herself to nod. "If it's what you want, then it's what you should do."

"You sure?"

"Yes. Congratulations. That's a big decision."

He grinned and returned to his seat. "I have it all worked out. I need a year to establish residency so I can pay in-state tuition. I'll get a job working for a charter company or at a marina. I want to sign up for an SAT study course and take the test again. I could do better on my scores."

"You have a plan," she said, impressed by how much he'd thought through.

"I'll apply this fall, start next fall. I'll be a year older than most of the other students, but that's okay." He flashed a grin. "The girls will think I'm hot."

"They will. Be careful with that."

438

"Mom, come on. It's me." He picked up another scone. "This changes things for you, back in Florida. Maybe you don't want to buy a house. You could get a condo, or rent somewhere and figure out your next act."

"You should both live here," Lillian said firmly. "I'd like the company. Austin, you can find work here just as easily as anywhere else. Robyn, you know how I feel about you staying." Lillian turned to Austin. "I've practically been begging her not to go on a daily basis."

"You've asked twice," Robyn said with a smile.

"Now you can think about it seriously."

"Let's take things one at a time," she said easily. "Austin, I'm really proud of you."

"Thanks, Mom." He turned to his great-great-aunt. "And thank you for letting me stay here. I'd like that a lot."

"Excellent," Lillian said with a sigh. "I'm very happy. Now to ask the awkward question, my dear boy. Have you spoken with your father?"

Austin shifted uncomfortably. Robyn held in a groan. Cord wasn't going to take the news very well. He'd never wanted his kids to consider military service. He would rather they worked with him.

"I was gonna call," Austin said, a definite whine to his voice. "It's hard with the time difference."

"He's not expecting you back anytime soon," Robyn offered. "You quit your job."

Her son nodded glumly. "Yeah, but we both know he expects me to come running and beg for it back. I'll call him later today."

"If it gets too bad, tell him to call me. I'll talk him down."

"Thanks, Mom."

"You're welcome."

Robyn excused herself and went in search of Mason. In the middle of the morning, he could usually be found in his office.

Sure enough he was seated there, typing earnestly, his focus on the screen in front of him.

He didn't notice her at first, so she had a second to study his face. She knew his moods now, could read when he was happy, annoyed or about to lose control in a vortex of pleasure that was thrilling to watch. She recognized his scent and his voice. She knew that while he was polite and restrained in public, he was more than willing to let go in private.

He was a good man, she thought, knowing that was a more rare characteristic than she would like to admit.

440

He looked up and caught sight of her. His mouth immediately curled into a slow, sexy smile. He was halfway across the room before she stopped him with a raised hand.

"Not so fast, mister."

One eyebrow rose.

"Austin's back," she said, putting her hands on her hips. "You didn't want to tell me he was interested the navy ROTC program? You didn't think that was information I should have?"

"I didn't talk him into anything."

"I know that. He's not a kid who's easily influenced, but he came to you with questions, and you knew where he was going."

Mason's dark gaze was steady. "I told him I wouldn't keep secrets. That he had to tell you what he was doing or I would tell you myself. He said he wanted to visit the ROTC office first, to make sure it was what he wanted, and if it was, he would tell you as soon as he got home." His expression softened. "He didn't want you worrying until he'd made a decision."

All of which made sense, but still . . . "You should have told me."

"I respected his request to stay quiet for a few days."

"But he's my kid."

"Yes, he is." His tone was cautious, as if

he wasn't sure how this was going to go.

Robyn wasn't actually angry — she was more interested in finding out how things had happened between Austin and Mason. While she liked him a lot, he still had to earn her trust.

"It was a judgment call," he said. "I did what I thought was best. If you don't agree, we should talk about it."

"He wants to join the navy. I don't know how I feel about that."

"The kid has potential. He's smart, he makes decisions with his head, and he's steady. He'll be a good officer. He wants to command a destroyer."

"So he'll be gone six months at a time."

One corner of his mouth turned up. "Not everything is about you."

She closed the distance between them and felt him wrap his arms around her. She rested her head on his shoulder. "I like having my kids close. He's going away."

"They grow up. It's God's way of saying go find a hobby."

She found herself laughing and crying at the same time. She grabbed his hand, then pulled him along behind her. She walked to the bookcase-lined wall, fumbled under a shelf until she found a lever, then eased it back and slid the bookcase to the side.

"Holy shit!" Mason stared at the man-sized opening. "Another secret passage? Where does this one go?"

"To the master bedroom. Lillian's still downstairs with Austin, so we can go from her room to mine."

She flipped the light switch. Mason followed, then pulled the bookcase back into the place. Together they went upstairs and came out, as she'd promised, in Lillian's sitting room. From there it was an easy walk to her room.

Once they were inside, she locked the door and turned to him.

"I need you," she said simply.

"You have me, body and soul. You should know that by now."

"Oh, Mason."

She had more she wanted to say — including the fact that he was the most unexpected, wonderful surprise. But once he started kissing her and touching her, talking seemed very, very overrated.

TWENTY-SIX

Harlow absently stroked the cat on her desk. Queen Mary, a stunning gray cat, had draped herself around Harlow's laptop, making it nearly impossible to type. Under normal circumstances, that would be annoying, but this morning Harlow was grateful for the impediment. Without it, she would be forced to answer the email on her screen, and she wasn't ready.

I'm going to have an opening the first of September. The charters vary. Fishing, sightseeing. We do a regular circumnavigation of the Key. We also do a three day trip up and down the Keys, but you'd have to work your way into handling that.

I'd be happy to talk to you if you're interested. I'm starting interviews in two weeks, so I'd need to know something by the end of the month. I know you're in California so we could talk via Zoom.

And there it was. A job offer. Sort of. Or at least an interview. She would be working in a different part of Florida, with another company. She wouldn't be her father's daughter — she would just be another captain, the newest hire, so the one getting all the undesirable assignments.

She continued to pet Queen Mary, wondering what to say. It was one thing to talk about leaving her dad's company, but it was another to actually do it. Her father would be pissed, maybe enough to say she could never come back. There was also the reality of relocating to Key West.

Kip couldn't come with her — not and keep his job. He was making good money where he was and had an established clientele. Would he want to start over somewhere else? And shouldn't she talk to him before even considering the interview?

Overhead the rhythmic banging of a headboard hitting a wall began again, slow at first, then faster and faster. Harlow groaned.

"It started last night," she told the cat. "About midnight. This is the third time. It's a little gross to think about."

She didn't care that Mindy and Payne were having sex, she just wished they wouldn't do it right above her head.

She saved her email as new, then closed her laptop and left her room. She made her way to the breakfast room, where Lillian and Austin were sitting at the table.

"Darling!" Lillian held out her hand. "I'm so happy to see you."

Harlow hugged her great-great-aunt, then poured herself coffee and took a seat. She looked at her brother.

"They're at it again."

"Mindy and Payne?"

Harlow nodded. "Someone needs to look at that poor bed frame. I think it's going to fall apart."

Lillian laughed. "I'll mention it to Salvia. She can put it on the maintenance list. However, we should probably wait until after our guests have left."

Austin looked at the clock on the wall. "I'm going to take a shower. If they're not done, I'll be back in fifteen minutes."

"Oh, they don't go that long, so you should be safe."

Austin grinned. "Old people. You never know what they'll get up to." He stood and circled behind Lillian. After hugging her, he whispered, "Thank you."

He left. Harlow added clotted cream and jam to a scone, wondering why her brother was thanking Aunt Lillian.

"You seem to have something on your mind," Lillian said as she sipped her tea.

Harlow stared at her. "You can't possibly know that. I've been here like five seconds."

"I've known you since you were a baby. So what is it?"

"I'm trying to figure out what to do about my job. Should I go back and work for my father, knowing he'll always see me as his kid?"

"Is that a bad thing?"

"He doesn't respect me." Harlow nibbled on her scone. "I'm not sure I've earned his respect, so maybe I don't have the right to complain. Now I wonder if I should quit and go somewhere else. I could earn my place in that company, get some real experience, then work for my dad later, when I'm more than a twenty-two-year-old with delusions of grandeur."

"You're being very hard on yourself."

Harlow wished that was true. "I kind of think I'm being honest with myself for the first time. It's not fun, but I'm hoping it builds character."

Lillian studied her. "How about if I mess up all your plans?"

Harlow laughed. "I don't think you have that much power."

"Oh, my sweet, how wrong you are." Lillian set down her cup. "I'm leaving you and your brother two hundred and fifty thousand dollars each. Before you joined us, I told Austin what I'm about to tell you. I'm going to give you both the money now. Why should you wait until I'm dead? I'm delighted to help him pay for college. So I say to you, if you want to buy your kayaking company, then you're about to have the money to do that."

Harlow stared at her wide-eyed. "What? I mean, are you serious? You can't give me that kind of money."

"Actually I can. I thought maybe you'd use some for your wedding, but maybe buying the company is a better option."

Harlow dropped her scone and flung herself at her aunt. "Thank you so much. That's incredible. You don't have to do this."

"I love you, child. What else would I do with it?"

Harlow's chest was tight, and she was having trouble thinking. Two hundred and fifty thousand dollars? She could do so much with the money. As Lillian said, she could buy the kayaking company herself. For cash! She could run it and keep all the profits! She could —

"I don't want to," she said, the words coming from deep inside. They shocked her,

448

but she knew they were honest. "I don't want to buy the company by myself. I'm not ready. I wouldn't know the first thing about running it. I'm twenty-two. I don't know how to be in charge of a bunch of employees or how it works. I would have to learn on the job, and that terrifies me."

With that particular truth came yet another wave of "what had she been thinking," expecting her father to buy her the business so she could play boss.

Harlow sighed. "I've been a fool. I don't even want to buy it when you hand me the money. I'm a fraud."

"You're young and finding your way."

A too-kind explanation for her behavior, Harlow thought. "I don't deserve your generosity."

"There is no 'deserve.' It's my money, and I get to decide what happens to it."

Harlow thought about how Lillian had said Austin would use part of his inheritance to pay for college. At least he had a plan. So did her mom and Enid, and —

"I want to help Enid. I could use some of the money to pay for part of medical school. That way she wouldn't have to take out so much in loans. As for the rest, I don't know. I'm overwhelmed."

"You don't have to decide anything now,"

Lillian pointed out. "That's why we have banks."

Harlow hugged her. "You're too generous. Thank you so much. You're right. I don't have to decide anything, but you've given me the gift of options." She smiled. "Now I want to talk to my mom about this."

Lillian patted her arm. "Yes, well, I would suggest you give her a little bit. She was going to yell at Mason about Austin wanting to join the navy. It might be better to let them deal with that first."

Harlow laughed. "You're right. I'll wait." She returned to her seat. "So, Mindy and her husband. Do you think they'll work things out?"

"I hope so." Her tone was wistful. "A good marriage is such a blessing. I hope you and Kip have that, my dear. And at least fifty years together."

Harlow smiled. "Me, too."

Because she loved Kip. He would be so excited about her inheritance and all the possibilities. They could use part of it for a down payment for a house.

"I'm feeling a little spry this morning," Lillian said. "Get me my cane, darling. Then we can walk in the garden and cut flowers for the table. This afternoon, Austin promised me a few games of backgammon. He

450

thinks he'll win."

Harlow laughed. "He always thinks that, and he never does."

Lillian winked. "Some people are optimistic by nature, even when they have no reason to be."

Once she regained her strength after multiple orgasms, Robyn returned to the music room to continue her inventory. While counting the number of flutes and guitars didn't need to be done, she wanted some time to herself.

She went through two cabinets and found piles of sheet music. A wooden box contained stacks of handwritten music by Bellini, Romberg and Puccini.

Robyn stared at pages and pages of what looked to be original sheet music.

"They can't be new compositions," she said to herself. "Just copies of known works." At least that was her assumption. What she knew about music and composers could barely fill an index card.

Still, she noted the find so that she could add to her list of required experts. It was growing by the day.

Close to noon, she dropped her notebook back in her room, then went downstairs. She was feeling brave enough to face everyone without her expression giving away her morning's activities. Because when it came to her and Mason, she was the weak link. Mason's face never gave away anything unless he wanted it to.

"A skill I should develop," she told herself as she walked toward Lillian's balcony.

As she approached, she heard voices. Lillian, of course, and Austin and —

She stepped through the open French doors and stared in disbelief. "Cord?"

Her ex-husband sat on the edge of a chaise, a drink in his hand. Lillian was next to him, and a very annoyed Austin was standing by the railing.

"Hey, Mom," her son said. "Look who just got here."

Cord flashed her his familiar I-prefer-to-ask-for-forgiveness-than-permission grin. "I thought I'd drop by and say hi."

Robyn had no idea what to say. "We're an entire continent apart. You don't just fly to California to drop by."

Lillian waved a hand. "It's fine, darling. Cord is always welcome. He's a charming addition to our little group. I do find it interesting how they're all following you across the country. You're a powerful woman."

"I should use my power for good," Robyn

murmured. *Charming* was not the word she would use to describe her ex. Yes, Cord could be great at a party, but this wasn't that. Plus, what was Mason going to think?

"Why are you here?" she asked, braced for a flip answer.

Cord shocked her by saying, "I needed to talk to you, and I didn't know how to do that on the phone. Plus the kids are here with you." His expression turned baffled. "I'm the fun parent. Why did they follow you to California?"

Her legs, already weakened by the whole orgasm thing, started to give out. She sank into a chair.

"You wanted to talk to me?" Better to ignore the rest of what he'd said.

"There's some stuff." He looked around. "Can we go somewhere private and have a conversation?"

"No," Robyn and Lillian said together.

Lillian smiled. "My house, my rules. Stay here and tell all of us, Cord. We're going to find out anyway."

Austin immediately took a seat. "Come on, Dad. She's right. Everybody knows everything."

There was low-grade anger in her son's voice, Robyn thought. But before she could figure out what to do about that, Cord sighed heavily.

"This isn't fair." He glared at his son. "You quit."

"Yup, I did, and I'm not coming back."

"You don't have to sound so cheerful."

Austin shrugged.

"What's going on?" Robyn asked. The sooner her ex told her, the sooner he would leave. At least that was her fantasy, she thought, glancing toward the door and wondering if Mason was going to show up. How was she supposed to explain the sudden presence of her ex-husband?

"Yes, Cord," Lillian said, sounding a little gleeful. "What is it now?"

Cord angled away from her and turned his attention on Robyn. "Zafina's pregnant," he said, his voice low.

Robyn started laughing. "Oh my God! Seriously? That's awkward."

"You don't sound especially sympathetic."

"I'm not. For years I begged you to get a vasectomy but you refused. Honestly, I'm surprised she's the first one of your women to turn up pregnant. The odds have finally caught up with you."

"Tell me what to do."

"No. This isn't my problem. It will never be my problem, and that makes me happy."

He glared at her. "But you always help. I

depend on you."

"That's unfortunate for you." She knew she should be upset, at least for Harlow's sake, but right this second, she was finding herself in awe of the irony of the moment. "You could have fixed this with one little snip, but you were too concerned about your manhood." She grinned. "You'll be sixty-two when this one graduates from high school. I hope no one mistakes you for the grandfather."

"Good one, Mom," Austin said.

Before Cord could react, Harlow walked out onto the balcony, her phone in her hand, her eyes wide.

"Mom? I just heard from Zafina and —" She came to a stop. "Dad? You're here?"

"Just got in. How are you? I've missed you."

He started toward her, but she stepped back.

"Is Zafina pregnant?" she said.

He grimaced. "She says she is, but I'm not sure. Or that it's mine. She's supposed to be on the pill, and —"

"Stop!" Harlow shook her phone at him. "Just stop it. Don't you dare say it's not yours. How could you not take responsibility? You're the one sleeping with my fiancé's sister, which is gross enough, but you're not weaseling out of this. If she's pregnant, you're the father, and you know it. Grow up, Dad. Just grow up."

Everyone stared at Cord, who seemed to shrink under his daughter's attack.

"It's just —" he began.

Harlow shoved her phone in her pocket. "You disgust me."

With that, she walked out. Austin followed.

Lillian looked at Robyn, her mouth curving into a smile. "Such drama. Do you think it's too early for cocktails?"

Mason sat on the balcony he shared with Robyn, Charles II on his lap. He supposed he should be trying to write, but that wasn't happening. Instead he was going to lounge in the sun and do absolutely nothing for the rest of the afternoon.

Robyn had worn him out, he thought with a grin. She was incredible — even more intriguing, sexy and fun than he'd imagined. He couldn't get enough of her, nor did he want to. If it were up to him, they'd be making love well into their nineties when they would have to be a bit more careful or risk breaking a hip.

He scratched the chin of the dozing cat, earning him a purr in return. "We both have a great life," he said. Charles stretched and purred in agreement.

He heard a bedroom door open. Anticipation brightened his already good day as Robyn walked through her room and out onto the balcony.

Damn, she looked good. Her long blond hair moved in the light breeze. Her jeans hugged her hips, and her T-shirt hinted at curves. One of these days he was going to convince her to go braless. Although probably not when the house was full of —

His fantasy faded as he caught sight of her worried expression.

"What?" he asked, carefully moving Charles to the chair next to his and coming to his feet. "Something happened. Is it one of the kids?"

She shook her head. "I'm just going to say it. I want to start by telling you I didn't know, and I have nothing to do with it. In fact, the only one who seems happy is Lillian, but I think that's more about enjoying the emotional show than —"

"Robyn," he said quietly.

She pressed her lips together. "Cord's here."

It took him a second to remember who that was. "Your ex?"

"Uh-huh. He just flew in, with no warning." She drew in a breath. "I had nothing to do with him showing up."

"You said that already."

"I don't want you to think that I invited him or that I want him here."

She was worried about him?

Deep inside he felt a rush of emotion he didn't dare identify. Rather than deal with it, he crossed to her, cupped her face and kissed her.

"I believe you," he said, staring into her beautiful eyes. "You don't want Cord here, and you don't want anything to do with him. He's in your past, and that's how you want things to stay."

Relief eased the tension in her shoulders. "Thank you for saying that. I wasn't sure what you'd think. Or if you'd be . . . I don't know. Intimidated, maybe."

"I'm not intimidated by your ex."

She laughed. "I'm glad."

"So let's go meet him."

She stiffened. "Do we have to?"

"We should get it over with."

She nodded and stepped back, then bit her lower lip. "Don't judge me, okay? I was really young when we got married."

"I'll never judge you. About anything."

Her gaze locked with his. "That's about the nicest thing anyone has ever said to me."

"It's true."

"I know that, Mason. You're the most honest man I know."

TWENTY-SEVEN

"Is anyone left in Florida?" Harlow asked, studying the contents of the refrigerator.

Robyn, exhausted, apprehensive and yet oddly relaxed, shook her head. "You mean of the people we know? Only a few."

"Enid and Kip and that's kind of it." Her daughter smiled. "You're a magnet, Mom."

"Apparently. Now tell me I'm right. There's nothing for dinner."

"Nada." Harlow closed the refrigerator door. "So it's you, me, Mason, Lillian, Austin, Dad, Mindy and Payne. We should get takeout from that Italian place. Lasagna and salad. It's easy, and everyone will like it."

"We're also going to need wine," Robyn murmured. "Lots and lots of wine." She sat down at the kitchen table, then patted the chair next to hers. "Come sit with me. How are you doing?"

Harlow settled next to her. "There's a lot going on, Mom. I can't believe Dad's here."

"I know. What was he thinking?"

Didn't the man have friends he could talk to? Why on earth would he simply show up in Santa Barbara? He'd met Lillian over the years, but they were hardly close. Imagine just waltzing into her house, expecting to stay. Of course, Mindy and Payne had done the same. Odd. Very, very odd.

Harlow rested her arms on the table. "Zafina's really pregnant. She texted me the, quote, 'good news,' right when Dad got here. She's Kip's age. Shouldn't she have been more careful? Dad's not exactly the most responsible guy on the planet." Her nose wrinkled. "And while I don't want to have this conversation, shouldn't he have gotten a vasectomy like years ago?"

"You'd think," Robyn said lightly. "Are you okay with the baby?"

"I don't know. It's surreal. Zafina and I aren't exactly tight, and —" Harlow's eyes widened. "Oh, crap! She's having a baby with my father. That makes their kid what? My half brother or sister *and* my niece or nephew? This is so twisted. Now they'll get married, and he'll be my father and brother-in-law. I'm going to need therapy."

"We all will," Robyn murmured.

"Why did she have to get pregnant? She should know better. And Dad! He's too old

461

to have a baby." She grabbed Robyn's hands. "Mom, make it stop."

Words her little girl used to beg all those years ago, when she'd been enduring cancer treatment.

"I wish I could." She squeezed Harlow's fingers. "I think for now, we just have to endure."

Harlow sagged back in her chair, then straightened, as if she'd just remembered something. "Mom, Aunt Lillian talked to me about my inheritance. She's leaving two hundred and fifty thousand dollars to me and to Austin."

Robyn smiled at her, not letting on she wasn't surprised. Lillian had mentioned her plan a couple of days ago. "That's very generous."

"She said she didn't want us to wait to get the money. Austin's going to use some of his to pay for college. He's being really responsible."

"He is." Robyn did her best to keep her tone neutral. "What about you? Do you want to buy the kayak business?"

Harlow shook her head. "No. It would have been different if Dad had been helping me. But on my own? I'm not ready. And it's not really calling to me, which makes me feel doubly stupid about expecting Dad to buy it for me."

Relief filled Robyn. She'd worried Harlow would want to jump at the chance — before she had the experience or possibly the drive. But her daughter had figured that out all on her own.

"I'm really proud of you, honey. You're so grown-up." And beautiful, Robyn thought. Harlow had always been a pretty child, but in the past couple of years, she'd completely blossomed.

"I'm trying," Harlow said. "I want to be smart about my inheritance. It's a huge amount of money, and I refuse to waste it on something stupid. I'm working on a plan."

"Good for you. Want to talk about it or dinner?"

"Dinner," Harlow said with a laugh. "People are going to be getting hungry. You choose the wine, and I'll call in the order. Austin can pick it up while I set the table. How's that?"

"Perfect."

Robyn started for the wine cellar, wondering if two bottles was enough or if she should get three. With luck, the weirdness of the day had passed, and dinner would be a quiet affair with only mundane conversation. That was the fantasy.

At least the meeting between Mason and Cord had been easy. Her ex hadn't known what to make of the other man, and after a brief greeting and handshake, Mason had pretty much dismissed Cord as uninteresting. She should have known not to be worried.

Mindy and Payne had made an afternoon appearance. They seemed to have worked through most of their issues and had asked to join everyone for dinner. Hopefully Cord, Mindy and Payne would head back to Florida in the morning, and the rest of them could get on with their lives.

She took three bottles of wine to the dining room. Harlow was there with Mason, pointing to the various dinner sets in the large hutches.

"It's Italian," she was saying. "I'm not sure which plates go best with Italian."

Mason stared at her helplessly. "Why does it matter? It's food on plates. Isn't that enough?"

Harlow patted his arm. "Silly man. Of course it matters."

"It really doesn't," Robyn said lightly.

They both turned to face her. Mason immediately looked relieved while her daughter appeared more disappointed.

"Oh, Mom, I was hoping to torture him a

few more minutes."

Mason stared at her. "You were playing me? You don't care about the china pattern?"

"Of course not, but it was fun to make you think I did." She grinned. "I have a wicked sense of humor. You're going to have to get used to that."

Robyn set down the bottles of wine and moved to him. "I think she likes you," she said in a low voice. "Teasing is a sign of affection."

"Then why don't you tease me more?"

She leaned close and whispered into his ear. "I show my affection in other ways."

"Good ways," he murmured back.

"Hey, keep it clean, people," Harlow said, pulling down dishes. "There are things I don't want to know about you two."

"That is very true," Mason told Harlow before crossing to her. "These plates?"

"Yes. They'll look lovely with the lasagna. See how the floral pattern will pick up the red of the sauce?"

He groaned. "You're killing me."

"Then my work here is done."

The odd mix of company made for an interesting meal, Harlow thought, passing her brother the last tray of lasagna. Mindy and Payne had been charming, acting like a regular couple rather than one who had spent the past four days trying to save their marriage through screaming fights and sex.

Lillian was perfect as hostess, entertaining everyone with stories about travels with Leo and adventures with Robyn as a girl. Even Mason, normally more reticent at the larger meals, had talked about his life in the army.

Her father, usually the center of attention, had been oddly quiet. She kept catching him looking at her, as if he wanted to say something. Harlow wasn't interested in whatever he wanted to tell her. The whole Zafina being pregnant thing made her want to throw up a little in her mouth, and she wasn't ready to talk about going back to work for him.

She understood the benefits — that she could learn about the business she loved and planned to take over one day. She mostly liked working for her dad, and because of her relationship as his only daughter, she got more flexibility than the other employees. She could pick the best assignments if she wanted. Not fair but very much her reality.

And that was how she'd seen her life going. She had a wedding to plan and a new life to start. Why would she want to stress about her job?

Only that didn't sound as right as it had a month ago. Everything she'd thought she'd known about herself and her place in the world had suddenly shifted.

She wanted . . . She picked at her salad, not sure how to explain the yearning inside. She glanced at Mason, who was telling a funny story about being in a broken Humvee on the side of an autobahn in Germany. Everyone listened, not only because he knew how to command a room, but because of who he was. Mason was the kind of person you respected. He was honest and careful, and she knew he would take good care of her mom.

She wanted to be like that. Oh, not the army or taking care of her mom, but more than a flaky kid who got by because her daddy let her.

She looked at Lillian who, in maybe her forties, had gone down South to register Black people to vote. She could have been beat up or worse, but she'd done it. And her brother, who took his time making his decisions, but damn did he get them right.

Nearly everyone was impressive but her.

Lillian leaned close. "You're looking very introspective, my dear. Tell me what you're thinking."

Harlow squeezed her hand. "I'm mulling over my options," she said quietly. "Thanks to you, I'm figuring out how to be a better person."

"I think you're already delightful and someone I always look forward to seeing."

Harlow suddenly found herself fighting tears. "You're so good to me, Aunt Lillian. I love you so much."

"I love you, too."

Mason gave her a quizzical glance. "You all right?"

She smiled at him. "Yeah, I'm good."

Her phone buzzed. She pulled it out of her pocket and glanced at the screen.

So your aunt's house. Is it really big and weird looking with a long, long, long driveway?

She jumped to her feet, waving her phone. "I think Kip's here."

Austin groaned. "Man, then it'll be three of us sharing a bathroom."

"The lovebirds can move to another part of the house," Lillian told him.

"Yeah, on the third floor," Austin muttered. "Where all the sex is happening."

Mindy flushed. "You knew?"

Payne appeared more smug than upset.

"The headboard bangs into the wall."

Mindy covered her face with her hands. "I'm so embarrassed."

"Don't be," Lillian murmured, picking up her wine. "Your enthusiasm was impressive. Made me miss my darling Leo."

Harlow excused herself and hurried to the rear of the house. Kip had come here? She wasn't sure what to think about that. Shouldn't he have told her was coming? Shouldn't they have talked about it?

Only the second she stepped outside and saw him, duffel bag in hand, sheepish grin on his face, all her concerns faded. She rushed to him, arms outstretched.

He caught her and pulled her hard against him.

"I missed you so much," he said, burying his face in her hair. "Harlow, I can't make it without you. I've screwed up so bad, and I know I need to fix that, but don't be done with me. Please."

She breathed in the scent of him and felt the rightness of being with him. After raising her head, she kissed him.

"I'm glad you're here," she said with a laugh. "I should have invited you myself."

"Yeah?" His gaze was hopeful. "I wasn't sure I should just show up like this."

"It's the best surprise. Come in. You'll

never guess who's already here. My mom's friend Mindy arrived about ten days ago, then her husband. Then my dad showed up earlier today. That was a much bigger shock than seeing you."

He picked up his duffel, then put his arm around her as they walked into the house.

"Are you upset about Zafina?" he asked.

"I'm not sure I can even grasp it. She's pregnant?"

Kip shrugged. "That's what she told me. Mom and Dad don't know. I think she wants to figure things out with your dad first."

Harlow thought about her father claiming the baby might not be his. "I hope he doesn't disappoint her."

Harlow tried to imagine what her future in-laws would say when they learned their twenty-six-year-old daughter was pregnant by a man two decades older. The father of their future daughter-in-law.

"We're like a bad TV script," she said, looking at Kip. "For a show no one wants to watch."

He set down his duffel and leaned close. "I think parts of it would be great to watch."

"Don't say that too loud. Both my parents are here. How's that for something you never thought you'd see?"

"I'm happy to see you."

She kissed him, then drew back. "Are you hungry? There's lasagna, if Austin hasn't inhaled it all. And salad and garlic bread."

"I'm starving."

"Then come meet everyone. After dinner, we need to find a different bedroom. Otherwise, we'll have Austin right next door, and given how sound travels in this house, we sure don't want that."

Despite staying up late the night before, Robyn woke before dawn. Mason was still asleep, so she crept out of bed and made her way across the balcony to her own room. The morning was cold and foggy. While she couldn't see the vast ocean, she could hear a distant foghorn and seagulls complaining about the weather.

Once in her own room, she showered and dressed. Breakfast for nine would take some planning, she thought. As would lunch and dinner. Hopefully Mindy and Payne would head home soon, and there was no reason for Cord to stay. Whatever he was looking for wasn't here. Unless he had a need for a used but beautiful grand piano. Or maybe a few teacups.

She was smiling at her own joke when her phone rang. It wasn't even six in the morning, she thought, reaching for it.

Her heart sank. Jase. Why?

She thought about not answering, but knew she would have to deal with him at some point.

"Hello?"

"Robyn. I wasn't sure you would take my call."

She gave herself a second to see if she felt anything when she heard his voice. But instead of regret or wistfulness, she only felt impatience. The man needed to stop calling her.

"It's pretty early here, Jase."

"Oh, the time difference." He paused. "I apologize. Did I wake you?"

"No. I was up."

"Still on Florida time." He chuckled. "You should probably think about coming home so you don't lose that."

"Jase, why are you calling?"

"I miss you."

"That's not possible. We were never that close, and now we're done. It's over."

"Robyn, please." There was a hitch in his voice. "I made such a mistake, letting you go. Please give me another chance. I'm in love with you."

Unexpected. She sank onto the bed she hadn't slept in.

"Jase, don't say that. We —" She didn't know what to say, then settled on the truth. "I'm seeing someone."

"What? How is that possible? Were you cheating on me?"

"No. I met him here, in Santa Barbara. He's . . ." She realized Jase didn't need the details. "I met him here," she repeated. "I don't want to hurt you, but we're finished. Stop calling. I won't answer you again."

Actually, when they hung up she was going to block him, but saying that seemed cruel.

"I see." His voice was curt. "All right. You've made your point. I'm sorry I bothered you."

Guilt swamped her, but she ignored it. If she was advising her daughter on a situation like this, she would tell her not to engage. That being friendly would only make him think she was playing a game rather than stating facts.

"Goodbye, Jase."

She hung up before he could say anything, then tossed her phone on the bed. She had breakfast to prepare and a day to plan. She didn't have time for her past — not anymore. There was too much present to be lived.

TWENTY-EIGHT

Robyn had barely finished breakfast cleanup when she started planning dinner. She figured everyone could grab lunch on their own. The morning fog had cleared, leaving the day warm and beautiful. Mason, Harlow and Austin had gone sailing. Mason had joked he was going to have the kids teach him some moves so he could impress her the next time they went out. Cord, Mindy and Payne were in their rooms. Lillian was watching CNN and talking back to the reporters.

She glanced at the calendar, surprised by how much time had passed. In a few weeks, she would need to get back to Naples and sign the paperwork to sell the house. And from there . . .

She smiled. Funny how she was back to not knowing what to do with her life.

Oh, the basics were in place. She was going to continue with her online classes and get a job where she could learn the antique business. That part was easy and set — it was the *where* that was more complicated.

"Knock, knock." Mindy walked into the kitchen. Her friend looked relaxed and happy.

"Breakfast was delicious," Mindy said with a smile. "You've been a very understanding hostess, as has your aunt. I wanted to tell you that Payne and I are grateful, and we're leaving for the airport."

Robyn tried not to show her glee. "You are?"

"Yes. We appreciate everyone's understanding while we hashed things out." Her smile faded. "You were right about Dimitri. I was a fool. I almost lost what matters most to me. But Payne wants our marriage to work, and I know now I want that, too. We're both committed to giving all we have."

Her humor returned. "And getting a good therapist."

Robyn stood and hugged her. "I'm happy to have been somewhere you could run to."

"Me, too. Thank you for everything. And next time I want to screw up my life, I promise to listen to you."

Robyn laughed. "I doubt that, but thanks for saying it."

"You'll see. Okay, I'm going to say good-bye to Lillian, then we're driving to the airport. Will you be home soon?"

"In the next few weeks. I have to get the house ready to sell."

"And after that?"

"I'm not sure. To be determined. Fly safe."

Mindy waved and left. Robyn turned back to her menu, but couldn't focus. Not on that. Her friend's question was the same one she'd been asking herself.

After she sold her house, then what?

She made her way to Lillian's study. Her aunt had turned off the TV and settled out on the balcony, in the sun. A colorful blanket was pulled up to her waist, and her ever-present cup of tea was beside her.

"Sit with me," Lillian said, holding out her hand. "I could use some good company."

Robyn complied, stretching out her legs on the chaise next to Lillian's. It was still a bit cool, but the sun would warm things up quickly.

"Mindy and Payne are leaving," she said.

"Yes, she stopped by a few minutes ago." Lillian's eyes crinkled with amusement. "Not that I don't enjoy all the company, but even this house was feeling a little crowded. You must be relieved she and her husband worked things out."

"I'm happy for her. I'm sorry she made such a boneheaded decision, but hopefully they'll get past it. I do worry that Payne won't be able to let it go as quickly as he thinks and she hopes."

"You speak from experience."

Robyn thought about how she'd felt the first time she found out Cord had been unfaithful.

"I tried to let go of the past," she said slowly. "To believe him when he said he was sorry and that it would never happen again, but I wonder if, in the back of my mind, I didn't actually believe him."

She looked at her aunt. "I gave up so much of myself to be married to him. I was too young. I got pregnant too soon. We were babies, pretending to be grown-ups."

"You were in love."

"Yes, but does that excuse bad decisions? I should have been more careful with my birth control." She smiled. "Not that I regret my kids."

"I know." Lillian studied her. "They are the light of your heart and always will be, but you think about what could have been."

"Cord was so excited to start his own business, and I wanted to make it happen.

His happiness was more important than mine."

Cord had wanted them to get going on building their life together. To support that, she'd worked sixteen-hour days, even while pregnant and with an infant. She'd let him decide when they could afford their first house, putting it off for several years so he could buy more boats for the company instead of telling him the business could wait so the four of them could get out of their one-bedroom apartment.

The first time she'd stood up to him had been when Harlow had been diagnosed with cancer. She'd walked away from the business to be with her daughter through every treatment. After work, when Cord showed up, Robyn had gone home to spend time with Austin, careful to make him feel he had her full attention.

"What are you thinking?" Lillian asked.

"That you and Leo saved us when Harlow got sick. Coming to stay with us kept the family together. Austin was little, and I had to be at the hospital all the time."

"You know we were happy to help. Poor Harlow. She was so brave."

"She was."

Robyn thought about how, after he'd cheated, Cord had shown up here, begging her to come home. She'd been torn between the life she could have with her aunt and uncle and what it would mean to return to Florida. In the end, she'd gone home because of her kids. So they could be part of a family. Right or wrong, she'd made the sacrifice. She could forgive herself for taking him back the first time she'd caught him cheating, but after the second, she should have known better.

"Then he bought that damned house," she murmured. "Without even talking to me."

"It was very beautiful," Lillian murmured. "Although not your style."

She still remembered the shock of it. The kids had loved their new rooms and the huge backyard with the massive pool. Telling him she didn't like it would mean breaking all their hearts. She wanted to say he hadn't trapped her on purpose, but even today, she wasn't sure he hadn't had a master plan.

"I can't surrender to a man again."

"Darling, what does that mean?"

Robyn turned to her aunt. "I can't make life decisions based on what someone else wants."

"Is anyone asking you to?"

"No. Not directly."

"Then indirectly?" Lillian smiled. "I assume we're talking about Mason."

"Maybe."

Her aunt laughed. "Is there another man in your life?"

Robyn grinned. "No, there isn't. Just him."

"That's what I thought. Now, how is he trying to control you? Has he asked you to stay?"

"No. I'm not even sure what he would think about that. Things would get awkward. I just don't know where it's going and what he's thinking. I won't be played. I want to be smart and make thoughtful decisions."

"Then do. And talk to Mason. From what I've seen, he's a very reasonable man. He's not the type to play anyone."

"What if he's not the problem? What if I'm blaming Cord for a lot of things that are my fault? I never stood up to him. Sometimes I even anticipated what he wanted and did it. I don't want to be like that again. I won't be."

"Hmm, so rather than take the chance, you walk away? If you're not with him, you can't make a mistake."

"I'm not walking away."

"Then what are you doing?"

"I have no idea."

Her aunt smiled. "They say admitting you have a problem is the first step. Now you just have to figure out the rest of them."

"Easier said than done."

"I know, and isn't that what keeps life interesting?"

Harlow found it surprisingly simple to avoid her father. She went running early with Mason. Given the choice, Cord slept in. He generally came downstairs for breakfast, but so did everyone else, preventing private conversation.

After breakfast, she helped her mom inventory the house or went sailing with Austin and Mason. Now that Kip had arrived, she had yet another excuse to avoid her father, even though she knew at some point she was going to have to talk to him. The problem was, she didn't know what to say.

Late in the afternoon, while Kip and Austin played video games, she picked blueberries in the garden for a pie. The morning fog had burned off, leaving the day glorious. There was something magical about the color of the sky and the palm trees and the wildness of the Pacific Ocean. That body of water had a lot more attitude than the generally tame Gulf of Mexico.

A ridiculous train of thought, but one that was easier than the constant refrain in her head telling her she had decisions to make. Big ones.

A couple of hours ago, Lillian had told her the money had been transferred into her account. Sure enough, when Harlow had checked, her balance had increased by two hundred and fifty thousand dollars. She couldn't begin to absorb that reality and felt both excited and shocked she was sitting on that much cash.

She still wanted to talk to Enid about helping her with medical school, but wasn't sure what to do with the rest of it. Open an investment account with some, she supposed. Put some in savings. Use a bit to help pay for the wedding.

What about Kip's debt?

A voice had been whispering the question in her head for a couple of days now. Helping him pay down his debt was the right thing to do. It would allow them to get serious about a budget and give them a chance to be on the same footing financially. Only . . .

She hadn't told him about the inheritance. She knew she should and she would . . . eventually. Keeping that kind of secret from the man she wanted to marry would be bad and wrong. She'd been telling him they had to be honest with each other, and here she was, keeping something really huge from him.

She continued dropping berries into her basket.

Just as bad, she thought, fighting yet more guilt, she'd gone online to find out if her inheritance would become a marital asset after they were married. According to what she'd read, as long as she kept the money separate, then it was hers alone and wouldn't be a marital asset even after the wedding.

She sank onto the grass and covered her face with her hands. She was a horrible person for not telling him about the money, and even worse, she hadn't told him about the potential job in Key West. She had a Zoom interview in two days, so at some point she was going to have to —

"There you are."

She sat up as her father walked into the garden.

"I've been looking for you," Cord said. "What are you doing?"

"Picking blueberries. Mom and I are going to make pies later."

Her father frowned. "When did you learn to make pie?"

"As a teenager."

"To make pie?" He sounded baffled by

483

the concept. "Why?"

"I like to bake."

He sat next to her on the grass and grabbed a couple of blueberries from her basket. After popping them in his mouth, he said, "These are really good."

"Yes, they are. If you want to eat some, pick your own."

He grabbed a handful from the basket. "They taste better when someone else does the work."

He stretched out on the grass and nibbled on berries. "I haven't heard from Zafina in two days. I don't know what that means."

Harlow really didn't want to have this conversation but didn't know how to get out of it. "How did you leave things?"

"I don't remember. We had a fight."

She resumed picking berries, wondering if her father had always been such a jerk in his relationships.

"Your girlfriend told you she was pregnant and you don't remember what you talked about?"

"I was in shock. It was the last thing I expected to hear." He pointed at her. "I was dealing with a lot. With you gone, I'm a captain short. When are you getting your butt back to work? You have responsibilities, Harlow. You can't go running off on vacation anytime you want."

"Why not? I'm just your overpaid kid, Dad."

"Hey, what does that mean?"

She looked at him. "It's what you said. I understand that you didn't want to buy the kayak business, but you let me believe you did. You treated me like a six-year-old whose dog died. You told me Fluffy had gone to live on a farm. I'm twenty-two. I could have understood your reasons, but you didn't even try to explain it to me. You let me act like a fool, and then you mocked me for what you'd told me to believe."

He sat up. "That's not what happened."

"Yes, it is. Lie to everyone else if you want, but don't lie to me."

They stared at each other. She watched the shifting emotions on his face and knew the exact moment he accepted that he'd been caught in whatever strange game he'd been playing.

"I didn't know what to say," he admitted with a sigh. "You were so excited, and I didn't want to disappoint you."

"Plus, Zafina," she said flatly. "You were busy with her."

"Hey, I get to have a life."

"So do we. I don't understand, Dad. You always talked like you wanted me to come work for you, but then you treated me the way you did. You did the same with Austin. He tried to talk to you a half-dozen times. He made appointments with you, but you always blew him off."

Her father looked past her. "Yeah, well, I didn't get that it was important. He talked to me yesterday. I guess he's going to college and joining the navy. Damned fool decision if you ask me. Who wants to be in the military?"

"You're not proud your son wants to serve?"

He swore. "Is that how we have to talk about it now?"

What had her mother ever seen in him? Harlow knew twenty-plus years ago her father had been a different man, but she doubted he'd ever been anything but selfish. Her mom must have loved him a lot to put up with that.

"When are you coming back to work?" her father asked again. "Or do you plan to keep pouting?"

She looked at him. "Pouting? Really?"

"Fine. Not that. Come on, Harlow, it's summer. I could really use you. Tell me what it's going to take. You want a raise? A different title?"

She didn't want either. She wanted to be

486

respected as a good captain who knew her job. She wanted to learn the business and earn her way into running it. But that wasn't likely — not right now. She was too young, she was his daughter, and he had way too much going on.

"What are you going to do about Zafina?" she asked, mostly to distract him.

"I have no idea." He groaned. "Why did she have to get pregnant?"

"Probably because you had sex with her. Ejaculation does that, Dad."

"Very funny. I'm too old to be a father again. I don't want to go through all the baby stuff." He grimaced. "Diapers, midnight feedings."

She laughed. "Because you did any of that when Austin and I were little? I don't think so."

"I was a good dad." His tone was defensive. "I helped."

Helped. Not partnered, but helped.

"What if she wants to get married?" he asked, sitting up. "I can't do it. I don't want a second family, and I was never going to marry her."

Harlow stared at him. "Then what were you doing? You're dating my fiancé's twin sister, and it was just about getting laid. That's gross, Dad, even for you. If you're going to act like that, at least keep it out of the family."

"She came on to me. It's not my fault."

"It never is," she said quietly. She stood and picked up the basket. She had enough for a couple of pies with leftovers for breakfast. "I need to get these inside."

Her father scrambled to his feet. "So you're coming back to work soon?"

"I'll be home in a week or so. We'll talk then."

She was putting off the inevitable, but knew there was no point in having the conversation now. Not when they were living in the same house and she had no way to escape him. And not when she was so disappointed by seeing her father for the man he was and not who she had always expected him to be.

Mason finished dressing and headed for the kitchen. One of the disadvantages of his early morning run was leaving Robyn alone in his bed. She was never still there when he got back. Of course, the two mornings a week he didn't run were pretty damned incredible, so there was that.

He was still smiling at the images of how they started their days when he didn't have PT as he entered the kitchen. Robyn was frying bacon and sausages. Harlow and Austin were helping their mother. Austin carried dishes into the breakfast room while Harlow cracked eggs into a bowl. Their conversation was easy, their body language relaxed. They were a team, and he liked that.

Harlow grinned when she saw him.

"Ack! Now I have guilt. You went running, didn't you?"

"Yes. Alone." He said the word pointedly. "Where were you two?"

"I got lazy," Harlow admitted. "Sorry."

"No excuse, sir," Austin added with a laugh. "I slept through my alarm."

"Enjoy that while you can." Mason stepped into the kitchen. "Put me to work."

Harlow pointed to a bowl of oranges. "Make juice, please."

He did as she requested, cutting the oranges in half, then using the manual juicer to fill the pitcher. Robyn smiled at him from the stove, her gaze warm and affectionate.

He liked feeling as though he was a part of their small family. He appreciated that they accepted and welcomed him. The thing he'd regretted most from both his divorces was losing the connection and sense of belonging. His parents had died years ago, and he had no siblings. Roots were important to him, and seeing as he didn't have any of his own, he was open to being grafted in somewhere.

At least he had Lillian, he thought with contentment. She'd made him feel as if he'd known her forever. His only regret was waiting too long to take her up on her offer to meet. He should have visited her years ago.

"What's the plan for today?" he asked, mostly to distract himself. What-ifs were a waste.

"I have a job interview," Austin said. "Just part-time, with a charter company."

"Good for you," Robyn told him. "I hope you get it."

"Me, too. It's not a lot of hours, but I think I'd like it. I'm also going to see about busing tables."

Mason knew the kid had just inherited a shitload of money. He could easily spend the next year sitting on his ass, but Austin expected more of himself.

"I'm going to be exploring the exciting world of sheet music," Robyn said. "I have a phone call with someone in New York later this morning. I found several handwritten scores. I'm assuming they're copies of original works, but I have no idea how to tell or where to start. A very nice woman is going to give me a crash course."

Harlow began to whip the eggs. "I think

I'm going to —" She frowned as Salvia hurried into the kitchen.

Lillian's companion's face was pale, her hands twisted together. Everyone stared at her.

"Salvia?" Robyn asked. "What's wrong?"

"It's Miss Lillian," Salvia said, her voice shaking. "She's gone."

Gone? Lillian never went anywhere on her own. In fact, she rarely left the house, and she —

Robyn's cry of distress told him he'd misunderstood. He instantly moved to her side and put his arm around her. She collapsed against him, starting to cry.

"When?" she asked, her voice trembling. He held her close, fighting sorrow and disbelief. Not Lillian. Not so soon.

"She passed in the night. In her sleep." Salvia wiped away tears. "I've already called her doctor, but it's too late. She's with Mr. Leo now."

Instinctively, he held out his free arm. Both Austin and Harlow rushed to him. They clung to each other, trying to make sense of the news. Robyn held on to Salvia's hand.

Lillian gone? Mason couldn't imagine it, didn't want it to be true. She was a gentle soul, a warm, caring person. He couldn't picture the house without her. She was the heart of it, the heart of all of them. He wasn't ready.

"No," Harlow whispered. "She can't be gone. She can't."

Robyn straightened. "I need to —"

"No," he said gently, meeting her gaze. "I'll handle whatever has to be done. You stay with the kids. I'll go with Salvia."

He wanted to say more, to explain that he was offering because he was good at logistics, at separating emotion from the job at hand, not because he didn't want to be with her.

She nodded slowly, then kissed him. "I knew you'd be a rock. Thank you."

She pulled her children close. He crossed to Salvia and patted her shoulder.

"It's on me now," he said quietly.

Salvia led the way out of the kitchen.

TWENTY-NINE

Robyn couldn't think, couldn't feel, couldn't do anything but continue breathing. She had no idea what was going on or what was expected. Soul-crushing sadness overwhelmed every other emotion. Yes, Lillian had lived a good, long life surrounded by those she loved, and of course everyone would want to pass away peacefully in their sleep, but what about those left behind? What about the sense of losing family?

Robyn stood in Lillian's office, telling herself to take a seat at the desk and pull out the bottom drawer. In there was a folder that was to be opened after her death. Lillian had told her so a dozen times. All the details of her funeral were planned, including the menu for the wake that would follow. There were lists of people to notify and oh, someone had to let the lawyer know.

But instead of moving forward, she wrapped her arms around herself and tried to keep her heart from spilling out.

She couldn't be gone, she just couldn't. The world couldn't function without Lillian's bright spirit, nor could Robyn. Lillian had been a constant her whole life — loving her, supporting her, always there for her. Lillian had played dress-up with her and read with her. Lillian had been the one she'd talked to when she got her period.

Later, when Leo had passed, Robyn had stayed for the summer, helping her aunt pick up the pieces. They were family.

"Mom?"

Harlow walked into the office. Her daughter looked as shell-shocked and stricken as Robyn felt. Pale, eyes red from crying. She seemed smaller, somehow. More frail and less capable.

"What are you doing?" Harlow asked. "Do you need help?"

"I need to go through one of the folders in her desk," Robyn said, wishing it wasn't necessary. "Lillian had everything arranged. The contacts, the instructions. All I have to do is call Gregory, her lawyer."

Harlow shook her head. "Mason's doing that."

"What?"

"In his office."

Robyn opened the desk drawer. It was

empty. Concern caused her to hurry downstairs. She found Mason in his office, paperwork spread out on his desk. His laptop was open, and there was a spreadsheet on the screen.

He stood as she approached, then walked to her and pulled her close.

"How are you holding up?"

"I'm shattered." She drew away and stared at him. "What are you doing?"

She heard the accusation in her tone, saw the confusion in his eyes, but didn't care. Who did he think he was, taking over like this?

"While you were with the kids, I pulled Lillian's after-death folder. She told me about it shortly after I got here. Once you arrived, she asked me to be the one to take care of things if she passed away. So you didn't have to. I've spoken to Gregory and the funeral home. Everything is arranged. Salvia has the menus. I've started calling people to let them know what happened. Austin wanted to help with that, so I gave him part of the list. He's in the library."

His voice was so calm, she thought. His words all made sense, and Lillian asking Mason to handle the logistics so Robyn would be spared was just like her. As for what Mason was doing — there were no surprises. He did the job thoroughly, seeing to every detail. There was no flinching from what was uncomfortable or difficult.

The anger — probably a mask for her grief — faded, leaving her with nothing but emptiness.

"I'm sorry," she whispered, feeling her legs start to shake. "I don't know why I was mad. It's ridiculous. I'm grateful you're taking over. I don't think I could do it."

He led her to a chair and waited for her to sit, then pulled up a seat and settled across from her. After taking one of her hands in his, he looked into her eyes.

"I'm going to be here through all the hard shit. Every second of it. Nothing you say or do will scare me away. I'm not interested in judging you, and I have no expectations beyond the fact that you lost someone you've loved your whole life. You deal with that. I'll take care of the rest."

She nodded, unable to speak. The tears returned, and her throat got tight. Everything hurt so much more than she thought it would.

Cord walked into the room. He glanced at them, then shoved his hands into his pockets. "So, ah, Robyn. I thought I'd, you know, ask if I could help or something."

Go home! That would be the biggest help,

she thought fiercely. Cord was nothing but dead weight. But before she could tell him that, Mason rose.

"Cord, Salvia needs to get food into the house. We're going to have a lot of visitors. She's not feeling up to dealing with that by herself. You're someone she feels comfortable with. Would you help her? I know she'd appreciate it."

Cord looked between them, then nodded slowly. "Sure. She's in the kitchen?"

"She is."

He shuffled out.

Robyn stared after him, then turned back to Mason. "You made him go away. How did you do that?"

He gave her a faint smile. "He said he wanted to help, so I gave him a job to do. Later I'm going to tell Kip to wash the serving pieces. Unless Harlow needs him." He raised a shoulder. "Lillian wanted an English high tea served at her wake. That's going to be a lot of coronation chicken."

"How do you know about coronation chicken?"

"I'm a well-traveled man."

She started to laugh, then sob. Mason was instantly at her side. She leaned into his strong body and knew he would take care of her and her children, no matter what.

"You're hurting, too," she whispered into his chest. "You loved her, too."

"Yes to both. She was a great lady."

She raised her head and met his gaze. "You were so special to her, Mason. She was so glad you were here."

They held on to each other and let the grief wash over them. Robyn knew it would be a long, long time until the healing began.

Four days after losing Lillian, Harlow carefully placed teacups and saucers on the rolling cart Austin had brought up from the basement. It was just the right size to fit on the dumbwaiter, so it could be lowered to the main floor. She'd already sent down stacks of plates and nearly a dozen silver trays. Kip had offered to shine up the latter, and Salvia had set him up in the laundry room with a tub of polish and a stack of clean rags.

Harlow counted the cups and saucers, not sure how many they would need. Her mom had said they were expecting about a hundred people after the funeral, so maybe a hundred and twenty cups and saucers?

Thinking about logistics was easier than missing Lillian, although she couldn't escape how terrible she felt every single second.

She heard footsteps in the hallway. Seconds later, Austin walked into the room. He looked awful, with dark circles under his eyes and slumped shoulders. She immediately moved toward him.

"I miss her, too," she said, hugging him tight.

"It's like losing Uncle Leo all over again," he mumbled into her hair. "But worse."

"I know."

He stepped back and swallowed. "Mason confirmed the catering staff will be here tomorrow, three hours before the wake. Salvia was going to supervise, but Mason told her she had to go to the funeral. She worked for Lillian for nearly twenty years. Mom and Mason were arguing over which of them was staying, but then Kip said he'd do it." He gave her a faint smile. "Your guy came through."

Harlow felt a rush of surprise and pride. "Good for him."

"I know that means you'll be alone at the funeral," Austin began.

Harlow shook her head. "I'll have you and Mom and Mason."

She didn't say anything about her father. She wasn't sure she could depend on him. Sad but true.

"What?" Austin asked.

"Dad. I don't trust him. I want to, but I can't."

Her brother didn't say anything. Harlow knew he was dealing with his own disappointment when it came to their father.

She thought about everything she'd learned over the past few months. Her father's cheating, how he'd only pretended to be interested in buying the business, claiming Zafina's baby wasn't his. Why did it all have to be so awful?

"I can't work for him," she said, fresh tears filling her eyes. "I can't. Not now. Not like this. I'm just his kid. All that talk about me taking over the business was just a story we told ourselves."

She wiped her cheeks. "I'm partly to blame. I expected too much. I assumed a lot, but some of it's on him."

"Most of it." Her brother's gaze was steady. "What are you going to do?"

"Work in Key West. Start over. Grow up. Maybe being away from Dad will be good for both of us. In a few years, we can talk about where we see things going with the company."

"What about Kip?"

She drew in a breath only to realize she didn't have an answer. "We've done the distance relationship before. We can do it again."

"Things are different now. You're engaged."

"We'll figure it out." They had to. She couldn't lose Kip, too. "I won't be that far away. There's the ferry from Ft. Myers to Key West. We have that, or the drive. It won't be that hard."

Austin put his hands on her shoulders and rested his forehead against hers. "You're lying, sis."

"I know, but let's pretend I'm not." She stepped back and pointed to the cart. "Would you please get these down to Salvia?"

"What are you going to do?"

"Find Dad."

Her father was in his room, on the phone with the office. When he saw her, he waved her in, then kept talking.

Harlow crossed to the open French doors. The past few days had been unseasonably gray and cold, as if the weather, too, mourned Lillian's passing. She shivered slightly in the breeze, then moved back into the bedroom and sat on the bench at the foot of the bed.

As her dad concluded his call, she tried to figure out what to say. She had a feeling that whatever it was, he would be mad at her. Something she would have to deal with. She'd made up her mind and would accept the consequences.

Cord dropped his cell phone to the desk. "We've got to get back to the office," he said, sounding grim. "Things are falling apart. Thank God the funeral's tomorrow. I'm taking off after that. What about you? How long are you going to hang around here? I need you back at work, kid. I've been more than generous with your time off, but enough's enough. You can mope just as easily back home."

"Mope?" she repeated. "I'm not moping, Dad. Lillian was an important part of the family, and she died. No one's moping."

He held up both hands. "Sorry. Poor choice of words."

"You think?"

She consciously drew in a deep breath and told herself to stay in her head. Giving in to emotions wouldn't make the conversation easier. She had to remember what was important.

"I'm not coming back," she began.

Cord glared at her. "What the hell? Are you serious? What are you going to do, sit around doing nothing? Did your mother put you up to this? I always knew she resented you working for me. She thought you should experience something more. I told her to butt out. That you and I had been planning your future since you were a kid. You belong with me."

Harlow was on the emotional edge. Too much had happened in too short a period of time. Kip's revelations, finding out about the business, having to figure out what to do about her career, then worst of all, losing Lillian. She had nothing left in her. No fight, no resources. She was raw and hurting, and she needed a father who understood that.

But as she stared at his angry expression, she knew that would never happen. He couldn't see past himself. He was only the "fun parent" because he wasn't willing to take enough responsibility to be anything else.

"I'm sorry it didn't work out," she said quietly, then stood. "I'll get you a formal letter of resignation by close of business today."

Cord's face drained of color. "You can't mean that. Harlow, you can't. I need you. Come on, baby, don't be like that. We're a team, you and me. You're my girl. How are you going to learn about the business if you walk away? Tell me what you want and I'll make it happen."

His shift in position gave her emotional whiplash. One second she was sitting on her ass and hanging out with her mother, and the next she was his baby girl and they were a team?

"This will be good for us," she told him. "I need to go be on my own and learn a few more skills. Maybe in four or five years, we can revisit the idea of me working for you."

She walked out, then downstairs. She found her mom in the kitchen, helping Austin unload teacups and saucers onto the counter so they could be washed.

Harlow walked directly to her. Without saying anything, her mother hugged her tight. After a few seconds, Harlow stepped back.

Her mom touched her cheek. "I'm sorry your dad was a jerk."

"I didn't tell you he was." She swallowed. "But you knew he would be. You knew all this time, and you protected him. He never deserved you."

Robyn gave her a sad smile. "Honey, no one is a hundred percent at fault in any relationship. I did a lot of things wrong. I let him get his way too much. I subjugated my dreams for his." She paused. "There's other stuff. Don't think it's all on him, because it's not."

"I know. I'm partially to blame for what went wrong at work. He doesn't make it easy, though."

"No, he doesn't."

Austin grinned at Harlow. "You could join the navy with me. We could go through training together. It would be great."

Harlow managed a smile. "That's not happening. But I'll be there to celebrate every accomplishment. You know that, right?"

His gaze met hers. "I absolutely know that."

The rain was so loud on the roof of the old Spanish-style church that no one heard the first song. But as the minister took her place in front of the congregation, the drops lessened, then stopped. By the time the eulogies began, the sun was out.

Robyn sat between her children, listening to all those who wanted to talk about how much Lillian had meant to them. Salvia spoke, as did the husband of Lillian's late best friend. Former students of Leo who had known her well flew in from different parts of the country to share how she had been like a mother to them, helping them, giving them advice, guiding them. Harlow spoke movingly about spending the summer here while recovering from cancer. And Mason read from several of the letters she'd written to him.

Robyn had cried so much in the past few days that there were very few tears left for the ceremony, so she was able to take in all the love these people had for Lillian. Knowing how her beloved great-aunt had touched so many helped start the healing.

After the short, family-only graveside service, they all went to Lillian's house for the wake. Their guests were there already, enjoying sandwiches and scones, fruit tarts and mini eclairs. In addition to tea, the catering staff offered a selection of Lillian's favorite cocktails.

Robyn escaped to her room to take a breath and freshen her makeup, then went downstairs to deal with the crowd. She found Austin, Harlow and Kip circulating, checking on drinks and food, and rescuing some guests from overly curious cats. Mason was comforting Salvia, who was still fighting tears. Robyn didn't see Cord anywhere, but also didn't have the energy or interest to deal with him.

She greeted people she knew and introduced herself to those she didn't. She was exhausted, but determined to represent Lillian as gracefully as possible. An hour stretched into two. She was starting to feel faint when Mason appeared at her side.

"If you'll excuse us," he said to two nuns Lillian had known. "Robyn's needed."

He ushered her toward the back of the house. Bypassing the kitchen, he pulled her into the breakfast room, where he guided her to a chair.

"You need to sit," he told her, his voice filled with concern. "You haven't slept, you won't eat, and I doubt you've had anything to drink."

"Trying to liquor me up?" she asked, hoping she could summon a little teasing tone for her voice.

He handed her a glass of water. "Let's start with this."

She sipped gratefully, the cool liquid helping her dry throat. "Thank you."

"You're welcome. Now stay there until I'm back."

She did as he requested, doing her best to clear her mind and simply be in the moment. Less than five minutes later, Mason returned with a plate of tiny sandwiches and a green salad.

"There isn't any real food in the house," he grumbled, putting the plate in front of her.

She managed a smile. "What do you consider real food? Bacon?"

He grinned and sat next to her. "It would be a start."

She nibbled on one of the sandwiches and picked at the salad, but had no appetite.

"I can't," she said, pushing away the plate. "I'm sorry."

"Hey, you tried." He took her hand and rubbed his fingers against her knuckles. "Tell me what you need."

Lillian not to be dead. Only she couldn't say that. He was hurting just as much, and he was only trying to take care of her.

"Why are you so good to me?" she asked.

He hesitated, as if weighing his words. Unusual for Mason.

One of the caterers stuck her head into the breakfast room. "I'm sorry to bother you, but someone just came in the back. She's not here for the wake. Her name is Zafina, and she's looking for someone named Cord."

THIRTY

Zafina? Robyn tried to take that in as she stared at the young woman standing in the breakfast room doorway. Her ex-husband's pregnant girlfriend? The ridiculousness of the moment combined with exhaustion and her soul-stealing grief. She looked at the pretty, dark-haired woman, saw the resemblance to Kip, remembered that Zafina was also her daughter's fiancé's twin sister, and started to laugh. The laughter burst out of her and grew until she couldn't control herself. She gasped for breath and laughed and laughed until suddenly she was sobbing, covering her face with her hands and not knowing if she would ever feel whole again.

Mason pulled her to her feet, then wrapped his arms around her. Then he looked past her and spoke.

"Hi, Zafina. You caught us at a bad time. Robyn's great-aunt passed away, and today was the funeral."

"Oh, I'm so sorry. I didn't know. I saw all the cars but didn't know why they were here."

"You couldn't."

Robyn managed to collect herself enough to wipe her face, then say to Zafina, "I'll get Cord."

Zafina looked confused, tired and wary. Robyn couldn't blame her.

She pulled her phone out of her dress pocket and quickly texted Harlow.

Please bring your dad to the breakfast room. It's important.

She put her phone away and smiled at Zafina. "He'll be right down. You can wait in here." She paused. "Would you like something to drink? Water? Herbal tea? We have plenty of food if you're hungry." She thought about the ingredients in high tea and figured they would probably be all right for a pregnant woman.

"I'm fine," Zafina said with a tight smile. "You're being very gracious. We haven't met, but I know who you are."

"Likewise," Robyn said. "You're right. We haven't met. You weren't at my dinner with your parents."

Zafina dropped her gaze. "I thought it would be awkward."

"What with you dating my ex-husband? I suppose, but I can get over it if you can."

Zafina looked her. She had lovely eyes, Robyn thought. Big and brown. She was a beautiful woman — just Cord's type.

"You're not angry with me?" Zafina asked.

"I don't care that you're dating Cord. That was over years ago. But I do worry about you dating the father of your brother's fiancé. Still, we can figure it out."

"Where are you taking me?"

They all turned at the sound of Cord's voice. He and Harlow entered the breakfast room, and he saw Zafina. In that split second, his expression was unguarded, his feelings exposed. Robyn was pleased to see genuine affection in his eyes, longing and a bit of hope alongside his surprise. At least he cared about the woman he'd knocked up. That was a start.

"Zafina? What are you doing here?"

Zafina glared at him. "Where else would I be? You took off without saying anything. I had no idea where you were until Kip told me. You scared me." Her lower lip trembled. "Cord, I thought you loved me."

"I do." He glanced at Robyn, then back at Zafina. "I do," he repeated. "But you surprised me when you said . . ." His gaze dropped to her belly. "I didn't know what to think."

"I want to have your child," she said defiantly. "I want us to be a family." She tossed her head. "What are you so scared about? That I'm trapping you? I'm not. You don't have to marry me, you just have to love me."

Harlow was wide-eyed, as if unable to grasp what was happening. Robyn thought it might be a bit uncomfortable to watch one's parent in the middle of a declaration like this one. She circled the still-talking couple and stopped by her daughter.

"Let's give them privacy."

Harlow nodded and walked out with her, Mason trailing behind. When they were through the kitchen and out in the hallway, Harlow stopped.

"That was weird."

"I know."

"She really loves him."

Robyn smiled. "There's someone for everyone."

Harlow's mouth twisted. "Dad's sure been doing his share of sampling. I hope they work it out. He's going to have to be there for her. Do you think he's capable of doing the right thing?"

"Maybe. We're kind of due for a miracle. Maybe it'll come from your father."

Harlow shook her head. "I think that's unlikely, but let's hope for the best."

Harlow woke up an hour before dawn. Her sleep had been restless, and more than once, Kip had pulled her into his arms to comfort her. But she hadn't been able to settle, and after pulling on yoga pants and a T-shirt, she crept downstairs to start coffee.

The house was quiet, and there was a sense of emptiness. Funny how one person could make such a difference, she thought as she scooped coffee into the machine. Lillian had been the true heart of this home. Without her it was just a ridiculously large, sprawling oddity that would never be anyone's idea of a place to live. Better to let the historical society have it, she thought, grateful Mason was committed to making that happen.

She opened the refrigerator for cream and saw leftovers from the wake. She and Austin were taking the food to a homeless shelter later that morning.

She heard footsteps and looked up as her father and Zafina walked into the kitchen. For a second, the three of them stared at each other, then her father offered her a quick smile.

"You're up early," he said.

"So are you."

He glanced at Zafina, then back at her. "We have a flight to catch. Back to Florida."

Harlow looked at him without speaking. No way she was going to make this more comfortable for him.

He cleared his throat. "I, ah, I'm sorry about our conversation before. I was dealing with a lot, and I should have been more understanding of what you were trying to tell me."

Zafina put her hand on his arm. Harlow wasn't sure if she was giving him a signal to keep going or offering support. She found she didn't much care.

"I don't want you to go," he said. "I want us to work together, to grow the company. But I understand your need to prove yourself somewhere else first. I want . . ." He drew in a breath. "You're my daughter, and I love you, and I want you to be happy. If you do take another job, maybe we can talk about how I can convince you to come back in a few years."

All the right words, she thought, not sure if she could believe them. Cord knew how to be charming, and part of that was faking sincerity. But he *was* her father, and she supposed based on that alone, she should give him the benefit of the doubt.

"I love you, too, Dad," she said. "Thanks. What about you two?"

He grinned. "Zafina's having a baby, and I'm going to be a father again."

Zafina gazed at him lovingly. "We're still working it out, but Cord understands what's important."

Harlow waited for them to say they were getting married, but they were all spared that by the sound of a horn outside.

"Our ride is here," Cord said. "We'll see you back in Florida?"

She nodded as she hugged him and Zafina.

Once they were gone, she took two mugs of coffee upstairs and crept into Austin's room. Her brother was asleep, sprawled across his bed. She sat in one of the chairs by the window and waited for him to wake up. He stirred almost immediately.

"Hey," he said, opening his eyes. "What are you doing here?"

She handed him a mug. "Hiding. Dad's gone. He and Zafina left for the airport. They seem to have reconciled." She wrinkled her nose. "I'm sure they'll be getting married. Yesterday she said she didn't care if they did, but I think she's going to want to have a ring on her finger before the baby's born."

Austin sat up and shoved the pillows behind his back. "What does that mean for you?"

"It's weird. And gross. I'm not sure Dad is capable of being in a relationship long-term."

"That's about him. I asked about you."

He was wondering how she would deal with her sister-in-law being her stepmom and her father being her brother-in-law.

She glanced at the ring on her left hand. The sparkling diamond was meant to symbolize her love for Kip and his love for her. They'd promised to get married and have a family. To be with each other until one of them died.

She'd been so sure, she thought. That he was the one, that they could be happy together. When had everything changed?

"Does he know?" Austin asked.

She shook her head. "I didn't know. At least, I wasn't sure." She wiped her cheeks. "How did you know I was going to end things?"

"There were too many secrets. He didn't tell you about his debt and Tracey. You haven't told him about the inheritance. Not exactly a great way to start a marriage."

"You're right."

"As usual," he teased.

She drew in a deep breath. "You're going to stay here?"

"I hope so. I'll ask Mason if I can rent a room or something. He's got the house for a year. He's thinking of keeping back a couple of acres and building a place. That will take some time. If he won't let me stay, I'll rent a room somewhere. I'll be working a lot and getting in shape, so it kind of doesn't matter where I'm going to live as long as it's in state."

She eyed him. "You're getting yourself in shape? What do you think you're in now?"

He grinned. "I'm okay for a civilian."

"You're taking the navy thing very seriously."

"Yeah, I am."

She sipped her coffee. "What do you think about Mom and Mason?"

"I like him. He's a good guy. He's crazy about her and would do anything for her."

"I like him more than I ever liked Jase. I always felt he was looking down on us."

Austin nodded. "It's all about appearances with him. He thought she was beautiful, but he never saw her as a person. Mason's not like that."

"Mom will need to inventory the house

before Mason sells it. She'll have to stay." Harlow ignored the jolt of pain that realization brought. "You'll be here. I'll be in Key West. Everything's different."

"You're for sure taking the job?"

"I'm going to call him in a bit and tell him. I can't work for Dad." She thought about what her father had said before he'd left. "Maybe in a few years, but not now."

"Want me to help you find a place to live?"

"You're sweet, but you'll be busy here. I'll manage."

She'd never rented a place on her own but knew she would figure it out.

She waited until after breakfast to talk to Kip. They went out to the back garden and sat on the grass in the sun.

"This is a great old house," he said. "Too bad no one can keep it."

"The historical society will take care of it."

"I guess." He looked at her. "I know you have to stay through the reading of the will, but I need to get back to work. I thought I'd get a flight out tomorrow."

She nodded. "You've been generous with your time. I appreciate it. I'm sorry we fought before. And for taking off. I should have talked to you first."

"It's okay. You had a lot going on. I know

you're glad you were here with Lillian. You know, at the end."

She didn't want to think about losing Lillian. Not right now. The sadness would distract her, and she had to stay focused.

"Kip, I have to tell you something." Her throat tightened, but she ignored the sensation. "I can't marry you."

He flinched. "What? You can't mean that. You love me. We belong together."

She slipped off the ring and held it out to him. He drew back.

"No. I won't take it. Why are you doing this?"

"I'm not ready," she said, thinking that was the kinder thing to say. "I can't deal with everything that's happened. I do love you, but I'm not ready to commit to you and to us. I'm not ready to get married."

He scrambled to his feet and glared at her. "What does that even mean? You're going to break off our engagement but still date me? That's not happening. Why are you acting like this? Is it because of Tracey? I told you that was nothing. Why can't you let it go?"

She stood. "You were married and didn't tell me. We've been together nearly a year, and you never once mentioned you had an ex-wife. That's big, Kip. That's huge."

"Okay, I was wrong, but you're not easy to live with either. You're moody and self-centered. I don't complain because when you love someone, you're supposed to love all of them. You're supposed to love my past."

"And Tracey?" she snapped. "Am I supposed to love her, too?"

"You're being ridiculous."

"That makes two of us."

They glared at each other. Harlow knew the argument was a perfect illustration of how neither of them was in a place to even consider marriage.

"I don't want to fight," she said quietly. "I'm sorry. This isn't going to work. I'll be home in a few days to get my stuff and move out."

All his anger disappeared, leaving him looking shell-shocked. "So we're finished?"

"I'm moving to Key West. I have a job there starting in three weeks."

His face tightened with rage. "You fucking bitch! You've known you were going to dump me for weeks, but you strung me along? You took another job and didn't say anything? Who the hell do you think you are? You don't play me."

The words came out in a roar. Harlow instinctively took a step back, not sure what

Kip was going to do. He raised his hand, as if to hit her, then froze.

Horror joined pain. "Don't," she whispered. "Don't make this the last thing that happens between us."

Slowly he lowered his arm. After snatching the ring from her hand, he stalked back to the house. Harlow collapsed onto the grass, pulled her legs to her chest and rested her forehead on her knees. There weren't any tears, not even when she started to shake.

THIRTY-ONE

Robyn ran her hands across the burled walnut desk. A small Waterford crystal vase held fresh flowers, and an assortment of pens filled a mug Harlow had made the year after she'd beaten cancer. At some point, Robyn would have to start going through the desk, but not today. Dealing with Lillian's death was hard enough without having to touch her things, knowing she was gone.

"I wish . . ." she murmured, then paused, not sure what she would wish for. More time with her aunt, of course, but that was her being selfish, although a case could be made that wishes were inherently selfish.

"I miss you."

An obvious statement, but one that needed to be said. She missed Lillian's laugh, her caring, her wise advice. Right now Robyn needed to talk to someone she trusted who would help her figure out what

522

to do next, or rather how.

All her plans had shattered, along with her heart, when Lillian passed away. Now she had only one very short year to get in experts, start sorting, decide on a location for her antique store, and learn how to run a business. She'd lost the gift of time. Even more upsetting, she had to do it all without Lillian.

But the larger complication was somewhere in the house, a strong, steady presence who made her happier than she had ever been while also making her more unsure. What about Mason?

She liked him. She enjoyed his company and having him in her bed. He was a good man, an honorable former soldier who believed in duty and service. There was no bad there — at least on his part. But . . .

But what if she lost herself in him the way she'd lost herself in Cord? What if their relationship was nothing but circumstances, and when they returned to the real world, it all faded away? What if he started expecting things of her — changes, really — that she couldn't do or didn't want to make happen? Suddenly there seemed far more risk than reward, and that scared her.

Her phone buzzed. She glanced down and saw a single word.

Marco.

She texted back a quick, In Lillian's office, then tucked her phone into her pocket. Harlow probably wanted to talk about the reading of the will. While Lillian had been clear about her plans, tomorrow it would be official.

She heard quick footsteps in the hall, then Harlow hurried into the room. She looked pale and shaken. Robyn instinctively moved toward her.

"What happened?"

Harlow voice trembled. "I broke up with Kip, and I thought he was going to hit me. He didn't, but I was scared, and it makes me think I never knew him at all. How could I have made such a huge mistake?"

Robyn guided her to the sofa and sat beside her. Anger burned, but she ignored it. Getting pissed wouldn't help her daughter.

"Start at the beginning."

Harlow explained how she'd woken up that morning and realized she couldn't marry Kip and that when she'd told him, he hadn't taken it well.

"He was so angry," she whispered, her body shaking. "He looked like he wanted to hit me."

"Where is he now?" Robyn asked, rubbing her daughter's back.

"I don't know. Somewhere in the house, I guess."

"He needs to leave."

Harlow nodded. "He does. I'm not sure I can tell him, though. Will you come with me?"

"Of course, but what about letting Mason tell him? He spent two years as a drill sergeant. I'm pretty sure he can handle Kip."

Harlow nodded. "If you think he wouldn't mind. I don't want to see Kip again. I was so wrong."

Tears trickled down her face. Robyn ached for her and was furious with Kip. Emotion on emotion, she thought, wondering how they would all get through this. She'd felt that Harlow and Kip were moving too fast and that they should wait on getting married, but she hadn't wanted it to end like this.

"You believed what he told you," she said. "You trusted him, and he betrayed you."

"I keep wondering how much else he's hiding," she admitted. "Now I'm doubly glad I'm moving to Key West. I don't have to worry about running in to him."

Robyn texted Mason, asking him to come

to Lillian's office.

Less than a minute later, he was striding toward them, his expression quizzical.

"What's up?"

Robyn looked at Harlow, who stood and squared her shoulders.

"Kip and I broke up. He wasn't happy that I wanted to end the engagement, and he kind of lost it when I told him I was moving to Key West." She swallowed. "He raised his hand and I thought he was going to hit me."

Nothing about Mason changed. Not his body language or his expression. Robyn marveled at his self-control.

"He was going to go home tomorrow," Harlow continued. "But I want him to leave now. I'm scared of him, and I don't want him in the house." She twisted her hands together. "I know I should be the one to tell him, but I can't." She looked at the ground, then back at Mason "Mom suggested that maybe you —"

Mason nodded. "Of course. Give me thirty minutes. I won't leave him alone until he drives away. Do you want me to beat him up first? I can do a little damage or a lot. Up to you." One shoulder rose and lowered. "It's not much of a challenge. Kip won't know how to fight back."

Harlow looked at her, then back at Mason. Robyn had a feeling she appeared as stunned as her daughter. Not just at the offer, but at the matter-of-fact way he made it and his assessment of the situation.

"Getting him out of the house is enough for now," Harlow murmured. "But thank you."

Mason's gaze sharpened. "Did he hit you, Harlow?"

"No. I'm not lying."

"Victims often don't want to get —"

"I'm not a victim," Harlow said, interrupting him. "Not ever."

Mason smiled. "No, you're not."

He left. Harlow returned to the sofa and leaned against Robyn.

"This has been a very sucky week."

"It has. I'm sorry about Kip."

"Me, too."

Robyn put her arm around her daughter and kissed the top of her head. "I do love you, and I'm very proud of you. Austin and I will be going back home in a few days. I need to get the house ready to sell, and he wants to pack up his stuff. How about if the three of us take a couple of days to drive down to Key West and help you find a place?"

Harlow straightened and looked at her. "I

appreciate that, Mom. I want to say yes, but I think I need to do this on my own."

Robyn felt a rush of pride. "I'll be around if you need me."

Her daughter smiled. "I know. Just like always."

The first time Mason had visited Gregory's law office, he'd been more concerned about what the attorney was saying than interested in the surroundings. Now, as he walked in for the reading of the will, he found himself aware of the wood paneled walls, the elegant fixtures and the quiet air of wealth and security.

He'd driven over with Robyn and her kids. Austin and Harlow looked as nervous as he felt. They were shown into a large conference room with a table for thirty and a view of a walled courtyard filled with stone benches and flowering trees.

Salvia was already there, as were several people Mason didn't know. He supposed some of them represented charities Lillian had supported over the years. Austin and Harlow sat on either side of their mother, and Mason settled across from them.

Since discovering the value of the house, he'd done his best not to think about his inheritance. It was too much for a guy like him to believe was real, and as it came at the price of losing someone he'd grown to love, he was fine not claiming any of it for decades. But now, waiting for Gregory to join them, Mason found himself wondering how much of this was real.

Had Lillian really left him a house he would sell for twelve-point-seven million dollars? No one should have that much money. It bordered on obscene. All he wanted was a nice little house and his military pension. That was plenty for him. Only what if it wasn't just him?

His gaze drifted to Robyn. She was so damned beautiful. He still couldn't believe she was willing to sleep with him and, in fact, seemed to enjoy his company. He knew every inch of her body and what her face looked like when she came. He knew what made her laugh, her favorite wines and that she loved deeply, from the soul.

Robyn deserved more than a little house and a guy with a military pension — not that he was assuming anything. Still, he also knew that she wouldn't care what any man brought to the table financially. She couldn't be swayed by money or power — she was interested in the essence of a person.

Gregory walked into the conference room and nodded at everyone. He settled at the head of the table and opened the folder in front of him. After explaining they were here for the reading of Lillian Holton's last will and testament, he told them he would start with the charitable bequests first, then excuse those representatives so the rest of the will was reserved for the family.

Mason told himself not to react to whatever he heard, then nearly fell off his chair when Gregory explained about a charitable trust, worth eight million dollars, that was to be divided equally among the eleven charities represented at the reading. There was a generous bequest for each of the gardeners and all the maids, and Lillian had made arrangements to pay off Salvia's mortgage, as well as leaving her a pension. All the staff were to be kept on for a year and paid their full salary.

That part completed, Gregory had the recipients escorted from the room. When the door had closed, he said, "I doubt any of this will be a surprise, but I'm going to read it anyway."

Robyn nodded.

Gregory read through the rest of the will. As expected, Mason received the house with the understanding that he wouldn't sell for a year. He was given funds for upkeep and was required to give Robyn and her agents access. Lillian requested he sell to the historical society on the condition that they pay him at least twelve-point-seven million dollars. If they offered less, he was free to sell to anyone else. He was also left Uncle Leo's papers and any books he wanted from the library.

He did his best not to react to the information — it wasn't new, and he shouldn't be surprised. Yet he was, because now it was real. Lillian was gone, and he owned her crazy, wonderful house.

Gregory moved on to the next section of the will. Lillian left Robyn the contents of the house, including her personal belongings, the cats and one million dollars.

"I'm sorry, what?" she asked.

Gregory paused. "Would you like me to read that part again?"

Robyn stared at him. "I, no. It's fine. I wasn't expecting any money."

Mason knew she'd been worried about her financial future. She blamed herself for not making smarter decisions after her divorce. She'd worked hard to come up with a sensible plan. Now she would be financially independent and wouldn't need anything from him.

Gregory explained that each of Robyn's children had already received their bequests, but she left several of Leo's watches to Austin and some jewelry to Harlow. A few minutes later, Gregory was done.

Back at the house, Robyn excused herself to go to her room. Mason watched her climb the stairs, wondering what she was thinking. There had been so much change in such a short period. While he had no reason to worry, he felt a hint of unease low in his gut. He was about to follow her, to ask what was going on, but Austin stopped him.

"You have a second?" the teen asked.

Mason nodded. "Sure. What's up?"

"I'd like to rent a room here, if that's all right. For the year. I won't be around much. Between my two jobs and working out, I'll be gone a lot. If you'd rather not, I'll get a place somewhere else, but I'd prefer to stay here."

"Still going to UC San Diego?"

Austin nodded. "I'll submit my application as soon as possible. I'm starting an online SAT review course so I can better my scores. I'll be applying to naval ROTC, too."

"You have a plan." Mason patted him on the shoulder. "You don't need to rent a room, kid. You can stay here until my year is up." He smiled. "Plenty of space."

Austin's face brightened. "You sure?"

"Absolutely. You're welcome to have friends over, but no loud parties. As for the rest of it, we'll figure it out as we go."

"Thanks, Mason."

Austin headed for the stairs, while Harlow hovered in the background. Mason turned to her.

"You want to stay here, too?"

She grinned. "No. I'm heading back home tomorrow." The smile faded. "I'm a little worried about what Kip is going to do with my stuff. My friend Enid is going to stop by the apartment and make sure it's not out in the parking lot."

"He didn't put up much of a fight when I told him to leave yesterday." Kip had folded in less than five seconds.

"He might be more emboldened at home." She shrugged. "I'll deal. What about you and Mom?"

"What are you asking?"

"Are you in love with her?"

"I appreciate the direct question."

She watched him without speaking.

Mason figured she was expecting an actual answer. "Yes," he said bluntly. "I haven't told her."

Harlow relaxed. "I won't say anything. That's between the two of you. I just wanted to make sure you weren't using her for sex."

"I'm not."

She turned away, then looked back at him. "You might have to fight for her, because of my dad and maybe Jase. I'm not sure she's going to trust so easily. I mean herself. I don't think she's worried about you."

"Giving me advice?"

She smiled. "Someone has to. Besides, I think it would be nice to have you in the family."

"I'd like that, too."

But it was a big ask, and Mason honest to God wasn't sure his luck was that good. Not when it came to a woman like Robyn.

Robyn changed into jeans and a blouse. She tried to focus on the basics, like fastening the buttons, then slipping on shoes, rather than admit her head was about to explode.

Lillian had left her a million dollars. She'd always known her great-aunt and uncle were well-off, but she'd had no idea they were rich. Although she supposed the house should have been a tipoff.

A million dollars. She'd expected to be left the cats and the contents of the house, but not anything else.

She sank onto the bench at the foot of her bed. The money offered her the financial security she'd recently realized she didn't have. It would give her start-up cash to open her own business selling antiques. It would cover the initial lease payments and remodeling of the retail space if needed.

Once her business was up and running, she would pay back whatever she'd used so the million dollars was made whole again. If she was smart with her store, she would never have to touch it and could leave it to her children. She should make enough to support herself, hire a couple of employees, and help pay for Austin's college and Harlow's wedding when she found the right guy.

Lillian had blessed her with the gift of peace of mind, and it was too much to absorb.

There was a knock at the door, followed by Harlow asking if she could come in.

Robyn opened the door. "Hey, how are you holding up?"

Her daughter smiled at her. "I want to ask you the same question. You all right?"

"No, but I'll get there. I'm having a little trouble grasping what just happened."

"You're going to need the money to pay for cat food."

Robyn laughed. "Possibly. Are you still leaving tomorrow?"

"I am. I have a lot to do before I move to

Key West, and I don't want to leave Kip alone with my things for too long."

Robyn nodded. "I get that. We both have a lot going on, but what we need right now is a distraction. Let's go to the store for taco and margarita fixings."

Harlow laughed. "I'd love that. I'll change my clothes, then meet you in the kitchen."

Robyn collected her purse and went downstairs. She didn't see Mason and had the brief thought that she should go find him, then decided not to. She needed a little time to figure out how she was feeling. She needed to process her grief. And maybe, just maybe, she was a little scared.

Lillian's death had accelerated all her plans. She had to move here to start on the inventory. Yes, Lillian had asked her to settle in Santa Barbara permanently, but Robyn hadn't decided yet whether she was ready to make the move. Now she saw no other choice.

What did that mean for her and Mason? Were they a couple? Was what they had real or a summer fling? She didn't know where he was mentally. Given the uncertainty, her instinct was to run and hide. Not exactly her proudest moment.

Before she could reach a conclusion, her daughter came down the stairs.

"We should check if we have tequila before we go," Harlow said. "The good stuff."

"Now you're a tequila snob?" Robyn asked with a grin.

"Absolutely. Once I get home and start on my new job, I won't be able to afford the good stuff, so I have to take advantage of you while I can."

"An excellent point. Let's look in the liquor cabinet. Given Lillian's love of a cocktail, I'll bet you'll have your pick from all kinds of tequila."

"She always did know how to throw a party."

Robyn blinked away tears. "She did, and we're lucky to have had her in our lives."

THIRTY-TWO

By six that evening, the ingredients for tacos had been prepped, and Robyn had made her guacamole. Harlow was putting ice into the blender while Austin and Mason argued over what kind of music to play. Austin wanted mariachi while Mason was a firm no on that suggestion.

Robyn listened to the friendly banter and felt herself relax a little. This was normal, she thought with relief. For a couple of hours, the four of them could pretend nothing had changed and that they would all be perfectly fine.

She told herself not to think about the fact that Lillian wouldn't be coming down the stairs or that Harlow was leaving in the morning, literally heading to the other side of the country, to start over in a new city. Harlow was stronger than either of them had realized. The summer had changed her, allowing her daughter to grow into the beautiful, capable woman she was always meant to be. There had been bumps along the road, but Harlow had figured it out. Robyn couldn't be more proud. As for her youngest, Austin was —

"Hello, Robyn."

Robyn looked up and saw Jase standing in the kitchen. The avocado she was holding dropped to the counter.

She blinked, but Jase remained right there, looking both sheepish and determined — an unlikely combination, but somehow he pulled it off.

"The back door was open," Jase continued, moving toward her. "I could hear everyone laughing and talking. I knocked, but I guess with all the noise . . ." He dropped the overnight bag he carried and crossed to her.

"I've missed you, Robyn. More than you know."

Before she could figure out what was happening, he grabbed her by her upper arms and kissed her. On the mouth. Like really kissed her. He tried for a little tongue action, but by then she'd restarted her brain and pulled back.

"Jase? What are you doing here?"

"I couldn't wait any longer." His voice was low and intense. "I can't let you go."

He glanced around, as if just now realizing they weren't alone. She assumed he would ask her to step outside, but apparently not, she thought, stunned when he kept talking.

"You're on my mind all the time," he continued. "I was such a fool. You're the most amazing woman I've ever known."

Then, right there, in front of God and everyone, he dropped to one knee. "Robyn Caldwell, you're smart and funny and caring, and I've been an idiot. Please give me a chance to make it right. Please let me spend the rest of my life showing you how much I love you and how I want you to be happy. Robyn, will you marry me?"

Everything moved in slow motion. She would swear there were five or six seconds between every tick from the clock on the wall. She stared at Jase's hopeful expression, at her children who were wide-eyed and openmouthed with shock, and at Mason, whose face, once again, gave nothing away.

She opened her mouth, then closed it. What was she supposed to say? *No* didn't seem strong enough. *Hell, no* was a little rude. How on earth could this be happening to her?

Just then, a black-and-white cat wandered into the kitchen and rubbed himself against

Jase's bent leg.

"Meow," the cat stated loudly and with expectation.

Jase frowned. "Robyn?"

This couldn't be happening. None of it. Not Lillian being gone, not the money, not everything with Harlow, and not Jase showing up with no warning and proposing while kneeling on Lillian's kitchen floor.

Robyn felt her lips twitch. Then she started to laugh. Harlow giggled a little, and Austin turned away to hide a smirk. Only Mason was expressionless.

Jase stood, looking annoyed and hurt.

"I fail to see what's so funny. I came a long way, Robyn. I canceled appointments with patients to be here."

Robyn nodded, trying to get herself under control, but she couldn't seem to catch her breath. She wondered if hysterical sobs were just a heartbeat away. She seemed prone to them lately.

"Jase," she managed, trying to stifle the laughter. "I'm sorry. I can't —" She sucked in air, then realized she wasn't trying to tell him she couldn't talk. She was telling him the answer to his question.

"I won't marry you," she said at last. "I'm sorry you came all this way. I was clear the last time we spoke and the time before that and when we ended things back home. We're finished. I don't want to see you anymore, and you really need to stop showing up in my life."

Austin patted him on the back. "*Clear* enough for you, bro?"

Harlow moved next to Robyn, arms folded across her chest. "Jase, seriously. This is bordering on stalking. We're asking you to leave. Don't make me get physical."

Jase seemed more startled than threatened, but he didn't protest. Instead he picked up his duffel and started for the back door. Once he got there, he faced her again.

"You're going to regret letting me go," he said stiffly. "Men like me don't come along all that often."

"I hope that's true," she said.

Jase glared at her, then walked outside, slamming the screen door behind him.

"He's a serious dick," Harlow said, flipping a switch on the blender. Instantly the sound of loud motors and blades crushing ice filled the room.

Austin joined his sister at the counter, and Robyn turned to Mason, hoping to see a flicker of amusement or something that told her he thought Jase showing up was a big, fat joke. Instead his eyes were hooded and his mouth a straight line. She had no idea what he was thinking, but he hadn't found the situation funny.

"So, that was weird," she said in a fake, hearty tone. "Now you've met my ex-husband and my ex-boyfriend. I'll have to have lunch with one of your ex-wives to even the score."

He looked at her with the cold, unwelcoming eyes of a stranger. "I have some things I need to see to. I'll leave you to spend the evening with your children."

And with that, he was gone.

Despite the fact that the house was over forty thousand square feet, Mason couldn't find a single place to hide. He wasn't worried about being found — that wasn't the point. His problem was he couldn't escape the memories he'd made in the damned place.

He couldn't go to his bedroom. Not only had he and Robyn fucked on literally every surface, but her room was right next door, and they shared a balcony. The office was just as fraught. They'd talked there, laughed there, even cried there after losing Lillian.

There was no room in the entire house that wasn't filled with her or her kids or the three of them. No matter where he went, she followed, blue eyes laughing, mouth smiling, hands pulling him close.

He couldn't escape the sound of her voice, the way she was so damned honest, or how no matter what was happening around her, she got dinner on the table every day. She welcomed everyone in need, listened, spoke truth, and offered unconditional support. She was everything he'd ever wanted times a hundred million, and he knew, he just knew, it was all going to shit.

He took the stairs to the fourth floor and searched for one fucking room where he didn't have any memories of her. Just one! But that room didn't exist, and he was left to stand in the hallway, desperate for relief from the five-ton boulder that was about to squash him like a bug.

She could have anyone, so why would she want him? She'd had a damned cardiologist flying across the country and proposing in front of people he didn't even know. Jase hadn't cared about anyone but Robyn. He'd put it all on the line. A doctor. She could have had a doctor.

Mason was clear on his place in the universe, even if his recent inheritance was messing with his head a little. But he would get over that. He would pick out his plot, sell the house, and live out the rest of his days with a view of the Pacific. It was a whole lot more than he'd ever dreamed he would have.

As for Robyn — he had to be realistic. He'd aimed well above his pay grade, and it made sense he'd fallen on his ass. Why wouldn't he? She was the moon and stars, and he was a grunt in the army. They'd had a great summer, and now it was time for them to face reality. Well, him anyway. He doubted Robyn had ever left reality behind.

He walked to the staircase and sat down. There wasn't a part of him that didn't hurt. He ached for her, body and soul. Losing her was going to be bad — probably the worst thing he would ever endure. But he'd get through it. That he knew for sure. The army had taught him how to handle adversity.

He would need every one of those skills to survive the next year. She would be here with him, doing the inventory. He had no idea how they were going to handle that. Would she want to continue their affair while it was convenient? Would she want to end things sooner, to keep things more neat?

He knew he was weak enough when it came to her that he would accept any crumb she offered. Humiliating, but facts were facts. What was that old line? She was his greatest weakness. Dying for her would be easy. He was willing to go beyond that and be her bitch.

"You're a difficult man to find."

He stood and turned, only to see Robyn standing in the hallway behind him. Just looking at her was enough to make him want to beg.

She slipped her hands into her jeans front pockets. "I'm sorry about Jase." She grimaced. "All of it. Him showing up, the proposal, me laughing. I think there have been so many emotions over the past few days that I'm incapable of being normal. Although I'm not sure what a normal response to him would have been."

"You might regret letting him go."

Her gaze was steady. "No, I won't. Not ever. We broke up months ago. I meant it then, and I've never wavered. I shouldn't have gone out with him in the first place." Her mouth twisted. "In fact, when I look back, I see that I've never had particularly good taste in men. Until now."

Her words were like a knife to the heart. He wanted to believe them, but somehow he knew he was going to end up with his guts spilling out on the floor.

"Yeah," he said slowly. "About that. I think we both know this was great while it lasted, but it was never going to be more."

Her eyes widened. "You're breaking up with me?"

"No. You're breaking up with me."

"I'm not."

"You are." He gentled his tone. "Robyn, you came here because you were lost and angry, mostly at yourself. You've worked hard to put yourself back together. I was a distraction. A reward, if you will. But you never saw us as more than that. You're going to be selling pieces of art and antiques to fancy museums and big shot dealers all over the world. You'll fly in experts and be a star. You'll love it. And I'm glad you're going to experience it."

"You're wrong about me. About us. I don't want this to end."

God, he wanted to believe her. He wanted her to feel the same way about him, but he knew better.

"What is this?" he asked quietly. "What do we have? Are you in love with me?"

She blinked several times, then took a step back. The two-by-four of the shit that was his life cracked him on the side of the head. Mentally he staggered, but physically he stayed standing. Her confusion, her withdrawal, told him everything he needed to know.

He forced a smile. "It's okay. I'm not

surprised. The question had to be asked. Like I said, you're the one breaking up with me."

"Mason, that's not what I meant. Love is complicated. I don't want to make a mistake."

"You won't. You know what you want, and you'll go for it. When you come back to work on the house, we'll figure something out. It's a big place. I'm sure we can go days and not see each other."

Her lower lip began to tremble. "I don't like this. I don't want to lose you."

"You won't, but you will move on. Oh, and when the year's up, I'm going to want to keep Charles II with me, if that's all right."

Tears spilled down her cheeks. "Mason, no. Please don't do this to me. I need you."

"I'll always be here for you." He crossed to her and pulled her into his arms.

One last time, he thought grimly. One last time.

She clung to him, crying harder now. Her whole body shook. He forced himself to step back. He lightly kissed her, then touched her cheek.

"Goodbye, Robyn."

With that, he went down the stairs, the sound of her crying following him until he walked into his bedroom and carefully shut the door.

Harlow returned home to find that Kip hadn't thrown her things out into the parking lot of their apartment building. Instead he'd taken them all the way to her mom's house and left them there — across the front lawn. Most everything might have been salvageable if the sprinklers hadn't destroyed her laptop and most of the clothes.

She got out of the Uber from the airport and stared at the wreckage. She'd taken her tablet with her to California, so that was saved. But pretty much everything else she owned was soaked and lying in sad piles.

The driver hesitated. "You going to be okay?"

"Fine." Kip didn't deserve her tears. Apparently she'd been engaged to a real bastard. That was on her, but no way was she going to cry over him. Never again.

She rolled her suitcase inside, then went to inspect her stuff. Most of the clothes could be salvaged, she thought grimly. Not many of the shoes. She moved closer to her laptop and saw not only had it been soaked by the sprinklers, it had also been run over.

She took everything she could carry into

the garage, where she quickly sorted her things into keep and toss piles. She stuffed her ruined things into large trash bags. She would put them into her car to dispose of later. Her mom was upset enough without knowing what Kip had done.

Luckily, Harlow had arranged her flight several days ago, so she'd been able to fly out before dawn. Her mom and Austin had followed with connecting flights that had them landing late that night. She had a few hours to clean up the mess Kip had left.

It took less time than she would have thought to sort through the remains and bring in what could be saved. She started a load of laundry and took the rest of her stuff to her room. At least when she moved, she would be traveling light.

After unpacking, she made a quick trip to the grocery store. Her mother hadn't eaten since Jase had showed up yesterday, but at some point she was going to get hungry. Plus Austin was always up for a meal.

Thinking of Jase made her think of Mason, which was much harder. Seeing Jase humiliated had been kind of fun, but knowing that Mason was in pain hurt her heart. She didn't know what her mom had said to Mason, but it couldn't have been what he wanted to hear. He was in love with Robyn, yet her mom was flying home. Mason had looked like he'd been diagnosed with a terminal disease.

When Harlow had tried to talk to her mom, Robyn had said she needed to be alone, and that was the last Harlow had seen her. She'd left before anyone was up.

By early evening, she was done with laundry and was looking at the remains of her sad wardrobe. She would have to do a little shopping before she moved, she thought. Just casual stuff and a few dresses. Maybe two or three pairs of shoes.

Her mom had told her to go through the house and take what she wanted. Harlow and Austin planned to rent a truck and cart her stuff down to Key West after she got an apartment. Places down there were tiny and expensive, so the less she took, the better.

She had a small sofa in her bedroom that would work, and her bedroom set was fine. She'd take the TV on the dresser. All she needed was a small table and a couple of chairs for an eating area and maybe a handful of end tables. There were plenty of those in the house.

She texted with Enid, then watched Netflix until close to midnight, when she heard a car in the driveway. She went outside and saw her mom and Austin getting their bags out of the trunk of the Uber.

"Welcome back," she said brightly, looking toward her brother, who shook his head.

"Harlow." Her mother sounded exhausted and looked worse. "How are you doing?"

"I'm fine, Mom. I have food in the house, if you're hungry, and I put fresh sheets on everyone's bed."

"Thank you." Her mother gave her a smile that trembled at the corners. "I'm tired, so if no one minds, I'm going to bed."

She rolled her suitcase down the hall and disappeared into her room. Harlow and Austin went in the opposite direction. She followed him into his room.

"How was the flight?" she asked.

"Okay. Long. She didn't say anything." He tossed his suitcase on the bed. "She was quiet the whole time. She didn't cry, she didn't read, she just sat there, looking out the window. It was scary."

"She'll be okay. She just has to figure out a few things. It's been a lot, Austin. Too much has happened. She has to take it all in."

He stared at her. "What about Mason? The man is shattered. Whatever they said to each other, it broke him. I think he's in love with her."

"He is."

552

"Does she love him back?"

Most of the time she thought of her brother as grown-up, but every now and then she remembered he was still a teenager. Now, with the worry and questioning in his tone, he sounded more like a little boy than an adult.

"I don't know," she admitted. "I hope so. He would be good for her."

"Love sucks."

She smiled. "You say that now, but one day you're going to meet a woman who changes your mind."

"Naw. I'm going to play the field. I'm never getting serious about anyone."

"Famous last words."

THIRTY-THREE

Robyn woke up a little after six — which would have been impressive, except she was now in Florida, and it was three in the morning back in Santa Barbara, so not exactly a full night's sleep. She couldn't remember the last time she'd felt rested — probably before Lillian had died. Regardless, life waited for no one, so she got up and headed for the shower. She stood under the hot spray until she felt human again, then dressed and prepared to start her day.

She thought maybe the routine would help, but she'd been gone so long, the house barely felt familiar. She'd lived here for years, yet nothing about the place was right. This wasn't home anymore. It probably hadn't been for longer than she'd realized.

She made the bed, then unpacked. She carried her dirty clothes to the laundry room, where she found a pile of Austin's clothes waiting for her. While Austin knew how to do laundry, it wasn't his favorite. She smiled. He'd have to take on the task when he moved in with Mason.

Just thinking the name stabbed her in the heart, but she ignored the sensation. She wasn't ready to deal with him just yet. When she felt stronger, she would do the deep dive into her feelings, first to figure out what had gone wrong and second to decide what she wanted enough to fight for.

Once the laundry was started, she went through the stack of mail, mostly junk. After that was done, she took a pad of paper and walked through the house. Some of the furniture would need to stay for staging. Some of it could be sold. She doubted there was much Harlow would be interested in, and Austin would stare at her in confusion if she asked him if he wanted to keep anything.

There were a few art pieces she knew Cord loved, along with the dining room table he'd bought without talking to her. It wouldn't fit in his current place, but if he and Zafina were going to have a kid together, they would need a house. His penthouse condo was too small for a baby, and there wasn't any backyard or . . .

She came to a stop in the middle of the dining room as an idea formed. It was insane, really. Twisted and strange, but it felt right. Okay, maybe that was the lack of sleep talking, but maybe not.

She pulled out her phone.

You have a second to talk?

Three dots appeared almost instantly.

Do you have any idea what time it is?

Yes, but so what? You get up early.

It's not even four in the morning where you are.

I'm back.

She pushed the button to call him.

"When did you get back?" her ex-husband asked when he answered.

"Last night. Cord, are you going to marry Zafina?"

He swore. "There's a question."

"Yes, it is. Are you answering it?"

"It's awkward talking about this with you."

She smiled. "Why? Come on, we've been done for years. I hope you two work it out. Are you going to marry her and be a dad to that baby?"

"I'm thinking about it." He sighed. "I haven't proposed or anything, and she keeps saying she doesn't have to be married, but we both know that's not true. What do you think?"

"My opinion shouldn't matter," she told him. "But for what it's worth, doing the right thing can feel really good. Maybe it's time to grow up."

"Low blow."

"But the truth."

"Did you call to tell me I shouldn't do it?"

"No, I called to say you should buy me out of the house."

His end of the call went silent, so she kept talking.

"Think about it," she said. "You love this place way more than I ever did. I'd throw in the furniture. You already own half of the house, so it would be a bargain. You couldn't find anything close to this nice for that price. There's room for the kids to visit, and when they have grandkids, we can all spend the holidays here. Harlow can have her dream wedding in the backyard, like she's always wanted."

He would easily qualify for a loan, she thought. After all, he had a successful business.

"You'd do that?" he asked, his tone hopeful. "I mean, Zafina would have to see it, but I know she'd be crazy about it. We'd ah, probably have to replace the bedroom furniture."

"Yes, I doubt your future wife wants to sleep in the same bed where you and I had sex."

He chuckled. "That's a blunt way of putting it."

"I'm speaking my mind more these days. Want to bring her by today? I'll make myself scarce. I'll also tell the kids to be gone, so there's no pressure."

"I can't believe you'd do this for me, Robyn."

"Like I said, this has always been more your house than mine." And having him buy it made things much easier for her. "Text me when you'll be by."

"I will." His voice was eager. "Probably around lunchtime, but I'll let you know for sure."

"Great."

She hung up. Cord had a way of being persuasive, so she was fairly confident he would get Zafina there at the first opportunity. She resumed her walk-through, now looking for what she would want to pack up for herself. Honestly there was very little. A few paintings, a couple of antiques that were meaningful to her. Otherwise, she would only take her clothes and jewelry. Harlow could take whatever dishes, pots and pans she needed for her new life. Zafina could keep the rest, or they could donate it.

By eight, Robyn was on the patio with her third cup of coffee. The sound of the waterfall flowing into the pool was restful but nothing like a view of the Pacific, and Florida was nothing like California.

The air was already hot and humid. She could hear the low hum of bugs, and even the air smelled different. This wasn't home anymore, and it was time she admitted it. She was leaving Naples.

There were a few things she would miss. Mostly being close to her daughter. But beyond that, Robyn knew she could easily leave the rest of it behind.

She leaned back in her chair and closed her eyes, and at last let down the carefully constructed wall she'd used to protect herself for the past forty-eight hours. Emotions rushed in, flooding her with pain and longing and sorrow. Her breathing got shallow and her chest tightened as she allowed herself to think his name.

Mason.

She didn't know what had happened, but she knew he was done with her. She'd seen it in his determined expression, had felt it through the distance he'd established. He'd pushed her away, basically told her they were over, and she didn't understand why.

He'd said she was breaking up with him, which didn't make any sense. She hadn't been. She'd thought — okay, assumed — that after Lillian died, she would come back and live there while she figured out what to do with the inventory. She'd even talked about buying some land from him so she could build a house next to his. She'd been so sure she mattered to him. That they would be . . . would be . . .

"What?"

She spoke the word out loud because she needed to hear the sound of it. What would they be? Lovers? Friends with benefits? What exactly did Mason want from her? No — that was the wrong question. She'd been so damned worried about giving up her dreams for a man, and here she was thinking about what he wanted? No! What about *her*? What did she want for herself?

The question propelled her to her feet. She circled the pool and the waterfall, went through the gazebo, then back to the patio, her mind spinning in all directions.

What *did* she want for herself? What was important to her? What would make her happy and fulfilled?

"I want to go through the house in Santa Barbara and enjoy the memories of Leo and Lillian. I want to find treasures and learn about sheet music and clocks. I want to sell pieces to museums and give others away, and I want to open a wonderful eclectic antique store."

She made another lap of the property.

"I want to travel."

Cord had never wanted to go on trips with her. He preferred being on one of his boats. She wanted to see New Zealand and those cats at that Japanese temple and do a river cruise through Europe.

There was so much more. She wanted a home that she loved. Something nice, but not ostentatious. She wanted flowers in the garden and a big kitchen with a six-burner stove so when friends and family came, she could cook whatever she wanted. It would have to be cat-friendly and open, with a large patio.

"I want grandchildren," she said, then smiled. Her kids were probably going to have a say in that one.

"I want to be happy, and I want to be loved."

She stopped by the waterfall, the spray hitting her arm. There it was — the most difficult one of all. She wanted love in her life. Strong, steady love, the love of a man who would always be there, no matter what.

Are you in love with me?

Mason had bluntly asked the question, because that was who he was. The man who would always ask the necessary question. She'd been so startled, so overwhelmed by emotion and the shock of Jase's proposal, she hadn't said yes. She hadn't *known* she wanted to say yes. And then he'd let her go.

"He let me go because he thought it was what I wanted."

He'd let her go because he'd thought it was what was best for her. He'd let her go because he loved her.

"Mom?"

She turned and saw Harlow stepping onto the deck. Her daughter wore a bathrobe and a sleepy expression.

"It's really early," Harlow said, stretching. "What time did you get up?"

"Six."

"That's like three in the morning according to your body clock. Are you okay?"

Robyn smiled. "Yes, I am. Do you think Mason's in love with me?"

Harlow hesitated. "Why do you ask?"

562

The question was an odd response. "Is he?"

"Yes, but don't tell him I said that."

Robyn nearly fainted. "He told you he loved me?"

"Kind of, but then you guys had a fight or whatever it was. You wouldn't say." Her daughter tightened her robe. "Mom, Mason's a really great guy. I know he's different from Dad and Jase, but he's strong, and he'd never hurt you."

Hope fluttered in her chest. Mason loved her? He'd been talking about his feelings?

Her first instinct was to rush inside and book a flight back to California. She could —

No, she told herself. She was going to think things through. She was going to make sure she knew her mind and her heart before she did anything. Besides, there were logistics to be worked out. When she went back, she wanted to be ready to stay there permanently. No running back and forth.

"Your dad's going to bring Zafina to the house later today," Robyn said, walking toward her daughter. "He's thinking of buying the house from me."

Harlow's mouth dropped open. "Seriously? But isn't that weird? Are you okay with that?"

"It was my idea. This is much more his house than mine, and she's pregnant."

"Let's not talk about the baby," Harlow said, following her inside. "I'm still getting past the gross factor of that piece of news."

"She could be your stepmother," Robyn said lightly.

"Yeah, that's more of a problem. I just hope Kip finds someone before there's a wedding."

"If not, I'll be your plus-one."

They walked into the kitchen. Harlow poured herself coffee.

"You'd do that for me?"

"Of course. You're my favorite daughter, and I love you. I was thinking of making pancakes."

"With bacon?"

Robyn smiled. "Yes, with bacon. Go wake your brother, and I'll get started on breakfast."

Harlow picked up her coffee. "What about Mason? Or are you going to tell me it's none of my business?"

"I'm going to tell you that I'm in love with him, but I need to think a few things through before he and I have that conversation."

As she said the words, she fought against fear he would be done with her by the time she got back. No, she told herself. That wasn't a concern. If he got over her so quickly, then his love wasn't real. She was talking weeks, not months. Besides, she had to do what was right for herself. She had to be willing to be strong. Loving Mason was one thing, but loving herself mattered, too.

"You have it all together," Harlow said with a sigh. "When I grow up, I want to be just like you."

"I appreciate the compliment, but try being your own person. That generally works out better."

A new lesson, hard-earned but powerful. Lillian would be so proud.

"It's nice," Enid said, looking around at the apartment. "But it's kind of small."

Harlow grinned. "How can you say that? It's nearly seven hundred square feet."

"Can you live here?"

Harlow thought about how expensive rent was in the Keys and that this place would cost nearly half her take-home pay. But the job was exactly what she wanted, and she was hoping to keep the rest of her expenses low. And be so dazzling that her passengers would tip her generously.

"I'll do great," she promised her friend.

Enid's expression remained doubtful, but

Harlow wasn't concerned. She was going to be just fine on her own.

As promised, her brother had helped her load the truck she'd rented to bring her things down from Naples. One of his friends had tagged along to help with the heavy stuff. Between the three of them, they'd had her things unloaded in a couple of hours.

Austin and his friend had left to return the rental truck, and her mom had shown up to help her unpack. Robyn had treated all of them to a night at a hotel — probably the last luxury Harlow would see for a while, so she'd enjoyed her lovely water view and roomy shower. She'd spent the last couple of days settling in. Enid was joining her for the weekend, before heading off to medical school.

"Come on," Harlow said, grabbing her bag. "I found a great little place around the corner. The cocktails are amazing, and the food is cheap."

Enid grinned. "I love cheap food."

"Me, too."

They walked the short distance to the restaurant. It was early enough that the place wasn't too crowded. They were shown to a quiet table on the patio. Harlow scanned the happy hour drinks menu, letting price as much as the description inform her decision. She was a bargain shopper now — something of a change, but not a bad one, she thought.

Once they'd placed their drinks order, Harlow smiled at her friend.

"Are you excited about school?"

"Mostly scared. I'm afraid everyone will be smarter than me."

"Not possible. At least one of them has to be as smart as you."

Enid laughed. "I was looking for more support."

"Why? You know you're uncomfortably bright. You're lucky I'm willing to be friends with you what with you being so freakish."

Enid studied her. "You seem okay. I thought you'd be more upset about Kip."

Harlow had told her about the breakup but not the final details. She wasn't hiding Kip's behavior so much as still processing it and trying to figure out if it mattered much beyond proving he really was a jerk.

"I got over him pretty fast," Harlow admitted. "I thought I was desperately in love with him. I thought I wanted to marry him. What does it say about me that I was completely wrong?"

Enid grinned. "That you're human?"

"Or that I'm an idiot." She held up a hand. "Not in an 'I'm pathetic' way, but you

567

have to admit, I had no idea who Kip was. Why didn't I ask more questions, or really take a look at his character? What made me fall in love with him to begin with? What if the whole relationship was based on the fact that I was getting close to graduating from college and the next obvious step was getting married? Am I really that shallow?"

"That's way too many questions," Enid told her.

"I know, but it's what I'm working through. I want to figure out what went wrong. What was my fault or at least my responsibility, and what's on him? Then I want to do better next time."

"You've really changed. Grown up, I guess." Enid grimaced. "Not that you weren't grown-up before."

Harlow laughed. "I know exactly what you mean. And you're right. I've changed a lot. When I think about fighting with my mom about having the wedding in the backyard, I'm so ashamed."

"But you've made up?"

Harlow thought about how everything was different now. "Yes. We're good. We're both moving on with our lives."

"She's going back to California?"

Harlow nodded. Hopefully her mom would have the courage to tell Mason how she really felt, and they could work it out. They were so good together, and she would, selfishly, like to have Mason as her stepdad. And speaking of stepparents . . .

"My dad's going to buy my mom's house," she said. "It's a whole thing with Zafina."

She explained how her father technically owned half the house and that he'd brought Zafina to see it.

"I left for an hour," she continued. "They were still there when I got back, and Zafina couldn't stop crying. I assume that was pregnancy hormones, because she doesn't strike me as the crying type."

Their drinks arrived. When their server had left, Harlow said, "They're getting married."

"You okay with that?" Enid asked.

"I guess. I'm going to have a half brother or sister. That's weird. Okay — we've only talked about me. Time for a subject change."

They talked about Enid's fall class schedule and whether or not she thought she could come back for the Christmas holiday. They ordered their dinner, then a second round of drinks. At a break in the conversation, Harlow reached into her bag and pulled out an envelope.

"So, I have something for you," she said, smiling at her friend. "Before I give it to you, I want you to know how much your friendship means to me. You're smart and kind and supportive, and you could be best friends with anyone, but you've chosen me. I know I don't always make it easy."

Enid looked confused and a little afraid. "What are you talking about?"

"Medical school. It's not right you're going to graduate with a hundred thousand dollars in debt."

Enid grimaced. "You're talking about my outburst from before. Pretend that never happened. I'll be fine. It's no big deal."

"It kind of is, and I want to help." She held out the envelope. "With this."

Enid took it and pulled out the check. Her eyes widened and her mouth dropped open as she stared at the amount.

"No! You can't. Harlow, what are you doing?"

"Giving you a check for fifty thousand dollars."

Enid started to cry. "You don't have this kind of money. This is crazy. No. I won't accept it."

"You have to. And I do have the money." She told her about the inheritance from Lillian. "I want to do this. Enid, you're my friend, and I love you. Let me do this for you. Please. It would mean so much to me if you'd accept it."

"But you can't."

"I can. I still have plenty for my future. You're going to be a doctor, and I want to be a part of that." She grinned. "Not the studying part, just the pride part."

Enid wiped her face, then flung her arms around Harlow. "Are you sure?"

"Yes. Take it, I beg you."

"Thank you." Enid hung on tight. "Thank you. This is changing my life. I can never repay you."

"That's not what I want. Go be a great doctor, and when you're rich and famous, do the same for someone else."

They both sat back and smiled at each other.

"I can't believe it," Enid said. "I've never seen a check for so much." She laughed. "I can't use my app to deposit it. The amount is too big. I'll have to go to the bank."

"A novel experience. We'll go in the morning first thing."

More drinks arrived, along with their dinner. As they talked about people they knew and maybe getting a pedicure tomorrow, Harlow couldn't stop smiling. She'd done a good thing for someone she cared about. She was proud of herself and happy for her friend. She had a new job and her very first ever apartment by herself. She didn't know where she would be in ten years, but she had a feeling she was going to be just fine. She was strong, like her mom — it had simply taken her a while to figure that out.

THIRTY-FOUR

Twenty-five years in the army had given Mason a healthy respect for routine. If you did what needed doing, regardless of how you felt, the day generally went better. There had been mornings he hadn't wanted to wake up at five, spend an hour on PT, or deal with whatever shitstorm was going to dominate his day, but he'd done it, and often the act of doing had improved his mood.

He'd put that theory to the test over the past few weeks. Since Robyn had left, he'd been forced to create a different kind of routine. He got up around six, went running, came back and started his day. He fed the cats, focused on his book every morning, and spent afternoons working in the house or out in the garden.

Neither was necessary, but they kept him busy and tired him out. The latter was required if he wanted to have a prayer of sleeping at night. No, not sleeping. Sleeping without dreaming of Robyn.

There were no words to describe how much he missed her. He'd loved and lost before, but not like this. It was as if she'd gotten into every cell of his body, and he couldn't breathe without thinking of her. Her ghost still haunted every room, every time of day. She was around every corner. He'd yet to find a single space she didn't occupy. And if that wasn't bad enough, her son was a constant reminder of her.

Austin had returned after spending nearly a week in Florida. Like Mason, he'd quickly settled into a routine of his own. On the days he didn't have an early-morning charter, he went running with Mason before heading to the gym to lift weights. His afternoons were spent studying naval history and navigation and brushing up on his math skills. He worked as a busboy most nights. He was a good roommate, quiet, clean, and he took care of his own meals.

On his nights off, he and Mason frequently went out to dinner. Mason talked about military life, and Austin told him which of the latest movies his friends liked. Neither of them ever mentioned Robyn. Sometimes Austin told him how Harlow was doing, but that was as close as they got to the delicate subject of Austin's mother.

Mason rinsed out his breakfast dishes and loaded them into the dishwasher. Salvia was only working a couple of days a week. He'd taken over most of the feline duty. He'd created a spreadsheet so he could make sure he inspected each of the cats every week. He fed them twice a day, and precisely at four in the afternoon, he emptied all eight litter boxes. While most of them took advantage of the grounds of the house, a few were too prissy to do their business outside.

He poured the last cup of the coffee before making his way to his office. He was determined to write at least three pages today. Yesterday morning he'd had a meeting with Gregory. The historical society had made a formal offer on the house. According to the paperwork, they were willing to pay fifteen million dollars. After closing costs and taxes, Gregory had said Mason would walk away with close to ten million.

He'd signed the commitment letter with the historical society, and the clock on his year in the house had started ticking. In one year, he would have to move out. He'd assumed he would find a place to rent while the house was being built, but Gregory had explained that based on the value of the land and the agreement with the historical society, Mason could get a construction loan, allowing him to start building now.

He'd researched the topic and had discovered the lawyer was correct. All Mason had to do was pick out the plot of land, get house plans approved by the city and hire a contractor. He'd gone so far as to hire someone to survey the acreage. That was happening next week. As for the rest of it, he wasn't sure he could pick out a house design. Not yet. Not when he'd secretly been hoping he wouldn't be living there alone.

He carried his coffee into Leo's office and set it on the desk, but instead of sitting down, he walked to the window and stared out at the view of the ocean.

He ached for Robyn, and not just in his bed. He missed her everywhere. He wanted to talk to her, hear her laugh, watch her hug Austin. He longed to hold her, just hold her, not have sex, although he wanted that desperately. She had become the best part of him, and without her he was becoming less by the day.

He knew at some point she was going to have to come back to deal with the inventory. So he would have her back in his life, but as what? A former lover? A distant acquaintance? He wasn't sure he had the strength to be around her and not be in her life.

Sometimes he tortured himself with the thought that she'd gone back to Jase. That when she returned, she would be engaged and that on weekends the asshole cardiologist would fly out and screw her right next door. The thought of that nearly made him lose his breakfast. Only steely self-control kept down the food.

He pushed away those thoughts and all the other ones of her, which left his mind blank. After seating himself at his desk, he forced himself to describe the use of mules to transport mountain howitzers in the mid-1800s. While mules didn't deal with the rigors of battle well at all, they were strong and could handle uneven and steep terrain.

Four hours later, he had written and deleted at least twenty pages, leaving him with a scant two that were passably readable, if not scintillating. He carried his now cold coffee into the kitchen and told himself he should eat something for lunch.

Before he could work up any enthusiasm, he heard a car driving around to the garage. Probably one of the workmen who appeared to take care of something going on with the house, he thought as he stepped out back, grateful for the distraction.

But instead of a work truck, he saw an unfamiliar SUV with Florida plates. His heart jumped into hyperspeed, thudding against his ribs so hard, he was pretty sure something was going to snap. Hope tried to spring to life, but he squashed it, knowing Robyn showing up wasn't necessarily good news. After all, she had a lot of work to get done. He'd always known she would come back — what he didn't know was if completing the inventory was the only reason she'd shown up.

The driver's door opened, and she stepped out. Wanting, love and a sinking sensation battled for dominance within him as she saw him and came to a stop.

She looked good. No, better than good. Her long blond hair fluttered in the breeze, and her mouth was exactly as he remembered. She was still the most beautiful woman he'd ever seen. He thought she was a bit thinner, as if she hadn't been eating enough. He would prefer her to put on a few pounds, but knew the most important thing was that she was here.

Sunglasses hid her eyes, so he had no idea what she was thinking. There was tension in her body, which didn't bode well for him. A sense of dread killed the last whisper of hope as he realized he had his answer. She wasn't here for him.

"Welcome back," he said, careful to keep his tone neutral with a hint of casual welcome. "How was the drive?"

"Long."

She pulled off her sunglasses, allowing him to see her stunning blue eyes. Emotions chased through them, but they were moving too fast for him to know what she was thinking. At least there wasn't a ring on her finger, so that was something.

Her mouth curved into a smile. "I've had three days to think about what I wanted to say when I saw you, and now that I'm here, I can't remember any of it. Which is probably for the best. You're the writer in the family, not me."

What the hell did that mean? He stifled his impatience and forced himself to pretend to relax. "I'm not writing as much these days. This morning I managed two pages about nineteenth-century cannons."

"Sounds interesting."

"Not really."

Could this be any more awkward? he thought desperately. Before, everything had been so easy. He hadn't worried about what to say because when he was with her, he'd been free to be himself. He'd been secure in his love for her, but now he was a mess.

"I can help you with your luggage," he said, mostly to distract himself from how awful this was.

She tilted her head as she studied him. "Mason," she began, then shook her head and walked toward him.

He didn't know what she was going to do, so he didn't move. He half expected her to go around him and into the house, but she didn't. Instead she stopped in front of him, grabbed a fistful of his shirt and pulled him toward her. He was so surprised, he let her tug him close, then nearly lost it when she raised herself on tiptoes and pressed her mouth to his.

She was kissing him, he thought in amazement, before the reality of her mouth on his caused his brain to shut down as his body demanded that he simply *feel* what was happening.

Her lips were warm and just insistent enough to make it clear what she wanted. He wrapped his arms around her so they were body to body. Her hands moved up and down his back before dropping to his ass, where she squeezed. Hard.

Wanting exploded, fueled by her heat and the way she was grinding her crotch against his suddenly rigid dick. Her mouth parted, and he pushed his tongue inside. She met him stroke for stroke before sucking on his tongue in that deep "take me now" way that always had him desperate for whatever she was offering. Was this really happening?

As he was trying to decide, she was pushing him into the house. Once they were in the kitchen, she maneuvered him into the breakfast room, where she drew back enough to start taking off her clothes. Responding in kind seemed like the most sensible course of action, he thought, nearly ripping off his shirt. He toed out of his shoes and shoved down his jeans and briefs, only to stop and stare at her.

"I don't have a condom on me," he said, barely able to speak through the haze of wanting. "They're in my room."

She gave him a slow, sexy smile that nearly drove him to his knees, before pulling one out of the back pocket of her jeans and waving it.

"I thought you might have less of a need to have one on you," she said, her voice teasing. "I got the extra-large ones. They seem to fit better."

He practically tore off the rest of her clothes before picking her up and setting her on the breakfast room table. She handed him the condom and looked into his eyes.

"I need you inside of me, Mason," she said

bluntly. "Forget about the rest of it. We can play later."

His hands shook as he tore open the wrapper. It took him two tries to get the damn thing on, but then he was pushing inside of her.

He felt his world right itself. When she tensed around him, her head tilting back, her mouth gasping for air right before she called out his name, begging him to never stop, he knew he was back exactly where he belonged. Whatever happened next, he would always have this moment, this time, this memory. And then he couldn't think anymore. He could only feel his release and the pleasure they gave each other, and hear the sound of his name as she screamed.

Robyn resurfaced to find herself naked on the breakfast room table. She'd spent most of her drive preparing what she wanted to say when she saw Mason, but instead of telling him any of it, she'd gone right to sex. He didn't seem to be complaining, but at some point they needed to have a conversation.

Once they could both breathe normally, they cleaned up and got dressed. Only then did they look at each other. She felt his questions, knew he had no idea what she was thinking. Her carefully organized speech no longer made sense, so instead of reciting it, she grabbed his hand and pulled him into the front sitting room.

When they were seated across from each other, she leaned toward him.

"Cord proposed to Zafina, and she said yes. He's buying me out of the house, which makes the most sense. He loves that place, and I think they'll be happy there. Harlow's settled in Key West."

She thought about mentioning the ridiculously high rents and how tiny her daughter's apartment was, but knew none of that was important. It was only something to fill time until she found the courage to say what really mattered. It was time for her to do what was right for her — to say what was important and hope that he responded in kind.

She looked into his dark eyes and prepared to lay her heart bare.

"I didn't come back for the inventory, Mason. I came back for you. Before, you asked me a question, and I didn't have an answer. That wasn't about my feelings so much as everything going on. There was too much, too fast. Practically everyone I know following me here, losing Lillian, having Jase show up in what can only be described as a boneheaded move. I couldn't answer you before because I needed to be sure. I am now."

She spoke clearly, so he wouldn't misunderstand. "I'm in love with you. You're a wonderful man, and being around you makes me feel safe and happy and strong. I want us to have a future together, and I'm hoping you want the same."

He stood and glared at her. "You need to stop talking. If you propose to me, I'll never forgive myself."

Not exactly the response she'd been looking for. "Why are you mad?"

"I'm not mad." He walked away two steps, then turned back to face her. "Dammit all to hell, Robyn. I'm not spending the rest of my life knowing you proposed."

He looked so serious, she thought, genuinely confused by his annoyance. Had she been wrong about him? Didn't he love her? "I thought you believed in equality between the sexes."

"I do. You know I do, but don't propose."

"Because you don't love me and don't want to marry me?"

He swore silently, closed the distance between them and pulled her to her feet.

"You know I love you. If Harlow didn't tell you, you're smart enough to have figured it out for yourself. I practically follow you around like a puppy. I worship you, Robyn. You're more than a fantasy. You're real, and for reasons I can't begin to figure out, you're claiming you love me."

Relief made her smile. "Not claiming. I mean it. I love you, Mason."

"Hot damn."

He kissed her, then pulled back and stared into her eyes. "I love you, too. All of you, for as long as I'm able to breathe. I've been looking for you my whole life. Whatever you want, whatever you need, I'll make it happen." One corner of his mouth turned up. "In and out of bed."

"I'll do the same," she promised. "Always. You're my fantasy and my hero. I don't know how I got so lucky, but I'm going to be grateful we're together every single day."

He buried his fingers in her hair, then kissed her again. A slow, melting kiss that had her wondering how far it was to either of their bedrooms. Before she could suggest they head in that direction, he drew back.

"So, about that proposal," he said. "I'd like to marry you, but if you don't want to go in that direction, I'm fine with it. But I do want us to build a house together. It's gonna need to be big, what with you having fifteen cats."

She smiled. "Fourteen. You were keeping Charles II."

"You're right. Fourteen of your cats and one of mine. We might need some kind of permit for that many of them."

"I was thinking we'd talk to a local rescue facility and see if we can rehome a few of them."

"There's an idea."

She touched his face. "Yes, Mason, I'll marry you."

"Don't say that!" He took a step back. "I wasn't proposing. I want to do that right. I was just asking if you wanted to do that. I'll propose later. Like at sunset, with roses and champagne."

"I had no idea about this whole traditional thing. It's kind of sexy."

"You're not taking me seriously," he grumbled. "You wait. You'll be blown away."

"I will be, I promise."

"I can't believe you said yes. Just like that. It's disheartening."

She laughed. "That is so sad. How can I make it up to you?"

He took her by the hand and started for the stairs. "I think you know exactly how."

"As a matter of fact, I do."

Three days before escrow closed on Lillian's house, Robyn walked through the mostly empty downstairs. Over the past year, she'd moved out hundreds of pieces of furniture and artwork. A sizeable majority of it had been sold to larger museums around the world, while dozens of pieces had been donated to small, regional museums that could never afford to buy the various items. The rest of it was in a massive warehouse she'd leased in preparation for opening her business in two months.

The remodel of *Lillian's,* as she'd decided to name her new antique store, was moving ahead. She had a great location on State Street, with nearby parking and lots of foot traffic. Although most of the pieces were exceptional and pricey, she would have plenty of inventory for the tourist crowd.

She'd made sure to leave nearly a hundred items for the historical society. Most of the bedroom sets were in place, along with plenty of artwork, dishes and a half-dozen clocks. The telescope was still on the roof, and beautiful handmade rugs were scattered around.

But for today, all that had been taken to other rooms. The main sitting room was set up with rows of chairs facing the perfect ocean view. Huge floral arrangements defined the space for the ceremony, while the foyer, dining room and library had been filled with tables and chairs. The catering staff was already setting up for the meal service.

They were expecting about sixty people for the wedding and reception to follow. Several of Mason's friends were flying in for the event, as was Harlow. Austin was up for the weekend, as well. For reasons not clear to her, Cord and Zafina had wanted to attend, bringing baby Kelli with them.

Robyn walked back to Lillian's office, now the unofficial bride's room. From here, she could almost see the house she and Mason had built. Thanks to the money from the sales to museums, they'd been able to move forward with the construction, offering their contractor a bonus for finishing in record time. When they got back from their honeymoon, they would move into the house.

Except for Charles II, all the cats had been rehomed. Mason was discussing his desire to get a puppy with his favorite feline. So far Charles wasn't saying much, but Robyn was sure he could be convinced.

The door opened, and Harlow stepped inside. Robyn's heart nearly burst with pride. Her baby girl was strong and tall, looking beautiful in the dark blue gown she'd chosen to wear as Robyn's maid of honor. Confidence and happiness radiated from her, which was all a mother could ask for, Robyn thought.

"Mom, you've got to get dressed. The valet service just texted to say guests are arriving."

"Except for the dress, I'm ready."

She'd already had her hair and makeup done, not trusting herself to do it on such a special day.

She shrugged out of her robe, then waited while Harlow picked up the dress she'd chosen. The elegant floor-length gown was an off-the-shoulder trumpet style with beading on the band sleeves that continued on the back of the bodice. The front had pleats to the waist. Then the champagne-colored fabric fell in soft gathers to the floor. She'd found a cute pair of sandals that wouldn't kill her feet and finished the outfit with diamonds Lillian had left her.

"Nervous?" Harlow asked as she zipped the dress into place.

"No. I'm marrying Mason. Nothing has ever felt this right."

Her daughter smiled at her. "I'm having trouble finding a guy I want to see more than three times. I'm a little envious of how much you're in love."

"You'll find someone."

"I know." Harlow grinned. "I'm only twenty-three. There's plenty of time."

Austin joined them, looking handsome in his tux. He hugged her.

"Mason's not nervous," her son told her. "I thought he'd be sweating or something, but he's completely calm. That guy can handle anything."

"He's marrying Mom," Harlow pointed out. "He's happy. What's to be nervous about?"

"That I'm so good-looking today," Austin joked.

"You do look good in a tux."

They talked until it was time. Then Harlow handed Robyn the larger bouquet before taking her own.

"I'm really happy for you, Mom," she said.

She walked out into the hallway and turned toward the main sitting room. Austin held out his arm.

"Ready to make him an honest man?"

"I am."

She was more than ready to be his wife and for them to continue on their journey together.

Austin guided her down the hallway. She could hear the music and smell the beautiful flowers. Anticipation made her want to hurry, but she kept her steps slow and even. They turned, and she saw the guests and the view of the Pacific beyond the deck, then turned her attention to the man standing, waiting for her to join him.

His gaze locked with hers, and she would swear she heard his breath catch. Or maybe she just knew that was what would happen, because whenever she dressed up, he acted like she was a treasured and beautiful princess. Come to think of it, that was how he treated her all the time.

He cared for her, loved her, supported her and had the most unexpected traditional streak. He'd spent the previous night in a hotel. Something she would tease him about later, when they were alone.

The guests rose. Austin walked her down the aisle. When asked, "Who gives this woman to be married?" he replied, "My sister and I."

As she stepped next to Mason, she felt an extra rush of love coming from somewhere beyond the confines of the room. She knew if she looked hard enough, she would see that they had been joined by two people who loved them. Which made sense. Leo and Lillian had always enjoyed a wedding.

She looked at the man she knew she would love for the rest of her life and breathed in gratitude for all that he was and all they would be together.

Mason smiled at her, then leaned close.

"We're going to have the best time," he whispered.

"I know. Honestly, I can't wait for us to get started."

■ ■ ■ ■

THE SUMMER GETAWAY: BOOK CLUB DISCUSSION GUIDE

■ ■ ■ ■

THE SUMMER GETAWAY:
PINEAPPLE CHICKEN

1 20-oz can of pineapple chunks in juice,
  divided
1/4 cup soy sauce
1 inch of fresh ginger, sliced thin
1 jalapeño, sliced
2 cloves garlic, smashed with the side of a
  knife
4 boneless, skinless chicken breasts
4 green onions, sliced
1/4 cup fresh cilantro or basil
salt and pepper
2 tbsp olive oil (if using a pressure cooker)
1 cup chicken broth (if using a pressure
  cooker)

Marinade: Combine pineapple juice with soy
sauce. Stir in sliced ginger and jalapeño and
smashed garlic. Place chicken in a glass dish
and pour marinade over. Marinate for at
least 2 hours but preferably 8 hours or
overnight.

Pineapple Slaw: Cut pineapple chunks into pea-sized chunks. Stir in green onions and cilantro or basil. Refrigerate until ready to serve.

Chicken: Remove chicken from marinade. Discard marinade. Liberally sprinkle breasts with salt and pepper. *In the oven:* Roast at 425°F for about 20–25 minutes, until the internal temperature registers 165°F. *In a pressure cooker:* On sauté mode, heat olive oil and brown chicken on each side. Remove. Add chicken broth to the pot and deglaze. Place the chicken on a trivet and cook on high pressure for 8 minutes, with 10 minutes' natural release. Whole baby potatoes can be tossed on top of the breasts if cooking this way.

Serve with pineapple slaw.

DISCUSSION QUESTIONS

Note: These questions contain spoilers. Lots and lots of spoilers. For the best reading experience, we recommend that you wait until after you have finished The Summer Getaway *to read the questions.*

1. Mother-daughter relationships can be difficult. Why do you think that is? What makes the stakes so high between mother and daughter? What were some of the reasons that Robyn and Harlow's relationship was complicated?

2. Why do you think Robyn stayed with Cord even after he cheated? Would you have stayed?

3. Cord surprised Robyn with a house, a grand gesture supposedly made in apology for his infidelity. Would you be happy if your significant other bought a house

for you that you'd never seen? Why or why not?

4. Robyn feels Harlow is too young to marry at twenty-two, even though Robyn herself married at eighteen. What's something you did as a young adult that you wouldn't want your kids or young relatives to do? Do you think twenty-two is too young to marry?

5. When Mindy talked about having an affair with her tennis instructor, Robyn tried to warn her against it, but Mindy wouldn't listen. What did you think was going to happen? Were you surprised that Payne forgave Mindy? What would you do if a friend told you she wanted to cheat on her partner? How would you react after she followed through?

6. Mason spent twenty-five years in the army, including two as a drill instructor. How do you think this shaped him as a man? What made him so appealing to Robyn?

7. Family dynamics are infinitely complex, as Susan Mallery has demonstrated with one bestselling family drama after another.

Each family is unique, and each relationship within that family is unique. How did Austin's and Harlow's relationships with their mom and dad differ?

8. What would you do if you inherited $250,000? What about $10 million?

9. Were you surprised when Lillian died, or did foreshadowing lead you to suspect it?

10. Robyn was the heart of her family, as evidenced by the way everyone followed her to California. Who is the heart of your family?

ABOUT THE AUTHOR

Susan Mallery is the #1 *New York Times* bestselling author of novels about the relationships that define women's lives — family, friendship and romance. *Library Journal* says, "Mallery is the master of blending emotionally believable characters in realistic situations," and readers seem to agree — forty million copies of her books have been sold worldwide. Her warm, humorous stories make the world a happier place to live.

Susan grew up in California and now lives in Seattle with her husband. She's passionate about animal welfare, especially that of the two Ragdoll cats and adorable poodle who think of her as Mom.

The employees of Thorndike Press hope you have enjoyed this Large Print book. All our Thorndike, Wheeler, and Kennebec Large Print titles are designed for easy reading, and all our books are made to last. Other Thorndike Press Large Print books are available at your library, through selected bookstores, or directly from us.

For information about titles, please call:
(800) 223-1244

or visit our website at:
gale.com/thorndike

To share your comments, please write:
Publisher
Thorndike Press
10 Water St., Suite 310
Waterville, ME 04901